CRITICAL PRAISE FOR TERRY C. JOHNSTON'S *PLAINSMEN* SERIES

"AN UNFORGETTABLE ADVEN-TURE!"
> —*Rocky Mountain News*

"A WINNER!" —*The Buckskin Report*

"MASTERFUL!"
> —John M. Carroll, historian and renowned expert on the Indian Wars

"EXCELLENT!"
> —Fred Werner, noted Western historian

"'COMPELLING . . . FASCINATING!"
> —*Topeka Capital-Journal*

"GUTSY ADVENTURE-ENTERTAIN-MENT!" —*Kirkus Reviews*

Terry C. Johnston is a two-time Golden Spur Award nominee, and award-winning author of *Carry the Wind*, the *Plainsmen* series and *Long Winter Gone*.

THE PLAINSMEN SERIES BY TERRY C. JOHNSTON

DYING THUNDER

THE FIGHT AT ADOBE WALLS AND THE BATTLE OF PALO DURO CANYON—1874–1875

TERRY C. JOHNSTON

St. Martin's Paperbacks

DYING THUNDER

Copyright © 1992 by Terry C. Johnston.

Cover art by Jim Carson.

ISBN: 978-0-312-92834-6

Printed in the United States of America

St. Martin's Paperbacks edition / July 1992

15 14 13 12 11

this novel is dedicated to
Ed Benz,
Director of the Hutchinson County Museum,
who time and again helped make sense
of the greatest Indian War on the
southern plains

The meadow at Adobe Walls at the time of the attack, June 1874

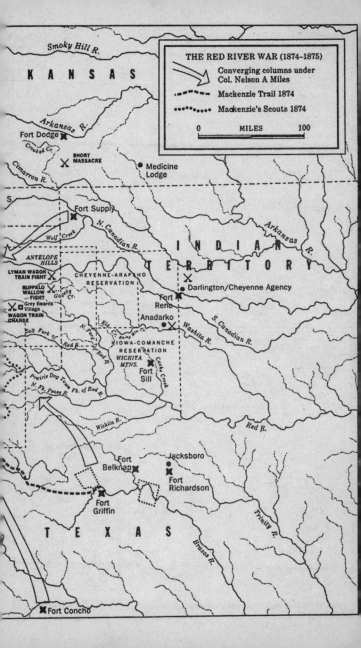

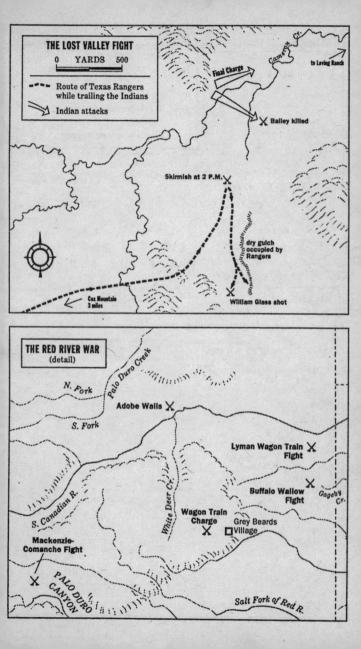

THE LOST VALLEY FIGHT

0   YARDS   500

- - - Route of Texas Rangers while trailing the Indians
→ Indian attacks

Cameron Cr.

to Loving Ranch

Final Charge

✕ Bailey killed

Skirmish at 2 P.M. ✕

dry gulch occupied by Rangers

✕ William Glass shot

Cox Mountain 3 miles ←

THE RED RIVER WAR (detail)

Palo Duro Creek

N. Fork

S. Fork

Adobe Walls ✕

Lyman Wagon Train Fight ✕

S. Canadian R.

White Deer Cr.

Buffalo Wallow Fight ✕

Gageby Cr.

Wagon Train Charge ✕

Grey Beards ☐ Village

Mackenzie-Comanche Fight ✕

PALO DURO CANYON

✕

Salt Fork of Red R.

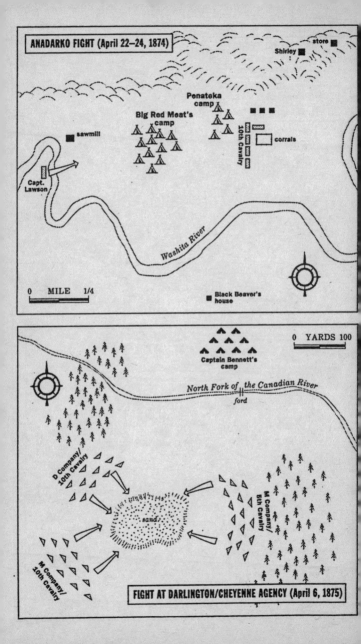

ANADARKO FIGHT (April 22–24, 1874)

store

Shirley

Penateka camp

Big Red Meat's camp

sawmill

10th Cavalry

corrals

Capt. Lawson

Washita River

0   MILE   1/4

Black Beaver's house

Captain Bennett's camp

0   YARDS   100

North Fork of the Canadian River

ford

D Company/ 10th Cavalry

M Company/ 5th Cavalry

sand

M Company/ 10th Cavalry

FIGHT AT DARLINGTON/CHEYENNE AGENCY (April 6, 1875)

Cast of Characters

Seamus Donegan

Civilians

Rebecca Grover*
Louis Abragon*
Henry Lease
Orlando A. "Brick" Bond
John Fairchild
John Miles—Cheyenne Agent at Darlington Agency
Charley Armitage
Jim Cator
Fred Singer
Prairie Dog Dave
Joe Plummer
Robert M. Wright
Cheyenne Jack
George Bellfield
Richard Coke—Governor of Texas
James Haworth—Kiowa/Comanche Agent
J. Connell—Acting Agent, Anadarko

William Shirley—government trader at Anadarko
Jacob Sandford—wagon-master, Lyman wagon train
James O'Neal—wagon-master, Mackenzie campaign
Dr. J. J. Sturm
Samantha Pike*
Frank Brown
A. C. "Charlie" Myers
Mike McCabe
Charley Rath
Bob Cator
Emanuel Dubbs
Dirty Face Ed Jones
Ned Sewell
Anderson Moore
Blue Billy
Henry Lease

Participants at Adobe Walls Fight

James Langton
Andy "Swede" Johnson
Tom O'Keefe
Hannah Olds
Billy Ogg
William Barclay "Bat" Masterson

Hiram Watson
James "Bermuda" Carlisle
Fred Leonard
Edward Trevor
Charley Armitage
Billy Tyler
Mike McCabe

"Frenchy"
Jacob (Shorty) Scheidler
George Eddy
Sam Smith
William Olds
Billy Dixon
Oscar Sheppard
Mike Welch
James McKinley
James Hanrahan
James Campbell
Seth Hathaway
"Dutch" Henry Born
Billy "Old Man" Keeler
Fred Myers
Issac (Ike) Scheidler
Juan

Texas Rangers at Lost Valley Fight

Major John B. Jones,
  Commanding, Texas
  Frontier Battalion
Captain G. W. Stephens
Ed Carnal
George Moore
Billy Glass
Walter Robertson
David Bailey
Lieutenant Hiram Wilson
Lee Corn
Richard Wheeler
William Lewis
Mel Porter
John Holmes

Army

General William T. Sherman
General C. C. Augur
Colonel John W. Davidson
Lieutenant Colonel Thomas
  H. Neill
Lieutenant Colonel George P.
  Buell
Major T. M. Anderson
Captain Eugene B. Beaumont
Captain Tullis Tupper
Captain Napoleon B.
  McLaughlin
Captain Wyllys Lyman
Captain Andrew Bennett
Captain S. T. Norvell
Lieutenant Frank West
Lieutenant Granville Lewis
Lieutenant William A.
  Thompson
Lieutenant R. H. Pratt
Sergeant Nicholas deArmond
Sergeant Reuben Waller
General Philip H. Sheridan
Colonel Nelson A. Miles
Colonel Ranald S. Mackenzie
Major William R. Price
Captain Peter Boehm
Captain Louis H. Carpenter
Captain T. A. Baldwin
Captain Sebastian Gunther
Captain William A. Rafferty
Captain A. S. Keyes
Lieutenant Frank Baldwin
Lieutenant Henry Kingsbury
Lieutenant H. W. Lawton
Sergeant John B. Charlton

Lone Tree Valley Massacre Civilians

killed:
Captain Oliver Frances Short
Captain Abram Cutler
Daniel Short
James Shaw
Allen Shaw
Harry Jones
John Keuchler

survivors:
Captain Luther A. Thrasher
Harry Short
S. B. Crist

German Family Massacre

John German
Rebecca German
Catherine German
Joanna German
Julia German
Lydia German
Stephen German
Sophia German
Adelaide German

Soldiers at Buffalo Wallow Fight

Sergeant Z. T. Woodall
Private John Harrington
Private Peter Rath
Private George W. Smith

Scouts and Interpreters

Sharp Grover
Amos Chapman
Horace Jones
William Schmalsle
Henry W. Strong—Fort
　Richardson post guide
Johnson (Lipan)
Job (Tonkawa)
Ben Clark
Ira Wing
Lem Wilson
James Butler Hickok
Henry (Tonkawa)

Comanches

Quanah Parker
Tonarcy
Paracoom (Bull Bear)
Wild Horse
Tabananica (Hears the
　Sunrise)
He Bear
Esa-Que (Wolf Tongue)
Cobay (Wild Mustang)
Big Red Meat
Cheevers
Mow-way
Isatai
White Horse
Ten Bears
Timbo

Old Man Black Beard Horseback
Horse Chief Quirts Quip
Sai-Yan (Rag Full of Holes)

Kiowas

Lone Wolf Guitain
Tauankia Long Horn
Mamay-day-te Big Bow
Mamanti (Swan) Howling Wolf
White Shield Big Tree
Dangerous Eagle Sun Boy
Stumbling Bear White Cowbird
Napawat Hunting Horse
Tsentonkee Lone Young Man
Loud Talker Tehan—white captive
Yellow Wolf Botalye
Poor Buffalo Satanta
Red Otter

Cheyenne

Little Robe Stone Calf
Sitting Medicine White Shield
Whirlwind Gray Beard
Red Moon White Horse
Medicine Water Iron Shirt
Stone Eagle White Wolf
Old Man Otter Belt Whirlwind
White Shield Spots on the Feathers
Hippy Elk Shoulder
Buffalo Calf Woman (Mochi) Yellow Horse
Gray Eyes Mad Wolf
Cedar Red Eagle
Long Back Wolf Robe
Black Horse Minimic

Arapaho
Yellow Horse

Delaware
Black Beaver

---

* indicates a fictional character

Prologue

Moon of Deer Shedding Horns, 1873

"There are only six of them, Quanah."

Quanah Parker nodded, still staring into the distance at the austere ocher and snow-covered ridges. The winter wind nuzzled his long, braided hair this way and that, gently clinking the silver conchos he had woven into that single, glossy queue that hung almost long enough to brush to the back of his war pony. The air was racy with the smell of late autumn's decay.

"You waited long enough to be sure there were no more inside?" Quanah asked the scout who had ridden back across the snow from the valley scooped out of the landscape southeast of where his Kwahadi warriors waited anxiously this bright, cold winter mid-morning.

"Six."

"How many of the white man's log lodges?"

"Two. One in front, the other in back—beside it, a wood pen for his horses and two of the spotted buffalo."

Quanah turned his nose up at that. Spotted buffalo. The white man's cattle. Docile and spineless. With less courage than even a buffalo cow. Good only for milking. And he wondered what the white man saw in milk anyway. If the Grandfather Above gave the milk to the spotted buffalo, why then did the white man drink it?

If he was so fond of milk, why didn't the white man suckle at the breasts of his wife?

It was not as if Quanah had never tasted human milk. He had. Many times. For a moment now, here in the cold of this open land, with the brutal wind moaning out of the west like a death song upon the Llano Estacado, it was

1

good to remember. At times he had thought about taking a second wife, but his first filled his life with all that he needed.

Tonarcy satisfied him even more now than ever before. Mother to their three children, he recalled how her belly had grown swollen with that first child. Thought about how he still made love to her when she grew as big as an antelope doe. How she had never been shy about expressing her hunger for him . . . the warm softness of her fingers as they encircled his excited flesh, kneading him into a frenzy. How he would roll her over, bringing her up on her hands and knees, that ripe belly of hers and those swollen breasts suspended beneath her as he drove his hard flesh into the moistness of her own warm readiness.

Quanah always answered her rising whimpers with his own growl of enthusiasm in the coupling, for none had ever satisfied him like she.

And after he had exploded inside her, Quanah would suckle at first one, then the other of her warm breasts. It seemed Tonarcy was never without milk from the time of the birth of their first child. And it had always been a warm, sweet treat for Quanah—after making warm, sweet love to his wife. This drinking of her milk from her small, swollen breasts—something that often made him ready to mount her again. And her more than ready to receive him as well.

He had never fully understood her appetite growing when it was he who suckled . . . yet had never questioned it either.

Quanah shook his head, aware of the cold blast of winter air once more. Something that reminded him that he was not in his warm lodge, wrapped in the furry robes with her.

Perhaps he needed her badly.

He acknowledged that he had been away from their winter village for too long, perhaps. He was thinking on his wife and that sweet, warm and moist rutting he shared with Tonarcy when he should be thinking about those six white men down there in that valley less than two miles away.

Many suns ago he had led a large hunting party away from their village to hunt buffalo. The Comanche were running low on dried meat. With a disappointing fall hunt, Quanah's Kwahadi band were forced to venture out on the hunt much earlier this winter than they normally would have. More than a moon before, he and the warriors had killed a few white hide hunters they found south of the "dead line," that place where the government's treaty-talkers said the white buffalo hunters were not to cross.

But more and more the Comanche, Kiowa and Cheyenne were discovering sign that the white man was venturing farther and farther south of the Arkansas River, come to the hunting ground guaranteed to the Indian as his own. A meaningless waste of time, this talking treaty with the white man, Quanah thought.

Ever since the autumn when the old chiefs had signed that talking paper up on Medicine Lodge Creek six winters before, it seemed the white hunters were crossing south of the Arkansas in greater numbers, crossing south of the Cimarron too. And Quanah feared they would one day soon come to the Canadian River—what he rightly believed was the last stand for his people: that northern boundary of the great Staked Plain, the Llano Estacado of the ancient ones who had marched out of the land far away to the south with their gleaming metal heads, the ones who first brought the horse to the People of the plains.

Besides those few hide hunters they found and killed more than a moon gone now, his scouts had also returned with news of a small group of soldiers marching northwest onto the Staked Plain. Quanah knew that killing the soldiers boded no good for his people. The army would only send more next time. Yet the yellowlegs never found the roaming warriors—instead the army's Tonkawa guides sought out the Kwahadi villages filled with women and children and the old ones.

Rarely were the young warriors punished by the white soldiers. It was their families who were made to suffer—losing lodges and blankets and robes, clothing and meat and weapons when they ran quickly to flee the white man and the Tonkawa trackers who led the soldiers to the valleys and canyons where the Kwahadi always camped to escape the cold winter winds or to find shade come the first days of the short-grass time.

No, he had told his warriors. We are not going to kill these soldiers. Which had made them howl in angry disappointment.

"But," he had instructed them, "we will drive them out of Kwahadi land—by burning the prairie!"

For miles in either direction along a north-south line, the horsemen set their firebrands to the tall prairie grass sapped dry by the arid autumn winds. The winter wind did the rest: whipping the sparks into a fury that forced the yellowlegs to turn about and flee to the east for their lives.*

However, in the days that followed, his scouts solemnly reported finding no sign of the soldier party. No charred wagon nor burned carcasses.

From time to time this mystery had made Quanah shudder: to think that those white men had merely vanished into the cold air of the Staked Plain. But if they had, he argued with himself, where still would they find food for their animals?

And besides, that great storm that had thundered down upon the plains, riding in on the bone-numbing breath of Winter Man, leaving behind tall snowdrifts and many hungry bellies, would surely have killed the white men so unprepared for such a blizzard.

While he was certain that storm had killed the retreating soldiers, it had also driven the buffalo even farther south. The little ones in Quanah's village cried with empty bellies. The women and old ones wailed as well. It was only the warriors who could not cry out in the pain of their gnawing hunger—for it remained up to them alone to go in search of meat to lift the specter of starvation from the Kwahadi.

After many days of endless riding to the south, Quanah and his hunters found themselves near the southernmost reaches of the Staked Plain, without having seen any buffalo or antelope. It was as if Winter Man had wiped all before him with his great cleansing, cold breath.

As the days of searching grew into many, they had come

* The Plainsmen Series, vol. 6, *Shadow Riders*

across a few old bulls partially buried in a coulee here, frozen in a snowdrift against a ridge there—no longer strong enough to march on with the rest. They were the few left to rot by the passing of the winter storm . . . like the white hide hunters left the thousands upon thousands to rot in the sun.

Where had the rest of the herds gone? Farther and farther south still—to the land of the summer winds?

If they had, they would likely not return until the short-grass time on the prairies, when the winds blew soft and the Grandfather Above once more told the great buffalo herds to nose around to the north in their great seasonal migrations.

"You wish to attack these white men today?" asked the young warrior sitting beside the Kwahadi chief.

He blinked, his reverie broken and brought back to the now. "Yes." Quanah turned to his scout. "You tell me there is a hill looking down on the place where the white man built his log lodges?"

The scout dropped quickly to the ground, his buffalo-hide winter moccasins scraping snow aside from a small circle. In the middle he formed up two frozen snowballs. Circling the snowballs on three sides, he mounded up some of the snow he had scraped aside.

"Yes, Quanah," he said, gazing up into the bright winter sun hung against a winter-pale sky behind his chief. "These are the white man's two lodges. And these, are the hills."

"Where are we?"

The scout pointed with the butt of his rifle.

"It is good," Quanah declared. "We will have the wind in our faces and the sun at our backs as we ride to the top of the hills."

After dividing his force of more than ten-times-ten warriors into four groups and instructing each in its role, Quanah led them away in silence, moving swiftly across the hard, frozen ground.

Behind the low hills he halted them, ordering off three of the groups, then sending away the fourth to guard the all-important opening in the small valley. If the white man was to flee, he told his warriors, it would be through that saddle. That group was not to attack. Instead, they were to wait for any of the white men to come their way once the settlers were flushed like a covey of quail.

When all was in readiness, Quanah took the small quarter of a red trade blanket that he sat upon and nudged his pony to the top of the hill. There he waved it against the pale background of the sky, watching the two white men turn from their work at some object in front of the first log lodge.

Immediately the three groups burst into motion, yelling, screeching, riding at a gallop for the two wood buildings.

The two men outside in the open, grassy yard threw down the tack they had been soaping and repairing, sprinting for the cabin.

Puffs of gray smoke began to rise above the warrior groups.

One of the white men skidded to a stop, reaching behind him to claw at his back before he fell face first into the dry grass dotted with wind-drifted snow. Some of the first warriors leaped their ponies over him, attempting to get to the second man before he reached the cabin. He grabbed his arm, crying out, and almost stumbled—yet he disappeared through the doorway and slammed it shut as the red horsemen galloped by, their bullets thudding dully into the heavy planks.

As that first wave passed the cabin, puffs of smoke appeared from the windows. From where Quanah sat, there were three windows used by the white riflemen. With one of the settlers already killed, his warriors had only to flush the other five.

Quickly Quanah brought the red blanket over his head and held it there in the steady breeze. Two warriors obediently broke off their attack and ordered their horsemen to a safe distance from the cabin while they rode to talk things over with the war chief atop the hill.

"Burn them out," Quanah told them. "If we attempt to ride past their windows and kill them—the chances are very small we will kill them. This would be a bad thing, for the odds are very good those five who are left will kill many, many more of us with their big buffalo-killing guns. Burn them out!"

The two returned to their bands, calling forth the Fire Carrier—the one who kept his hot coals smoldering in a protective gourd when they marched from camp to camp, fire to fire. A dozen of the warriors quickly made firebrands using the dried, belly-high prairie grass.

The torches glowed and smoked smudgy trails against the blue sky as the warriors raced in. This was the most dangerous work of all, Quanah admitted. His men were riding in defenseless, not shooting arrow or bullet while their hands carried the crackling firebrand. And the horsemen had to ride close—very close—to drop the torches through the windows—into the earth and wood lodges where the white man squatted like a badger in his hole . . . with those big-barreled buffalo guns of his.

Rider after rider swept past the windows. Some of the torches fell short. One horseman was knocked off his animal and dragged across the ground to safety by the long rawhide rope lashing him to his pony. Most of the firebrands fell against the sides of the log lodge. Only two of the torches made it into the cabin.

They were enough.

It did not take long for the smoke to begin wafting from the chimney, pouring thick and greasy from the three windows Quanah could watch. Then as the smoke darkened and grew thicker, boiling black as if it rose from a grease fire, he instructed his warriors with his blanket to await the bolting of their prey from its den.

A few minutes more and two of the white men burst out of the cabin, coughing, their rifles still held up at the ready.

Warriors hammered their ponies into action, intending on running the white men down. But first one, then a second horseman fell to riflefire. And from the looks of it, those deadly guns were being fired from the second of the white man's log lodges.

So. A pair of white men had been in the second log lodge all the time and his scouts had missed them. Quanah grew furious inside, his hatred seething for these settlers come to Kwahadi ground.

The two who had fled from the cabin sprinted across the wide, grassy yard and found safety in the barn. Three more white men appeared at the door of the cabin, driven out by the thick columns of dark smoke issuing from every window.

As the Kwahadis galloped in to make the kill, the three white men bolted headlong for the barn while the four already there laid down a covering fire.

His anger grown to a rage, the war chief became a warrior once more. Without waiting for any of the rest to take the initiative, Quanah put heels to his pony and raced off the hillside for the cabin. At a full gallop he reined his pony toward the front window, leaning off the side of the animal to sweep up one of the burning firebrands that had not made it inside the first log lodge. Bringing his pony around in a broad circle, Quanah rode for the barn with the torch smoking and hissing, sparks sputtering on the cold winter breeze.

Bullets whined angrily overhead like noisy yellow wasps on a spring day. He felt the sting of one of those bullets at the moment he pitched the firebrand through the narrow opening at the back of the barn where the white man had stacked a tall pile of grass.

The muscles that lay banded along his arms and shoulders like woven wire grew taut. Sawing the rawhide reins hard to the left, Quanah urged his pony away from the white man's guns—but not quickly enough.

He sensed the flutter in the pony's heart . . . a misstep, then the animal pitched forward suddenly, throwing its rider clear.

Quanah rolled and rolled across the dry, smothering grass and frozen, crusty patches of snow, coming at last to a stop far from the white men who had just killed his favorite war pony.

On all four sides of the small valley, his warriors set up a great cry of rejoicing, for the firebrand had gone in and quickly ignited some of that dried grass the white man foolishly stored to feed his stock.

With white smoke billowing from doors on both sides of the barn, the seven white men darted into the open in a

8

tight group, hurrying for the skimpy timber along the little nearby creek.

With their quarry flushed into the tall grass, the young warriors had great sport with the settlers who no longer had any place to hide.

It was over quickly.

Quanah watched as the noisy young men laughed and joked over the eight bodies, counting coup and scalping, stripping them of their clothing to try it on, then cutting off hands and feet, and finally the manhood parts. Each of the eight were left facing the sky—for they had fought hard to the end and were worthy enemies. Their courage had not shriveled in the face of the Comanche horsemen, shriveled up like last summer's stalks of buffalo grass.

"Do you claim any of the white man's horses, Quanah?" asked one of the older warriors.

"I should look over the animals in the log corral. If I don't find one that will let me ride it on this hunt—I will have a long walk home!"

"That gray one looks strong," suggested the warrior.

"Quanah!" yelled a young scout tearing across the crusty snow, racing in off the nearby hill. "Soldiers—they come!"

"Where?" he asked. "How many!"

The scout pointed to the east, his face grave. "Ten times ten. More," he replied, striking his left forearm twice.

"Tonkawa trackers lead them?"

The scout nodded, his eyes filling with great concern.

Sweeping his red blanket from the ground, Quanah turned to some of the others. "Open that horse pen and bring the big gray horse. Drive the others away before you when you leave." He brought the blanket over his head, waving it swiftly from side to side. "Ride, my brothers—soldiers come! Ride now!"

Two mounted warriors brought the prancing gray horse up, its eyes wide with fear at the foreign smell of the Kwahadis, its nostrils flaring as it tested what was brought it on the cold wind.

"You do not like the smell of Comanche, do you, my new friend?"

Quanah tore the shiny concho slide from the yellow bandanna at his neck and looped the bright cloth over the horse's eyes, tying a knot securely behind the animal's jaws. As the two warriors held the big stallion, the Comanche war chief leaped on its bare back.

When it attempted to rear, Quanah instead drove his heels into its rear flanks. The horse bolted off, followed by the last of the raiding party to leave the scene of the attack.

"You will do, my new friend," Quanah whispered into the horse's ear, leaning forward as they raced up the snowy slope. "We will learn much from one another.

"Between now and the short-grass time when the Kwahadi will join the Cheyenne and Kiowa in one great fight against the white hide hunters, you and I will kill many buffalo together and learn much about each other."

The cold breath of Winter Man whipped tears from his eyes as the great gray horse easily surged ahead of the other ponies, its hooves tearing up clods of frozen ground and crusted snow.

"Then will come the time I will proudly ride you as I lead a thousand warriors down to drive all white hide hunters from the Staked Plain—for all time!"

I

January 1874

Already the Kiowa and Comanche were slaughtering their ponies to feed their starving families.

Warriors who had once felt the free wind blow through their unfettered hair as they galloped knee to haunch with the bulls and cows of those great herds were now reduced to butchering their own ribby, starving ponies.

Reuben Waller felt himself shrivel up and cry inside for them. Especially the little ones among Kicking Bird's Kiowa or old Ten Bears's Comanche bands who had willingly given up the old ways and obediently did as the white man told them: stay on the reservation; do not hunt the buffalo; believe in the white agents and soldiers, that their families will be fed with enough to fill the bellies of the crying children.

But the blizzards had come. Not just one, but one on the back of another. And then the monthly allotments for the reservation bands were delayed. Some flour, filled with wriggly weevils, did make it through just after the first of the year. Much of the rest never arrived at Fort Sill, nor farther north at the Darlington Agency for the Southern Cheyenne. Sergeant Waller was growing convinced that the government traders and contractors were simply waylaying the shipments, selling the goods on the side, and then double-billing an ignorant, apathetic Indian Bureau back in Washington City.

"They don't give a good goddamn for these Injuns," Waller muttered to himself as he brushed down his mount with the other soldiers from Company H among the stalls at Fort Sill, I.T. Indian Territory.

He had just led them north across the Red River from Texas with their two prisoners. White men both. Caught after an exhausting chase that had taken Waller's Negro soldiers all the way to eastern New Mexico, tracking a small band of white horse thieves who had stolen the pride of the Kiowa herd and pointed their noses west. Two were all Reuben ended up bringing back alive. The rest of the white thieves he and his Company H, Tenth U.S. Negro Cavalry, had left in shallow graves among the foothills of New Mexico. Along with two of Reuben's men.

Now Sergeant Waller had sworn he would see the two white men swing from the end of a rope for their crimes—if for no other reason than the hanging would show the restless, angry warriors that the army was serious about the growing unrest among the reservation bands. If the army and the agents weren't able to put an end to the horse thieving and the whiskey trading, then the army was sure as hell destined to have its hands full come green-up.

Spring would see the warriors slipping off the reservation for the open country to the west. Out there to the Texas Panhandle. The no-man's land south of the dead line where no white man was supposed to tread. The home of the greatest light cavalry the world had yet to see. That was the Staked Plain, home to the Kiowa and the Kwahadi Comanche.

Reuben turned at the sound of the familiar voice coming through the far doorway of the long company stable standing at the edge of the Fort Sill parade. Captain Louis H. Carpenter strode through the frosty breath of men and animals that made for a fog this sub-freezing January afternoon.

"Thought I'd find you with your men, Sergeant," said Carpenter, the white commander of H Company, Tenth Cavalry.

With a salute and that wide smile of his creasing a well-lined face, Waller replied, "Looked you up when we rode in late morning, Cap'n. Figured I could report in after we got squared off."

"That can wait, Sergeant." Carpenter presented his

12

hand in a show of genuine affection. "Good job, Reuben. Damned good job."

He felt the tug at his throat, knew his heart was rising to it with a heavy, sour lump. It had been this way many a time for Sergeant Waller, a youngster come of age in the Civil War, who joined up to fight Indians out on the plains not long after Appomattox. From the very first day of the newly-formed Tenth U.S. Cavalry, Reuben Waller had been out here on the central and southern plains. Riding beside Captain Carpenter, himself a man who inspired great loyalty among his brunettes, as the Negro troopers were called by their white counterparts.

Known as buffalo soldiers to the warrior bands of the great plains, wherever the Negro regiments were serving with unrelenting distinction.

"Thank you, Cap'n," he said, his voice heavy as his throat constricted. His eyes misting slightly with the nagging bite of the cold, Reuben watched some of the rest of his detail wander close. "We . . . we—"

Carpenter put a hand on Waller's shoulder. "It's all right, Sergeant. We can't always bring back all the men we take with us when we march away from post. Many a time, so many a time . . . well—you've heard me talk of Sandy Forsyth and me down in the Shenandoah, haven't you?"

He nodded. "Major Forsyth. Yes, Cap'n."

Reuben doubted he would ever forget those stories of Phil Sheridan's Shenandoah campaign, tales of heroics and blood, battles and gripping fear he had come to know like the fragments of his own life. How Forsyth had taken three pieces of Confederate lead during those long weeks of that Union campaign to squeeze off the rebels' supply lines, yet Forsyth still gritted his way into the saddle for every major battle.

It was that same George A. Forsyth, friend and fellow officer to a young Louis H. Carpenter, who had led fifty woolly civilians onto the trackless high plains of western Kansas and eastern Colorado Territory some six years before, stalking the fearsome Dog Soldiers of the Southern

Cheyenne. Until Roman Nose and Pawnee Killer turned and snapped back at those fifty frontiersmen.*

They had been cut down to twenty-eight who had not been wounded, all huddled on a sandbar in the middle of the Arickaree Fork of the Republican River, in a stinking ring of bloating horse carcasses and puddles of river seep the civilians had dug down into the sand to stay alive for those nine days of siege.

It was Captain Louis H. Carpenter's H Company, those shiny black faces of young soldiers anxious to prove themselves every bit as good as white cavalry, who were the first to raise the siege at the Arickaree. And it was none other than Carpenter himself who was first to cast his shadow over an old friend who sat at the bottom of a rifle pit grittily holding out against the pain of his three wounds, each inflicted by the Cheyenne in the first day's fighting.

It was there at the edge of Forsyth's pit, the blood dried at the bottom after days of relentless summer sun, that Reuben himself recognized the face of an old friend, the tall Irishman called Seamus Donegan.

Later that winter of 1868–69, Reuben had once more run across the gray-eyed plainsman out on the mapless expanse of the Texas Panhandle when Major Eugene Carr dispatched Donegan and a young Bill Cody out to search for Penrose's Negro soldiers. The two scouts did locate the buffalo soldiers, starving, despairing of surviving long enough to be rescued.†

And since that time, Waller had seen ever more of the central and southern plains, stationed first out of Fort Wallace, then Camp Supply, and now out of Fort Sill itself. It was where last fall, after some four years, Reuben had once again crossed trails with the long-haired Irishman with the ready grin and the sparkling gray eyes. He had been going south of the Red River with Jack Stillwell, another veteran of that famous fight at Beecher Island on the Arickaree. South to see what there was of the country around Jacksboro, Texas, where veteran scout Sharp

* The Plainsmen Series, vol. 3, *The Stalkers*
† The Plainsmen Series, vol. 4, *Black Sun*

Grover had settled down. Then months later, to the surprise of them all, Waller had bumped into both Donegan and Stillwell out on the aching expanse of the Staked Plain following the first blizzard of the winter. Waller was marching east with his pair of prisoners when his army posse ran across the white plainsmen and their military escort, stranded by the howling fury of winter come to the plains.*

Carpenter breathed deeply of the shockingly cold air, pursing his lips as if to hold down the pain of remembering the men who he had himself been forced to watch die in the many years he had devoted to the service to his country. He cleared his throat as if something thick threatened his forthcoming words. "Well, Sergeant—we're marching south come morning."

"South?" Waller asked as the rest of the black soldiers inched closer.

"Camp Augur."

"On the Red River. Yes, sir. I hear some war parties been sniping into the stockade there, firing at wood and water details—making everybody nervous as a bitch in heat. How long you figure we'll be dutying there?"

The captain shrugged. "No telling, fellas. All I know is I hope it will be a quiet winter. Give us time to put some meat on the ribs of these skinny mounts."

"And us too, sir!" Waller replied with a laugh, patting his own ribcage.

Carpenter nodded. "One thing's for certain—we'll all need to be in riding form come spring, fellas. Way everything is pointing, we'll be busy when warm weather arrives."

"War parties, sir?"

"These Kiowa and Comanche can't sit still for long watching their families slowly starving, living on the ponies they butcher to make up for what the government doesn't give them. I figure we'll have our hands full, Reuben. That, and more come spring."

Waller straightened and saluted. "Company H will be saddled and standing to horse at sunrise, Captain."

* The Plainsmen Series, vol. 6, *Shadow Riders*

Carpenter answered the salute and smiled, his eyes slowly crawling over the bright faces of his brunettes as wisps of foggy breath-smoke clung over their heads like frozen garlands of wispy gauze.

The captain nodded. "A change of scenery might do us all some good, fellas."

Reuben watched Carpenter turn and leave into the bright, cold afternoon sunlight beginning to stab the western doorway with streaks of artificial warmth. Suddenly, Carpenter stopped and turned.

"Oh, I almost forgot. Meant to tell you that rumor has it Lone Wolf is grieving something fierce. We're to be on the alert tonight. Colonel Davidson and Haworth have no idea how the chief is going to take the news."

"Grieving, Cap'n?"

"Post interpreter Horace Jones claims Lone Wolf's just got word his son was killed last month down in Texas."

"War party off the reservation," Reuben said. "We'd heard Lone Wolf's boy and nephew was leading a bunch south to Mexico."

Carpenter nodded, sullenly. "They were caught on the Double Mountain Fork of the Brazos last month. Nine warriors killed."

"Lone Wolf won't sit around camp grieving for long, Cap'n."

"We all figure for the worst of it. He'll cut his braids, kill some ponies, slash himself up a bit. But when it comes down to it—Lone Wolf's the sort who'll ride off the reservation to salve his wounded spirit."

"By getting the bodies of his boy and nephew?" Waller asked.

Squinting, Carpenter licked his lower lip. "The only way I figure Lone Wolf can salve his wounded spirit is to shed some white blood. His warriors will have to cross the Red River somewhere, Sergeant."

"And H Company will be down there at Camp Augur when they do, Cap'n."

Carpenter nodded one time, his face gone solid as late winter ice. "See you at sunrise, Sergeant."

"Yes, sir."

Word around Fort Still had it that new recruits were on their way from Jefferson Barracks. The Tenth Cavalry was finally being brought up to fighting strength—for only the second time in its eight-year history. New men were on their way, to arrive before spring found the Tenth marching off to war again.

Besides the new recruits, Carpenter had assured his company that new weapons were bound for the Tenth as well. Replacing the old, well-used Spencer carbines handed down from white regiments would be brand spanking new 1873 Model Springfield carbines. And for their hips would be the much-talked-about Colt's breech-loading revolvers.

Reuben Waller shuffled his men back to their work of currying and mucking and soaping down both saddles and tack. He turned back to his own mount, a sore-mouthed mare with a good heart.

No matter what, the sergeant thought as he began to gently brush the aging mare, the Tenth would be ready, by God.

If the Kiowa and Comanche and Cheyenne wanted to start a war in earnest . . . then, by God, the Tenth Cavalry would be ready this time.

He had mourned for the full waxing and then waning of the moon. And now it was the Moon of Ice in the Lodge.

Lone Wolf felt as if it were the moon of ice in his heart —so cold with grief and anger and rage did his chest feel.

The prescribed time of mourning was now complete and he could do as he had promised: take the trail south to recover the bodies of his favorite son, Tauankia, or Sitting in the Saddle, and his nephew, Guitain, Heart of a Young Wolf. Together with his brother, Red Otter, Lone Wolf had grieved piteously for the deaths of the two young warriors at the hands of the soldiers.

Both fathers had chopped off fingertips, hacked off their long braids, dragged knives across arms and shoulders and bellies and legs, praying that with the seeping of their own blood they might find some relief to their excruciating, unending grief. But all the wailing and fasting and praying and maiming did was to give the old chiefs more resolve than ever to see to it that not only were the bodies recovered, but even more so that the soldiers would pay for the murders.

Back in the Moon of Deer Shedding Horns the young men had slipped off from the reservation, a combined war party of Kiowa and Comanche. The survivors told the story that they had made their successful raid south into Mexico and were almost home when they had bumped into a strong reconnaissance force from Three-Finger Kinzie's Fourth Cavalry. Eleven warriors had fallen during a bloody, running skirmish with the yellowleg soldiers. Besides Lone Wolf's son and nephew, a well-known Comanche chief had fallen to the white man's guns. The uncle of a powerful, rising young Comanche shaman named Isatai.

Lone Wolf was certain Isatai would not let the murder of his uncle go unanswered.

Once again this afternoon he stopped at the greasy ring where his buffalo hide lodge had stood a month before. But in the prescribed ritual of mourning, Lone Wolf had burned it and most of his possessions, forced now to live with his wife's relations until they could once more secure hides in the spring hunt. As he kicked at the scattering of collapsed, charred lodgepole and rawhide and fragments of buffalo-hide lodge cover, Lone Wolf knew he would not be joining that hunt for the great shaggy beasts. Instead, he would be riding with the young men as they hunted the white man—both yellowleg soldiers and the Tehan buffalo hunters.

His eyes were a dull, slate-colored pair of murky windows that clouded up with hate.

Had not the treaty of Medicine Lodge Creek guaranteed that the last great buffalo herd on the southern plains belonged to the Kiowa and Comanche and Cheyenne? The chiefs had touched the pen to that treaty more than six years before, after hearing the promise of the white peace-talkers that no white man would be allowed onto the great buffalo range. That was Indian land. And those buffalo were promised to the Indians.

But in the past two winters, the white man was venturing farther and farther south of the dead line—that imaginary boundary that marked the northern extent of the no-man's land. Originally, the hide hunters had been forbidden to travel south of the Arkansas River. Then they pushed south to the Cimarron, and later south to the North Canadian. And now, stories told of small groups of white hide hunters occasionally seen in the country of the South Canadian. Come to steal what belonged to the Indian. Pushing, ever pushing, farther and farther south until they had reached the land of the Llano Estacado. The Staked Plain.

To the land of the whispering walls of mud.

When Lone Wolf had been but a boy entrusted with others to guard the great herds of the Kiowa warrior bands, the traders had come from far up the Arkansas River to the land of the Kiowa and Comanche, where they built their mud trading houses. Blankets for hides. Beads and pots and vermilion for hides. Whiskey for hides.

Yet the white man knew little of the legends of that very place where they raised their mud walls. Lo, the stories told by the old ones around the fires, tales passed down to them from the bands who had inhabited this land even before the coming of the Kiowa. Fables of the metal-heads who had marched out of the south on foot or rode the first horses the Indians had ever seen. Long columns of fair-skinned tai-bos with their shiny metal breasts and gleaming helmets that frightened the old ones who kept out of sight and watched in awestruck wonder the progress of these men who could remove their heads at each night's encampment. With their long lances aflutter with colorful pennons, the old fables stated that the metal-heads strode ever northward on some meaningful purpose.

Riding what those old bands first took to be large dogs—elk-dogs. What later came to be the ponies of the Kiowa and Comanche. They carried and used from time to time the loud roaring fire-sticks that spat smoke and belched in monstrous, fearsome reports that made the old ones tremble behind their sandy hills. The metal-heads pointed their fire-sticks at antelope and deer, killing their game the way the Indian pointed his arrow at what he needed to eat.

And the metal-heads walked on to the country beyond the South Canadian, then turned east, marching into the land where the sun rose each morning. Some of those were never to be seen again, like some mythical, many-headed and fearsome beast that was swallowed by the far horizon.

Come to search for the golden splendor of the Seven Cities. Then gone as mysteriously as they had appeared out of the south.

In all that time, in all those many generations gone since that long-ago time, Lone Wolf again realized as he stood looking over the greasy, blackened ruin of what had once been his lodge, no man had ever realized the full extent of the great wealth to be had out there in that land once traveled by the greedy, gold-seeking metal-heads . . . a land where the Kiowa and Comanche had struggled against one another before forming an uneasy alliance against all the rest.

No man realized what wealth lay out there at the edge of the Staked Plain.

At least, no white man knew the riches to be won.

2

March 1874

Seamus Donegan tore his eyes away from the shimmering surface of the red whiskey in his glass and glanced once more over the motley collection of customers in this Dodge City saloon. Winter was quickly soaking away into the first warming of the spring earth.

The more time he spent on these far, lonely plains, the more he enjoyed these all too brief visits to what passed for civilization here at the edge of an immense frontier. It wasn't just the whiskey. A man could take enough of that along if he were of a mind to. And he had to disagree with those who said it was for the company of a soft-skinned, honey-smelling woman that he had come to this hive. There were few like that soft-hipped, well-rounded Samantha Pike. Fewer still the likes of the mysterious Jennifer Wheatley . . . wherever the world had swallowed that auburn-haired beauty.

He tossed back the whiskey to kill the hurt of missing

them both and poured himself another before digging into a coat pocket to drag out his corncob pipe and a beaded pouch in which he carried his tobacco. He stared at it a moment—a gift from Bill Cody. The pipe from trader McDonald at Fort McPherson, Nebraska Territory. Up on the Platte where that mulatto renegade nearly had the Irishman stuck and gutted like a hog to slaughter . . . had it not been for young Bill Cody's curiosity and fast pistol hand.*

Buffalo Bill, he had been called for the first time in that winter of 1868. Killing buffalo for the railroad and the army had brought him a little fame in the ensuing years. And it had brought the rest to Dodge City on the Arkansas. Out there at the end of this street where saloons and chippie nests stood shoulder to hip lay the huge sod corrals, crowded with the huge mountains of buffalo bones destined for shipment east, there to be ground into fertilizer. Farther still stood the long rows of hide ricks, some fifty to sixty hides high—the stacks of dried flint hides a man could smell as far as he could see as the weather grew warm and the wind shifted out of the southwest.

As slow as spring was to make its full, tantalizing appearance, winter had not worn well on this town, nor its many temporary inhabitants. What with the numerous blizzards that kept the men hunkered down for weeks at a time with nothing to do. Or the fact that the buffalo appeared to be gone far, farther still to the south this year than ever before. On top of that, none of the merchants were making all that they normally made come this time of year with the first rains of spring mixed with the last snows of winter. Too few were in need of a new outfit before he rode off for buffalo ground.

Trouble was, as young as Dodge City was, it seemed the town had already seen its heyday. Time was, Jack Stillwell had told him, there were buffalo hunter camps strung up and down the Arkansas in either direction from Dodge City like glass trade beads on a gigantic necklace. And a man would be hard pressed to ride out of hearing of the

* The Plainsmen Series, vol. 4, *Black Sun*

big guns the hunters used, the booming heard from gray of first light until well past the falling of the sun. Those were the days the buffalo came to drink at the Arkansas and every man with enough money to buy a Sharps rifle could make himself a small but quick fortune.

But inside of three years the fates had begun to frown on the likes of the hide men in Kansas. A good number of those who had hunted through '72 and '73 had already seen the elephant and given up, bucking back east, some perhaps gone on west to try something different out California way.

Only the tough had stayed on, squeezing out their last few dollars through their fingers this past winter, waiting until the time came that they could wander south from Dodge, south far enough to find the buffalo ground. Word had it in Kansas that these were the toughest of their breed —the toughest that ever would be. The holdouts, knowing little else but skinning knives and buffalo loads, Sharps and needle guns. They were the toughest, if for no other reason than every man jack of them knew where the buffalo ground would be come this season.

Down in Indian country. On the Staked Plain. Home of the Kiowa and Kwahadi Comanche.

The smelly men in their bloodstained clothing and long, greasy hair which draped past their shoulders huddled at their tables or lounged against the wobbly bar, regaling one another with one story after another of past hunts. And no season better than the year just gone. It had been the peak, they knew. So, why wouldn't the hunt of '74 be all the better?

Last year had seen better than a quarter-million buffalo hides hauled east by the Atchison, Topeka & Santa Fe Railway alone. A million and a half pounds of buffalo tongue. Two and three-quarter million pounds of bone gone east for fertilizer. Estimates from the railroads had it that in the last two seasons, more than 3,698,730 buffalo had been killed.

"While there's buffalo," those holdouts waiting in the Dodge City saloons toasted one another, "there'll be hide hunters!"

"And when you shoot your way through the last of the herds?" asked Seamus Donegan more than once. "What then?"

The question usually brought a smile and a sweep of a hand to brush the long hair from the shoulder of their thick, woolen coats which had taken on the patina and character of countless campfires.

"Then a buffalo hunter finds something else to do till there's some other critter to hunt. Something else to do— like drinking bad whiskey, my friend!"

They were of a breed that Donegan had to admit he liked, if not admired. While a few were of a kind that no man could call friend, the sort that drew trouble like honey drew flies, or caused it wherever they trod, Seamus had found most to be likable, honest, hardworking and downright enjoyable folk. A few were even the sort he would not question at his back in a serious fight of it.

Men like that young Billy Dixon, who stood among a gaggle of others against the bar. It had been last summer when first he met Dixon, here in Dodge City. And therein learned that Dixon was a friend of Sharp Grover's, back when the old frontiersman had scouted for Custer's campaign down to the Washita in '68. Dixon had been nothing more than a wet-eared teamster back then, but learning all the time because he was the sort to keep his mouth shut, eyes and ears open to the likes of Sharp Grover.

Some five and a half years later now, wasn't a man in this part of the country who didn't know who Billy Dixon was, who hadn't heard of his prowess with a Sharps rifle, a man who didn't like his ready smile and offer of a friendly hand.

Dixon's long hair gleamed like a shiny coal shuttle in the greasy light of the oil lamps glimmering against the fading afternoon light as he pantomimed a shot, throwing an imaginary rifle to his shoulder, squinting down the barrel of this make-believe octagon barrel, cocking the hammer and easing back on the trigger to make that boasted kill. Others listened in rapt silence, men like Jim Hanrahan, a noted frontiersman in southwestern Kansas in his own right; men like the fiery-headed "Brick" Bond and the cruel-faced "Dutch" Henry Born, who, while he had a reputation as a man-killer and a horse thief, had harmed no man that Donegan knew.

Guns.

Out here, one way or another, a man always made his living with a gun. Or kept his life with a gun, Seamus thought, sipping at the whiskey that scalded his tongue no more.

Word up from the Darlington Agency where the Southern Cheyenne were penned up had it that the bands were getting their hands on better and better weapons all the time. Down on the Kiowa and Comanche reservation too. Seemed there were always the white traders who preferred to barter for buffalo hides rather than hunt the buffalo. Whiskey and weapons. Liquor and gunpowder traded on the shadowy fringes of Indian Territory.

Donegan didn't doubt it. Where there was a chance to make a dollar, someone would be there to steal that dollar. And if the whole dirty business meant selling the latest in rifles or that new Colt's breech-loading revolver to the tribes corralled on the reservations—the young warriors would have those weapons.

Lovingly, Seamus touched the butts of both pistols belted at his waist, a separate belt for each holster astraddle his hips. The army .44's had seen him through a lifetime and more since coming to Indian country back in '66, when he had a hunger for gold and the Bozeman Road had beckoned him north through Red Cloud's country.*

These old pistols with their scratched barrels and well-rubbed grips would do nicely, thank you, he thought.

As well as doing nicely for those men who in the next few weeks would finally venture south of the dead line, stepping foot into that no-man's land of Indian country to search for the southern herd. They were to be admired, he offered. If only for the size of their balls. A hundred miles or better south and west of Dodge City they would have to go to find the buffalo.

Yet it would be there too that the hide men were sure to

---

* The Plainsmen Series, vol. 1, *Sioux Dawn*

find the warriors jealously guarding the last of the great, shaggy animals. Something to admire in the likes of Billy Dixon and the rest of these men, each man of them willing to walk into that lion's den like modern-day Daniels.

The remembrance made his eyes smart more than the heavy pall of thick, blue smoke in this stinking place ever could. Just that gentle prick of his childhood memory on a biblical story of old made him remember his mother. He drained the glass and stared at the last drop left against the thick, opaque bottom.

A'times he felt just like that. Without much left at the bottom of his soul. What did he have to show for all these years in Amerikay? he asked himself. Here he sat in a dingy sod hovel hard by the Arkansas River, among hard men more resolute than he in grabbing at their dreams.

He had tried, Seamus commiserated with himself. Lord knows, he had tried. But here he sat, drinking bad whiskey, waiting out his chance to go chasing after some dreamed-of fortune.

"You should be working for your daily bread, Seamus," he whispered into the glass, then flicked his tongue at that last drop of red whiskey slowly coursing its way toward his lips.

"And I've found work for us."

Startled at the surprise of the familiar voice, Seamus jerked around as Jack Stillwell seated himself at the tiny table beside the Irishman. Stillwell was every bit as curly-headed as he had been that day more than five years ago when he had signed on as the youngest of those who would ride out into Cheyenne country with Major George A. Forsyth's fifty scouts.* He had proved himself a genuine hero, slipping away from the Arickaree under cover of darkness and crossing more than a hundred miles of high plains wilderness to carry word of the survivors' plight on that bloody island where the warriors of Roman Nose had the white men huddled behind the bloating carcasses of their dead horses and mules.

* The Plainsmen Series, vol. 3, *The Stalkers*

"Don't tell me—you're guiding more government men, is it, Jack?"

Stillwell smiled, his eyes merry. "Be some time before I'll get myself talked into guiding for the likes of those treasure-hungry bastards, Pierce and Graves."*

"Makes no matter what it is, Jack—count me out. I've my own business to attend to. And attend to it at last I will," Seamus replied, pouring himself another brimming glass of whiskey.

"Count you out? Before you've heard me out?"

"All I know is that in the last few months of traveling with you, I've nearly been roasted to death in a prairie fire, then nearly froze to death in the first bleeming blizzard of the season. It's time I relax a bit." He hoisted his glass to Stillwell. "And relax is just what I intend on doing."

Stillwell watched the Irishman bring the glass to his lips. "Scouting: just what you was cut out to do from the start."

He dragged his big, scarred hand across his lips, swiping the droplets from his shaggy mustache that hung over the groomed Vandyke beard. "Drinking whiskey and slipping my hand inside a woman's perfumed blouse sounds more to me liking, Jack."

"Scouting's in your blood. Liam was one of the best—" Jack stopped mid-sentence.

He could tell Stillwell had realized his transgression. "It's all right." Seamus topped off the glass and raised it. "Here's to the memory of me uncle Liam—a finer man never guided the U.S. Army across this trackless wilderness."

"You're blood of his blood, and always will be, Seamus. Chances are, you'll be even better than Liam ever was."

"If scouting was something I wanted to do with the rest of me life."

Stillwell leaned back in his chair and sighed. "Whiskey and women. That's it? For the rest of your life?"

"What you're offering isn't anywhere near as much fun, is it, Jack?"

* The Plainsmen Series, vol. 6, *Shadow Riders*

He plopped his elbows down on the table as he leaned forward. "Working for Colonel Miles."

Seamus eyed him thoughtfully for but a moment. "He's up at Larned, is he not?"

Jack's head bobbed. "With about half his regiment. The Fifth Infantry. Miles is beginning to call in most of the rest from the other posts where they've been on duty."

With a squint he asked, "Another campaign?"

After glancing around and leaning forward, Stillwell replied, "Too much happened for the army to let go unanswered. From reports of the Cheyenne raiding into Kansas, on down to Texas where the Kiowa and Comanche have been striking here and there."

"Can't say as I blame them, Jack. What with the white horse thieves waltzing right in and rustling Indian stock from under the noses of the army and agents both. I'd get riled too. Reuben and the rest down at Sill got their hands full this time: keeping the whites away from the Indians and keeping the Indians from striking back at the whites. Thank you, but no, Jack."

"I figure it will be the army's loss, not having the likes of Seamus Donegan riding out come the spring campaign."

"They're going after the bands for sure?"

"The smart money has it that it's only time before the Comanche and the rest are crushed once and for all."

He nodded. "Aye, only a matter of time, isn't it?"

Seamus remembered the last few weeks he and Jack had taken traveling north from Fort Richardson, when he had finally torn himself from Samantha Pike and Sharp Grover and made his excuses about leaving, made up what he thought would be lies about returning to Jacksboro when this business on the Canadian was done and over with.

But the more he thought about Samantha, how her kiss had been like a lick of flame sucking into a piece of over-dry tender that first night in Grover's pole-and-shake barn. Just looking at her, remembering the shape of the shadow her naked body cut in the moonlight, was enough to put drool on a dead man.

But he had convinced himself it was best to leave that woman who could raise more hell in him than any number

27

of average blanketings he had enjoyed. Or so he told himself all the way north from Texas, crossing the Red River to Fort Sill. From there on he had sensed something almost tangible, something of an uneasy feeling to the crisp winter air that nudged the leafless branches of the blackjack oaks and alders along the water courses. More than winter itself had given the land the odor of things dead and dying.

"The wrinkled old medicine doctors been thumping their drums and whirling their rattles," Reuben Waller had explained one winter evening during their brief layover at Sill. "Those old men in the council lodges been praying for the game to come back while the young men try to dance back the buffalo." The Negro sergeant had wagged his head morosely. "They're down to eating their ponies."

"What ponies don't get stolen by the likes of those bad characters you tracked all the way to New Mexico, Reuben," Donegan had replied in the Fort Sill mess hall where they shared many a cup of black, potent army coffee.

While the white horse thieves emptied the tribal pastures of horses, and the harsh winter worked its evil to empty the bellies of the reservation bands. The Kiowa and Comanche and Cheyenne hearts were being sucked dry as a milkweed pod of all hope. All hope, that is, save for leaving the white man's reservations and returning to the old way of life on the buffalo ground.

If the agents weren't admitting it, then at least the army was openly talking about the fact that this growing despair one day would likely bloom into outright frenzy. And Colonel Black Jack Davidson's Tenth Cavalry would be right at the heart of whatever would come to rock these southern plains. Time and time only would tell when this land would tear itself apart.

"So it's still the gold you're after, Irishman."

Donegan's gray eyes quickly flashed their warning at Stillwell. "You promised you'd still your tongue about it when you said you wanted no part of this treasure hunt."

Jack grinned. "I did. And I got out because I got to thinking how crazy a tale it was. You really believe you'll find a fortune in Spanish gold out there?" He pointed west, toward the Staked Plain. That fabled Llano Estacado of Coronado's conquistadors.

"Time was, I thought you believed in it too, Jack."

"Perhaps I still do," he sighed. "But, I'll not die chasing that gold like a madman."

"A madman am I now?" He snorted and drained his glass with a quick toss.

"Easy money, eh, Seamus?"

"By the saints! Been nothing easy about it, Jack."

"But scouting—"

"Scouting's easy work? You're bloody well daft!"

Stillwell pushed back from the table a bit. "You'll not ride with me to Larned to see what Colonel Miles has on his mind?"

"Not while there's the chance that there's a fortune to be found out there, Jack. Gold is what brought me to this bleeming wilderness to begin with eight winters gone now. And gold is what I pray I'll still find."

Stillwell stood. "You eaten today?"

Donegan finally shook his head, staring into his glass.

"C'mon. Least I can do is buy you supper."

"I'll stay here. Thank you anyway."

Slipping his hand beneath the Irishman's arm, Stillwell said, "We're eating over at Louis Abragon's place tonight."

A sudden heat crossed his cheeks as a fire leapt to his heart. "The Mexican's back?"

"Heard he came in this afternoon from Leavenworth. Brought him back some new girls."

Donegan stood with a clatter of chair legs on the uneven floor planks. "Supper, and by glory some new soft faces to look upon. What in blazes are we waiting for, Jack?"

3

Moon of First Eggs, 1874

The new grass was raising its head across the hillsides as far as a man could see. For more than three moons now Lone Wolf had stared into the distance, looking south and west. Where lay the bodies of his son and nephew.

He could wait no longer.

Their ponies had grown strong enough to make this journey. Tonight would be the dark of the moon. He would ride south with the young men, elude the patrols along the river and cross into Tehas to recover the bodies.

His wives did not want him to go. Grief was strong enough to keep other men at home. But not Lone Wolf. His normally grave face had been chiseled even more deeply now with the scars of mourning, every bit as deeply as were the fresh scars that tracked his arms, scored his legs. His once long hair, the pride of a Kiowa warrior, now hung in ugly tatters. Hair he had hacked off then burned in the same fire that had consumed his lodge and most everything he had owned.

Lone Wolf would complete this vow he had made to the Grandfather Above. First to recover the bodies. Then to exact revenge on the white man for the murders.

They were but boys, he thought now as the cool breeze of evening brought with it the smells of blossoms along the creek bottom. The yellowleg soldiers had murdered exuberant boys gone on a raid to Mexico. Nothing short of murder.

For sure the Comanche and Kiowa war party had stolen some Mexican horses, killed some Mexican herders, and were bringing north some Mexican prisoners—but what business was that of Three-Finger Kinzie's white soldiers anyway?

Better that the army use their guns to keep the hide hunters away from the buffalo ground.

With the coming of each winter, Lone Wolf had watched in growing alarm the gradual disappearance of the great herds that had once blanketed the southern plains. Come now the crying of the children with empty bellies, and the long faces on the old ones who had too little to eat, the going of the buffalo was no longer only a matter of starvation. The white man was stamping out the Indian's spiritual existence.

Rising up when and where they could, the bands gathered around Lone Wolf struck back. In February they had attacked some white surveyors northwest of the Anadarko

Agency, killing one and driving the rest back to the agent's buildings. A month later some young warriors boldly fired into a squad of buffalo soldiers near Fort Sill itself. The brunettes returned the fire and chased the warriors until they scattered and disappeared. But several trails of blood were found on the ground, along with a Kiowa war bonnet. And ever since the first leafing of the trees this spring, snipers had been firing into the Camp Augur stockade of buffalo soldiers at the Red River, from as close as eighty paces. Tensions were clearly growing.

It would soon be time to strike with more muscle. But first Lone Wolf had to recover the bodies.

As was the Kiowa custom in such matters, Lone Wolf asked another chief to lead the expedition. Mamay-day-te agreed, for he had been a close childhood friend of Tauankia, Lone Wolf's son, and as well a member of the *on-de,* the highest caste among the Kiowa. There was no question in his agreeing, especially in light of the fact that he had been one of the leaders of the raid returning from Mexico when the warriors were killed. Another survivor of the fight with the yellowlegs, Long Horn, declared that he knew where the bodies had been abandoned—he volunteered to guide the Kiowa south into Tehas.

Beneath the black of the moonless night they led their ponies away from the Cache Creek campsite, stopping to climb aboard the animals only when they were a handful of miles from the agency. With nothing more than starlight, memory of the terrain, and their prayers, the two dozen warriors pointed their noses south to the land of the Tehannos, where the Kiowa were forbidden to go.

Seeking cover when the sun rose each day, emerging from hiding only when twilight darkened the land, the Kiowa took three nights to reach the Red River. Crossing the following night to avoid the patrols of buffalo soldiers, the warriors crossed into the land that would bring them sure death were they spotted by the yellowlegs. It was here that Long Horn pointed their noses west by southwest, moving out of the lush country for the more open landscape as the horsemen climbed ever on toward the Staked Plain. The warming days passed endlessly as they waited out the crossing of the sun. Each night's travel seemed all too short while Long Horn led them beneath the dark sky, taking his bearings from nothing more than the glittering clusters of stars overhead.

Two suns past the White River, the guide led them into a shallow canyon where he informed the warriors they would await sunrise, and sleep out the day.

"How far now?" Lone Wolf asked the question he had given voice to every morning of their journey.

"We will be there tonight," answered Long Horn.

He had not expected the answer. So close now to the body of his son. The body of his nephew. Lone Wolf looked at Red Otter, his brother. The warrior nodded.

"Those of you who came to recover the bones of our relatives, do not climb down from your ponies," Lone Wolf told them.

With a hushed silence heavy like the still air trapped in that narrow ravine, the two dozen gathered close, ponies snorting.

"We go on, Mamay-day-te. Do you agree?" Red Otter asked, turning to the expedition leader.

The young warrior looked first at the two grieving fathers, then glanced quickly over the rest, assessing their will. Finally he nodded. "We go on. Long Horn, take us to the hillside where we left the bodies of our friends."

A warm spring sun hung nearly at mid-sky when Long Horn reined up and pointed a finger into the distance. He traced the path of the brush that rimmed the narrow thread of a creek leading into the timbered hills.

"There. You will find the bodies of your sons," said the guide.

Lone Wolf looked at his brother. Then he turned to the rest halted behind them. "You can stay, or you can come. It matters not. Red Otter and I will not be long in gathering the bones of our loved ones."

He did not have to look behind him as he tapped heels to his pony's ribs to know the rest were following in respectful silence. Red Otter halted at his side among the stunted piñon. Their moccasins touched the ground together as some of the animals snorted, the stench of death still strong on the breeze.

It was heavy in his nostrils as he knelt beside what was left of the first body.

What had not been brutalized by the winter storms and spring rains had been discovered by predators. Little flesh remained on the bones picked over by the four-leggeds and the flies-above. Nonetheless, the stench of death's own decay hung over this place, and would forever remain in his nostrils.

"This is my son," Red Otter said quietly as he lifted a shred of leather legging from the new grass, a bit of colorful quillwork adorning that scrap of clothing.

With a sigh, Lone Wolf rose shakily as Red Otter fell to his knees and began his wailing. He moved off a few yards, his eyes searching. Then he spotted something white sticking up from the green of the new grass and those rainbow colors of an array of prairie flowers draping the hillside.

It was a bone. A long, heavy leg bone looking so profane and out of place here among the new life of the prairie. And near it the shreds of clothing that showed it was Tauankia's moccasin. Among the scattering of bones, Lone Wolf collapsed to his knees, beginning to wail and keen, his voice sharp against the midday air. Down the slope, Red Otter's grief was growing as well.

Lone Wolf crawled clumsily on his hands and knees, scooping bones and bits of torn clothing from the sandy soil and new grass, clutching the remains of what had been his firstborn son in the crook of one arm, the tears flowing freely.

Mamay-day-te wordlessly came to his side.

Blinking his eyes clear, Lone Wolf looked up into the spring sky at the tall young warrior. The expedition leader spread his own blanket on the ground, then stepped away out of respect and his own mourning. Down the slope, Long Horn was spreading a blanket for Red Otter.

Onto Mamay-day-te's blanket Lone Wolf carefully laid the bones of his son. He felt colder inside with each new fragment he located in the grass of that piñon-studded hillside. Yet, it amazed him that it was a cold fire he sensed in his breast as he performed this necessary ritual. While cold, the flames of his fury for the white man grew higher still as he gathered these last tangible shreds of his favorite son.

First one bone, then another . . . Lone Wolf held them to the sky, to the sun, crying out over them, releasing his grief, vowing to avenge the dishonor, the death, the murder of his flesh. The spilling of his blood—

"Red Otter!"

Down the slope that voice lanced through the Kiowa chief's mourning. He blinked tears free and looked downhill at his brother. Mamay-day-te was hurrying to Red Otter's side.

"Lone Wolf!" the young warrior shouted up the slope. He was pointing to the south.

"Our sentries—they see yellowlegs coming!"

Lone Wolf stood. "The soldiers?" He was gripped with despair—yet hope took wing that his fury might here be unleashed. His heart beating wildly in that next instant, he asked, "How many?"

Spreading five fingers, Mamay-day-te tapped his left forearm once with a right hand, then tapped the right with his left. Five-times-ten. Then he brushed his fingers along one forearm.

"And a few more," Lone Wolf whispered to himself as he knelt quickly, his eyes jabbing across the nearby grass to see if he had missed any of the bones.

There were more soldiers than this small band of warriors should attempt to fight off.

"We go!" Lone Wolf shouted as he folded in the corners of the blanket and cradled it in his arm, hurrying down the slope to where Red Otter and the rest awaited him.

Handing the clumsy blanket to Long Horn, he clambered atop his pony and took up the rawhide rein before accepting the blanket bundle once more. As soon as Red Otter had mounted and again held the bones of Guitain, Mamay-day-te waved his arm.

They took off in a clatter across the sandstone and rock, down the narrow creek that would lead them south, farther still into the land of the Tehannos. Lone Wolf smiled grimly. He approved of the bold move taken by the young war chief. Heading south and east was the only course offered them at this moment, the only way they could escape the army patrol.

"They are heading for this place," Red Otter said breathlessly as he brought his pony alongside his brother's mount.

"They knew we would come," Lone Wolf replied, fury rising in his voice.

So much in his life had led to tragedy. An accomplished warrior, every bit as good an orator as Satanta himself, Lone Wolf nonetheless had been forced by circumstances to play a secondary role in the life of his people. While Satanta enjoyed much greater prestige, Lone Wolf almost gave his life fighting for the honor of his people eight winters before, when Yellow Hair Custer came to drive the tribes back to their reservations. And now as the white man encircled that Kiowa reservation more tightly than ever before, with Satanta's influence on the wane, it appeared the boot-licking peace chief, Kicking Bird, held most of the tribe in his hand.

Lone Wolf's heart cried out as the wind whipped his short, shaggy hair from the corners of his mouth. Arrrgh! He could not even bring home the bones of his son without the yellowlegs harassing his journey.

For the next two days the Kiowas' heels were dogged by the soldiers, having little time to rest, graze or water their ponies. It was the evening of that second day when Red Otter signaled a halt and reined up beside his brother.

"There, Lone Wolf," he said, pointing toward the ocher bluff rising above them more than a hundred feet.

Lone Wolf glanced at their backtrail, seeing the dust of the pursuing soldiers. "You want us to take our ponies up that steep slope?"

Red Otter wagged his head sadly. "No. We must leave the bones of our sons here."

Again he glanced at the nearness of the dust hung beyond the hills. The soldiers were driving them south. There was a fort of yellowlegs farther south. How far, he did not know. But one thing was certain: the soldiers were squeezing Mamay-day-te's war party between them and the soldier fort. The trap might close tomorrow. Perhaps the next day. But soon . . .

"Leave them here?" he asked, already knowing the answer in his heart.

"I do not want to leave the bones where the soldiers will know where," Red Otter replied.

For a moment he studied the narrow clefts in the rocks above them on the red and brown ridge. He sighed. "Yes."

They slid from their ponies quickly and shuffled clumsily up the steep slope, dragging behind them the heavy blanket bundles lashed with rawhide strips. When he had neared the top, less than ten feet from the lip of the bluff itself, Lone Wolf halted near a narrow crack in the rock wall.

Turning the bundle on its side, he was able to shove it into the mouth of the crevice with difficulty. Then it became easier as the blanket disappeared into the shadowed darkness. Before it was totally out of sight, Lone Wolf bent his head and kissed the hem of the dirty blanket.

"Good-bye, my son. One day I will return for you," he whispered. "Wearing the scalps of many white men on my shirt and leggings to show you. Good-bye."

Immediately he shoved the bundle into the crevice, burying it the length of his own arm so that no man would ever be able to see a hint of the red blanket. Then he turned and slid down the steep slope in a flurry of dust and rocks tumbling into the creek bottom.

"These ponies are weary," Mamay-day-te said as he tossed Lone Wolf the reins to the chief's animal.

"We will find others soon." He leaped atop the pony and reined about, hammering heels to its ribs.

"White settlers?"

Lone Wolf nodded. "If not them—we will steal soldier horses."

It was as he had promised—two hard, trail-pounding days later, after a nonstop chase that left little bottom in their war ponies. Smoke smudging the horizon to the south gave away the position of what they thought would be the white man's fort called Concho. But in bellying up to the crest of a brush-covered hill, the Kiowa warriors saw the smoke did not come from the soldier fort some three miles farther down the valley. Instead, the smoke came from the cookfires of a camp of buffalo soldiers. And nearby grazed their herd of cavalry mounts.

Smiling, without a word, the warriors nodded to one another and descended the hill.

"I will take the ponies toward the fort," Mamay-day-te offered.

"You will act as a decoy?" Red Otter asked.

The young war chief nodded. "I am responsible for the lives of all of you. I will make it look as if we are all mounted and skirting around the soldier fort to avoid the yellowlegs."

"I will count on you doubling back after you have freed all our ponies to be on their way—once you are past the fort," Lone Wolf declared.

"I will rejoin you in a day," Mamay-day-te said.

Lone Wolf turned to the others, waving his arms, hollering his orders. "Strip your ponies. Bring bridles and blankets with you. We will wait down by the creek until nightfall, when we will sneak in among the soldier horses. We can ride some off, driving the others before us so that the yellowlegs cannot follow."

"To the soldiers who follow us already, you will make it look as if we are giving wide berth to the fort the soldiers call Concho?" asked Long Horn, turning to the war chief.

Mamay-day-te swept to the back of his pony. "May the Grandfather Above make you as invisible as the wind tonight when you take the soldier horses. Hep-hah!"

He brought his pony around, waving a noisy piece of rawhide that startled the other animals he began driving on down the creek bank. Two dozen riderless ponies and one young warrior bringing up the rear, galloping toward the soldier fort.

"He has the heart of a mountain lion," Red Otter said quietly as the ponies disappeared from view.

Lone Wolf turned on him, his face grave. "If he had truly had the heart of a mountain lion, Mamay-day-te

37

would not have left the bodies of our sons on that moun-
tainside."

Pushing past his brother, Lone Wolf signaled the rest to
follow him on foot down into the dry creekbottom, where
they would hide themselves until nightfall.

With a prayer in his heart and a curse on his lips, Lone
Wolf vowed he would leave at least one soldier dead this
night before the cavalry horses belonged to the Kiowa. It
would be but one death against the death of his son.

But it would be the first of many deaths he hoped would
drive from his bowels the aching fury he suffered.

4

Late March 1874

"It's a sure way to make yourself some money, Seamus,"
said Billy Dixon to the tall Irishman seated at his table in
Hoover's saloon. It had the roughest of reputations, perhaps because it sold the strongest of whiskey.

"Sounds to me like it's a sure way to get myself killed,
Billy. No thanks."

Dixon sighed. "You're a good man with a rifle, I've
heard tell. Many a lesser man's made himself a small fortune out on the buffalo range. That's country so open you
can see three days behind and a full week ahead of yourself. But if you're of a mind not to give it a try . . ."

"I've other plans," Donegan replied. "And they don't
include making myself a target down on the buffalo
range."

"I just come in from that country—didn't see a feather
or sign of smoke one. Shit, if those Injuns make any big
stink over the hide men coming down there, why I'll kiss
your ass till it barks like a blue fox."

Donegan eyed the young buffalo hunter. "You been
down there lately, have you?"

"Circled down to Palo Duro, 'round to Buffalo Springs
and the Red River, 'round about to Adobe Walls and back
to—"

"Adobe Walls, you say?"

Dixon was suddenly taken aback by the interruption and intense interest glowing in the Irishman's gray eyes at the mention of the place. "Yes," he answered slowly. "You heard of them?"

"Heard they're the ruins of an old trading post. Anything left of them?"

Dixon wagged his head, scratching the back of his neck. "Walls nearly washed away—only some four foot high now. Why?"

Donegan averted his eyes, staring into his whiskey. "Just . . . interested. You see anything—unusual."

"Strange questions a man to be asking me."

"Never you mind then, Billy," he said before he drank from his glass.

"It damn well may be the last hurraw on this part of the plains, Seamus," Dixon pressed on, trying to sell the Irishman on the idea of throwing in for the trip south. "Don't you damn well feel the sap of spring running in your veins?"

"Whiskey is what I'm feeling, Billy. And I ain't empty-headed enough to go somewhere asking for trouble. Damn, but don't it always find me where I'm hiding anyway."

"Seamus, I went south to smell things over, see where I'd want to camp come the time the herds wander back north."

"You was lucky you didn't lose your pretty hair."

Dixon shrugged. "Perhaps luck does have something to do with it. The way that big outfit got shot up down on the Palo Duro last month. But the hide wagons of Mooars—filled to the sidewalls with prime winter hides—sure did make a lot of us sit up and take notice. Made me start thinking."

"And made you ride down to that country on your own to take a look around."

Dixon leaned in, slapping the table with one hand in excitement. "The best part is the traders are coming with us, Seamus!"

"Traders?"

Billy's head bobbed. "Men like Charlie Myers."

A. C. "Charlie" Myers had been a buffalo hunter of a time himself, then of recent began a general mercantile business. His specialty had been the sugar-curing of buffalo out at the smokehouse he had built on Pawnee Fork. He had a profitable business shipping to eastern markets. After sugar-curing each buffalo "ham," Myers smoked it and sewed it in canvas to preserve it for its journey east. He was the sort, Dixon knew, who had not only the money, but the savvy, to make a grand scheme work. And opening up a full-scale trading post south of the dead line was a grand scheme indeed.

"None of the traders been moving a whole hell of a lot of their goods here in Dodge, so Myers made a number of us an offer. If we'd go down into buffalo country after that Texas herd, he'd set up shop for us right down there on the Canadian."

Donegan nodded. "Myers got every reason in the world to talk you boys into going, don't he?"

"Better having a trader down there than one way up here over a hundred miles away from the buffalo ground. Times've changed, Irishman. No more are the big shaggies close by Dodge the way they once was."

"Myers only got two wagons. How's he figure on hauling enough goods south to make it worth his while, yours too?"

"That's the beauty in it, don't you see? Myers will pay every hunter with an outfit—wagons and teams—to haul his goods south for him. We'll all be going south empty anyway, and Charlie will pay us the going dollar for freight to get his truck down there for him."

"It all makes some sense to me now," Donegan replied, looking toward the door.

"So, you'll throw in with us?"

He shook his head, grinning. "Not that, Billy. I was saying it made sense that this town suddenly had some life pumped back into it. I wondered why for the past few days —just what all the excitement was."

"Folks like Myers and Emanuel Dubbs aren't taking just anybody down."

"I'd figure they'd want all comers—sweeten their share of the proceeds."

Dixon shook his head. "Myers going to sell everything at Dodge City prices—he swore he won't gouge a one of us. But in return, he wants to be sure that no one is going but those who got the sand and tallow to make a stand of it—if it comes down to it."

Donegan smiled, licking drops of whiskey from his lips. "Oh, it'll come to it, no doubt. But it's a smart man will back himself up with only those who got the grit to stare trouble in the face."

"There's no running this time, we figure. Far enough from Dodge City where we'll be. Too far for troops to reach us. We're on our own down there if the Kiowa and Comanche want to stir things up south of the dead line. Yessir—it's fight to the last ditch and victory to the strong I say."

"It's their buffalo ground."

"No it ain't, Irishman. That's ground open to any man what's got the balls to make his claim on it."

"Sounds to me like you're so all-fired set on heading to that Injin country because it's the last place to make buffalo hunting a paying proposition, Billy. You know where you'll be having Myers set up for business?"

Dixon wagged his head once. "Not for sure. Anyplace there's good water and grass, enough timber too."

"And buffalo," Seamus said, musing on it a moment. "Your enterprise got a lot of takers?"

"Some of the best, Seamus. Just yesterday Jim Hanrahan rolled into town from the north country and signed on soon as he heard tell of our plans."

"He a good man?"

"Hanrahan? One of the best buffalo hunters in this part of the frontier. He's been in on the hide trade from the first day and runs a good outfit. Was a big boost when he said he was heading south with us."

"Sounds to me like you'll have enough grit along with you to stare down any Injin trouble . . . as long as you aren't filling your ranks with the likes of that one at the bar," Donegan replied, thumbing the greenhorn propped against the wobbly bar.

The easterner clearly stood out. "Fairchild? Just a lawyer from back east out to see the woolly west, Donegan. I don't figure he'll be going along."

As much as he hoped it, Dixon could not be sure. Something about the tenderfoot's shiny, store-bought suit and plug hat nestled squarely atop his well-groomed head, that brilliant spray of colorful vest there beneath his silk cravat, which made him stand out garish and ungainly among the rougher men of this town.

"You got a blacksmith going, haven't you?"

Dixon leaned back, assuredly. "Damn if we don't."

Donegan appeared genuinely surprised. "You don't say?"

"Fella by the name of O'Keefe. Got a wagon hired to carry his bellows and forge. There'll be plenty of work for him down there—not only on the wagons coming to and fro, but what with setting up the shops: hinges, hardware, and all the rest."

"Now, let me see if I get this right," the Irishman said, grinning widely. "You're taking enough trade goods down to supply every hunter in the surrounding country."

"Right."

"And with it, enough ammunition to supply a small army."

"Which is what we'll have to be—poking our sticks down there in that hornet's nest."

"And Myers is taking some whiskey along as well?"

"Knew I'd interest you, Donegan."

"Whoa—wait just a minute. Tell me how close you'll be getting to the South Canadian."

Dixon waited a moment, his one eyebrow lowering. "Oughtta be damn close. Why, what's pulling you down there, Irishman?"

"You'll be going to that country, you say?"

"Well," he thought of it, the way the Irishman was near whispering, his eyes gone shifty too, "come to . . . yes. By damn, we'll be in that country."

42

He held out his hand to Dixon. "I'll throw in with you after all, Billy."

"Damn, if that ain't good news, Irishman! Lemme buy you dinner on it."

Donegan wagged his head, suddenly glancing at the falling light streaming through the western windows. "Can't this night, Billy. Promised myself to another."

"One of those new girls down the street, fresh in from Leavenworth I'll bet," Dixon said, grinning.

"Naw. Louis Abragon. I'm buying him dinner at Kelly's place, in return for a little of his help."

"Help? A business deal?"

Donegan rose and shoved the rest of the bottle across the table to Dixon. "Let's just say that Abragon is going to help me with my Spanish."

"You're learning to speak it? What good is that palaver gonna do you, Irishman? Planning on riding on down to Mexico to visit the greasers?"

"No. Planning on visiting only one—and his name is Abragon. We got some business to talk over. I'll see you tomorrow."

"Louis Abragon? What's he offering you in the way of a business proposition that Charlie Myers can't?"

Donegan got that impish look on his tanned face. "Did I use that word—business? My mistake, Billy. Like I said, Abragon is helping me translate some Spanish."

"Never figured you for a man of languages, Donegan," he said, wagging his head in disbelief. "So be it. Just remember, we leave day after."

"Don't worry, me young friend. I'll be rid of this hangover of mine by then," he called out as he shouldered his way through the crowd and disappeared into the growing dusk.

Dixon pulled the bottle toward him and lifted it to his lips. Damn if it didn't burn. He just might have to give himself one last good and rollicking drunk before he pulled out of Dodge. Perhaps more than that—he'd call on at least one or two of those new Missouri girls Abragon just brought down from Leavenworth.

Hell, he shuddered with the thought. There was going to

be damned little chance of finding a warm, willing, white-skinned gal down there south of the dead line in Injun country.

A far better chance of leaving his scalp hanging on some Comanche's lodgepole.

He was too tired to really care that the town wasn't quieting down. Dodge had that sort of reputation. It hooted and hollered from sundown clear to sunup.

Seamus tugged off the second boot and let it fall where it would beside the cot in the narrow, canvas-walled room. Throughout the past several hours spent with Louis Abragon, he had been exerting his brain like an overworked muscle, and now it seemed to be complaining for the lack of sleep and the soaking he had given it in Abragon's potent alcohol.

"I waited more than a month to meet you, Louis," Donegan had said days ago upon first meeting the short, spare Mexican at Abragon's dingy, smoky saloon. But as he had looked around the squalid surroundings, Seamus had been one to admit that the businessman did know his women. Abragon's reputation of having the best to offer in the way of girls was not at all unfounded.

Abragon had seated himself, indicating a chair for the Irishman beside him at the saloon owner's table. "I take it you approve of my . . . employees?"

"Truly a marvel, Louis. Finding so many of such beauty out here."

"For some time I have wanted to offer the very best a man could find, Mr. Donegan. Every color . . . something to please any taste, you might say. I do so want to give these rough but wealthy men something to think long and hard on when they are many weeks on the prairie shooting their buffalo. Something soft and sweet-smelling that just might make a good number of these hard men come riding back here to Dodge earlier than they might plan otherwise."

"You sound like an educated man."

Abragon had nodded, signaling the bartender over. "I spent more than a dozen years in the southwest traveling with a missionary. The Jesuits were very kind to share their knowledge with me."

It was then that Donegan had forged ahead with his discussion of the Spanish language, and a particular Castilian dialect in particular.

"Yes. Jack Stillwell was perhaps right when he said I am the one man for many hundreds of miles who might know something of that dialect."

"Did you ever help the Jesuits do any translating?"

Abragon's brow had furrowed for a moment, something dark crossing those deeply brown eyes, before he caught himself and let his face become a mask once more. "I did, from time to time."

When Seamus mentioned the existence of the ancient map and that it covered an area stretching from the northern provinces of Old Mexico to the central plains of what appeared to now be the United States, Abragon became clearly excited. He suggested they take their discussion to his private office.

The more Seamus had described the map, the more Abragon became excited about seeing it.

"It would be an honor if you would allow me to look at it, Mr. Donegan," he had gushed.

"It's back in my room at Kelly and Beck's. I'll go get it if you—"

"I will go with you," Abragon had interrupted, his hands busy with one another. "This piece of Spanish and Mexican history I must see."

Seamus took him to what passed for a cheap hotel in Dodge City. Inside the narrow cubicle formed of timber with walls of whitewashed canvas hung from rafters, a narrow hallway only feet away, the Irishman unlashed his bedroll to retrieve the leather map tube. From it he had carefully pulled the ancient map. When it was unfurled across the low cot, Donegan had once again looked at the Mexican's face.

Abragon had his hand to his mouth. Above it, the wide, dark eyes were lit with a liquid fire as they bounced over the figures and lines and fading words.

"You can translate this for me?" the Irishman asked.

Abragon's eyes had flicked to the doorway, then back to the Irishman's face. "I can. But tomorrow is soon enough."

"Why not tonight—"

"Tomorrow," he had snapped hurriedly. "I must return and attend to my place of business. Shall we say, noon?"

"Noon it will be."

After Abragon had left and Seamus had gone back out for his usual toast to the early morning hours, and perhaps a tumble with one of Dodge City's soft-skinned attractions, the Irishman had answered the voice inside him that said he should take the map tube with him now that others knew of the map's existence. When he decided to call the evening short and returned to his cot, the nagging doubts still troubled his whiskey-numbed brain. Bothered that he found a pair of faces becoming familiar to his in every saloon he visited that night as he sought out the company of Billy Dixon.

His second boot dropped to the dirty canvas that served as a carpet over the hard-packed earth. Donegan turned down the wick on the oil lamp and lay back, wadding up his wool mackinaw for a pillow. Deciding he was cold enough that he might need a second blanket, Seamus sat up suddenly, reaching for the end of the cot, when the blast of a shotgun ripped through the peaceful fog of his mind, as well as shredding the canvas wall beside the bed.

Without much more than a glance at the tatters the buckshot had made of his mackinaw and the canvas cot, Seamus swept up one of the gun belts and pulled free the pistol just as an arm and a head poked their way through the gaping hole the shotgun blast had made beside his bed.

"The bastard oughtta be—" snarled a voice like slow water over gravel.

"Just get it and be quick, goddammit!"

There were two of them.

Without conscious thought, he knew he dared not wait.

Drawing back the hammer as fast as he ever had, the Irishman unloaded the first three cylinders, sure that one of the shots hit something with the sound of a smack on wet clay. He was answered by a grunt of pain, like a boar hog rubbing on a stump—then quickly thumbed a fourth and fifth, but held the sixth in ready as a second frightening spray of buckshot spat into the tiny cubicle.

He fired the sixth cylinder from the floor, his last shot, then went groping in the dark for the second gun belt he had dropped upon returning to his canvas cubicle.

Muffled, furious and frightened shouts pierced the whitewashed wall nearby. Just outside the shredded canvas footsteps dragged and shuffled across the hard earth. They were getting away and he wasn't about to let them—

"Stay where you are!"

Seamus whirled around to the doorway at the sound of the voice as the canvas hung like a curtain door was pulled aside, exposing a gunman.

The Irishman started to ask, "Who are—"

"Put the gun down."

"I doubt that I will till I know who you are and what your bleeming business is, friend. I've just had the hell shot out of me—"

"You will put your gun down—until we can sort out what happened here."

Wagging the pistol barrel at the gaping canvas wall, Donegan said with a grim smile, "It's bloody plain to see I'm the one someone wanted to kill. Not the other way around. Suppose you tell me who the divil you are and why you're here so goddamned quick after the shots."

As the stranger pushed on into the cubicle, eyeing the gaping hole in the side of the wall, Donegan looked across the crowd of faces straining to get themselves a peek into the doorway.

"Seamus!"

Blessed Mary, a familiar voice. And with it a familiar face pushed into the tiny space Donegan rented from the innkeeper.

"Billy, what brings you to—"

"Curious. Ain't often a man hears a shotgun in Dodge City. Much less a two-shoot gun."

"Took all of you long enough to come help."

Dixon shrugged. He crossed the narrow room and stood with the stranger at the gaping hole.

"You know this one?" the stranger asked of the young buffalo hunter, wagging his pistol barrel at the Irishman.

"He's all right, Zeke." Dixon turned around to Donegan. "Only trouble he's ever gonna cause will be to the Kiowa and Comanche."

"He going with you?"

Dixon nodded. "Part of my outfit, Zeke."

The stranger straightened. "All right. Looks like someone wanted you out of the way, mister. But if you're leaving with Dixon when Myers pulls out, I suppose we won't make any more of it."

"Any more of it?" Seamus asked, incredulous. "Someone just about took my head off!" He scooped up the tatters of his old mackinaw coat. "I'll bloody well find out who—"

"Not in my town you won't."

"Zeke!" called a voice from just beyond the torn canvas wall. "Looks like the Irishman hit something out here."

"You found some blood?"

"Damn if I didn't."

"There," Zeke said, turning to Donegan. "Seems to me you evened the score. He ruined your coat, and you ruined his night."

Still in disbelief, Seamus watched the gray-faced stranger push his way out the doorway, past the curious faces.

"Damn, Seamus," Dixon said, turning from the empty rifle case splintered by buckshot. "I was going to light your lamp, but it's blown all to hell. Whyn't you come bunk with me till we pull out day after tomorrow."

Donegan wagged his head. "I'll bloody well be ready to get out of this crazy hole. Who was this Zeke anyway?"

"Oh, him? Just the fella some of the local businessmen pay to watch over things for 'em."

"Thought you had a marshal?"

"This town does. But some of the businessmen pay for a little extra protection, you might say."

"Protection, is it?"

Already something in his weary brain was telling him this was the work of Abragon. It had to be because of the map. And as far as he knew, Abragon was the only other man in town who knew of the existence of the old map. Whatever those faded words said on the map—it was evidently worth killing for.

"Hell," Seamus muttered to himself as he bent to scoop up his bedroll, "more than one man's been killed for that map and its secrets already."

"What're you growling about like a sour-rumped bear?" Dixon asked, tossing Donegan the Henry repeater.

"Just said I'm going to have to see that fella Abragon again in the morning."

"Don't think so," Billy said. "Saw him leaving town while ago."

"In the middle of the night?"

"Yeah, thought it strange myself. But he said he had urgent business to attend to up at Fort Larned. C'mon, I'll buy you a drink, Irishman."

Donegan shook his head, eyes narrowing. "No, I might take a ride up to Larned meself."

Dixon wagged his head. "Listen, Irishman. It's gonna be Larned . . . and Louie Abragon. Or it's me and the Canadian River down there in buffalo country. Which is it?"

For a moment Seamus ground his teeth together in disappointment and fist-pounding frustration verging on rage. "Whiskey, me friend. That, and a ride south of the dead line with you."

5

Late March 1874

"Billy!"

At the call of his name from an aging skinner named Frenchy, Dixon turned from one of his many checks of the two wagons he and his outfit were taking to Indian country. Nearly every one of the fifty-odd men had stopped what they were doing up and down Front Street and were either staring gape-mouthed or nudging one another and outright guffawing at the sight of the greenhorn fresh out of Illinois.

"Lookit Fairchild, will you?" shouted another of the

crowd pushing onto the plank boardwalks lining the storefronts.

"Damn, if he don't look the sight," Dixon had to admit.

Whereas only two days before, Fairchild had been dressed in his shiny broadcloth suit, flowery vest and plug bowler, fresh from the east, the former barrister was now outfitted from head to toe in what he evidently considered a costume appropriate to the woolly frontier. At least that frontier he had recently been reading of in the dime novels of the day so popular east of the Missouri River—the same novels that had so excited Fairchild that he abandoned his law practice in southern Illinois to come to the buffalo country and take part in making history himself.

Up and down the street he paraded on his horse, bouncing ungainly atop his saddle, nonetheless whooping along with the crowd lining Front Street. At the end of his arm he waved a white, stiff-brimmed sombrero big enough for an umbrella. A tan canvas suit covered him top and bottom, with the pants stuffed down the stovepipes of the favored high-heeled boots Fairchild had adorned with brand-new spurs, the huge, menacing rowels rattling like cymbals as he throbbed up and down atop his new horse. At his neck was tied a brightly printed bandanna, and around his waist bounced both pistol and cartridge belt, along with a huge butcher knife. As Fairchild reined up near some of the buffalo hunters, he held aloft his new Sharps rifle.

"What caliber you get, mister?" asked Jim Hanrahan.

"Fifty," Fairchild answered, a smile brightening his face. Although in his mid-thirties, the barrister nonetheless appeared almost boyish in his delight and enthusiasm to forge his way south with these hardened hide men.

"How much you pay for it?" pried Frenchy, the greasy-mopped skinner who had hired on to work for Billy Dixon.

"Eighty-five dollars."

"Lordee!" someone exclaimed as general laughter broke out.

"Trader musta see'd you comin'," allowed Frenchy.

"Doesn't matter if I paid a little more than I should have," Fairchild bristled instantly. He stroked the breech and action. "This old girl is bound to make meat and raise hair."

At that contention arose more catcalls and hoots.

Billy shouldered forward so that he could stand near Fairchild's horse. "What do you mean by 'raise hair'?"

Fairchild looked evenly at the young, black-haired hunter. "Just what I said. I believe that is the term I've read about in the books. Meaning: to kill me a redskin. Make him a good Injun. See this here knife," he said, patting the huge butcher knife at his belt and affecting a real frontier roll to his words. "Well, boys—I aim to pack at least one Injun's scalp home to Illinois!"

Dixon caught Hanrahan looking at him, and they both wagged their heads in disgust. Dixon backed away from the wild scene.

"That one, he'll cause plenty trouble for you."

Billy turned at the low rumble of the familiar voice, a sound like a splash of water over parched ground. "Chapman. Oh, him? He's harmless, I suppose."

"Mark my word, Dixon. That one make trouble for you." But then the young half-breed scout finally touched the young buffalo hunter with his black eyes and graced him with half a smile. "But then—I suppose you don't go stick your nose down to buffalo country and not expect trouble, right?"

He nodded at the half-breed who served as post interpreter and a sometime scout down at Camp Supply in Indian Territory. "That's right, Amos. We're likely fellas and we're bound for where the buffalo can be found. You ought to think about throwing in with us."

Chapman snorted. "Me? I got honest work to do, Dixon."

"Army work, is it?" Billy knew the scout had a Cheyenne wife, probably children by now. And he could count on Chapman's family being back at the Darlington Agency. "You helping keep things quiet for us, are you, Amos?" Over Chapman's shoulder he watched the Irishman walking up.

"Nothing I say, nothing I do, can keep those warriors from going after your scalps—they take a mind to, Dixon."

"Your words don't carry enough medicine with 'em—
that what you're saying?" Billy declared, then immediately
looked away so that Chapman would not have a chance to
answer. "Seamus! C'mon over here—want you should
meet a honest-to-goodness scout."

Chapman turned, his dark eyes measuring the tall Irishman as Donegan came to a halt and held out his hand to
the half-breed.

"Seamus Donegan."

"Amos Chapman." He turned to Dixon. "He going with
you, maybe lose his long, curly hair too?"

Billy chuckled. "Yeah. Seamus is going to buffalo country too."

"Too bad," Chapman said without emotion. "That pretty
scalp of his will look real good on a Kwahadi lodgepole."

"Crazy Horse and Red Cloud already tried," Seamus
snapped, hooking his thumbs inside his gun belts. "Then
Roman Nose did too. There's been others—but none's had
the medicine to raise this scalp of mine."

Without his face betraying his thoughts, Chapman nodded, perhaps with something close to approval. "You talk
good, Irishman. Maybe your medicine was stronger back
then. Just you pray your medicine stays strong in the days
to come."

They watched the sullen half-breed part them and move
off through the crowd that for the most part made way for
him.

A. C. Myers and his partner, Frederick J. Leonard, were
clambering up into one of the tallest freight wagons, standing on the seat above the crowd, where they began to wave
their arms, whistling for attention. Myers shouted for attention then, quieting the clamor as the spring sun finally
made its appearance at the far edge of the prairie. Referring to some papers he held in his hand, Charlie Myers
called out trail assignments to the teamsters of those forty-
plus wagons lashed behind their hardy, restive bull teams
anxious for the trail. Better than sixty men would be rolling
south in outfits that would mess together and camp together, he told them, for the sake of securing enough grass
for the animals.

"Don't this make a fine show of it, Seamus?" Dixon asked, feeling the pride surging through him as he peered over the group spread up and down Front Street.

Donegan nodded. "Got to admit, Billy. This bunch looks like it can handle itself, trouble comes calling."

"Damn right, we can. Look at these fellas. This whole damned outfit could fight its way clean down to the Rio Grande, we had to. And cut a path through the Kiowa and Comanch' on the way back if we need to."

Donegan chuckled. "Don't doubt it a bit."

At least fifty thousand dollars in trade goods were spread among most of those sturdy freight wagons. And when it came time for Charlie Myers to open shop somewhere down in Indian country, he would not be displaying trade goods meant to make a settler's eyes shine. Nor those geegaws meant to quicken the pulse of a settler's wife. No, this trip to buffalo country meant that Myers had carefully planned and purchased his stock. Only those goods he knew from experience would be highly desired by that rare breed of hunter had he packed beneath the heavy canvas tarps in the many wagons he contracted to haul his investment all the way to the Canadian. Besides rifles and pistols, lead, powder, knives and reloading equipment, Myers made sure he brought along the usual blankets, tenting, tin cups and plates, in addition to coffee, sugar, flour and assorted tinned foods. But there was as well a wide assortment of rugged clothing, pinch and slouch hats, bandannas, tobacco, pipes and decks of cards. In addition, Myers had packed the supplies he would need for the construction and operation of a full-blown trading post, located more than a hundred fifty miles from the closest place that could even be remotely called civilization.

Besides Dixon's well-respected outfit, and that of Jim Hanrahan, Emanuel Dubbs had thrown in with the grand procession to march south of the dead line. Dubbs had long been a success at the buffalo business, but had heretofore always done his hunting in the fall through the spring. This would be the first time he had thrown in for a summer operation. And to make the whole scheme complete, blacksmith Tom O'Keefe had his heavily laden wagon

53

ready to roll with the others. With plans to establish more than a frontier outpost in mind, these men clearly had their sights set on erecting a small community of their kind right in the heart of the Staked Plain.

"Let's roll!" came the shout from Leonard's lips.

An instantaneous roar burst from the throats of the near sixty hunters and skinners. It was answered by shouts and whistles and cheers from the crowd of Dodge City citizens, store owners and saloon girls who lined Front Street for the raucous departure.

Up and down the dusty, rutted path, drivers called out hoarsely to their teams, "Hi-ya! Hi-ya! Hup-hup, hi-ya!"

Above the wide backs and sturdy yokes, more than forty long, silken-black whips cracked the dry, spring air. Bulls snorted as they leaned into their yokes and traces. Horses whinnied as their riders brought them around in the growing orange light of that Thursday morning, the twenty-sixth day of March, eighteen and seventy-four.

It was enough to make the hair stand on the back of Dixon's neck and give him a case of goose pimples. Damn, if he weren't proud to be leading this procession south, his heavy-barreled .50 across his thighs, a good horse beneath him, and the smell of spring blowing in off the far prairie.

The hide men were coming to buffalo country. And they were coming to stay.

"You wanna come along when I take him out there with me, Bat?" Seamus asked of the young, handsome twenty-year-old hunter.

William Barclay Masterson nodded eagerly, an even-toothed smile adding to his good features. To any who met him, he was just what his best friend, twenty-four-year-old Billy Dixon, proudly called him: a chunk of steel, and anything that struck the young hunter drew fire as sure as sun. They were the youngest of the bunch, those two.

"I figure it time to haze him from hell to breakfast before he causes us trouble," Masterson declared.

"Every one of us thinks Fairchild's got it coming," Dixon said, a comment that elicited approval from the dozen or so who had gathered to discuss the increasing concern over the greenhorn's eagerness to have him a go at an Indian, any Indian.

Across the last four days out of Dodge, the more hardened hunters had grown weary of the tenderfoot's boasting that he would be the first to raise hair in Indian country. With each mile that brought them closer and closer to the dead line, those same experienced plainsmen grew more anxious that Fairchild would himself prove the spark of real trouble. For the past day a handful of them had even been talking over plans to teach the greenhorn a lesson about both Indians and courage that Fairchild would not soon forget.

"He's bad medicine from the forks of a creek, all right," Charlie Myers grumbled.

"He's the fancy-pants sort that wants the rest of us to jump the buckets, and leave us to pay the fiddler when it comes due," agreed Dutch Henry Born.

Hanrahan snorted. "I'm in, Billy—for certain. That Fairchild's a wolf with hydrophobia, a goddamned blizzard in July."

Their plans quickly laid during that noon stop to rest the animals, Donegan asked for two others to accompany him onto the prairie and away from camp once they had finished supper that coming evening. Word that Fairchild was due for his comeuppance quickly spread among the rest of the teamsters, hunters and skinners through the long afternoon. An air of anxious expectation settled over their encampment on the South Canadian as twilight came down in fits and starts on the land.

Tonight, like every night gone before it, a few of the men brought out some stiffened buffalo hides and pegged them out atop the new grass. Others dragged fiddles from battered cases, a few squeeze boxes or mouth harps, and began the evening ritual of music and dancing. The hides provided secure footing for the lively jigs and gyrations of these hard men on a joyful lark. What a sight it had been for Seamus Donegan that first night they camped on Crooked Creek, watching the likes of Shoot'em-Up Mike dancing arm in arm with Light-fingered Jack, or Shotgun Collins performing a genteel bow in front of Prairie Dog

Dave before they tripped the light fantastic, energetically clogged a mountain step or stomped through a favored Virginia reel. Those who didn't dance ringed the buffalo-hide dance floors, clapping and singing along in merriment.

Firelight and starlight, rollicking music and likable companions. Throughout those crisp spring evenings each man was required to entertain the others in some manner: be it playing an instrument, singing a favorite song, dancing or merely a rendition of a remembered story. And while some like Billy Dixon were hard pressed to come up with any manner of talent in those areas, night after night the Irishman regaled one and all with his recitation of Irish poetry and songs, sung a cappella. Without fail, Seamus brought tears to the eyes of these hardened men, with an unexpected remembrance of home to their hearts. Then as quickly he was up and stomping his big boot, roaring out a bawdy Irish drinking song learned in those smoky pubs dotting Boston Towne.

Their second day's march had seen the outfits cross the turbulent, red-tinged and spring-swollen Cimarron. A brackish and most capricious river that concealed sinks and a swirling bottom laced with sucks and quicksand, the teamsters spent much of the afternoon locating a suitable ford, then driving their nervous beasts across the tumbling, ever-shifting torrent.

"Keep your team moving," Billy Dixon had instructed his two skinners atop their plank seats after they had double-teamed Frenchy's wagon. "Whatever you do, keep these damned oxen moving. You stop, they're likely to sink."

Donegan had sat there in the saddle, watching as the Dixon's skinners moved their wagons down the slope. "Never seen anything like this before—I only heard of rivers the nature of this, Billy."

"The Cimarron'll swallow a tree or a buffalo, it gets the chance. Don't you doubt it will make a grip on a horse or those wagons of mine." He immediately read the hesitancy and shouted at his timid skinner. "Be at it, boys! Let 'em have the reins and don't spare the whip! Don't stop now!"

Frenchy and Mike McCabe obeyed, whipping the reluctant bulls across the Cimarron, hollering and cursing the snorting, bellowing oxen through the boiling red waters, the first teams to lead the way to the south bank, where the hunters were determined to make camp for the night.

"We're in Injun country now," Dixon had told Donegan on the south bank of the Cimarron that night as the sun sank a'red in the west.

Donegan had sniffed the breeze in a long draught, then grinned impishly. "Wondered why the air smelled different, Billy."

A third day's march took them squarely into no-man's land and brought them to Beaver Creek, the primary tributary of the North Canadian River. To that night's camp came the first of the buffalo hunters like the English brothers, Jim and Bob Cator, and others like Fred Singer, hide men who had already ventured south on their own hook, all of whom were most happy to bump into such an impressive army of well-armed frontiersmen. It was from that point on that Myers and Leonard asked the hunters to begin scouting in earnest for a suitable location for their trading post.

Past the mouth of Palo Duro Creek and on to the fast-running, steep-banked Moore's Creek they drove their long procession of wagons. A pretty place with good timber and water, but not nearly enough grass for what they knew would be the demands of so many hunters coming to and fro from their planned post. Myers decided they would follow Moore's Creek on south and thereby strike the Canadian.

It was here they camped near the ruins of the old Adobe Walls their first night by the Canadian. And cemented plans to pay their respects on Fairchild, the unsuspecting easterner who had long been claiming an unrequited fondness for Indian scalps.

6

Late March–Early April, 1874

As the stars blinked into sight one by one overhead, Seamus Donegan sighed and leaned back against the saddle and blanket. This appeared to be the end of their journey south.

And later in the evening they would pay their respects to the tenderfoot in hopes of giving him enough of a scare that he would likely forget he had ever hungered after an Indian scalp.

The place was beautiful, Seamus had to admit. Here, near the ruins of the adobe walls that had once enclosed an old trading post, two small streams flowed in from the north while another came in from the south. Whereas the rest of the surrounding countryside was pocked with high, steep-banked streambeds, those three streams gave this particular valley a smooth, more gradual slope. It had been an ideal setting chosen by the traders working for the Bent brothers, who wandered into this valley back in 1838 to establish some business relations with the Kiowa and Comanche.

For better than four years William and Charles Bent had already conducted trade with many of the southern tribes from their mud fortress located on the north bank of the Arkansas, just across the river from what was then Mexican territory. Yet because the Cheyenne, Arapaho and occasionally the Ute would come in to trade at Bents' Fort, the Kiowa and Comanche, and even the Apache, had never ventured that far north and west. Therefore the Bents would go to the tribes living with the buffalo on the Staked Plain. Here, as they had done on the Arkansas, the traders built their much smaller post of adobe—mud and straw. Two commodities of which there was never a short supply. A modest trade was carried on for a handful of years before the simmering hostility of some of the roving warrior bands forced the Bent traders to abandon the buildings. It was, in fact, none other than veteran mountain men Kit

Carson and John Smith, both then employed by the Bents, who decided to pull out and strike for the Arkansas when a large war party of Kiowa raiders killed a Mexican herder and drove off all but three of their horses, threatening to make things hot for the white men if they remained.

Across the next two decades, the crumbling walls were visited only by a passing war party, the curious antelope or turkey, or an occasional field mouse escaping the diving pursuit of a swooping red-winged hawk. But in 1864 the Civil War finally came to the Staked Plain, played out in high drama among the crumbling remains of what was even then coming to be known as the Adobe Walls.

Ever since the beginning of the war of rebellion, Kiowa and Comanche warriors had vigorously attacked commerce plying the Santa Fe Trail that linked New Mexico's forts and cities with the east. At long last the army ordered an expedition into the field, under the old mountain man, Kit Carson, to punish the warrior bands that had threatened to close down travel along the now-famous trail. Marching his dragoons east from Fort Bascomb, Colonel Carson led a sizable contingent of both California and New Mexico volunteers, along with some Ute mercenaries anxious to chastise their ancient enemies.

Carson's scouts led the soldiers to a village upstream from the old ruins, and the battle opened. During the running skirmish that found the soldiers chasing the Indians down the creek valley, the white men and their Indian allies were suddenly surprised to find even more villages boiling with angry warriors. Carson was forced to order a retreat and seek a defensible spot. The crumbling adobe walls offered him just that. With their horses corralled and his two mountain howitzers wheeled into action, the unshakable old mountain trapper held the enraged warriors off until the Indians tired of the contest.

While the bands did dog his retreat back to New Mexico, they never did any serious damage to the Fort Bascomb column.

For the last ten years, the Kiowa and Comanche had ruled this valley like sovereign kings. Only an occasional knight errant, some courageous buffalo hunter, had ever laid eyes on the ruins of the adobe walls. But with the falling of the sun that March afternoon, some sixty bearded and long-haired white men rode into the valley of Bent Creek. Without any man really having to give voice to the sentiment, most realized they had arrived. The grass was tall, even at this early season reaching for the bellies of their horses. Here timber stood aplenty for firewood and rafters and cross-beams. Besides, the timbered bottoms held a great assortment of deer and turkey and other wild game. And water—not only the creek and its small feeders, but a number of springs bubbled on the nearby hillsides.

"You got any idea what went on here?" asked young Bat Masterson of the rest that afternoon as they slid from their saddles and in silence peered over the overgrown ruins.

Dixon shook his head. Myers and Donegan muttered in wonder. Others began peering on tiptoes over the remains of the old mud walls.

"I bet this was a old Spanish mission," ventured Sam Smith.

That had pricked Donegan's curiosity. "Any particular reason you say that, Sam?"

The hunter just shrugged. "S'pose it's as good a idea as any, Irishman. Bring the church to these damned red heathens, don't you see?"

Some of the others chuckled as Smith strode off, then entered the walls themselves with a few others.

"Lookit this, will you?" shouted Fred Singer.

Donegan and some of the others joined the hunter inside. "What'd you find?"

Johnson plowed at the grassy soil with his boot heel. He knelt and brought up a palm filled with dirt, and a few multicolored beads. "Traders were here, I'd say."

"Not Dodge City traders, that's for sure," Myers said.

"Injun traders," Singer declared. "No one else got a need to offer beads like these'uns."

The valley of Adobe Walls had been the ideal location for a trading post more than twenty-six years before, and that valley remained a paradise here in 1874 at the northern edge of the Staked Plain.

Later that evening as he settled beside Seamus at their

mess fire, young Bat Masterson counted himself in—eager to have himself a major part in the joke they had planned for the tenderfoot now that the stars were out in full array and the music had begun drifting over the encampment. Here and there around the circle of fires men danced and whirled and jigged atop the buffalo hides pegged down on the new grass. Few showed any visible worry that by venturing this far south they had now plunged their fists far down the throats of the Kiowa and Comanche.

"I figure we ought to seize time by the forelock," Billy Dixon said quietly to Donegan.

The Irishman nodded and arose, stretching. "You fellas see all those turkeys roosting in those cottonwoods up from camp?"

Several of the conspirators answered enthusiastically.

"You think we can bag us a few tonight?" Fairchild asked, his face no mask to his boyish delight.

"I figure we'll clean up, we do it right," Charlie Myers said.

Fairchild rubbed his hands together with glee. "I can't wait, Irishman. Let's be to it."

"Whoa," Donegan called out. "I think the others will agree with me. We got a few more minutes till it gets slap-dark and the turkeys all roosted in the tree branches for the night. Then we can fetch our rifles and go on our turkey shoot."

He winked at some of the others then watched as Billy Dixon, Jim Hanrahan and Andy Johnson nonchalantly slipped away out of the firelight and into the darkness, unseen by the eager Fairchild, busy discussing the hunt with Masterson and Myers.

Within a half hour Myers led Fairchild and Masterson out of camp toward the distant stand of cottonwood where the three other jokesters had just built a particular sort of fire that could not be seen from the hunters' camp. Then Dixon, Hanrahan and Johnson slipped quietly back into the brush to watch the show begin, awaiting their next cue.

Masterson halted and turned on Fairchild, saying, "I'll go first. Charlie, you bring up the rear. Now, we all got to be quiet or we won't sneak up on them turkeys roosting up yonder."

Fairchild bobbed his head eagerly as Masterson led off, the other two following in single file. After something on the order of two hundred yards, young Bat rounded the bend of the creek, stopping suddenly as he threw up his arm in surprise. Fairchild bumped into him, Myers into the tenderfoot. All three gaped at the discovery of a campfire. Bat quickly whirled about, motioning first for complete silence, then pointing down the backtrail that would take them toward camp.

"God, you don't suppose it can be?" Masterson asked in a harsh whisper after they had quietly shuffled back into the brush.

"I ain't so sure that it don't look like no white man's fire to me," Myers hissed.

Masterson shook his head, from the corner of his eye seeing how wide Fairchild's eyes were growing. "None of our boys would be camping out here anyway," Bat went on, making a grand show of the frightened swallow he took.

"In—Indians?" Fairchild gulped, his face gone ashen beneath the rising moon.

Masterson nodded, knowing the others were hiding in the brush, barely feet away. "You bet that's a Injun fire. Damn, but now I know why I been having nightmares last few nights—woken up in a cold sweat, getting chased by them red fiends."

"God bless!" Fairchild whimpered, lips trembling.

"What? You turning yellow, Bat?" Myers said, playing it up big. "I don't think that's a Injun fire in the first place— and if it was . . . Fairchild here has said he's gonna raise hair on the first warrior he lays his hands on. Ain't you, Fairchild?"

The easterner began to snivel, "Well . . . I—"

"Looks to be you're rattled, Bat. But I ain't a damn bit scared," Myers plunged ahead. "You can run if you got a streak up your back. I'll stay right here with Fairchild and let him get his Injun scalp. Maybe more'n one—right, Fairchild?"

The tenderfoot swallowed hard, his eyes wide already, unable to speak for the moment.

"With that rifle and skinnin' knife of his, Fairchild could whip all the Comanche in the whole damned Panhandle, you give him a fair show of it. And I want to be here to watch Fairchild lay into 'em for certain!"

"N-Now," Fairchild sniveled, "let's not be too hasty about this here!"

"We best get our own scalps out of here while we can, fellas," Bat said. "I don't have a good feeling about this—"

At that moment Masterson pulled his hat from his head, the signal to Donegan and the rest.

One shot, then a heartbeat later more rattled over the heads of the would-be hunters, whistling out of the night, crashing through the leaves and branches behind them.

"Lord God Almighty!" Fairchild shrieked as he crumpled to his knees.

"Injuns!" Masterson yelled, leaning over to pull the greenhorn to his feet.

Playing his role perfectly, Myers wasn't anywhere close to reply. He had already bolted off at a full sprint through the brush along the creek, hollering his bloody alarm with every leap.

"Just like I always say," Bat hissed in Myers's direction, "there's five miles of nerve between pointing a gun and pulling the trigger. Run, Fairchild!" Bat suddenly hollered as he pushed the tenderfoot off in the direction of camp, dropping to his knee to fire off a few shots with his pistol. "Run for your life!"

The greenhorn did not need any more coaxing, bounding away from Masterson like an antelope, hurtling headlong through the brush on Myers's heels. It took but a few yards until Fairchild passed the trader, careening toward camp as if the devil himself were on his heels. For more than half a mile he kept up that wicked pace until he tore into camp, collapsing on a pile of blankets and bedrolls, heaving, his tongue lolling from his wild escape.

Many of the others, also in on Donegan's and Masterson's practical joke, quickly gathered around, each one shouting a multitude of questions.

"What happened?"

"Where's Bat?"

"Why'd you leave Myers behind?"

"Who fired them shots?"

With his eyes bugging and his breath coming harsh and hammered, Fairchild was a few moments before he could get the single word past his trembling lips. "I-Injuns!"

"Injuns?"

"Timber . . . it's crawling with 'em!" declared the shaky tenderfoot as the others pulled their weapons up, readying for a fight.

"It's us or them, boys," someone declared.

"I knew it'd come down to it," another declared. "Been good riding with you."

"Oh, God . . ." Fairchild whimpered. "Myers and Masterson, they're surely . . . surely dead!"

"You're shot!" screamed Frenchy, suddenly kneeling over Fairchild. With a flash, the skinner yanked his butcher knife from his belt and ripped through the side of Fairchild's shirt, pushing the easterner over on his belly.

Emanuel Dubbs had a coffeepot ready, pouring the warm dregs over Fairchild's bare back.

"You can't feel your own blood?" Frenchy asked.

"Oh, sweet Jesus!" Fairchild moaned. "The Injuns got me. Got me!"

"Get some water!" Dubbs hollered into the crowd. "We got to pry that bullet out!"

"B-Bullet?"

"We can't let it set in there too long," Frenchy said gravely. "Blood poisoning."

"Just dress it for now!" Charlie Myers huffed as he darted into camp. "You got more ambition than a mustang stud in spring—and we got Injuns to fight!"

"Charlie! Fairchild claimed you was dead!"

"Would've been," Masterson said as he too came to a halt. "Fairchild run off from us—left us to fight alone."

"How many?" Frenchy asked.

Masterson shook his head. "Woods is alive with 'em. We ain't got time to yank that bullet out now, Fairchild."

"I say we head for Dodge City!" Prairie Dog Dave hollered.

"They got us surrounded. We'd never get out," Masterson said dramatically. "Grab that big Sharps of yours, Fairchild—you'll stand guard on the edge of camp like the rest of us."

"I say we try for Dodge City," Fairchild whimpered. "They can't follow us at night."

"We'll never make it through the noose they've thrown up around us." Bat whirled on the rest as they swept up their rifles. "Sell your lives dear, boys. Take some of those bastards with us!"

"The devil's here to pay—and no pitch is too hot, fellas," shouted Seamus Donegan as he, Dixon and Hanrahan rushed into camp as if just answering the call to arms. "We expected trouble—and it's found us. Rally forth!"

They all spread out as planned, making sure the frightened, half-naked Fairchild was taken to the far edge of camp where there would be some timber between his sentry post and the main fire.

"You must keep a vigilant watch here, Fairchild," Seamus said with all the seriousness he could muster. "The rest of us are depending on you—despite your wounds. You mustn't allow those bloodthirsty h'athens to ford the creek and plug you for good. Keep your eyes moving and your nose in the wind, boy."

Fairchild nodded, more than nervously.

"Your rifle still loaded?" Masterson asked.

Again the easterner nodded.

"We'll be back to relieve your watch in an hour," Dixon said as the three turned and left the tenderfoot in the brush along the creekbank.

Back at camp, fresh coffee was a'brew and muffled laughter greeted each new "guard" who quietly slipped back in, unbeknownst to the terrified Fairchild, abandoned at his solitary post by the stream. Time and again someone new would arise in the firelight and mimic the tenderfoot in word and action, until they all suffered aching bellies from suppressing the laughter.

"Got him—slick as the inside of a willow whistle!" Frenchy roared with laughter.

That hour passed as the stars whirled overhead and the moon climbed out of the east, and still no Fairchild.

But when another hour had passed and still no guard came to relieve him, Fairchild's curiosity overcame his crippling terror. Cautiously he inched his way back to camp, there to find every one of the traders, hunters and skinners sharing their merriment around the fires.

He stood trembling at the edge of the firelight. No more was he frightened. Now he was beyond angry, realizing he had been made the butt of their joke.

Donegan was the first to spot the greenhorn at the edge of the light.

"Fairchild! C'mon on in and have yourself a cup of Frenchy's coffee."

"Him?" the tenderfoot shrieked. "He's the one ripped my shirt—thought I was shot."

"Frenchy's coffee is about as bad as being gut-shot sometimes!" Dixon roared, ducking the skinner's swinging arm. "But you are one bad actor."

"You sonsabitches!" Fairchild yelped with blood in his eye, dropping his rifle and bolting into a dead run for Masterson.

Donegan and Andy Johnson caught him, holding the smaller man back as Fairchild's legs continued to pump, his arms flailing, sputtering his curses at them all.

"We was damned worried you'd go off half cocked and get us all in a world of trouble," Dixon tried to explain.

"We're sorry if there's any hide wore off," Masterson said.

"No hide," Donegan said, having lifted Fairchild's shirt. "Just might've rubbed raw the man's pride a wee bit is all. Will you quit your squirming!"

"When I get my hands on one of—"

"We done it for your own good," Masterson said.

"You let me go and I'll show you for your own good."

But he eventually calmed down enough for Donegan to release him. And then Fairchild accepted a cup of Frenchy's coffee.

One by one the ringleaders of the great practical joke came up and offered their hands in peace. With a self-deprecating grin, Fairchild accepted those hands.

"You'll make a damned good hunter after all, you will," Seamus said, clamping a big hand on Fairchild's shoulder as they drank coffee beside that fire, near the ruins of the old adobe walls beneath a spring moon, deep in the heart of buffalo country. In the land of the Indian. "Not a bad sort for a friend either."

"You . . . you mean you still want to be my friend—after I made such a damned fool of myself?"

Donegan pounded the tenderfoot on his back. "We're all friends here, Fairchild. 'Cause down here in the land of the Kiowa and the Comanch'—a man needs all the friends he can find to watch his backside."

7

Early April 1874

West Adobe Walls Creek coursed through the valley from the northwest, creating the broad, open meadow. Along its banks grew a profusion of bluestem and beargrass, poke-weed and sage, hackberry, chinaberry and willow. Overhead towered the sheltering cottonwood.

For some time Charlie Myers and Fred Leonard simply stood in silence at the center of the meadow that lay on the west side of the creek some two miles north of the main branch of the Canadian, a mile or so upstream from the ruins where they had camped the 'ght before, their sixth coming south from Dodge City. The more they considered the location, the better it seemed. By erecting their stockade here, they would command a broad field of fire in the event they would have to defend their lives and property from the warriors most of these men knew would come. Only a matter of time. One day the warriors would come.

The two traders nodded to one another, shook hands, and announced their decision. It was here they would raise their trading post. And they would pay all those hide men who would stay to help build the post, making their offer before the hunters and skinners scattered across the surrounding countryside.

When the hurrawing throats and the hearty backslapping died down, the work of off-loading the wagons began. The hide men had come to stay.

Although few white men had ever crossed the meadow until that time, it was far from being an unknown speck on the mental map of those red men who traveled the great expanse of the buffalo country known as the Staked Plain. Here, just north of the Canadian River, this broad meadow allowed for an easy crossing of the river, while in either direction the banks proved much steeper and more difficult to negotiate for horse and travois.

The second morning in the meadow saw Myers contracting with Dirty-Face Ed Jones and his partner Joe Plummer, both accomplished teamsters, to officially blaze the trail that would be used by Myers and Leonard freighters between the trading post and their store in Dodge City. It was bound to be a well-used route, bringing in merchandise and trade goods from Kansas, freighting back a fortune in buffalo hides for the eastern markets.

"You're sure now you won't throw in and come along?" Billy Dixon had asked Seamus that third morning.

Donegan had shaken his head. "I know you're like a boy with a new gun, wanting to look over that buffalo country south of here again."

Dixon had smiled. "I want to be the first to find them." Wistfully he had looked off into the distance across the Canadian. "They're out there. I can feel it."

"And they'll come soon enough," said Seamus. "I think I'll stay for a while and help the rest get these buildings raised. It's good pay, and the work ain't half bad. Besides, I want to have a better look at those old ruins back down the creek. Get to know them a wee bit better, Billy."

Donegan stood back now, gazing again at the immense Myers and Leonard stockade, remembering how it had looked after those first few days of work plowing up the grass at the far ends of the meadow, throwing into the empty wagons those sod bricks they had carved from the earth, using a special plow made by Dodge City blacksmith

Patrick Ryan, hauling the sod to the site where Myers and Leonard had staked out the dimensions of their new domain. While the first buds were swelling in the sunnyside places along the creeks and watered places, brick by sod brick, the foot-thick picket walls were slowly raised, some two hundred feet wide by three hundred feet long on the east and west. Small loopholes were placed four feet from the ground, at intervals of every ten or so feet, which would allow riflemen to fire from the safety of the stockade walls.

At the northeast corner of the immense rectangular stockade stood the store itself, some seventy feet long and twenty feet wide. After a center ridgepole was laid across the entire length of the store, supported by upright posts, cross members were laid, extending from the sides of the walls. Atop that was laid a thatching and a layer of sod.

At the southwest corner stood the mess hall with four separate entrances, where Billy "Old Man" Keeler would soon serve as cook. Near it, along the west wall, they built a covered stable with stalls for seventeen animals. Completing the entire rectangle, roofless bastions were erected at all but the southeast corners of the stockade.

An unusual gate was placed across the large opening in the east wall, itself balanced on an immense cottonwood trunk the men sunk deep in the ground. This gate "floated" from this single pole, counterbalanced by a large cage made of wooden pegs, in which the men placed heavy rocks dug from the meadow or hauled up from the creek bank. This ingenious floating arrangement made it possible for a single man to open or close the immense, heavy gate. Timber for these pickets and gate were found along Reynolds Creek, some six miles down the Canadian.

When the major work had been completed on the walls, Seamus spent a day working with fellow Irishman Tom O'Keefe to erect a blacksmith shop about a hundred feet south of the rectangular stockade. Together they first dug a trench of about twenty-four feet by twenty-one feet in which they buried their eight-foot pickets, then over it all the two laid a thatch roof. Besides what circulation could be provided by the two doorways, O'Keefe did not daub any mud between the wood pickets, so that the constant breeze blowing through the meadow would make his work over the glowing forge just a little cooler.

It was near the end of the third week in the meadow that another small wagon train was spotted rumbling into the valley of Bent Creek.

"Looks like Rath is making good on his promise," Charlie Myers said to his group of laborers as he came to a halt by them, dusting his hands across his dirty canvas britches.

"He say he was coming down to give you some competition, did he?" Jim Hanrahan asked.

"He did," Fred Leonard said as he strode up to watch the arrival of the wagons coming past the far buzzard-bone ridges ringing the meadow.

"There's enough business for two outfits," Donegan said.

Myers nodded grudgingly. "Aye. There'll be so much business soon enough that we'll all be rich by autumn."

While Charlie Myers and Fred Leonard had been the first to seize the opportunity, there were others who had been just as anxious to seize upon what appeared to be a safe bet. Longtime Dodge City businessmen Charles Rath and Robert M. Wright threw in together with a young Irishman named James Langton and outfitted a train for the buffalo country. They had followed the wagon tracks south, passing Jones and Plummer on the teamsters' trail-blazing journey back to Dodge City.

"By Jesus, Myers—you damn well knew we weren't going to let you have all the business!" Rath sang out, standing in the foot well of his high-walled freighter as he rolled to a halt in the meadow and legged-down on the brake handle.

"You're late, Rath!"

"And I see you doing a land-office business, do I?" Andy Johnson called out from his wagon as employees of both outfits began to shake hands. Johnson had a reputation as the most reliable and trusted of the Rath employees.

"Get down here, Swede—and you too, Rath. Let's have a drink to the hide business!" Myers growled.

"Now you're talking," Rath replied. "Where's Hanrahan?"

"Here I am," Jim Hanrahan answered, emerging from the brush where he had gone to relieve himself.

"Button your goddamned fly and get over here, Jim," Rath said. "I got a proposition for the likes of you that will keep you so busy, and make you so much money—you won't need to think of shooting another buffalo."

The next day, while Myers and Leonard and their employees returned to finishing their stable, store and mess hall, and while Rath and his bunch began work erecting their modest store, some twenty-two by sixty feet, along with a corral and an outdoor privy, all constructed south across the meadow from the other structures, Jim Hanrahan strode over to ask for Donegan's help in his new venture.

"Blessed Mary!" Seamus exclaimed that morning over strong coffee and soda biscuits while the wiry cut of the spring breeze made a sound like mocking laughter in the new leaves. "Your bleeming building will be the most important of all. A saloon. By the saints, a saloon!"

Another fifty feet south of O'Keefe's blacksmith shop, Hanrahan selected a level piece of ground to stake out his rectangular sod house, twenty-three by thirty-nine feet. A door they left at the east and west ends, with a single glazed window on the south wall, along with two open windows each along both east and west walls.

Meanwhile, Charlie Rath had no intention of giving the restaurant trade over to Myers and Old Man Keeler. From Dodge City, Rath brought Mrs. Hannah Olds to serve as cook, along with her husband, William, who had already been a Rath employee for some time. Therefore the Rath & Company store was divided into three rooms: the kitchen, the sales room, and a small partitioned area that served as private quarters for William and Hannah Olds.

Once the store was erected and stocked with approximately twenty thousand dollars in trade goods, a private privy for Mrs. Olds was constructed to the west some distance across the meadow. Only then did work begin on the Rath & Company corral itself. For weeks now the men had expected the appearance of Indians, but as each new day failed to bring a showing of feathers, the men grew more and more relaxed. Rath suspended work on the corral when the sod walls were but three bricks high.

Tonight, Seamus promised himself, he would again drag his aching muscles back to the ruins by starlight and once more walk among those walls, now no more than some four to five feet tall. Digging here. Digging there, in the silence of the night when none of the others knew of his absence.

Perhaps, he likewise vowed, one of these nights he would be rewarded by the glint of something shiny beneath the blade of his shovel. And then—by the saints—yes, then . . . Seamus Donegan would no longer have to worry about using his muscles to make a living.

The cold rains had started in the waning days of winter and continued into the spring. Not the sort of thunderstorms the Kwahadi had come to expect out of the season. No boiling black clouds racing overhead, gone as quickly as they came. Instead, this was a time of cold, endless gray days. The prairie sucked at a pony's hooves and a man's moccasins. Children cried in the lodges. And the buffalo had not returned.

Quanah Parker prayed.

It was the first time in his young life that he had asked the Grandfather Above for answers. About the rains. About the cold. About the buffalo not coming back when they should. But mostly Quanah asked those questions he did not give voice. He wanted to know about Isatai.

From a different band of Comanche, and nearly the same age as Quanah, this young shaman was not yet a rising star among his people. Yet when two of his major predictions came true, word of Isatai began to spread across the southern plains. Just last spring a fiery comet had burned its first path across the night sky. For three more nights it made its appearance before the young medicine man predicted that the comet would perform its nightly fireworks five more times then return no more. The fire-tailed comet had obeyed Isatai.

72

Not long afterward he predicted the beginning of a great drought that would parch the southern prairie and especially the Staked Plain. Creeks dried up. Game wandered far in search of water. The sun seemed like a dull, brass button suspended overhead as each day seeped into the next with no relief from the blistering heat. Isatai told the people to hold on, the winter would bring rain—before another great time of dryness.

The rains had come. As if the skies were obeying the shaman. Here in the waning days of the Moon of Geese Coming Back, Quanah prayed, asking for answers.

Isatai. His name meant "coyote droppings" to some, "ass of wolf" to others. Of late he had claimed not only to control the elements, it was said he was curing the sick and raising the dead. Then, a few days ago, word came to Quanah's band that Isatai had performed the greatest of all miracles—proclaiming that it was time to finish off the white man, he had then vomited up enough rifle cartridges to fill a wagon.

Unable to believe this great feat, Quanah had questioned the message bearers. Yes, they had seen it with their own eyes.

"Does Isatai now possess those cartridges?" the Kwahadi war chief asked. "Will we use them against the white man?"

The message bearers shook their heads and one replied, "Isatai swallowed the bullets again."

"The whole wagonload?"

"He said he would produce them again when the time came to make war on the tai-bos," answered one.

The second message bearer nodded. "And he will make medicine to keep the tai-bo guns from doing our warriors any harm."

"How is it he can do these wonderful things?" Quanah had asked, not really expecting an answer.

"Once Isatai was sleeping when he was taken into the spirit world of the sky by the Grandfather Above and told he would be given these powers to help our people," the young Comanche went on. "His rising to the sky to talk with the spirits was witnessed by many. When he returned,

73

Isatai said the Grandfather Above wanted all his children to do as Isatai would command them."

With that invocation, Quanah had grown suspicious. Any man wanting too much power of a proud and independent people like the Kwahadi aroused his gravest doubts. And of late, Isatai was not only demanding obedience of the Comanche, but attempting to spread his influence over the Cheyenne and Kiowa as well.

Perhaps he was only jealous of such great power in the hands of another, Quanah brooded, here beneath the first stars emerging from the deep purple of twilight above the multihued canyon walls. Eight hundred feet, some higher still, those walls rose above him and the camp of his people here among the trees and brush and gurgle of the spring-swollen creek.

Yes, he was suspicious—for it seemed to Quanah that Isatai had in his heart not the good of the people, but the burning need for revenge. Many moons ago, in the time of the Deer Shedding Horns, Isatai's uncle had called together a few young Comanche and a handful of Kiowa warriors to follow him on a raid into Mexico. Upon their return with horses and captives, the soldiers discovered the war party and attacked. Among the dead who were reluctantly abandoned on the battlefield were the Kiowa sons of Lone Wolf and Red Otter. Seven more lay mortally wounded as the survivors rode off and escaped—among them Isatai's uncle.

But, in his heart, Quanah understood revenge. His father, Peta Nocona, had taught him that well enough. Since that winter when the Tonkawas and white Tehas rangers had recaptured Quanah's mother, Peta Nocona wandered in search of Cynthia Ann, his blond wife known as Naduah among the Comanche. It was a search that eventually brought death to the Kwahadi chief. But not before Quanah had learned the value of fury and revenge, of life-long love.

He shivered with the chill wind knifing through the canyon, the smell of rain heavy on the air in its passing. Quanah would soon make his way back to the warmth of his lodge and the smooth heat of his wife's flesh. Nothing warmed him so like driving his own hard lance deep within Tonarcy as they tumbled and grappled and scratched and bit in a furious dance of coupling. Quanah Parker knew love.

If he did not always understand the ways of men and magic and making war, he did understand women and making love.

And perhaps even more, Quanah understood himself. He realized he could enlist Isatai's help in fighting the white man. If the shaman's powers were not real, no more than breathsmoke in a winter wind, then at least Isatai had proved his worth by bringing together the warrior bands of all the tribes to wage this last great struggle to drive the white man from the land that had belonged to Quanah's people since time began its journey across the stars.

And if the shaman's power proved to be real—so much the better.

All the better too that Isatai had called for the first-ever sun dance to be held by the Kwahadi. True enough, they had visited the Kiowa and Southern Cheyenne and had witnessed the great sun-staring dance for many generations. But Isatai had announced it was time for the Kwahadi to hold their own, in preparation for the last great fight against the white man. Such was the power of the young shaman's medicine.

Eager to do anything that would hasten along their plans to make war on the hunters and soldiers and settlers, Quanah had immediately dispatched pipe bearers to all the bands of Comanche and Kiowa, Cheyenne and Kiowa-Apache, carrying word in every direction. From the reservations to the far reaches of the Staked Plain the word was raised: *war* was coming.

"Come join us in driving the white man far from the buffalo ground. Bring your fastest ponies and your weapons—we will kill as many whites as we can, and those we don't kill, we will drive beyond the rising sun."

His words ringing in their ears, Quanah had watched those pipe bearers ride to the four winds with the Kwahadi call for a sun dance and war.

Powerful medicine.

Alone now with only the land and the wind, Quanah vowed, "Together, Isatai—we will see the buffalo hunters fall and the white ground-scratchers driven from our hunting ground. We will watch the soldiers' hearts turn to water, and the white hunters soil their pants in fear of our power." His voice was seized from his lips by the cold wind as quickly as his words were uttered.

"Our power comes from the heart!" Quanah flung more words into the face of the first drops of driving rain hurtling down from the rim of the canyon. "Hear me, white man! This simple Kwahadi warrior knows the power of love. As well, he knows the power of hate."

8

Moon of First Eggs, 1874

Stone Calf was doing his best to walk the white man's road in order to keep his people fed. But his heart remained out on the prairie.

For many moons the white horse thieves had come and gone at will, slipping across the unguarded boundaries of the Cheyenne Reservation. The outlaws laughed in the face of the army's puny efforts to protect the Indians' herds. Men like Jack Gallagher and Robert Hollis, and the most infamous of them all—William A. "Hurricane Bill" Martin. It was his bunch that rode down out of Kansas early in March, striking Little Robe's herd.

Turning the stolen ponies north toward Kansas, Martin's men began their escape while Little Robe and other warriors caught up what horses they could to pursue the white thieves. Even though they were driving the stolen ponies before them, Martin's gang nonetheless began to widen the distance, causing Little Robe to call off the chase.

Angrily, some of the young men refused to give up the pursuit of the white men. Chief among them—Sitting Medicine, Little Robe's son.

When they found themselves unable to catch the thieves, who had escaped well into Kansas territory, the young warriors decided they would lick their wounds by doing a little raiding themselves. They struck the first settlement they happened upon, stealing some horses and cattle, along with making a lot of noise. They succeeded in turning south without harming anyone.

That all changed when the victorious warriors bumped into some cavalry under Captain Tullis Tupper out of Camp Supply. In the brief but hot skirmish, the stolen horses and cattle were recaptured by the buffalo soldiers, and two warriors were seriously wounded.

Sitting Medicine was barely able to stay atop his pony by the time the young warriors limped back to the reservation.

Among the various camps surrounding the Darlington Agency, the word quickly spread. Retaliation was called for. The army was clearly protecting the horse thieves instead of the victims. The same army that had guaranteed food for the hungry families was slowly starving the proud Cheyenne.

In an electrifying council little more than a moon ago, the chiefs met and argued which path to take. But in the end the Southern Cheyenne tore themselves apart. Vowing to stay on the reservation where the army would not hunt down the Cheyenne, Stone Calf was joined by White Shield and a reluctant Whirlwind.

"You are old women!" Gray Beard had shouted into the faces of the three peace chiefs. "You sit here while Cheyenne horses are stolen and are offered for sale to the buffalo hunters on the streets of Dodge City. You are worse than women. You are fools too! Open your eyes and see the destruction brought us by the white whiskey traders who sell their poison on the outskirts of our camps. Our warriors are no longer allowed to be men who can hunt and raid—so they drink to fill that hole inside them where their spirit used to be. And when a man is no longer a man, he no longer feels the need to feed his family.

"I am taking my warriors away from this slow death," Gray Beard vowed. "No more will we sit by while the white man poisons us with his whiskey. No more will we numbly watch our people starve because the agent and army don't keep their empty-mouthed promises. And we will hold onto our ponies. My warriors will ride them when the buffalo return north this season. We will ride our ponies when we drive the white man far from the Indian country. Sit on your hands if you will. But as for me—my hands are raised to fight!"

While the promised rations were in short supply on the reservations that winter and into the cold, wet spring, the trade in guns and ammunition flourished. Not only did Gray Beard's warriors seek revenge, but young warriors from the other bands hungered to even the score by crossing into nearby Kansas. The chill winds of spring brought with them the stench of blood and death.

Three white teamsters were butchered near Medicine Lodge, where seven winters before the tribes of the central and southern plains had signed a momentous peace treaty with the white man.

A few days later, another group of teamsters were corralled on the road between Fort Dodge and Camp Supply and overwhelmed by a large Cheyenne war party.

Detachments of cavalry traveling the road to and from the Territories were struck, raids made swiftly before the warriors disappeared, leaving wounded and dead soldiers in their wake.

More and more, small groups of buffalo hunters sighted or even skirmished with war parties of feathered, painted warriors roaming the country between the reservations and the Staked Plain.

Stone Calf lay awake most nights in his lodge now, listening to the hard rain falling against the hides like the soul-numbing rattle of gunfire.

He saw their angry faces in his mind. Said their names in his heart. Those young warriors who, one by one, left the reservation nearly every day. Riding off to the west to join the war parties, to live the free life that had been his own as a young man. Only in the darkness of the lodge, with his wives and older children all asleep, did he allow the tears to come. Knowing not what else to do, Stone Calf wanted desperately to believe the white man would keep his word and keep the Cheyenne fed.

But more and more he was beginning to see this was not only a matter of the belly, full or not. This was becoming a matter of the spirit. To have the warrior spirit meant to ride away from this place of despair before the white man fully crushed what little fire he and the old ones still possessed.

True enough, a flame still lingered in his old breast.

"The buffalo herds do not survive where the white man builds his cities, lays his railroads, plows his fields," Stone Calf had admitted time and again in council. "First the buffalo hunter comes. Behind him the railroad and then the settlements. Spreading from those settlements are the houses of those white men who scratch at the earth."

"To me it is clear," said young Red Moon, a warrior of note who had early on slipped away from the reservation. "Clear to me that to stop the earth-scratchers, the city-builders and the railroad men—we have only to stop those who clear the way for all the rest. We have but one choice —and that is to stop the buffalo hunters."

In the night silence of his lodge, Stone Calf's tears burned his cheeks, for he knew the young warriors were right.

From the buffalo the Indian drew his physical and spiritual existence. From head to tail, the Cheyenne and the others realized if the buffalo were driven from the plains— so too would the Indian cease to exist. Horns were boiled to fashion spoons and combs. Those shaggy hides the white men stripped from the warm carcasses provided clothing, lodge covers, rawhide shields, and wrapped their infants in cradleboards. The long hair they wove into rope, while his people used tendons to sew clothing and fashion sturdy bowstrings. Hooves provided glue to strengthen the war shields of the young warriors. Liver and brain were pounded to a pulp to soften hides. Paunch and bladder were dried to serve as containers. Even the tails served as fly swatters.

Little went to waste. And what was left behind by the women and old ones on the prairie after a hunt served to feed the carrion eaters in the great circle of life.

"The circle has been broken," Stone Calf whispered in the darkened silence of his lodge, listening to the rain beating on the side of the buffalo hides like the hammering of pony hooves in the chase.

His first wife turned against him, nuzzling her head into his shoulder, grunting in her sleep. Her breathing soon became regular and deep.

Stone Calf wondered about his friend, Ben Clark, the army scout who had long ago married one of Stone Calf's sisters. He was a man who could be trusted, although many of the young warriors never would forgive Clark for acting as one of the scouts who led Yellow Hair Custer to Black Kettle's village on the Washita many winters before. When soldiers would attack a sleeping village camped under a peace chief—there was truly no peace left for any of them, he decided.

Ben Clark had quit scouting back then and now worked only as an interpreter out of Camp Supply. Time and again through the terrible winter he had visited his wife's people at the agency, his own eyes saddened by the great hunger he saw. What ponies weren't being stolen by white horse thieves, the Cheyenne had to butcher to fill the empty bellies. Clark understood why the young men were leaving the reservation, most abandoning their families to hunt and make war on the buffalo hunters and soldiers.

"Yet I hear that White Horse has come in with his band," Clark had said during his last visit with the aging chief at the Darlington Agency.

Stone Calf had nodded. White Horse, the chief who four winters ago had assumed leadership of the most feared of the Cheyenne warrior societies—the Dog Soldiers. At the battle of Summit Springs, the famed Tall Bull had been killed by Bill Cody, the warriors scattered to the winds by the Fifth Cavalry.* White Horse and his band had held out as long as possible.

Stone Calf remembered the sadness he had clearly read in Ben Clark's eyes when the white scout learned that even the famed Dog Soldiers had no option left them but to come in to the agency in order that their families would have food for their bellies.

* The Plainsmen Series, vol. 4, *Black Sun*

I only pray the agent can feed us all, Stone Calf brooded in the cold of his lodge. More than five hundred lodges of Cheyenne and Arapaho now. And Agent Miles complains that he does not have enough coffee and sugar and flour to go around. There has been no beef for so long, I forget the way it tastes. How the white man's food hurts my teeth.

"If the government contractors cannot supply us with what we need to feed your families," a disgruntled Miles had told Stone Calf and the others, "I will have no other choice but to free your people to move west, to hunt the buffalo."

The sting in his old eyes also burned in his chest. Stone Calf knew it was what his people would want most to hear. But, that meant the Cheyenne would have to go west to locate that last great herd of buffalo, the same southern herd the white hide men from Kansas were very likely already hunting.

The catfish and perch had been a most welcome change for Seamus from the steady diet of venison and antelope and turkey. The nearby creeks throbbed with the fish. And there was a morning or two when the Irishman decided he would take the day off and sit beneath the shade of the willow and cottonwood and doze, listening to the drone of the horseflies and dragonflies and yellowjackets while the rest of the men finished the last details of their settlement here in the meadow beside Adobe Walls Creek.

That is, those few men who had remained behind when the rest pulled out to find the great herd.

"This damned weather is likely keeping them south longer than normal," Charlie Myers said one evening as a group of them had stood outside, staring to the south as rose-colored twilight came down easy on the land.

"All they've brought in so far are a few bull and a some cow hides," added James Langton, Myers's young partner.

Donegan often eyed the growing ricks of dried "flint" hides outside the Myers and Leonard compound or across the way near the low walls of the Rath & Company stockade. Each stack stood some forty to fifty hides tall, giving the appearance of clusters of small buildings dotting the outskirts of the stockades.

Nearly every day now saw the arrival of a new outfit, hunter and skinners having followed what had become a well-worn trail south from Dodge City. In either store, the hide men bought powder and primers, lead and cartridges, patch paper and gun oil. Food was next on the list for highest demand among the hunters: canned tomatoes, soup and peaches; crackers, pickles and dried apples. Others items moved more slowly—Castile soap, strychnine wolf poison, axle grease and stomach bitters.

While Charlie Myers had promised the hunters he would hold the line on Dodge City prices, most items did cost more when they crossed the counter at Adobe Walls. In Dodge City bacon had cost fifteen cents per pound; twenty cents in Indian country. Coffee that was thirty-six cents a pound in Kansas was selling in Texas for at least forty-five cents. And tobacco cost a man at least twenty-five cents more by the time it made it to buffalo country.

Upon arrival at the trading post, or during their infrequent visits to purchase supplies, most of the hunters took their two hot meals a day in one mess hall or the other for the enviable price of fifty cents per meal. Most of the time Seamus would avoid the closed-in buildings when the hide men came in off the range, preferring to eat or do his drinking when he could do it alone. Although soap was available to the skinners, most did not take advantage of mixing it with water. Theirs was a life requiring that they work up past their elbows in the great carcasses, some of which were becoming putrefied. Blood, body fat and the parasites that infested the buffalo all were the lot of the skinner—lowest in the hunting echelon.

Dried sweat on a frontiersman was one thing, Donegan brooded. The telltale stench that clung to a buffalo skinner was something else altogether.

It was on the long late-spring nights like this that the men of Adobe Walls congregated to drink, play cards, tell stories and dance, besides regaling one another with their lies and windies. And because of some of the company a man was required to keep in either of the two stores,

Seamus ofttimes preferred his own company. The solitude of the night beneath the stars and the sliver of that gold moon as he dug and drank, letting long draughts of the whiskey tumble down his throat before he set the bottle back atop the crumbling adobe wall above the new hole he was currently excavating. Still hoping. Talking to himself and God and any of the saints who might be listening—telling them that he needed their help as night after night he had been coming down here, slipping away in the darkness lest anyone become suspicious of the Irishman's need to be digging up the old ruins.

And tonight he just did not have the grit to work long at his obsession. Whether it was the nagging warning of something unknown by the great white scar across his back, or only the bone-weary fatigue settling into his muscles after these weeks of labor during the day, digging at night. He was no longer a young man able to work and drink as long as he required of himself.

Ah, though the spirit were willing—his flesh no longer was.

Secreting the shovel back in a copse of willow and hackberry, Seamus strode back to his tent, pitched close by the stakes and twine that marked what would soon become the walls of Jim Hanrahan's saloon. With the completion of the Rath & Company compound, Swede Johnson had only recently begun raising the newest of the settlement buildings.

Tracing an icy finger along the scar down his back, the wind made him shudder. Donegan glanced at the clouds scudding across the thumbnail sliver of a moon as he hunched over to enter his tent. And instantly froze.

Everything lay scattered.

He dropped to his knees, digging through the jumble of what few possessions he owned. The Henry was here, he could feel it with his hands without any light. The extra pistols as well. They hadn't wanted his weapons.

Hurriedly he dragged a lucifer down the tent pole and lit the crude lamp he used—a wick standing in buffalo tallow in a tip cup.

They were after something else.

Pulling the painted rawhide pouch into his lap, he knew before he even lay back the flap. It was untied. He never left it untied. But even then he knew they had not come to steal his money. It had been just a plus to going through his things.

Whoever it was had wanted something else. Something more valuable than that last hundred dollars Seamus Donegan had in the world. Back at the walls earlier that evening the warning at his back had told him, and he hadn't paid attention to the ghostly whisper.

Now, like a cold wind come to frighten a man on a hot mid-summer day, the questions and fear eddied and rustled through his weary, troubled mind. His heart thundering in his ears, furious and wanting more than anything at this moment to put his big hands on whoever had violated him, Donegan nonetheless knew that there was someone among these men he could not trust. And, in all likelihood, it had to be someone newly come to the meadow. One of the new arrivals—hunter, skinner or company employee.

Eyes gone dark with instant suspicion, his temper flaring hotter than a rope burn, Donegan knew he would have to watch his back now. Never giving any man among them a chance to even suspect where he had buried the map.

Worse still, now he would no longer be free to wander off at night. No more could he feel certain of his own safety, alone beneath the stars and moonlight. Whoever had violated the unspoken trust and bond between these frontiersmen might very well be the sort of predator who would stop at nothing short of killing him to get what he wanted.

Someone sent by Louis Abragon to do everything he could to get his hands on the Irishman's map.

9

Moon of Fat Horses, 1874

The first day of the new moon. And when that first moon of the summer had grown full and fat, they would attack the white hide hunters while they slept in their earth lodges.

As decided by the chiefs, the bands had come together a few days ago at the mouth of Elk Creek on the North Fork of the Red River. It was there, within the bounds of the Kiowa-Comanche Reservation itself, that Isatai had directed the construction of the sun-dance lodge. Even Quanah was impressed by the size of the gathering. A wildly independent people, often led by extremely jealous chiefs, the Comanche had never before joined in such numbers for any purpose. Even the avowed peace chiefs like Horseback and Elk Chewing had journeyed south to the great sun-praying with their bands.

Perhaps even more telling, many of the Kiowa and Cheyenne warrior bands rode in to take part in the great Comanche celebration, afterward to hold a council of war with the Kwahadi war chiefs. To that camp on Elk Creek came the Kiowa under Satanta and Lone Wolf, along with the Cheyenne under Medicine Water, Iron Shirt and Gray Beard, each chief carrying the war pipes sent them by Isatai. Little Robe, on the other hand, had immediately taken his people to the agency, fearing most what everyone knew was coming, while Stone Eagle sat arguing with himself on what path to take.

For most the path was clear.

As much as he had initially doubted this magician and his sleight of hand, Quanah found himself reluctantly beginning to believe in Isatai: perhaps this shaman was truly more than a magician. Perhaps through the prophet Isatai, the Comanche truly could drive the white man from their ancient hunting ground, for all time to come.

If for no other reason, Quanah thought, Isatai was extremely smart—in the way a wolf is smart. By assembling the various bands, the shaman was consolidating his power in a way few others among the Comanche could ever think of doing. But something about that, something right down in the pit of him still nagged the young Kwahadi war chief —worrying over any man who wanted so much power. Still, Quanah had to admit as he argued with himself night after night as the lengthening days turned warm, then hot, Isatai was accomplishing exactly what Quanah himself wanted: gathering a large force of proven warriors with one concerted end in sight.

So it seemed fitting that the Comanche had chosen to immerse themselves in more of the symbolism of the sun dancing, forgoing many of the "formalities" practiced by the Kiowa and Cheyenne. And that symbolism of the sun dance had for many generations been unequivocally tied to the buffalo. Now more than ever, the threat posed by the white buffalo hunters had become most real.

The extermination of the buffalo clearly meant the extermination of the Comanche.

Across four days the bands had gathered the poles and branches for the great sun-dance arbor. At the center they raised a tall, forked ridgepole which had been selected for cutting by a virtuous captive woman who had been faithful to her Kwahadi husband. Ringing the outer circle stood twelve shorter poles, connected to the center with long streamers decorated with scalps and scraps of fluttering calico and trade cloth. All but one of the openings between these twelve poles were filled in with brush—the easternmost remained open to admit the dancers. A newly killed buffalo calf, its body cavity emptied then stuffed with willow branches, was raised to the top of the huge center pole. There it would symbolically look down upon the dancers, granting its blessing upon them.

At the same time as warriors were raising the sun-dance arbor, masked clowns who had smeared themselves with mud and tied small branches of willow about their bodies cavorted and swirled among the villages, throwing mud balls at the unsuspecting and generally giving a carnival atmosphere to the predance activities. These were the Comanche "Mud Men," the *sekwitsit puhitsit*—a purely Comanche addition to the sun-dance practice, in all likelihood something picked up from the *koshare* dancers of the Pueblo Indians near Taos.

To Quanah's way of thinking, the Mud Men were a comical diversion to an otherwise deadly serious act: invoking the power of the supernatural to bring about the salvation of a dying way of life.

On the final day of preparation a group of warriors constructed a fortress and stockade of brush that simulated the earth buildings inhabited by the white hide men to the northwest on the Staked Plain. Then the young warriors rode down on this mock fort, destroying the hated enemy to the last man. Only then did the dancing begin at the sacred arbor where the buffalo calf looked down upon those who prayed.

While he did not himself join in the dancing, Quanah nonetheless fasted the four days of scorching sun and long, chilly nights, taking no water and sitting through the endless drumming and singing by the old men. While dancers among the northern tribes hung themselves from the rawhide tethers or dragged buffalo skulls from skewers driven beneath the muscles in their backs, the Comanche dancers did not believe it necessary to torture themselves to be heard by the Spirit Above. Still, like Quanah, the dancers took no food or water for the duration of the celebration of the sun. While these warriors danced, men and women both came forward and hung small offerings of food and tobacco and scalps from the center pole. Young boys hoping one day to become full-fledged warriors tied their gifts to their tiny arrows and shot them into the sun-dance tree, far above the dancers.

Quanah prayed as he sucked on the bark of the slippery elm, something that softened the torture of his thirst—prayed that the coming war council would bring together as one the tribes and warrior bands.

On the morning after the fourth day of dancing, there arose a great celebration that stirred Quanah's heart to believing his prayers had been answered. He called for his warriors to dress as for battle and mount their finest war ponies. Then he led them on a mock charge on the Kiowa and Cheyenne camps—riding through the villages screeching their war cries, shaking their shields and scalps and lances, firing their weapons into the air before returning to their own camp.

In no time did the Kiowa respond in kind, riding down in a mock attack on the Comanche villages. The warrior bands of Lone Wolf and Satanta and Big Bow were ready to take up the battle against the white man. All waited expectantly for the Cheyenne answer to this flamboyant call for war.

And just as he was beginning to fear the Southern Cheyenne would not join the Kwahadi in driving the white man from the Staked Plain, Quanah heard the pounding of the hooves. In a swirl of dust and a deafening cacophony of screeching noise and trilling women, the Cheyenne warriors tore into the Kwahadi camp, shaking their scalps and firing their rifles.

"We are ready to join you, Quanah!" shouted Medicine Water as he brought his snorting pony to a halt beside the lodge of the Kwahadi war chief in a spray of yellow dust.

Quanah had rarely felt more proud, wishing that his own father stood beside him at this moment as he looked into the paint-streaked faces of those Cheyenne and Kiowa warriors, their voices raised exultantly to the heavens, the hot summer breeze toying with their feathers and braids and unbound hair. Were that his father could be here to see this great union of fighting men.

"Tonight!" Quanah replied, his voice booming across the great gathering. "Tonight Isatai and I will host a grand council for all chiefs."

"We talk of strategy for the coming fight!" Isatai echoed.

"Yes," Quanah replied with the hunting yelp of the prairie coyote. "We talk of war!"

And war was all they spoke of that evening as the early summer sun sank in the west, far beyond the great canyon called Palo Duro.

Isatai began with his long harangue about the Caddos and Wichitas, bands that had accepted the white man's reservation life and no longer lived as true Indians.

"Are not their numbers diminishing?" asked the shaman of that great gathering beneath the summer stars. "Are they healthy? Eating the white man's food instead of the meat of the buffalo?"

Slowly, dramatically, he strode around the interior of the huge circle formed by the head men of each warrior band. "Is this what the Comanche want? What the Kiowa and Cheyenne want?"

There arose a general muttering, until Isatai turned suddenly to look at the young Kwahadi war chief.

"What say you, Quanah?"

"We want to follow the buffalo herds as in days of old!" he replied, his voice booming. "We wish to stay a strong people, needing nothing from the white man!"

Isatai quickly strode to Quanah. "I have been to talk to the Spirit Above. He has told me that the strong of heart will prevail in the coming war. He has told me that if we go on the warpath and wipe our land clear of the white man—only then will the buffalo return to blanket our hunting ground. Unless we drive the white man out now, the buffalo will disappear."

"The white man must go!" Quanah shouted.

"No," Isatai snarled. "The white man must die! All of them. Man . . . woman . . . child!"

Reluctantly, yet magnetically, Quanah felt himself drawn to the charisma of the shaman, unable to think of nothing else at that moment but killing all whites. But as much as he hated the white man, a small voice inside reminded him that had the Comanche killed all whites—man, woman and child—his mother would not have been Cynthia Ann Parker. And he would not be who he was this night, standing before this greatest gathering of war chiefs the southern plains had ever seen.

"How do you answer, Quanah?" Isatai demanded. "Bull Bear, the old war chief of the Kwahadi, lies dying of the great lung sickness in his lodge. Will you take up the war banner of Bull Bear? Will you lead the Kwahadi back to greatness!"

His eyes quickly went to Bull Bear's second chief, an older warrior named Wild Horse. Quanah could see the jealousy in the warrior's eyes, the threat there. Yet even Wild Horse refrained from protest.

"I will lead the Kwahadi," Quanah said boldly.

"And I say we first wipe out the Tonkawas," Isatai told the assembly, turning away from Quanah. "They lead the white man down on our villages. They are evil Indians, wearing the white man's clothes, eating his food and leading his soldiers. And, the Spirit Above told me that this is true: the Tonkawas eat the flesh of their dead enemies!"

Many of the warriors and chiefs quickly clamped their hands over their mouths. Quanah himself was surprised by this sudden declaration, although it had long been suspected that the Tonkawas did practice cannibalism.

"No!" shouted White Wolf, a powerful Cheyenne war chief. "These Tonkawas are not our concern."

Isatai's face glowered at the taller, powerfully built warrior. "I say we wipe out the Tonkawa first."

"I too answer no," added Old Man Otter Belt, a warrior of great distinction among the Cheyenne. He rose to stand beside White Wolf, then strode over to Quanah. "This medicine man is no warrior, Quanah Parker. But you—you are a pretty good fighter. Too bad you are still young and don't know everything."

White Wolf joined Otter Belt before Quanah. "We think the Kwahadi need first to wipe out the buffalo hunters gathered on the Canadian River. Kwahadi go do that first. Then your hearts will be ready for war. You kill all the buffalo hunters—then the Cheyenne follow you to war in Tehas. All our young men gladly follow you anywhere then, Quanah."

Otter Belt tapped a finger against his heart, then against Quanah's. "In there, we both know the Tonkawas are no threat to our peoples. Don't we, Quanah? In there, in your heart, you know the real threat to the survival of our peoples are the buffalo hunters. We stop them—then we stop the white man."

Quanah had to nod, almost reluctantly. The older Cheyenne had stripped it bare, like he himself did when he cracked open a large bone to expose the marrow. Gone to the heart of the matter. "Yes. We stop the buffalo hunters now. The rest will not bother us: these settlers and the workers for the smoking horse. We will fill the hunters' camps with dead, bloating bodies until no white man will ever again venture onto the buffalo ground."

"What about the hunters' camp I told you about on the Canadian?" White Wolf asked.

"Your scouts have seen them?"

"Yes. They come and go as if the land were theirs to use up and throw away," Otter Belt answered for them both.

"No!" shouted Isatai, leaping forward to confront the two Cheyenne war chiefs, his hand working like claws before him. "Forget those buffalo killers. We must first wipe out the Tonkawas—they are the eyes and ears for the soldiers who killed my father!"

"The Tonkawas are not the cause of our problems, Quanah," White Wolf repeated in turning away from Isatai. "You must stop the buffalo hunters first."

Otter Belt agreed, but with a reservation. "The white man will fight, staying hidden in those lodges he has raised with earth for their walls."

"The white man fights hard when he gets behind his walls," Quanah reflected thoughtfully, then had his attention snagged as Isatai lunged toward the Cheyenne chiefs, his hands gripping and releasing, as if suddenly possessed, gesturing angrily.

"Those walls are nothing to my power!" the young shaman growled. "Haven't I told you of my recent visit to the Spirit Above? He told me he would put all the white men to sleep before our attack. Don't you see?" he gushed enthusiastically. "Our warriors will only have to ride in and club them on the heads, like the white man's stupid spotted buffalo are clubbed to death."

"Those hunters have guns that shoot a long, long way," came a voice filled with doubt from the council ring.

Isatai whirled on the doubter, slapping his chest with his two hands. "Let them shoot all their bullets at us! Do you dare talk against my powers? Do you doubt that I can make a medicine so powerful that it will protect our warriors as they ride down on the white man's earth lodges? Tell me!" he shrieked, scurrying around the center of the gathering, yelling his words into the faces of the chiefs. "Do you doubt the power of my medicine to turn their bullets into water?"

"No," Quanah answered firmly. He had decided. It would not be the Tonkawas. It would be the white man. It had to be the white man. Down in the core of his marrow, Quanah knew he had to confront the white blood in him,

91

and defeat it—as surely as he had to ride down on the white buffalo hunters and defeat them. One and all.

When Quanah answered Isatai, the rest had little choice but to respond in kind. They muttered their assent to the plan the Kwahadi war chief now gave his strongest voice. "The tai-bo hunters will fall beneath our hooves and hands like newborn calves, their hearts turned to gall and their courage gone the way of winter breathsmoke."

"So you will wipe out the settlement on the Canadian?" White Wolf asked, stepping before Quanah in a challenging way.

Surprising the Cheyenne warrior, Quanah snagged the front of the calfskin vest White Wolf wore and hoisted the warrior off his toes. "Do not play with me, Cheyenne. I am not so stupid nor am I a child, as you might believe. If your warriors are not the men they used to be before your people went to stay on the reservations—then move aside and let the Kwahadi and Kiowa pass through to drive the white man out."

In slowly lowering the Cheyenne war chief to his feet and smoothing the calfskin vest, Quanah continued, his words barely audible at the center of that great assembly. "This will be great sport, this challenge you present us, White Wolf. This is the land of my people, where the Kwahadi ride free and proud—ever since life was in the womb of time itself. But, we have seen too much sorrow in recent winters, so Kwahadi hearts are ready for this fight. Where once the great herds roamed and drifted before the seasons, I now see only death, White Wolf. While our children and old ones go hungry . . . the bellies of the big-winged predators grow so heavy with rotting meat that the birds cannot fly. I myself have stood and looked down on a field of death that stretches far beyond where my eye can see. My nose has so filled with the stench that my heart becomes angry, thinking of the little ones." His eyes narrowed on the Cheyenne chief. "Do you have little ones gone hungry in your camps placed in the shadow of the white man's forts, White Wolf?"

"The flour does not come," replied the Cheyenne.

"When it does, the sacks are filled with weevils and dead mice. There is never enough of the white man's spotted buffalo to feed our families. Many of those who live on the reservation are too old or sick to hunt for themselves. They are reduced to begging at the back doors of the kitchens from the soldiers at Camp Supply. No—you do not hate alone, Quanah," White Wolf growled. "I am sorry if I offended you. I knew of your white blood, and distrusted it. Forgive me: White Wolf wanted only to be sure it would be your Comanche blood that would guide your heart in the coming fight."

"Quanah?"

They both turned, finding the old and venerable Comanche chief hobbling into the bright firelight.

Ten Bears said, "Paracoom is dying, Quanah. Chief of your Kwahadi band. It now falls on your shoulders to lead this fight. Take not the counsel of the shaman or the owl-puffing wizards. Listen only to your heart, young one. And do what it tells you."

The strength of the old chief's words filled him with the power of prairie lightning. "I will do this for my people, Ten Bears."

"When the white man wanted to put us all on a reservation, six winters ago—he wanted us to live in one place as he does." Ten Bears licked his dry lips, the pink tip of his tongue flicking out between gaps in his worn teeth. "I do not want a house like these buffalo hunters build for themselves. I was born on the prairie, where the wind blows free and there is nothing to break the light of the sun. I was born where there are no enclosures and every living thing draws a free breath. I want to die here, and not within walls." His old eyes grew moist as he peered up at the young war chief. "Make this so, Quanah."

"No Comanche must die a captive of the white man. A warrior dies on the prairie, Ten Bears. He dies riding into the face of his enemy. We will take the magic of Isatai with us to the buffalo hunters' settlement. But we will also take our weapons as well. The white man's days on the prairie are numbered."

Quanah slowly made a tight fist before the old man's smiling, watery eyes. "I hold those last days of the white man in my hand."

10

Early June 1874

Billy Dixon was not the kind to sit on his thumbs, or to grovel in the dirt and sod when there was money to be made shooting buffalo. But that was just the problem. The buffalo had been slow in moving north that spring.

Almost from that thud of the first hammer or the grating of the first saw, Dixon eagerly pulled his three-man outfit from the meadow beside Adobe Walls Creek and headed south to scare up the herds. Instead, all they got for their two-week, wide-ranging trip were some saddle galls and a few bulls.

Billy tried to explain his view of things to his skinners in a way that would keep them from losing heart. "Season's too damned early for the cows and bulls to start mating and running together, boys. We'll be in better shape soon."

Buffalo outfits ranged in size from the sort of man who was a loner, bent on doing his own hunting and skinning, to outfits numbering several hunters who would join together in one base camp, then each of whom would range out in different directions every day of the hunt. Most hunters could easily keep three to four skinners busy as they worked through a sizable herd.

Usually able to get no closer than three or four hundred yards to a herd before the sentinel bulls grew restive, a hunter would belly down in a likely spot with his canteen to cool the big-bore barrel and cartridge belt and often an extra rifle should the one become overheated. Then by carefully selecting his targets on the fringe of the herd, or by putting down those animals that were tending to wander away from the stand, the hunter could keep the dull-witted beasts confused as one after another of their kind collapsed onto the prairie. And such work always made social misfits of the skinners, working up to their elbows for weeks at a time in the blood and gore, their unchanged clothing time and again soaked with tallow and slicked with blood. A gamy sort of character that most men kept downwind.

After having left Adobe Walls and swinging as far east as Cantonment Creek on that first sojourn, Dixon brought his crew back in to the meadow to find most of the buildings nearing completion, and Charlie Rath's store not lagging far behind. It proved a joyous few days that third week of April: drinking, singing, dancing, regaling one another with their stories of past hunts or bloody battles fought in a faraway war not quite ten years gone. Indeed, it was good to see new faces, and those familiar, like Donegan's—but again, after only two days of company, the boredom became nettlesome to Dixon and he itched to ride out once more.

Having had enough company to last him for a while, Billy headed west up the Canadian this time, as far as Hell's Creek, where they caught up the Old Fort Bascomb Trail and followed it as far as Antelope Creek. Near there Dixon ran across the path he had taken the previous winter. Taking it, they recrossed the Canadian and marched north to Grapevine Creek, running across small bands of bulls along the way. Some they shot, mostly for camp meat. But, for the most part, Dixon did not disturb the few buffalo they found as he pushed his outfit eastward while the lengthening days took them into the month of May and the weather invigorated the randy blood of the young men.

From time to time Dixon or the others would find a patch of lamb's quarter where they made their evening camp. They ate wild greens most every night as the stars came out to sparkle against a brilliant, nighttime canopy. And every morning they arose to the smell of coffee brewing as the sunrise splayed orange lances into the sky from somewhere still far to the east.

Eventually deciding not to push their luck by pressing farther south than they already were on the North Fork of the Red River, Dixon led his wagons north by west, returning a second time to the sod buildings of the settlement at Adobe Walls. Yet once more the boredom wore on

Billy after no more than a week. That, and the unaccounted absences of the Irishman each evening. Donegan just up and disappeared not long before nightfall—to where, no man seemed to know.

"Being downright unsociable," Billy had muttered to himself more than once when gone in search of the Irishman, asking after Donegan at each of the buildings. "Not like him at all," he decided. Not like Donegan to miss out on the drinking and singing and dancing in such a way. Something was clearly amiss, and it bothered him not a little. Almost as much as not finding the herds. Getting later and later the way it was . . .

The end of May, Dixon pulled out again.

On this third trip, with but two skinners along, he struck due south for the mouth of White Deer Creek, following it until the stream took him directly into the heart of the plains. There was no doubt of it—the place even had the smell of it: they were in buffalo country, when the buffalo decided to come back north. But, they were undoubtedly in Indian country.

Finding a place that offered good grass, water and firewood, Dixon proposed making a permanent hunting camp. Not only was Frenchy a skinner, but camp cook as well. The trio was rounded out by another skinner, Charley Armitage, recently arrived from England to immerse himself in the life of the American frontier.

For three days now Billy had been riding far out to the south in a grand circle trying to locate the herds, without success. But as coffee water boiled that fourth morning, the summer sun rising early out of the east, the low, thundering rumble came carried to him on the clear prairie air. For any hide man who had ever heard that sound, he instantly knew in every fiber of his body that his time was at hand.

"You hear it, Billy?" Armitage asked, kicking on his leather-split broughams and standing in the crumple of his blankets, looking like something a dog would drag in off the prairie.

"They're coming, boys," Dixon replied. "Keep an eye on that pot and I'll be back shortly."

96

He strode off on foot to the south, ascending to the highest hill. There his eyes strained into the early light streaming across the wide, rolling land. Still nothing. He waited, listening through those long minutes. While his eyes failed him, his ears did not. The buffalo were coming.

By the time he was back at camp, Frenchy had some meat frying in one pan, a Dutch oven with johnnycakes browning nicely. Dixon hurriedly shoved his breakfast down, swallowing several cups of coffee before he swiped a hand across his shaggy mustache and saddled up.

No more than five miles south of their camp, Billy ran into the first small bunches of buffalo—bulls. Migrating slowly to the north, each and every one eating and bellowing as they plodded their way in the seasonal imperative. It was now the breeding season, when the bulls roared and snorted and raised their challenges to the cloudless summer sky.

His heart leaped in his chest the farther south he rode. Another eight miles and Billy Dixon reined up suddenly atop a low knoll. Below him, in all three directions, stretched a brown-black carpet undulating gradually to the north. The excitement of this great land and of the life he had chosen once more sang through his heart, causing his limbs to tingle as he sawed the horse about and raced back to camp to spread the news.

Before noon, within sight of their tents, Billy dropped forty buffalo, putting Frenchy and Armitage to work with their long-bladed skinning knives. By sundown the fringe of the herd had begun to pass within a gunshot of their camp.

At work by first light the next morning, it took little time for Dixon to shoot enough buffalo to keep his pair of skinners busy for several days before he hitched up the mules to one of his light wagons and pushed north, heading back to Adobe Walls.

"What brings you back here, with that shit-eating grin on your face?" asked Charley Rath as Dixon tied the reins around the brake handle and hopped down from the wagon. "You found some buff, didn't you?"

"Damn if I didn't, Charley!" Billy cried.

"Whooeee!" Rath hollered as more of the settlement's inhabitants hurried to gather close. "They're coming in, boys!"

"Where's Donegan?" Dixon inquired, craning his neck.

"He's coming over now," Billy Tyler said, pointing across the meadow as the tall Irishman loped up.

"Say, Donegan!" Dixon hollered. "I need all the hands I can get. You want to make some good money skinning for me?"

The Irishman bellowed loudly at that as he came to a halt. "You're bleeming daft, Billy Dixon! That's what you are. If you think I'm going to squat my arse down in blood and splash that blood up to my elbows day after day—you've gone out on the prairie without a hat one too many times, you have!"

"Money's good," Dixon tried again. "More'n enough to keep any dozen of you busy under my gun."

"Just the same, I'll stay here until my plans change, Billy."

"What is it you're planning on doing—if not eating and drinking and sleeping away the summer?" Dixon prodded, both his hands on his hips.

Seamus leaned in, a wide smile cracking his well-seamed, wind-eroded face. "Just what's so bad with a man spending his days doing nothing a'tall?"

Dixon laughed, then asked the group, "Any of you? Want good money? Twenty-five cents a hide. That's top money for skinners. I need you and I need you now."

"I'll go with you," replied one man.

"What's your name, mister?"

"Sewell," he replied. "But I can only go for a few days. Got a partner coming in with a full load of hides, and then we'll be taking off for Dodge City soon's he gets back."

"You'll do. I'll bring you back here in a week or so, if that sets with you," Billy said, turning from the new man. "How 'bout the rest of you?" His eyes scanned the silent crowd.

Rath clucked sadly. "The rest that was here a day ago heard the same news, I s'pose."

"Yeah," agreed Charlie Myers, who was edging up to the

circle. "Every outfit that could hit the prairie has already took off. We won't see nobody back in here till they've got wagons swaybacked under hides. Ain't that right, Rath?"

"By damn—won't it be a pretty sight when them hide wagons start wheeling in here, groaning under all that pretty flesh? We'll punch some life into this settlement real soon, we will!" Rath exclaimed as the rest cheered the arrival of the herds.

Dixon quickly worked out a trade with Charley Rath for some more lead and powder, flour and coffee, along with some tinned vegetables and fruit before he and Ned Sewell climbed aboard the light wagon and turned the team south.

For more than a week Billy worked his three harder than he had worked any of his skinners: rousting them out of their blankets in the predawn darkness so that they could have breakfast eaten and be at the killing ground before the sky had turned gray. And he kept them at it, not bringing the wagons back around for the bloodstained trio until the last vestige of light had drained purple from the evening sky.

Wearily all four men wolfed down their corn dodgers and lean buffalo meat seared over the merry flames where the coffee bubbled and boiled to a heady, fragrant brew, its aroma lifted on the air of each summer evening. Overhead the night sky deepened into coal-black, the color of a well-worn kettle bottom as they smoked their pipes in silence, perhaps wandering a few yards onto the starlit prairie to spray the sage before climbing into their bedrolls without a protest. The next morning always prodded them early, and the day's labor took care of itself. Every man was in the process of making himself a small fortune that hot summer as the days lengthened perceptibly. And no one really thought about Indians, much less worried to keep an eye on the far horizon.

It was man against the buffalo for now. And the hide men were clearly winning.

When the time arrived that Dixon was to take Sewell back to Adobe Walls, Billy drove Frenchy and Armitage out to the killing ground and left them with plenty to do while he turned the wagon due north, striking for the Canadian River. Upon reaching the unpredictable river, both hunter and skinner found its banks frothing and swollen with spring runoff.

"She's damned well got her back up, don't she?" Dixon said as he sat there on that plank of a wagon seat, those reins slung loosely through his fingers and across his palms, as he stared down at the boiling, turbid, muddy water.

"Banging and smashing everything gets in her way, that's for sure," Ned Sewell groaned. "How we get this wagon across that?"

He wagged his head. "We don't. Be suicide to try, I'm afraid. We'll push on over to White Deer Creek and see if that isn't a better place for us to ford."

But the mouth of the White Deer wasn't all that much better, although Dixon knew it offered their best chance in many a mile should they ride in either direction. Billy quickly stripped off his clothing and eased down into the cold, swollen river, moving slowly, leaning against the flow as his feet sought out the footing his mules would need in crossing. Inside of twenty bone-numbing minutes he was back on the south bank, shivering and blue-lipped as he yanked on his boots, explaining to Sewell that they could make it, with a little luck and the cooperation of the mules, Joe and Tobe. They had become seasoned by Dixon across the last three seasons, and should be able to ply those frothy, reddish waters.

"Only fifty . . . maybe sixty yards," Billy regarded. "That's all Tobe and Joe will have to swim. Then they ought to be across the sand and up on some pretty solid footing."

"You fixing to take the wagon over?" Sewell asked, wide-eyed and tight-mouthed.

"Naw. We'll leave it here. I can get you back to the Walls on the mules, then bring 'em back to fetch up the wagon when the river's run itself down a might."

They both turned at the sudden sound of hooves, grabbing up their rifles as a pair of white men appeared out of the cottonwood and willow from downstream.

"Ho, Dixon!" one of the riders shouted in his unmistakable booming voice.

"That you, Donegan?"

Billy Tyler and Seamus Donegan reined up.

"You going in to the Walls, ain't you, Dixon?" Tyler asked.

He nodded. "Got to get Sewell back for his—"

"You still got men back in your camp, Billy?" Donegan asked in a gush.

Dixon nodded again, something gnawing at his belly with that pinched look on the Irishman's face. "What you got to dust off, Seamus?"

"Riders just come in from Chicken Creek. They found two hunters butchered there. Been a couple days back, likely."

Dixon squinted to the east. "That's twenty, twenty-five miles off."

"We're riding out to tell the other camps," Tyler announced.

"You figure to get everyone in?" Sewell asked, slow to tear his eyes off the gray-eyed Irishman.

"We just figure to let everyone know that Injins're riding this country," Donegan answered, his own eyes seeming to study Sewell's hard smile.

"We're obliged, Seamus," Billy said finally, not liking the way Sewell raked his gaze over the Irishman. Long enough he had been around his share of men on this frontier to catch a whiff of trouble brewing between a pair of them. And this smelled. But, he figured, he'd be shet of the hired man, and Ned Sewell would soon be on his way back to Dodge City—where there wouldn't be a threat of something starting between Donegan and Sewell. Something bloody.

"See you back at Adobe Walls, Billy," Donegan said, finally bringing his eyes from Sewell's challenging sneer.

Dixon watched after the pair of riders for only a moment before he turned to his hired man. "I don't figure to leave this wagon here now—not with Injuns in the country. We'll float it across with us. Help me get the mules hitched."

When he had pulled the first animal around in a tight circle, Dixon inquired, "Just what you got against Donegan?"

Sewell seemed to jerk in surprise, then shrugged. "Him? Nothing, goddammit. Don't even know the man. Never talked to him."

As Billy backed the first mule into harness at the single-tree, he said, "You two was both at the Walls long enough to know one the other."

"I just figured I'd stay out of his way," Sewell said, backing the second mule into harness. "Heard he was bad medicine down the pike."

Dixon had to laugh as he patted Tobe's neck. "Donegan? He's as good a heart as they come."

"He don't like me," Sewell huffed.

"He got any reason not to like you?" Billy asked, his eyes climbing over Joe's back. The sudden fire in the other man's eyes gave him some caution.

Sewell finally looked down and put his hands at work on the traces. "Never did I give one single man a reason not to like me. No man I ever worked for."

"You two don't seem to hit it off—"

"Why the hell don't we talk about something else?" Sewell snapped, more than a hint of iron in his tone.

That drew Dixon up so abruptly it was like Sewell had just yanked on his short hairs. "Yeah—let's see about getting these mules swimming this wagon."

Billy had enough to think about for the moment. A man of the plains knew the odds were against him bucking a wagon across a swollen river like the Canadian, but with a little savvy and a lot of luck, they could make it. And for the moment, he wished he had someone working with him he trusted. Sewell was no longer a man Billy trusted.

Dixon squinted across the rippled, sun-glimmering water, choosing a point on the far bank where he wanted to bring the mules and wagon out. The odds were against them: a mule had smaller hooves than a horse, so it wouldn't work to ply their way across the bottom of a river ford the way a horse would; and once a mule got its ears filled with water, he quickly became frightened and worse than useless.

But this was far from the first time Billy Dixon had played himself against house odds.

"Hang on, Sewell. Here we go. Hep, hep! Hee-yawww!"

Slapping leather down on mule hide, Billy drove Joe and Tobe down into the muddy water, which instantly nudged and shoved against the high sidewalls with a groaning might that surprised him. The mules were in the current sooner than he had expected. Their eyes wide and nostrils flaring, Joe and Tobe were swimming already, yanking the wagon along in spurts as they caught a hoof here and there on the shifting bottom, struggling against the current.

With a frightened snort, old Joe, the upstream animal, fought the first big wave as it swamped both mules.

"We're going over!" Sewell shrieked. He stood and lunged for the muddy river.

Dixon was standing at the same instant, sensing the footwell shuddering beneath his boots. With a prolonged creak, the wagon started to ease over, then as he cleared the seat, the wagon tumbled in a full, free circle and tumbled again. Billy was swimming on the upstream side to stay clear of the huge, iron-rimmed wheels, clawing at the red, boiling water in an effort to reach the hee-hawing mules as they bobbed up and down in the White Deer Crossing.

Pulling himself inch by inch along the traces, he got on the upstream side of that gee-ward mule, snagging a death grip on Joe's bridle to yank his head out of the water with all the strength the hunter could muster. Behind the mules the wagon pulled and spun on the end of the singletree like a child's string toy. Except this bobbing, groaning toy repeatedly yanked two mules and a man beneath the muddy surface of the Canadian each time it spun against the surging current.

"Sewell!" he shouted at the skinner's head bobbing just ahead of the wagon atop the surface. "Help me cut 'em loose!"

"Let 'em go!" he yelled as he swam away with the current.

"Damn you!" he roared against the braying of the mules and the roaring river. "I'll kill you myself if the Canadian doesn't!"

Evidently the look on Dixon's face was enough. In but a

moment the skinner was wildly flailing away with his arms, struggling back through the few yards of murky, angry water to reach the haw-side mule.

"Cut him loose, dammit!" Dixon said, his own knife sawing at Joe's thick leather harness.

More than halfway across, the animals were freed and finally came up snorting. The wagon itself went tumbling on downriver, lost in the sunlight around a bend sheltered with willow and overhung with the rattling green leaves of cottonwood.

Billy hung on, murmuring to Joe, clinging to a bit of its severed harness, urging it through the terror of that river. Then he felt the first hoof scrape bottom. Joe got a hold, then lost it against the powerful current. He fought with his arms, pulling as hard as he had ever swam, sputtering water, choking on it, his eyes burning with sandy grit as he struggled to keep them open. Then the mule got a second hold with a hoof. And held on this time. With everything Joe had left in him, the animal pulled against the current with those small hooves until it had all four down on something more or less solid.

Hanging to those severed traces for his life, Dixon was dragged from the Canadian River, his boots and clothing filled with water and sand. He dropped to the muddy bank, gasping as the mule eased down on its front haunches, eyes rolling back and wheezing. Joe suddenly collapsed onto its rear haunches and sputtered as he eased onto his suddenly motionless ribs.

Billy watched the animal die without a struggle, its lungs already filled with sand and river water. Crawling across the muddy bank, Dixon dragged his old friend's head against his leg and stroked the wet jaw, the sopping forelock, wishing he weren't crying but knowing that with his own dripping hair, Sewell wouldn't notice anyway. Besides, the skinner lay on his back, gasping for air beneath the other mule's belly. Tobe. The younger mule had made it alive and stood shuddering from exertion and fright. But, Tobe had made it.

Reluctantly, Billy looked back at Old Joe. It was hard keeping it down, this hollow feeling inside him at this moment. The soles of his boots lapped by the river that had taken the wagon, his rifle and everything in it. And it had just claimed one of his two mules, the two friends that had seen Dixon through so many seasons beneath so many skies.

But now Old Joe was gone.

And just when things had seemed they were going to work out for this summer's hunt, the Indians had started raiding again.

And now, Old Joe was gone.

I I

Late June 1874

June was growing old, and he with it, Seamus cursed sourly.

No fool like an old fool.

And he had been as big a fool as any man, chasing after the merest wisps of dreams harkening from untold wealth. Just like any other addle-brained Irishman who believed in rainbows and leprechauns and pots of gold just waiting to be discovered.

Myths, legends . . . nothing more than a dream dispelled come the morning's light.

Damned foolishness is what it had been for him to stake so much on finding a treasure near the old ruins of the adobe walls. Yet something at the pit of him kept nagging Donegan nonetheless, ready to convince him again and again that if there were no substance to the rumors and legend about the place, if there were nothing tangible come of that old map and the hefty chunk of gold bullion two crazed civilians had died for—then why had a man like Louis Abragon wanted him killed in Dodge City?

And if unable to kill Donegan there, then why had Abragon for certain assigned someone to follow the Irishman all the way south to Adobe Walls?

Work. It had always been one form of work or another for him. And that was the wellspring of all his dreams of treasure and fortune and the soft life. For certain Seamus damn well knew what it was like, knowing nothing but work and want. Work and want.

Then with Donegan's growing doubts concerning his own venture came the troubling belief among the others that their combined fortunes at Adobe Walls were about to go belly up. Back there on the first of May, after the buildings were completed and both trading posts opened for business, along with O'Keefe's blacksmith shop and Hanrahan's shady saloon, things couldn't have looked brighter. But with the passing of each new day gone without sighting many buffalo, much less the great herds they had ventured south to hunt—the mood over the meadow grew increasingly somber.

But of a sudden, just as if Lady Fortune was playing them all like the fickle bitch she so often proved herself to be, they awoke one morning to the distant, but distinct, lowing of the bulls, presaging the return of the great southern herds. That very day, Seamus had watched every outfit pack and leave as if the life itself of the settlement were being sucked out of Adobe Walls. Any and all men there who called themselves hunters or skinners mounted up and were gone before the sun set on that meadow ringed by buzzard-bone ridges and leafy cottonwood where the deerflies buzzed and the air grew suffocatingly hot late each afternoon.

Dame Fortune had once again smiled on those ragtag bands of free-roamers who made their living on the comings and goings of the buffalo. Them, and smiled too on the traders who catered to their every need, except one. Charlie Myers had made it clear as crystal when he organized this entire endeavor back at Dodge City that there would be no women come to buffalo country. Fine it was that the only woman had been brought here by Charley Rath, along with her husband, and both of them clearly getting on some in years. But Myers had little time for any man who wanted to argue about his decision not to bring whores to buffalo country.

"You wanna get some honey on your stinger, boys," Myers told them, "saddle up and make that long ride back to

Dodge. Plenty of whores up there. But down here—we come to work."

Damn that trader's hide anyway, Seamus had thought more than a half-dozen times in the last week alone. He was needing to get himself a woman, be her copper-skinned, coffee-skinned or Irish pink. As long as she knew what it took to please a man and just didn't want to lay there beneath him. So much better when she joined in the celebration of all that bare flesh and moist, sweaty exertion.

The very thought of it made his mouth go dry. Yet those thoughts on other women failed to long pull his thoughts from her.

From Samantha Pike and how she had wrestled with him, scratched him, bit him and held him locked inside her arms and legs until he was for certain they were one heaving animal that first night in Sharp Grover's barn. Indeed, she had been like an animal unleashed, and her pot like the warm, sweet honey he had long craved, were he to admit it now to himself. Seamus the bee, and Samantha Pike the hive that beckoned to him beyond the miles.

"Sweet Mother of God!" he exclaimed, physically trying to shake off the thought of her, those large breasts exposed with her blouse and bodice opened, that pair of sweet, ripe melons heaving with every rapid breath she took, shuddering as he kissed and licked and kneaded their juicy firmness.

Hard, so hard it was, not to remember how he had struggled so with the many buttons on her skirt until she had laughed at him in that way of hers, eyes like fire, and ripped both skirt and the many petticoats off herself, like a madwoman tearing the bloomers down to her ankles and kicking them over her boots—the only thing she kept on, the only thing from her feet all the way up to that welcoming moistness that beckoned his rigid flesh.

"But she wants a husband out of you, Seamus," he scolded himself. That's why Sharp himself wrote you that goddamned letter you got last summer.

And if that husband-molding wasn't a cold jolt of January ice water down Donegan's spine, nothing else ever could be. Just the merest mention of marrying and settling down and having to contend with but one woman for the rest of his days—why, the thought of it . . .

That wasn't true either—is it? He had dreamed of many tomorrows with that dark-haired colleen in Boston Towne who had ushered a big, overgrown youth into the wonders of women and ecstasy. And thought of the very same thing again with sweet, auburn-haired Jennifer Wheatley, she of the beautiful freckled shoulders and breasts that he had gazed upon but had yet to touch. But Samantha Pike—hers was the sort of body that begged him to touch and fondle it, taking as much pleasure as Seamus in his growing madness, in the boiling froth it brought to his passion as Donegan had ripped such wild, fragrant pleasure from her soft, rounded body.

"Perhaps she'll just come to understand I'm not the marrying kind," he told himself as he stood from his fire and tossed the dregs of his coffee into the nearby grass.

Coals dying in his fire pit, lamps blinking on in the trading houses and Hanrahan's saloon, Seamus decided he'd go over there and see if anyone new had shown up today. More hunters coming and going each day now, here to trade or get the latest bits and fragments of news—what with the recent Indian scares. The hide men came and went, sharing what they knew, asking questions about what they didn't know and feared most. And making plans to gather here should there be a general outbreak.

They reminded Seamus of lone bulls by instinct gathering in a crude circle, rump to rump, horns out and to the ready when confronted with the packs of quick, lithe prairie wolves. Men who preferred being alone or in small groups, come together here in a time of danger to ensure the safety of all.

Felt to be summer was aging fast. While all of spring had been unseasonably wet, June had turned dry as baked rawhide. The grass gone brittle. Prairie flowers drooped and withered. The ground underfoot went dusty as fine talcum powder, then shriveled up and cracked like a brittle puffball shell.

"And if she truly understands, then perhaps she'll be

willing to live with a man like Seamus Donegan: poetry in me soul and fire in me heart," he whispered as he strode across the meadow, rounded the corner of the Myers & Leonard stockade and walked on to the saloon where the noisy voices were rising against a background of squeaky fiddle and plaintive mouth harp, a French harp twanging rhythm as someone else pounded on a table.

You could do worse, Seamus. Hell, you've done a lot worse, he told himself as he strode through the semicircle of greasy yellow light thrown out from that door at Hanrahan's. Samantha's a real looker, city, settlement or prairie. And for certain she knows how to make a man feel good climbing atop her. Damn, if she didn't push him down not long after they had finished that first time, her gentle hands kneading his limp flesh into readiness then climbed atop him. He remembered that with a genuine smile as he stepped through the open doorway—how that half-dressed Samantha Pike had climbed into the saddle there atop him and took that long, furious ride until they both collapsed, exhausted.

And slept until the next time she awoke him with her insistent fingers. Suddenly acquainted with the joy that could be experienced between man and woman, Miss Pike was not to be denied her pleasure.

"What the devil you smiling so about?" Billy Dixon asked, waving the Irishman over to his table.

Young Bat Masterson, Jim Hanrahan, Billy Ogg and Billy Tyler, along with Dixon's skinners, Frenchy and Charley Armitage, all sat on crude benches pulled around the table. Other hunters and skinners called out their halloos to the newcomer then went back to their tin and china cups.

"Bet he's been thinking of women—like we been thinking of women," said the handsome Masterson, slapping Donegan on the shoulder as the Irishman plopped down beside the young hunter. "Have yourself a drink and let's all be miserable together."

"Miserable, is it?" Seamus asked.

"Aye," said Billy Ogg. "Injuns riding over the countryside, scalping, driving stakes through the bodies of our friends—"

"And us down here with no women to poke!" shouted Billy Tyler.

That brought a round of cheering coupled with many a growl of disappointment from the other tables.

"Just drink up, boys!" Hanrahan called out to the room. "Drown your sorrows, I say!"

"And make Jimmy Hanrahan the richest man in buffalo country doing it!" Masterson replied, leading the rest in loud laughter.

"Don't know if you really look any better than you did a few days back, Billy," Seamus said to Dixon, who sat across the table. "You were the sight that day you and Sewell dragged in, like something I'd find at the bottom of a buffalo wallow."

"Poor Old Joe," Dixon said, eyes dropping to stare into his china cup filled with red whiskey.

"That mule of your'n is as much a casualty of the Injuns as was Dudley and Wallace," replied Charlie Myers as he strode into the saloon.

The two men had been working as skinners for Joe Plummer when they were attacked on Chicken Creek while Plummer was away at Adobe Walls for supplies. Finding the butchered bodies upon returning to his camp, Plummer had galloped back to the settlement to spread the alarm. When Dixon had straggled in later that day after crossing the swollen Canadian River, there was but one thought on his mind—to get back to his own outfit. With only a mule, no horse or rifle, he was in sad shape for Indian country.

Nonetheless, Charley Rath did have a round-barreled .44-caliber Sharps, and Billy Dixon had quickly snatched it up on his good credit. And that very evening while the young hunter was putting together a new outfit, another hide man name Anderson Moore arrived on a lathered horse announcing that two men had been killed in his camp over on the Salt Fork of the Red River.

"Cheyenne Jack?" Rath had asked of Moore. "The Englishman was working skinner for you?"

Moore nodded.

"And Blue Billy?" asked Dixon himself. "He was that German fella, weren't he?"

"Didn't speak but a handful of words of English," Seamus commented, remembering the young man who had so enjoyed the singing and dancing, recalling how caught up the German could get in the entertainment that he sang along at the top of his lungs, mimicking the sounds while not understanding the words, as he clapped and plopped 'round and 'round in those oversized dry-split broughams of his.

But for many the playing had grown old during the past few days of waiting out the Indian scare. Some horse racing. A lot of cards and drinking. But very little of the shooting at a mark that had kept them occupied so often before. If there were to be a general outbreak of the warrior bands, then a man need save all his powder and lead for that serious business.

It was during the past few days that some of the hunters had captured a wild mustang colt that had become separated from its mare and been lost among the settlement's stock. They proudly presented the colt to Hannah Olds, the one woman at Adobe Walls, the one person around whom every man became suddenly well-mannered and respectful and downright docile.

Like men would around someone who reminded them of home and a mother . . .

As much as he wanted to smile at that thought, the vision of two more dead men—their bodies in all likelihood mutilated, as he himself had seen the mutilation of Dudley and Wallace in Plummer's camp—came crowding in on Donegan. From far up on the Bozeman Road to the high rolling plains of that Kansas Territory, Seamus had seen his share of Indian butchery. But, never before had he witnessed mutilation such as what beheld his eyes at Joe Plummer's hunting camp on the Staked Plain: the skulls of both Dudley and Wallace had been cracked open, brains removed, and the seeping cavity filled with prairie grass; eye sockets gouged out and filled with sprigs of sage; tongues skewered with sharp sticks; huge stakes driven through the skinners' groins, pinning the bodies to the ground.

"Might'n been the same bunch tried to jump us," Hanrahan said.

The rest nodded in solemn remembrance of that bloody day when warriors attacked Hanrahan's own wagon outfit returning from Dodge 150 miles away with a load of whiskey, warriors who succeeded only in running off their horses. They were fortunate that the warriors did not press their advantage, lucky too that Charlie Myers showed up the next day to share his mules with the muleless Hanrahan. Had the horsemen known that the entire shipment was barrel upon barrel of crazy water . . .

"Much as you fellas think so, I still can't figure that what few scalps these damned savages been lifting and a little hell they been raising works out to be an Injun war," Billy Dixon said.

"Dixon's right," Masterson agreed. "A few scalps ain't a war. Any of us can hunt north and west of here and not see a feather, by damn. But if you stick your nose south and east of the Canadian, you're liable to get your nose chopped off. That's Injun ground, for certain."

"That's why you're all sitting here, isn't it?" Donegan asked, swiping whiskey from his mustache. "Because you don't want your scalps hanging from some warrior's belt?"

Hanrahan nodded, chuckling. He had the saloonman's insight and knowledge of all the sins of men tucked into every one of the knowing wrinkles and crevices of his face. "We're all here because we know the red bastards won't be crazy enough to try this place on for size—right, fellas?"

"Damn right!" Charlie Myers cheered. "There's safety in numbers, by God."

"And look around at these walls," James Langton said. "No Injun would dare try to attack us when we can hunker down behind these walls."

"Here's to being safe as you would be in your mama's arms here at Adobe Walls, boys!" Hanrahan cheered, lifting his cup. "No place safer unless you're rocking in your own mama's lap."

* * *

Isatai was finally satisfied.

They had been on the move for three suns now, using every bit of daylight to march northwest from the Elk Creek encampment. The Comanche scouts had led the entire war party up the North Fork of the Red River until they reached the Staked Plain. Once there, the great procession of more than seven hundred warriors struck almost due north for the Canadian River and the white man's settlement of earth lodges.

A few bands of young Comanche warriors, a band of Kiowa too, had grown eager and hurried ahead of the rest. One war party returned with two scalps. Later that day a second group rode in to celebrate the taking of two more white scalps. Sign everywhere showed there were many more buffalo hunters in the country. It would be a glorious victory, Isatai told them, so enjoying the answering fury of their war cries.

Now they were drawing close to the white man's earth-lodge settlement. Very, very close.

He could almost smell the stink of those hide men. They smelled of death, smelled of this killing of the buffalo. Soon these tai-bos would reek of their own death.

This very morning as the sun had risen, Quanah had ordered all warriors to stay with the main party before selecting seven scouts to find the exact location of the earth-lodge settlement and count the white men who would defend it.

There were a few Kiowas along, those riding under Lone Wolf and Swan, Big Bow and Howling Wolf. And some Cheyenne under Stone Calf and Crazy Mule, Medicine Water, White Shield and Whirlwind. Even the handful of the old Cheyenne chiefs who had openly refused to go on the raid had been held in that great sun-dance encampment by the Bow String soldiers, some of the Cheyenne tribal police, for fear they would alert the agent or soldiers of Isatai's great war.

As the week of celebration continued at the mouth of Elk Creek, a few Comanchero traders had even wheeled their carts in, selling whiskey to a thirsty clientele. Adding to the festive atmosphere, a few Arapahos under renegade

Yellow Horse had slipped off the reservation to join the sun dance and the coming fight too, although most of the Arapaho bands resolutely stayed to the white man's road.

He had to laugh at that, Isatai did. The white man's road led only to self-destruction. It was just as he harangued the warriors at the fires every evening they stopped to rest the ponies.

"Look at the Caddos!" he would shout at the gathering come to hear the great shaman speak. "Have you not seen the Wichitas? Both once great peoples. And look at them now that they have taken the white man's road, scratching in the earth like the white man. Wearing the white man's clothes. Reading from the white man's holy book. Would any man of you claim the Tonkawas are holy people? The white man and his ways are evil! He wants only to destroy us—if not with war, then the white man will destroy us with his religion . . . pulling us away from the Spirit Above!"

Some unquenchable flame within Isatai had compelled him to call the hundreds together each night at the cooking fires. To keep the young men whipped to a fury. To assure them of their forthcoming victory over the hide men asleep at the earth lodges.

"You will fight with us?" asked Wild Horse, a noted Comanche war chief. "With your own hand you will club the white hunters as they sleep?"

Isatai knew a veiled challenge when it was thrown at him. But he refused to rise to the bait the way the catfish hungered for what was on the end of his string. This was his fight, and his war—make no mistake about it. Isatai believed he would right the terrible wrong done when the soldiers killed his uncle in last winter's first moon. He had been given powers of magic and sleight of hand by the Spirit Above, had he not? Then surely the Spirit Above would expect him to use all his powers of magic and persuasion and threat and presence to gather behind him a great fighting force to wipe the land clean of the white man's stain.

"No, I do not fight. I am not a warrior. The Spirit Above has called me to walk a different path," he declared to the hushed assembly, surprised at his calm. "I alone walk this road of the spirit. You cannot walk this road. I alone make it possible for your great victory. I alone will turn the bullets into puffs of air and make the white man's rifles useless, Wild Horse. My prayers will drape each warrior with power, just as I will mantle myself with a sacred yellow paint."

"Surely you will want to see for yourself how brave Kwahadi warriors kill the white buffalo hunters," challenged Wild Horse.

"Soon enough, we will all see how you kill the tai-bos . . . but only if you believe in the word of the Spirit Above —told you from my lips. Why do you doubt me?" he asked them strongly, his voice raised so that every one of them was stunned speechless. "Ask those who have seen my powers—they will tell you I can make bullets come from my belly. Ask, and they will tell you I can raise the dead with the power of my breath blown into their mouths."

Isatai stepped before the Comanche war chief, looking up at Wild Horse's face. "Did I not predict a great dry time for this summer?"

"Yes."

"Is that dry time upon us, Wild Horse?"

Again, "Yes, it is."

Isatai enjoyed this, watching the war chief squirm like a crawls-on-his-belly. "Our war camps swelled with the recent converts as the air grew hot and the grass drooped for want of rain. Don't any of you dare to question me, for my powers are the powers of the Spirit Above! And all those who stay on the reservation will mourn with empty bellies and sad hearts that they too did not join me in wiping out the tai-bos!"

When this killing of the hide men was done, Isatai told them, he would lead them on to the first of the soldier forts in the land to the south. There they would attack the white and buffalo soldiers while they slept, clubbing them as they would do with the buffalo hunters. He had been assured by the Spirit Above in the most recent visit Isatai had made to the land of the clouds that the soldiers' guns would be rendered useless, as would the long-shooting buffalo rifles of the hide men. This settlement of earth lodges on the Canadian was but the beginning.

Killing the white men who reeked of blood and death would merely be the opening chapter to a long and glorious war to drive the white man from Indian country. And those tai-bos who would not flee the buffalo ground?

They would die where the Comanche found them.

1 2

June 25–26, 1874

"Just who the hell is this Amos Chapman anyway?" Donegan asked.

Billy Dixon motioned for the Irishman to walk with him. If he was going to talk about Chapman, it had best be done in private, away from the saloon, the buildings and the rest of the hide men.

"You remember—you met him up at Dodge the morning we was pulling south. He's a half-breed," Dixon explained in a low voice as they walked toward the setting sun. "Army scout and interpreter. Works out of Camp Supply mostly."

"I remember him all right," Donegan replied. "Recognized him a week ago when he come in with that army escort, them five soldiers. What I want to know is what he's told you and why's it so damned important."

Dixon sighed, looking over his shoulder and coming to a halt to face the Irishman. "Two fellas named Lee and Reynolds—they're contract traders at Camp Supply—they had a Kiowa from Kicking Bird's band come in to tell them the warriors was up to no good."

"We damn well know that, Billy. It's summer and that means it's time for raiding. And they've raised four scalps . . . four is all we know of."

Dixon shook his head. "This is something bigger, Seamus. The warrior said the Kiowa was joining the Cheyenne and Comanche to make war."

"They're riding north into Kansas again—like they did back to 'sixty-eight?"

"No. This time word has it the war party is heading this way. Lee and Reynolds paid Chapman their own money to come tell us. They both know Robert Wright, Charley Rath's partner—so they convinced the commanding officer at Camp Supply to give Chapman an army escort for the trip."

"Whoa," Donegan said. "Wait a minute. You said that war party is coming our way?"

"No telling how big this will be." Dixon watched worry etch the Irishman's face.

"You don't know how many . . . so, do you know when?"

"Chapman brought word that them traders think it might come in the next couple days."

"Tomorrow?"

"Day after—twenty-seventh."

"Why's this such a damned secret anyway, Billy?"

"The traders don't want word getting spread around and it running the hunters off—bad for business. Besides, it'd leave 'em with no way to defend their investments."

Donegan snorted. "Ain't that just like 'em? Not sharing news of a coming fight to save their bleeming business!"

"You gotta keep it quiet—I'm trusting you."

"I ain't so sure that attack will ever come, Billy."

"Rath and Myers and Hanrahan all think we'll be attacked."

Donegan wagged his head. "It don't make sense. I asked one of them soldiers with Chapman what they was doing down here. He said they were on the trail of horse thieves. Now, who's lying?"

Dixon shrugged. "All I know is Chapman said the soldiers was told by their commander to lie if they were asked anything about what they was doing out here—so I figure they made up that story about tracking horse thieves."

Gazing for a long moment at the distant saloon, stars making a cloudy glitter overhead, Donegan finally said, "I don't know. I figure the rest of them fellas what know this Chapman just might have that half-breed man pegged. Like them—I figure he's the liar. He's got him a Cheyenne wife, so like Billy Ogg says: Chapman's here spying on us for them Injins. If there's any war party coming our way, likely Chapman's already gone and give 'em news of what's here for the taking."

"Damn you, Irishman, if you'd just listen to me—"

"That half-breed is a spy for the Cheyenne, Billy . . . or Chapman damn well did bring those soldiers here looking for horse thieves. I figure there's some in this jailhouse bunch what wouldn't be above pinching a horse here or there."

Dixon had to agree with that. "It's for certain some of these boys have stolen a horse a time or two, but of all the things Chapman might be—he ain't a spy for the Cheyennes and he ain't the sort to lead them soldiers down here to arrest anyone. That'd be a sure death sentence for him when word got out."

With a sigh, Donegan conceded, "I suppose you're right. Still, some of this bunch was ready to string Chapman up that very night, wasn't they?"

"Hanrahan himself covered for Chapman and got the half-breed out of the saloon before those drunk hunters tied Amos to Hanrahan's ridgepole. Chapman hid out with the Mooar outfit and that next morning told Hanrahan that he gave John Mooar word about the war party headed this way."

"So that's why Mooar hurried out of here."

"To fetch his brother, Wright, and the rest of their outfits —before the Injuns ran across 'em. John Mooar figured he had less'n a week to do it and get high-behind back north to Dodge with all their hides. The Mooar brothers still run the biggest outfit in the country, Seamus."

Donegan nodded like it was beginning to come together in his whiskey-soaked mind. "That Mooar bunch pulled back through here a day later telling us those stories of getting sct on by warriors three times between their camp and the Canadian." He scratched at his chin whiskers. "Now it makes sense why John Mooar suggested Hannah Olds go back to Dodge with 'em—saying it would be for her own good."

"I heard Mooar asking Mrs. Olds to come with 'em—get

her sore tooth pulled. But she said if it got bad enough, she'd let one of us pull it with some pliers. Better than that whiskey-soaked dentist they got up at Dodge, she told him."

The Irishman snapped his fingers. "Why, those bloody cowards!" he rasped. "Rath and Myers running out on their clerks and the rest! Both of 'em left here about the same time as the Mooar bunch, didn't they?"

"Only man left what knows of the attack coming is Jimmy Hanrahan."

"And you, Billy."

"That's only because Jimmy confided in me—we're partners now, and he figured I ought to know."

"If he knows what's coming—why's Hanrahan staying?"

"Simple: he's got everything he owns in his saloon business. Got nothing else now that he threw in with Rath. Jimmy figures he best stay and fight for the whole pot."

"Damn good man, I'd say," Donegan replied. "Still, it's hard to figure, though. After the Mooars' outfit had their scrape a few days back, we ain't seen a feather or a bit of paint one."

Dixon chuckled. "What was it you say Jim Bridger once told you, Seamus—up on the Bozeman Road?"*

His teeth gleaming in summer's early twilight as lantern light from the nearby windows and doorways scoured yellow channels of brightness through the coming darkness, Donegan answered, "It's when you don't see Injins that you best be worrying."

"And you believed that old trapper, didn't you?"

"Damn if I still don't, I suppose." Seamus looked toward the bluffs to the west that rose hard against the fading light. "The twenty-seventh, you say?"

"That's when word from Camp Supply has it. It makes sense, don't it? Come the full of the moon, Seamus."

Donegan squinted, seeming to Dixon to look somewhere off into the distance. "That's right. And the full of the moon is good time for war parties to ride: moonlight at night, enough light before dawn for them to get into posi-

* The Plainsmen Series, vol. 1, *Sioux Dawn*

tion for an attack. Yeah, Billy—the full of the moon is coming on the twenty-seventh, ain't it?"

"And when it comes, I sure as hell don't count on being here—Billy Dixon's scalp hanging from no Comanche's smelly breechclout string!"

"I doubt Horace Jones is a man any of us can really trust," declared Louis H. Carpenter, captain of H Company, Tenth U.S. Negro Cavalry.

Reuben Waller wagged his head in frustration. He wanted Carpenter to believe him, if not believe in Jones, Fort Sill's post interpreter. "He ain't been drinking this time, Cap'n."

"Too many times Colonel Davidson has known Mr. Jones to blow things all out of proportion, Sergeant."

Waller pursed his lips, looking at the handful of his soldiers from H Company who had accompanied him to Carpenter's quarters, requesting an audience with their company commander. "It ain't just what Jones says about the Kiowa being split in half here, Cap'n."

"We've known the Kiowa have divided loyalties for some time. Kicking Bird and his bunch are trying their best to stay peaceful—if the horse thieves and whiskey peddlers would just give them a chance." Carpenter sighed, breathing deep of the warm summer air of this evening. "And on the other side of the equation stands Lone Wolf and Swan and all the rest who scamper off the reservation whenever it damn well suits them."

"They've gone and run off now, Cap'n," Waller told him. "And this time they've joined up with that Comanche medicine man who's been beating the drum for to start a war."

"A small, fanatical bunch, I assure you, Sergeant. Colonel Davidson is well aware that some of the Kiowa were down at the Comanche sun dance last month. Why, Kicking Bird admits to being down there himself with his people."

"But Kicking Bird scooted right on back here as soon as the war chiefs started talking about killing soldiers and buffalo hunters. The Penateka Comanche came running back here too."

Carpenter smiled. "Kicking Bird and the rest do know which side their bread is buttered on, don't they?" He placed a hand on Waller's shoulder. "You're a good soldier, and you've made a fine officer, Reuben. But, why don't you let Colonel Davidson worry about things. If there were something for us to really be nervous about, don't you expect the colonel would have patrols out or have the post on alert?"

"Cap'n, it ain't just this post."

"What do you mean?"

Waller licked his lips in the deepening twilight. "I hear tell that up at Supply there's a buzz of it too."

"What sort of buzz, Sergeant?"

"The Cheyenne have took off to join up with the Comanche and Kiowa."

Carpenter narrowed his eyes, face gone grave as a cemetery stone. "Where did you learn this, Reuben?"

"M Company, Cap'n. They rode in for rotation a week or so back."

"I know." Carpenter considered, staring at the ground beneath him. "What's the mood up at Supply?"

"From the sounds of it, not much better'n here."

"Ugly, is it?"

"This could be something big, Cap'n."

Carpenter straightened and took a deep breath. "Yes. It could, Sergeant. I'll pass your concerns on to the colonel. Thank you for coming to see me this evening. Good night."

Reuben returned Carpenter's salute and watched the captain stride back to his quarters, wondering if Carpenter's talk with Davidson would do any good. Time and again Reuben had followed the chain of command, like other good soldiers always did. And somewhere along that chain things always seemed to grind to a halt. Nothing was ever done with those scraps of news the soldiers passed among themselves.

He was beginning to believe it was Davidson's self-appointed job to do nothing about the growing war scare. The colonel would just as soon wait to dispatch some troops to put out a fire—rather than stopping the fire before it began. That was the army way. And so that made it his job to wait and do nothing until they got orders from farther up the chain.

Again it became the job of soldiers like Sergeant Reuben Waller to sit and wait. Wait until they would be asked to mount up and ride out. Marching somewhere in that great wilderness to the west, where they would be ordered to fight and die.

It was Friday night, June twenty-sixth.

Another hot, sultry night on the southern plains. Buffalo country.

Why, the meadow itself was so dry, the Irishman figured a man could raise enough powdery dust to choke Billy Dixon's dog Fannie just by spitting on the ground.

The full moon had come up hours ago and had now ridden just past mid-sky. Seamus Donegan stood staring at it for a moment as he relieved himself outside Hanrahan's saloon, hearing the moisture splatter on the bone-dry crust of this drought-ravaged land. Time to find Dixon's wagons, and Billy himself. Time to find his bedroll and sleep off all the whiskey he poured down his gullet.

The company had been good and the music worth a listen. Along with it were a few stories told among new friends and old. Some dancing to that scratchy fiddle and wheezing squeeze box. All of it well greased with Hanrahan's whiskey; "sweeter'n honey and stronger'n iron," that's what Jim Hanrahan claimed.

"Ah, the pure. My beloved cottheen," Seamus often purred over the red whiskey served at the saloon. "Nothing finer is there in this whole world for sinking your sorrows in . . . or for raising your joys!"

"Sing for us, Seamus!" Hanrahan had hollered above the clamor.

"Yes, sing, Irishman!" others had called out.

Even though he could not carry a tune in a perfectly sound bucket, for some reason they enjoyed the life he put in every song he bellowed out for them—be they sad and tragic tales, or be they full of joy and zest and a love of life. Like the popular "Hangman":

Hangman, hangman, hold your rope,
Hold your rope a little while.
Thought I saw my father a'coming,
From many, many a mile.

Father, father, have you gold,
Have you gold to set me free?
Or have you come to see me
Hung upon the gallows tree?

Oh, son, oh, son, I have no gold,
Have no gold to set you free.
I have come for to see you
Hung upon this gallows tree.

Or the lover's lament in "Molly Van":

Come all you young men who handle a gun,
Beware of your shooting just after set sun.
Jimmy Randall went hunting it was all in the dark,
He shot his sweetheart and he missed not his mark.

Stooped under a beech tree a show to shun,
With her apron pinned around her he shot her for
a swan.
Young Jimmy went home with his gun in his hand,
Saying, "Father, dear Father, I've killed Molly
Van!"

Then just before the Irishman had risen to go, leaving
the hardy handful who would likely drink till first light,
Seamus sang the very old "I'll Hang My Harp on a Willow
Tree."

I'll hang my harp on a willow tree
And off to the wars again;
My peaceful home hath no charm for me
The battlefield no pain.

One gold tress of love's hair I'll twine
In my helmet an able plume,
And then on the field of Palestine
I'll seek an early doom.

And if by the Saracens' hand I fall
'midst the noble and the brave;
A tear from my lady love is all
I ask for a warrior's grave.

Seamus weaved a bit now, the clean, pristine air helping to clear his head of the remnants from that smoky saloon resplendent with the stench of buffalo men. He ground to a halt, trying to make out the dark lumps on the ground beneath the moonlight. Then he tried focusing on the four wagons set against the starlit sky, their loads covered by canvas, their long tongues disappearing in the tall grass surrounding O'Keefe's blacksmith shop.

By God, if it didn't appear Dixon was ready to pull out. He snorted quietly.

"That you, Donegan?"

"Billy?"

"It's me," Dixon replied from the ground. "Your bedroll's over here. Climb in."

"You're going in the morning, are you now?"

"Hanrahan needed a hunter he could count on—so we're partners. I'll get fifty percent of everything because he knows I can keep his skinners busy. Our wagons're loaded and ready for hitching at sunrise."

Donegan plopped noisily onto his bedroll. "Why don't Hanrahan go himself?"

"Too much to worry about here."

Seamus snorted. "Oh, yeah—the Injins you was telling me about yesterday. Aren't you feared they'll raise your hair?"

"No. I'm taking the outfit north toward no-man's land."

"That ground between here and the Arkansas, is it?"

"Yes—there's been no trouble up there."

"And damned little buffalo," Seamus growled as he sank back on a pillow he made of his new blanket mackinaw bought from trader Rath the day before the caravan left Dodge City last spring.

"The Schiedler brothers just come down from Dodge."

"Saw 'em come in today meself," Donegan replied sleepily.

"Said they saw enough buffalo to make it worth a man's while, Seamus."

"That why they're heading back in the morning? To hunt buffalo—or because they're afraid too?"

"No," Dixon replied. "They aren't afraid. And they ain't hunters either. Just teamsters—hauled goods down for Myers, and now they've got two wagons loaded with hides, ready for the return trip. Ike and Shorty want to take off first light—so, I'll pull my outfit out with theirs."

"Can you use another hunter, Billy?"

"Someone needing a job?"

"Mother Donegan's whiskey-sucking rounder of a son, that's who, God-blame-it!"

"You? You want to hunt buffalo now?"

"If there's nothing better for a man to do than kill his way through a herd of buffalo—then I suppose I'll bid farewell to Jimmy Hanrahan's saloon. I'm broke. Dead broke, Billy."

"Besides, it might be safer for your long and curly hair if you was long gone from here when the Comanche and the rest ride down on this settlement day after tomorrow—right?"

Donegan cleared his throat. "I suppose you're right. Might be a little more healthy for us both, Billy."

"I been wondering, Seamus. Maybe this scare from those traders and Amos Chapman was all some kind of joke the traders are playing on each other."

For a moment Seamus considered that, listening to the owls hoot in the timber down by the creek. Nearby the horses and mules snuffled and grazed on the dry grass. "Maybe Amos Chapman's playing the joke on the lot of you."

"No, I don't think the half-breed would do a crazy stunt like this. It about got him killed for it. No," Dixon mused, "Chapman ain't to blame for the joke that's been pulled on us."

"Just the same—we're going to be long gone before any warriors ride down on this place . . . right, Billy?"

"If I don't see this place for another month, it'll be too soon. We'll hunt to our heart's content, Irishman. Which reminds me, I left that new .44 Sharps of mine over at Hanrahan's. Got to get it and the cartridges I left with Langton in the morning before we pull out."

"You? Without a big fifty to shoot?"

"The .44 is the best I can put my hands on for now."

"Since you drowned your other one in the river!"

"Well, I'll make that .44 work for me—and come back here only when we need powder or lead for it."

"Or coffee or whiskey," Seamus said softly, starting to drift off to sleep.

"A little less whiskey for you, my friend. And a little more work might do you some good—"

Seamus sat bolt upright, instantly awake again. His head hurt, his mouth dry and pasty. There were loud voices coming from the saloon. Beside him, Dixon had come up at the same instant—with what sounded like a gunshot.

A rifle. A sharp crack, just like a rifle shot.

Dixon was pulling on his tall boots. Seamus reached down to pull his on and was surprised to discover he hadn't taken his off, as hot as the night was.

The voices grew even louder. A lamp went on in the Rath store. Muffled shouts came from the distance where the Myers and Leonard compound stood in the moonlight.

"I been asleep?" Seamus asked.

"You just got here," Dixon growled. "C'mon—we'll see what the trouble is over at Jimmy's."

"Dixon!" a voice came out of the prairie blackness.

"Over here," Dixon replied as he dragged the Irishman along by the arm, getting closer and closer to the smudge of yellow light spilling from Hanrahan's windows. "What's the shooting about?"

A dozen or more men were soon milling about the saloon. Oscar Sheppard and Mike Welch bolted from an open doorway, shouting that they would find something for a prop.

"No shooting," Jim Hanrahan said as he appeared out of the moonlit night. His eyes were red with whiskey and worry, and as furtive as an animal's.

For the moment, Seamus thought they reminded him of a badger's eyes. A trapped, cornered badger.

"No shooting," Hanrahan repeated, smiling as big as his face would allow. "Welch and Sheppard are getting something to prop the damn thing."

"What they have to prop?" Donegan demanded.

Hanrahan gestured toward the saloon. "Can only figure it was that ridgepole cracking in my place."

13

June 27, 1874

It was the full of the Moon of Fat Horses. And Quanah was leading the ten-times-ten he could count on seven of his fingers, leading them out of their last camp some five miles due south of the earth-lodge settlement. He swore they were close enough to smell the wood smoke of the tai-bos' fires.

The thought made his hooded, gray-tinged eyes go dark with hate.

Not quite six feet tall, Quanah nonetheless stood taller than most Comanche and Kiowa warriors. Too, his long, straight hair, now tied in a single braid at the back of his neck, was not as black as a raven's wing. Instead, there was clearly a touch of brown to it, perhaps a reminder of his mother's hair—hers the color of buffalo grass kissed by the first frost of autumn.

They had started west from the mouth of Elk Creek with some four hundred warriors. But by the time Quanah and the rest had reached the Staked Plain, their fighting force had nearly doubled. In four days almost three hundred warriors had hurried from the reservations to catch up, to take part, to be included in this glorious victory.

And that fourth day, yesterday, Quanah had carefully selected seven scouts to find the exact location of the settlement and determine the strength of the tai-bos. The old Cheyenne chief, White Wolf, had asked to go along with the young scouts. Quanah had agreed. If the Cheyenne chiefs wanted these hide men rubbed out first, then let White Wolf see where this war would begin.

And just this morning at dawn, a Kwahadi sentry atop a hill above the warriors' camp called down.

"The scouts—they return!"

On foot Quanah had dashed anxiously to the top of the knoll. Many other warriors had followed. From the top they watched the seven scouts and the old chief circle their horses four times.

"They have found the earth lodges!" Quanah shouted.

The rest of the warriors yipped and sang, cheered and cried out their war songs. Some leapt into impromptu dancing, whirling, kicking up tufts of grass and puffs of dust from the baked, cracking, drought-stricken earth. Even the tall one they had captured from the buffalo soldiers three summers gone, the one with coffee-colored skin who had ridden the trail with Quanah's Kwahadi for more than two winters now—even he with the bugle slung over his shoulder danced like a true Comanche warrior, screaming out his own war song.

Then Quanah stopped before the smirking countenance of Isatai.

"Is it as I told you?" asked the young shaman.

More than once he had wanted to smash the flat of his hand into that sneer. But, again, he held himself—reminded that he needed Isatai, perhaps as much as Isatai needed him.

Before he answered, Quanah glanced down at the warrior village below. Already there was an exciting throb to the frantic activity of those warriors and the few women who had followed their men on this war path. Finally he gazed back at Isatai's face.

"It is as you told it. We have found the hide hunters."

Quanah pushed on past the shaman, eager to be away from that smirk he wanted to claw from Isatai's face.

In the war village, the Kwahadi camp police had finished arranging the warriors and women into a long gauntlet by the time Quanah reached the meadow. He strode to the end of the two long lines, signaling Old Man Black Beard that he would have the honor of formally announcing the scouts' return.

Like the dead Kiowa chief, Satank, Old Man Black

Beard preferred the idea of some facial hair. He had cultivated a tuft of coarse, black hair on his chin—like a buffalo bull.

The seven scouts and White Wolf halted at the far end of the gauntlet. When all grew quiet, Black Beard signaled that they were to follow him down the opening between the hundreds of warriors and women. When at last the old Comanche had stopped the eight before Quanah, Black Beard turned to the party's leader.

"Tell us, with the honor in your heart—what did you see?"

The young scout drew himself up. This was a great honor to announce the news. He was expected to tell the truth, without the slightest embellishment. "We circle four times, beyond the hill, Black Beard."

"We saw," Quanah replied. "Four."

"Four earth lodges," continued the young scout.

"Any ponies?"

"Some," the young scout answered. "Spotted buffalo. Wagons too."

"How many tai-bos?" asked Black Beard.

The scout held up five fingers then struck his other arm six times.

Quanah smiled, satisfied. Three-times-ten. And they would be asleep. With their bullets useless and their guns like limp manhood unable to answer the Comanche challenge. He laughed loud, and in but a moment the hundreds were laughing with him.

"We have had our last sleep before riding down on the tai-bos," he told them. "Go ready your ponies. Pull your shields from their cases and string your bows. We ride to the river, where we will wait until the new sun."

By the time they had struck camp and were on the move to the Canadian, it was late morning, the bright, hot summer sun nearing mid-sky. They traveled slowly, scouts widely ranging on their flanks, carefully marching in a wide arc to the west as they inched their way across the broken country toward the river where the white man had raised his earth lodges. It was some time after mid-afternoon that Quanah halted them, sending word back through the many that here they were to stay until nightfall. Scouts were sent up and downstream now, to assure that they would not be seen by any white men and their surprise spoiled.

No fires were allowed as the warriors sat clustered in small groups, eagerly performing their toilet, that private ritual of grease and earth pigment before a fragment of a mirror stolen from some settler's soddy or wagon. Braids were loosened then re-bound, perhaps wrapped in trade cloth or ermine skins. Silver conchos traded from the Comancheros were shined and hung from scalp locks and clothing. Special protective medicine, perhaps a special stone or the dried skin of a kingfisher, was tied to a warrior's hair. Then each man moved to his favored war pony, where a sprinkling of puffball dust or red mud from the creek bank was smeared near the animal's nostrils to give it extra wind for the coming fight, smeared up and down each of the four long legs to give the pony strength for what would be required in the coming hours.

As he stroked his hands up and down the graceful limbs of the big gray horse he had stolen from the white settlement last winter, Quanah thought of how he stroked Tonarcy's strong, thin limbs. Throwing the buffalo robes back so he could stroke them winter or summer, how he loved the feel of her legs. Supple and strong and oh, so willing to open and accept him. As quickly as they opened, they always wrapped back around Quanah to hold him firmly locked in her moistness.

The warm breeze jostled the single golden eagle feather he had tied at the braid. It brushed his shoulder, reminding Quanah of the way Tonarcy brushed her fingers over him, kneading his muscles with musk oil from the glands of the big rats that lived in the marshes. In the red firelight of their lodge, their children asleep, the woman would then roll him over on his back, kissing his manhood into readiness, murmuring to it softly with her hot lips before she would settle down atop him and continue rubbing the oil onto his flesh—this time across the taut muscles of his chest as she moved up and down, up and down upon him.

Quanah found it impossible not to grow excited, thinking how her breasts felt in his hands, the nipples rigid as he thrust himself up into her.

He tried to shake off this heated remembrance of Tonarcy and think only of the coming fight. Gazing into the sky to the west, he watched the clouds gathering along the horizon, below where the sun would soon settle. They were the color of flint, streaked with the gray of his own eyes. Quanah hoped there would be no rain this night, that the clouds would dissipate from the sky so that his warriors could see by the light of the full moon that had already risen far to the east. It was a good omen.

All about him the warriors prepared. Some smoked their small pipes, talking in low, excited voices. Others sat in silence, like he, remembering those back in the villages. Villages either on the reservation or those out on the mapless expanse of the Staked Plain.

With the coming of the sun he would lead his own Kwahadi warriors into battle. Not only they, but also Kotsoteka and Yamparika Comanche, as well as Kiowa and Cheyenne and a handful of brave Arapaho.

Although they had followed him here, Quanah knew that when the battle was enjoined, the warriors would listen only to their own war chiefs. Such independence in making war did not matter now. The only thing of consequence was that they were here, a handful of miles from the white hide hunters, and in a matter of hours the tai-bos would all be dead. Some things were just not important when thrown up beside this matter of death.

"Put your saddles in the trees," he had told them when they arrived at this spot hours ago

Now the branches above them were heavy with saddles and other property the warriors and women did not want animals dragging off before the humans returned to reclaim it. Coyotes and badgers, even skunks, had a way of doing that—dragging off a man's things, hiding them so that a man never would find them again.

For the first time since they had arrived at this place, he saw Isatai. The young shaman was strutting through camp on foot, leading his pony. Completely naked except for a special pair of yellow-painted moccasins, Isatai had carefully covered every inch of his body with ocher earth paint. His pony was smeared a dull yellow as well. In his hair the medicine man had tied sprigs of gray sage for their power to protect and heal. In his free hand he carried a long lance, its shaft adorned with scalps of many colors.

Isatai strutted boldly, flaunting his bare flesh and uncovered manhood, without invitation telling those who stared too long that he needed nothing to stop the white man's bullets—not even the thinnest of antelope clothing.

At least his manhood will stay cool, Quanah said to himself and turned away with a smile.

Even if Isatai's medicine did not prove strong enough to keep the white man asleep as the warriors rode down on the earth lodges, even if Isatai's medicine were not strong enough to make the tai-bos' guns useless, even if the bullets did erupt from those weapons . . . Quanah was nonetheless convinced they would quickly overwhelm the two dozen white men at the settlement. In his mind he quickly scratched at the calculation, something he had never been good at . . . and still came up with more than twenty warriors for every one of the tai-bo hunters in that evil place.

Dark came at last, and the biting bugs came out with the cooling of the air. Quietly he passed along the word to move out once more. They were to lead their ponies on foot from this point on until mounting at the moment of attack.

"Riding ponies, the white man will hear," he explained to them. "Walking, the tai-bo cannot hear."

They crossed the Canadian, then moved east once more. At the southern end of the valley Quanah halted them near the red hill that rose beside the little creek.

"Sleep now," he told the war chiefs. "Have your warriors sleep with their reins in their hands. We will wake them when it is time to mount for the attack."

He did not sleep, his mind so full of many things as the stars whirled overhead. Thoughts of the little ones and old ones in the villages far out on the prairie—how they hungered for the meat that should have filled their bellies, but instead lay rotting on the ground, beneath a sky blackened with buzzards, stripped of the hide and tongue before the white man moved on.

Too, he thought of those who in despair had limped back to live on the white man's reservations, with hopes of having enough to eat, a warm blanket to replace a warmer buffalo robe. But there was far too little to eat, and what the white man gave them was rancid and full of bugs. Too often the warm blankets did not arrive for the winter, and when they did, the blankets were thin and full of holes.

No, long ago Quanah had decided he would die here on the free plains. Never to die cooped up on the white man's reservation. Some might take their last breath in their blankets, perhaps like old Paracoom was dying at this very moment. But Quanah wanted to die like his father, the Wanderer, had died—like a warrior.

With horse thieves and whiskey traders sucking the very life out of the tribes—Comanche, Kiowa and Cheyenne all —the reservations had become prisons where the white men could prey at will upon the Indian. Sucking the last bit of life from the Indian just the way the drying prairie winds drew the last bit of moisture from the great stalks of buffalo grass in the autumn of every year.

The same grass that fed his brother, the buffalo.

"May I sit with you, Quanah?"

He looked up in the dark, beneath the travel of the full moon, recognizing the face of his young friend, Timbo. "Sit beside me." He patted the ground beside him, then offered some of the cooked buffalo meat from the small herd they had bumped into just that morning on their march west of the white man's earth-lodge settlement.

"My heart is glad I did not let you talk me out of coming," Timbo said quietly after a few moments of silence.

Quanah had tried to convince the young warrior to stay behind and protect the village. "This will be your first time under fire, Timbo. It seems nothing I said was enough to convince you to stay behind. Not even what the owl told me."

"Told you that my medicine was not right?"

"Not yet strong enough, Timbo." How Quanah wished the young man, related distantly to his wife Tonarcy, had stayed behind with some of the rest to protect the Kwahadi village.

"Is your medicine not strong enough for us both?" Timbo asked, then before Quanah could answer, he continued. "I know that it will be, Quanah. There is powerful blood in your veins—enough medicine to protect us both come this fight."

His eyes misted in the moonlight as he looked upon the brave youth. Praying that his medicine would be strong enough for two, now that the owl had spoken to him of death. "Wait here . . . with me, Timbo. Until it is time to ride."

The great patterns of light overhead slowly whirled until He Bear and Tabananica returned from the meadow where the white men had their earth lodges.

"It is time," He Bear told Quanah.

"Tell the others to mount," Quanah said, rising with Timbo. "At the edge of the meadow beside the red hill, we will make a line." As the other two older warriors left to inform the rest, Quanah turned to Timbo. "You ride beside me."

Timbo beamed proudly in the graying light of predawn seeping into the summer sky. "To ride near your strength is a great honor!"

Quickly the Kwahadi war chief rode the big gray horse among the hundreds, searching out the other war chiefs, reminding them to restrain their hot-blooded young men in a solid, unbroken line until the order was given to charge.

"We go slow at first, walk," he told them. "When we see the earth lodges clearly—then I will order the charge."

Without disagreement, Quanah led the great gathering along the cottonwoods and brush, pointing the big gray's nose to the north. In the moonlight, they passed the ruins of Hook Nose's old trading post. Its mud walls now stood only four to five feet tall in places, slowly weeping from many winters of rain and summers of scouring wind. The dust of this land itself silvered his sweaty body in the milky moonlight.

Quanah prayed his people had the strength to prevent

such a crumbling of their culture. As warm as the morning was, nonetheless he shivered as he looked over the empty ruins, windows and doorways like the empty eye sockets of a buffalo skull. He tore his eyes away and looked north across the meadow.

In the murky, graying light, he could barely make out the dark shadows of the four buildings they were told the white man would hide within. And off to the side of the closest, he saw a fifth, but much, much smaller than the others. Without speaking, he halted the hundreds, spreading one arm to the right and the other to the left. The warriors obeyed, forming a long, compact phalanx, ready for the charge.

Off to their right the two great hills limned blue-gray before the coming of the sun. He would not wait for the orange streaking of the sky. Still, in a matter of heartbeats there would be enough light to make their swift ride across the meadow, closing this last gulf between them and their victims—and club the white men in their sleep.

Among the cottonwood and chinaberry lining the creek, a bird called. Another answered. Then a trio of them took to the wing, swept overhead, and suddenly darted back to the north, having discovered the long line of feathered horsemen waiting in the darkness atop their snorting ponies.

It was a good sign, these birds.

The dawn fell silent again among the trees and brush, clear across the meadow to the white man's earth lodges. As much as he strained his eyes, Quanah could not see much across that distance. Then as he watched, the air seemed to take on a gauzy texture. Eventually he could make out the wisps of smoke above the white man's lodges, like ghostly entrails, remnants of last night's untended fires.

As he watched, he saw a dark figure emerge from the side of a wagon and stand motionless for a few moments while the man relieved himself on the ground. At the corner of a far building, Quanah watched another shadowy figure ambling toward the meadow. Between that white man and his warriors grazed the tai-bo horses and mules.

He sniffed the air, filled with the ghosts of old fires as it was. Good, for the breeze was in his face at this time of day, with the cool air rushing down the valley toward the Canadian. The white man's horses had not smelled them.

That solitary tai-bo kept moving toward the horses.

Then a third far-off figure stood, and in the growing light the man hacked and coughed and spit on the ground.

Soon his blood would moisten that very spot, Quanah vowed.

"It is time!" he hollered, waving his rifle.

From the throats of seven hundred burst a war cry that rattled the valley and sent a thousand birds winging from the trees. Hooves hammered the dry, drought-seared earth as the line erupted into uneven motion, the old men trying their best to hold the young men back in a concerted charge.

In a matter of heartbeats they were among the white man's horses, scattering the frightened animals.

The yelling was deafening. The pounding of the hooves like a hailstorm on a buffalo-hide lodge.

Quanah felt the wind whip the tears from his eyes as he peered over at Timbo beside him. The young man smiled, throwing his head back to scream at the lightening sky.

Around them a few of the riders began to go down, their ponies stumbling in prairie dog holes. Horses screeching in fear and the pain of broken legs, riders crying out in tumult as others vaulted over them in the gray light. Dust was everywhere, kicked up by hooves, stived up by the tumbling beasts and falling men.

And still they rode on, gathering speed. Ever faster. Ever, ever faster.

It was good to see the white men running now. Turning away and running.

Death was coming.

Death was coming on the summer wind.

14

The air was sticky. Billy feared last night's clouds had fore-boded rain.

He glanced up at the sky to the west, across the flat meadow in the direction of the ruins at the distant flash of some heat lightning streaking from the ground into the heavens with a ghostly light, green and phosphorescent.

The air was still and heavy, portentous of the coming thunderstorm.

After Hanrahan had some of his men climb up on top of the saloon to hurriedly throw dirt off the overburdened roof, and had the others muscle a stout prop beneath the huge cottonwood ridgepole that the saloonkeeper claimed had cracked in the middle of the night, awakening at least a half-dozen men sleeping off their cups inside the soddy, Jim Hanrahan invited everyone to belly up to the bar for free ones. And while about fifteen hunters and skinners were drinking to their red-eyed health, the saloonkeeper suggested that Dixon get a head start on the day.

"Since you're up, Billy," Jim said, "whyn't you get on the road north afore the sun catches you and your crew sleeping? Have Billy Ogg to catch up our animals for you."

Dixon had thought a moment on it, then decided it sounded as good as any idea. After all, the moon had eased on out of the sky about the time all that ridgepole commotion got started. True too, every one of the outfit's wagons were loaded. All that was needed was to bring in the stock from the meadow and roust the rest of his men. With Masterson and Donegan along as hunters, the three would surely keep more than nine skinners busy. It was bound to be a profitable summer hunt, moseying along as they followed the herds north.

"Ogg! Roll out!" Dixon shouted, nudging the skinner's stockinged foot, having found Ogg sleeping just outside the saloon door, likely able to get no farther than that with his blanket after last night's late celebration followed by that early scare with the ridgepole.

"Shit, Billy! I just laid down four winks ago," Ogg grumbled, coming up slow but rubbing his face briskly with both hands. "What time is it anyways?"

"I figure it can't be too much after four from the looks of the sky to the east. Jimmy figures we ought to leave soon's we can. Go fetch up the stock."

"The stock?"

"We're rolling soon as we're hitched."

With his folding pocketknife Dixon shaved off a sliver of chew and plugged it in his cheek as he turned to the north. The Scheidler brothers had their two wagons parked some distance from Myers's stockade, their tongues still down.

At least I'll get a jump on Ike and Shorty, Billy thought to himself. Hell, even that big damn dog of theirs was sleeping sound as sowbugs.

He whistled for Fannie, and when the dog came to him from the direction of the Scheidlers' wagons, stopping between his legs for a vigorous rub, the breeze shifted a moment, and Dixon thought he heard something out of place, a sound from somewhere off across the meadow to the south. He raised his nose into the breeze, like a hide man would. Disgusted, he went back to scratching Fannie, his nose only able to smell the cinder and charcoal of O'Keefe's forge which stood nearby, on the far side of Dixon's wagons.

There was the sound again, almost like hail rattling through dry cottonwood leaves. But he convinced himself as quickly that he was just hearing things.

Billy told himself he was just spooked. What with all that talk the last few days, and then Hanrahan pulling that damned stunt a couple hours ago. There was no goddamned crack in that ridgepole—Billy and Bat had seen that with their own eyes. Jimmy looked sheepish enough when they asked him about it, saying with that smile of his that at least if any trouble did show, they'd now have the whole durn settlement up and ready for what came.

He knelt beside Fannie and let her lick his cheek as he

listened to the peep-frogs down in the trees. Then they went quiet and the air was still.

The east was growing red. Like Hanrahan's eyes this morning. Jimmy had been punishing the bottle pretty hard the last few days. Hell, Dixon thought. Hanrahan had everything he had ever owned tied up in that saloon now. Billy couldn't blame the man for being worried about that rumor Amos Chapman had carried all the way in from Camp Supply.

"That coffee?" he asked Masterson as the young hunter strode up from the saloon, a steaming cup in hand.

"I ain't got the belly like them others to be drinking Hanrahan's saddle varnish this time of the morning," Bat replied, hoisting his tin mug.

"Whyn't you roll Donegan out with that coffee of yours. It sure smells good."

"Want me fetch you some?"

"Get some soon as Ogg gets back with the stock. G'won and get Donegan out—but be gentle about it. He made a rough night of it," Dixon commented as he turned away from Fannie and went to lash up his bedroll.

"So the Irishman's going with us after all?" Masterson asked as he wheeled slowly, stomping over toward the sleeping form darkening the ground. Donegan was snoring with a flat-back, hung-over rumble.

"Says he'll tie in with us. Wants to hunt buffalo now. Not just his next round of whiskey."

Masterson knelt to nudge Donegan. "Time to open them bloody eyes of yours."

As Billy turned from the rear gate of the wagon where he had just thrown his bedroll, he knelt to retrieve his new Sharps. A bullbat swept overhead, keening quietly as it disappeared in the darkness. Something brought Dixon around slowly, to look at the awakening meadow. And at that same moment Dixon thought he heard that sound again, sound carried on the breeze as it shifted out of the south, rustling the long hair at his shoulders. It was . . . Billy Ogg. He was yelling something. Probably having him a bit of trouble with some of Hanrahan's stock.

Dixon watched the murky light shift, like the sandy bottom of the Cimarron, revealing a wide fan of dark objects throbbing at the nearby horizon. Nearer still, Ogg was yelling at him. Then, straining his eyes, Dixon saw them.

Seamus growled as he rose beside young Masterson, one hand against his shaggy head, hawking and spitting to clear the night-gather from his throat. "Too bleeming old to be—" He blinked. "Just what the hell time is it, you two rousting me out? I ain't in the goddamned army no more. You two rounders out to—"

"Jesus, Mary and Joseph!" Dixon roared, thunderstruck, his voice as tart as pickling brine.

He stood gape-mouthed three heartbeats more as the cries of the warriors set the hair on the back of his neck to standing. He had never seen anything like this before. Likely, his mind fixed on it suddenly, no one else had ever seen anything like this before—and lived to tell the tale of it.

"By the saints!" Donegan bellowed, clambering to his feet, weaving unsteadily and grabbing for the seven-foot-tall wagon wheel.

"Billy—come back!" Masterson shrieked.

"I gotta get my horse!" Dixon shouted as he ran straight for Ogg, who was galloping on foot in a beeline away from the oncoming charge.

He felt his insides draw up just as if they had been salted. There were hundreds of them—more than he had seen since . . . since the government peacemakers had that October parley with all the tribes seven years back up on Medicine Lodge Creek.

Now he knew what it had been. That faint noise, not so faint now. The sound had grown—almost deafening, the thunder those hooves made. Suddenly ponies shrieked as they spilled their riders among the prairie dog village in the meadow.

The war cries of those horsemen were enough to make a lesser man's heart turn to water. As he reached his frantic, plunging horse, Billy snorted. It wasn't that he wasn't afraid—because he damned well was. He was just fool enough to try to save the horse he had a genuine affection for.

Then he swallowed hard, convincing himself the warriors were just making a charge on the herd—simply to run off the stock.

Ogg sprinted past him as Dixon pulled up the picket pin, his mouth pumping faster than his legs. It was all Dixon could do to get the tether freed from the pin and drag the rearing, frightened horse over to the wagon wheel, where he lashed the animal.

"They ain't turning!" Dixon found himself shouting, more thought than intent to speak.

"They come at us without turning—our meat's cooked! Godblame it, Dixon—c'mon!" Donegan's rough brogue cut through the shrieking war cries. "The bastirds coming for the buildings!"

In that next instant, Seamus was yanking on Dixon's arm with one hand. Then he stopped, whirled and levered a cartridge in that brass-mounted Henry. The Irishman brought it calmly to his shoulder, nestled his cheek against the stock and fired.

Dixon wasn't long in acting behind him. That space between the cracks of the Irishman's Henry was suddenly punctuated by the boom of Billy's single shot with the .44 Sharps. Dixon stood there in awe for a long breathless moment.

"It's almost beautiful." Billy finally found words for this bowel-numbing sight as he drove home a cartridge, watching the onrushing cavalcade as the sky lanced red-orange arrows out of the east. "Look at them feathers and lances and shields—"

"Shut up and run!" Donegan growled, dragging the younger man back toward the saloon and the greasy yellow light spilling from the east door. "We ain't got time for talking or shooting!"

They both heard the door slam shut against its rough-hewn jamb. Inside the saloon men were yelling in surprise and fear. Outside, Dixon thought it was nothing less than how Hell itself must sound on a man's ears, just as he and the Irishman reached the plank door.

"Open up!" Donegan boomed, his big fist hammering against the door.

"It's Dixon!" Billy hollered. The first bullets were beginning to kick up dust around their feet. Slap the earth walls around them. "And the Irishman—let us in!"

Seamus brought the Henry back, preparing to ram the rifle butt against the door when it suddenly opened. A bullet whined past them, snarling somewhere into the saloon's interior. Billy Ogg dove between them, coming out of nowhere on the fly, the first to lunge across the threshold. He stumbled and fell facedown, climbing onto his knees as he scrambled into the interior of the saloon.

"Damn! I ain't got but a handful of cartridges!" Donegan moaned as he collapsed against the wall, pulling the brass casings from his canvas britches.

"Where'd you leave your gear?" Dixon asked, settling next to him and patting his own pockets.

Seamus nodded north. "Myers's place. When I walked over last night to have a drink—"

"Jesus, Mary and Joseph—I'm low on ammunition myself," Dixon interrupted. "Enough to keep me shooting for a while, but—"

"Well boys, I can stay here and watch the rest of you fellas stand these h'athens off," Donegan hacked as he rolled over onto his knees in a crouch. "Or, I can make a fight of it back to Myers's place while I still have some cartridges left me."

Dixon grabbed the Irishman's sleeve. His palm was sweaty. Keeping the older plainsman there beside him might be just his brand of luck. "You'll be a damned fool to try it out there now, Seamus."

"I wait another minute more and I won't stand a whore's chance in mass." He was crouching toward the doorway now, flinging his voice over his shoulder. "Close the door behind me!"

Donegan was gone.

Hanrahan flung the door shut as angry wasps of bullets stung the doorway, slapped the side of the saloon, whined incessantly outside.

Still the war cries did not cease. Nor the whinnying of the hide men's horses, answered by the screams of the war ponies as the white men hunkered down and put those powerful buffalo rifles into service for the first time, yellow-orange flames spurting into the murky light of dawn this Saturday morning.

The frightening, bowel-puckering shrieks of those countless warriors grew in volume . . . drew closer and closer still.

And Dixon knew they were in for a long siege of it.

An old cavalryman like he had reacted on instinct. And right at this moment as he reached the back wall of the Myers stockade where the shadows hung thickest, Seamus Donegan was downright amazed he had made it this far without being picked off or ridden down in all the mad confusion.

By the time he had dashed away from the scant safety of O'Keefe's shop, dragging a broken wagon wheel bouncing across the sage behind him, the phalanx of warriors had engulfed the Rath compound.

His heart in his throat, Seamus squeezed down the fear. More so the memory of fear: surrounded and outnumbered and on the verge of being overrun in that hayfield corral a handful of miles from Fort C. F. Smith.* The foggy image of his uncle Liam swam before his eyes as his breath caught high in his chest. Once more he had become surrounded and outnumbered by the screaming hordes who appeared out of the last gray moments of night beside a sandbar in the middle of a nameless river.†

Hearing the hoofbeats hammering closer and closer, Seamus realized he could wait no longer in these shadows. Instead, he had to chance climbing into the new day's light to clamber over the wall.

The toe of his boot found the wheel hub. His left hand sought a grip around a stockade picket here behind the Myers & Leonard stable. Unsteadily, his leg craned his weight upward. His left foot found a shaky rest at the top of the broken wheel he had dragged from O'Keefe's just as his left hand screamed out in pain—a splinter almost the

---

* The Plainsmen Series, vol. 2, *Red Cloud's Revenge*
† The Plainsmen Series, vol. 3, *The Stalkers*

size of a wiping stick burrowing itself in his palm. That hand grew warm and wet as he dragged himself to the top of the stockade and hurled himself over, landing in a heap beside the stable.

Bullets rattled the wooden pickets behind him, scattering splinters and chunks of dried mud.

Those bullets hadn't come from outside the compound —they were fired from the store . . .

"Hold your fire!" he shouted, holding the Henry up, waving it at the end of his arm. "It's Donegan, by damned! Don't shoot!"

"The Irishman!"

He recognized the voice.

"McCabe! It's me—Seamus!"

Of a sudden the redheaded skinner stood in the doorway at the back of the store with that surprised look of a turkey gobler peering over a downed cottonwood log. "If you're fixing on joining us—best you do it now, Donegan!"

He was off and running before McCabe had finished.

"Lord, but you do look a sight," growled Seth Hathaway as Donegan slid to a stop and McCabe slammed the plank door closed.

"Where the hell were you?" asked Charley Armitage, Dixon's skinner.

"Sleeping, when Masterson woke me up—just before the bleeming Injins come calling," he wheezed, his heart a ringing, anvil beat in his ears as he sank against an inner wall.

Seamus gazed around the room quickly, taking a count. Besides Armitage and McCabe, there were another nine men in the store. Fred Leonard, Myers's clerk and partner; James Campbell, a skinner; Edward Trevor, hunter; Seth Hathaway, another hunter; "Dutch" Henry Born, a hunter; Billy Tyler, skinner; Billy "Old Man" Keeler, Myers's cook; Fred Myers, another hunter but no relation to Charlie; and Frenchy, also a Dixon skinner.

As he clicked them off in his head, Donegan almost felt sorry for those he left behind at Hanrahan's saloon, as it appeared that the best shots and the calmest heads were gathered under this roof. Better than half of them weren't dressed, crouched at the walls and doorway in their long-handles, gun belts around their waists, bandoleers of Sharps ammunition slung over their shoulders. Yet most still hadn't taken the time to pull on their boots.

"Ah, Jesus . . ." groaned Leonard at the east wall, where he peered through a loophole he had chiseled between the pickets.

To a man, the others came to the wall and gazed at the open meadow in the gray light of dawn, watching the brown horsemen swarm over the Scheidler brothers. Ike grappled with three warriors in the back of a high-walled freight wagon, tripping and falling backward over the loose canvas shroud. Shorty bolted over the side of another wagon and was sprinting for the stockade, hollering at the top of his lungs when he suddenly skidded to a stop and started clawing at his back, screeching in horror.

When Shorty turned to look behind him, Donegan and the rest saw the arrow buried halfway to the fletching between the teamster's shoulder blades. In the next instant a huge horseman atop a tall gray horse appeared out of nowhere with a huge club, the head of which was made with terrifying iron nails, swinging at the end of his arm. Prancing across the meadow so gracefully, standing more than sixteen hands high—Seamus was reminded of the huge gray horse he had once owned. The General.

A piece of Donegan's heart had been ripped out that day the renegade North had killed The General during the Irishman's frantic race to a sandy island that already had about it the smell of cold sweat as the warriors closed in, drawing their noose ever tighter. Remembering the smell of cold sweat dripping down a man's spine . . . if not the stench of death itself.*

"Uncle Liam," Seamus whispered, blinking his eyes clear as he peered like a shabby voyeur through the earth-coated pickets. "God bless you wherever you are . . ."

The huge warrior brought the terrible studded club down into Shorty's face and came away with the top of the white man's head, screeching his glee as he shook the skull

* The Plainsmen Series, vol. 3, *The Stalkers*

and gore free then wheeled his huge gray horse about in a prancing circle, rearing the animal as he retreated from the stockade walls.

Donegan grew sickened, watching the spray of blood and brain as the body quivered, still standing for some reason. Then Shorty finally sank to the ground in a heap, where his body trembled for a moment. Seamus had to turn away.

It brought back memories of that rain-soaked bowl among the Lava Beds, just beneath Black Ledge where the Modocs had come down to do their evil work on the soldier dead. And found some, like Donegan, still alive. And again his soul caused him to wonder why the Modoc leader had called off his warriors, sparing the undead that day.*

"Virgin Mary, Mother of grace," he muttered, and crossed himself. Then looked around to find some of the others staring at him, their faces sharp-stitched with lines of hard living every bit as white as he felt his to be.

"How many of us are there?" asked the Irishman.

"Here?" someone asked from the darkness across the room.

"No—here at the two posts," Seamus replied.

"Twenty-five or so," Leonard spoke up.

The clerk would know, Seamus thought. A man precise with numbers. "Now with those two gone . . ."

Donegan did not want to finish his thought. "Well, that just about takes the rag off the bush. Looks like our work's cut out for us, fellas."

He turned back to the wall, shoved loose some chinking between the tall pickets and pushed the blued barrel of the Henry through.

"Virgin Mary, full of grace . . . hear me in my time of need . . ."

15

June 27, 1874

Billy was certain the sonsabitches were going to come hurling in through the doors of the saloon at any moment.

Outside, the warriors closed to within an arm's length of the walls, backing their ponies up to the doors, driving rifle butts and buffalo lances—hammering, pounding, screeching like banshees at the door of Hell itself.

Others, hundreds strong now, closed within a pistol shot's distance in the next six heartbeats. For those first frantic moments at Adobe Walls, it was the white hunter's sidearms that held against the red onslaught while the horsemen pressed their advantage of surprise. Before the hunters could even think of scrambling for their rifles, they yanked pistols from gun belts hurriedly buckled over longhandles, then fired into the painted faces of warriors no more than three arm lengths away at most.

So close a man could almost smell the grease and sweat on the bodies. Damn near close enough in the murky, semidarkness to smell that morning's jerky breakfast on the breath of every warrior.

While some two dozen of those most brave dared make it all the way to the earth walls, most chose to drive their ponies in a wild, furious circle, ringing the buildings, slipping down the off side of their animal, hanging on with only a heel locked on a rear flank and a hand caught up in the mane, firing their pistols and rifles from beneath the heaving ponies' necks. Scalp locks of brown and red and blond fluttered from bridles and the rims of shields or at the muzzles of their rifles. In the coming light of day the many-colored hues of horse and warrior streamed in a brilliant blur like watercolors splattered in the first moments of a thunderstorm as the ring tightened around those hide men outnumbered more than twenty-to-one.

Still, some of the finest marksmen at that time on the frontier grimly set about to defend those three earth buildings at Adobe Walls that hot June day in 1874. Men who made a living truly knowing their weapons. Men who cast their own bullets, loaded their own shells, treated their buffalo rifles like a friend. These were men used to killing at long range. These were men truly in their element, men who time and again would turn the onrushing red tide throughout this long day.

"Ain't this something? Look at all of this," Dixon said, flannel-mouthed in wonder, and under his breath just loud enough that the young hunter next to him heard.

"Your brains must've seeped out your ears," Masterson replied, chewing his tobacco like a glass-eyed cow. "You getting all such excited to see such a thing—when here we are about to lose our hair!"

"Good shot, Jimmy!" someone shouted as another of Hanrahan's bullets hit their mark. He was hell on those horsemen with that pistol barking steadily in his sure hand.

By laying down a heavy, concerted fire, the riflemen in Hanrahan's saloon momentarily parted a thick phalanx of brown riders making a second charge on the building.

"Whoeee!" shouted skinner Oscar Sheppard. He stood and pranced light-footed for a moment as if he were jigging on a flint hide stretched flat upon the prairie. His right arm went out. "Gents to the right." Then his other arm swept in a wide bow. "Ladies to the left!"

The saloon defenders laughed wildly, like men staring death in the face yet still able to enjoy a joke made by one of their own, a joke that drew up images of the raucous saloon-hall dances in Dodge.

Then more bullets slammed against the thick earthen walls, smacked the wood frame of windows, splintered thunderously at the door planks. A few stray shots made it through the open window, splattering lamps and bottles and china cups in a tinkle that served as a counterpoint to the roar and shriek and scream and fury.

Damn, but he prayed this wasn't the cork in the jug for them.

His gut twisted in a knot, Billy didn't know how long that first deadly assault lasted, those warriors daring to ride right up to the walls themselves. Inside there was a controlled, fevered pitch of activity while most of the white

148

men piled what they could against the windows and doors: sacks of grain and flour, overturned tables and other furniture, barrels and kegs and saddles. That attention to barricading themselves finally assured, the hunters and the rest returned to their weapons, sorting through the various pouches of cartridges while Hanrahan distributed a limited number of pistols to the other eight men. If it came down to a close-quarters scrap of it, they would damn well hold back the red tide as long as any men could.

Dixon turned at the same time some of the rest paused in their frantic activity.

"You hear that?" Jim Hanrahan asked.

The rest seemed to hold their breath. There it came again.

"A bugle, by God!" Hiram Watson swore.

They were peering through the loopholes with greater interest in that next moment. Trying to find the bugler.

"You see 'im?"

"Naw, he must be back there some—off a ways with the rest," James "Bermuda" Carlisle growled. "Some bastard what knows how to blow—"

Another blare of that brass-lunged horn rose over the meadow.

"Sonuvabitch knows his calls," Hanrahan commented. "That's 'assembly.' He wants them bastards to pull back!"

He ought to know, Billy thought. Jim would know bugle calls.

"We got us some red bastard out there with a captured bugle," Mike Welch moaned.

"No. Not no red bastard. That there's gotta be some turncoat renegade," growled Oscar Sheppard. "Some soldier's gone over."

"I heard tell there's a Mexican greaser been living with the Comanche since the sixties," Hanrahan told them. "Heard the story of it that he can blow a bugle good as you'll hear on the parade at Fort Dodge itself."

The horn's notes changed their call—from the plaintive cry for assembly to—

"That's a charge!" Hanrahan warned.

"I knowed of a man said he visited the Kiowa back to

'sixty-six," Carlisle replied calmly, his teeth the color of pin oak acorns. He eased over on his knees to peer through a loophole. "And he told of a half-breed Mex fella what blew the bugle—"

"Here they come!" Billy Ogg hollered, announcing the next assault.

By that time the warriors realized their element of surprise had been foiled and they would not be able to breach the walls of the sod buildings. Many of the horsemen decided to abandon their ponies and charged forward on foot.

In anxious wonder Billy watched as first a handful, then a dozen and finally many more abandoned their animals, whirled and sprinted toward the saloon, zigging then zagging as they hurled themselves into the muzzles of the buffalo hunters guns. Those powerful weapons erupted in a spray of orange in the gray light of coming day, smoke filling the saloon, blanketing the province of no-man's land just beyond the walls. Time and again a warrior fell. Some never to rise again, others crawling back to safety, still more who called out to others to come claim them.

Again and again more of the hundreds flung themselves into the jaws of those terrible, powerful weapons put to work by the buffalo hunters. In wave after furious wave as the sun emerged red and angry from the bowels of the earth, the Comanche, Kiowa and Cheyenne sought to divine Isatai's prophecy by sheer numbers alone. Flanks of brown bodies and screaming, wild-eyed ponies pressed out of the new light like a whirlwind of crimson death. Yet it was their bravery in the face of those buffalo guns that made Billy Dixon truly admire his enemy this sultry morning already heavy with the stench of death.

As many times as the warriors charged in on foot or horseback to rescue their fallen dotting the ground of that smoke-shrouded no-man's land close to the walls, it never ceased to amaze young Dixon. This was true courage, he thought as he rammed home another cartridge in that .44 Sharps, true courage of the highest order. He doubted he would ever find men braver than these naked horsemen who had come riding out of dawn's darkness.

"Shoot that sumbitch!" Carlisle ordered as he fought to ram home more cartridges in the loading tube for his .56–52 Spencer.

Out in the yard a few of the horsemen had grown very brave and pulled out of the circle of death ringing the saloon. Approaching daringly close, they yanked their breechclouts aside, exposing their manhood, turning to show their brown rumps, slapping their flesh and gesturing profanely.

"They say we're women," Hanrahan explained.

"Blow that'un's balls off!" Welch demanded as he poked his barrel out the loophole once more.

On and on went the daring, luring, provocative challenges of a few of the braver warriors. A time or two one of these courageous ones who ventured from the cover of wagons or hide ricks to provoke the enemy would end up getting knocked off his pony. Likely as not, they retreated unscathed after delivering their profane message to the white hunters.

For those white hide men this was in no way qualified as a romantic encounter with the red cavalry of the southern plains. On the contrary, this was a bloody, terrifying, cruel and immensely ugly moment in their lives. If only he lived through it, Billy Dixon thought to himself as he tapped his finger on the Sharps barrel. Hot to the touch. If he lived through it, he would never glorify this day, nor the killing of Indians. Among these hardened men, Dixon knew that to be anxious, even scared of dying, was no sign of weakness. What mattered most at this moment, like many others to be faced in the life of a plainsman, was that these men did what they had to do.

And for the moment Billy wondered if he would see his twenty-fifth birthday.

His nose stung with acrid gun smoke.

It amazed Seamus how quickly the day was turning hot. Most of the defenders had not even dressed, sleeping and completely surprised when the horsemen rode down on the meadow. They sat at their loopholes now in their greasy long-handles and grimy underwear, ammunition belts slung around their bare waists or strapped over their shoulders. Little did it matter; no man seemed concerned enough to take the time required in searching for his britches or his shirt.

With every passing minute the heat climbed. Both doors shut against the assault, little breeze could sneak through the Myers & Leonard store. In a matter of moments it had come down to close, hot, sweaty work—this business of death and dying.

In those first few moments of fear and uncertainty, Fred Leonard had dragged out a sealed case of Sharps rifles. Using a huge butcher knife, the clerk cracked open the case, prying off the lid. The twelve shiny new rifles, still in their oil, were quickly passed around the smoky room. It was some time before the defenders loaded those rifles, however, interrupted as they were with the matter of close-quarters fighting at the pickets and in the stockade as the warriors swarmed over the walls.

Outside, a few of the horsemen reined their snorting ponies to a halt beside the store walls then stood atop the horses to pull themselves to the sod roof.

"Get in the bastions!" Leonard was shouting, nervously tearing open boxes of cartridges for the riflemen. He spilled a box at his feet.

"Don't go getting fouled in your own harness now, Fred. No man gonna try crossing that open ground," sneered Old Man Keeler.

"Them bastions is useless," agreed Mike McCabe. "Worse'n tits on a boar."

Seamus paid little attention to the ill-tempered bickering between the sweaty gunmen. He and the rest were at the walls, knocking out some of the uncured mud chinking between the upright pickets. Shoving first one pistol out a loophole, then the other, the Irishman joined the rest in laying down a fire they prayed would keep the warriors from overwhelming them.

"Listen, ever'body. Quiet, dammit!" Frenchy shouted, his chin climbing toward the ceiling, pointing overhead with his pistol.

Donegan cocked his head, sorting out the sound. He

rose quickly. Dutch Henry Born was slowly stepping across the room as well, listening to the sounds from the earthen ceiling. A sudden shower of dirt and grass rained down on Born as a warrior poked a hole through the roof.

On instinct Donegan sprayed the hole with three quick bursts from his army .44. He watched the last hit the warrior for certain, driving the Indian backward, his face gone in a bloody spray. Then he made out the sound of footsteps hurrying to the side of the roof, a pause followed by a heavy thud that led Seamus to believe the warrior had fallen off the roof near the outer wall.

More rooftop footsteps scurried out of hearing as Born swiped his eyes clear with a dirty hand, his well-seamed face now tracked with grime and sweat. He was cursing under his breath, eyes like huge white rocks in his dark face.

"Shit!" cried Fred Myers. "Help me! Dammit, help me!"

He sat crouched at the wall in the tattered rags of his old butternut uniform, the mark of a southern infantryman, his pistol stuffed through a loophole. The warriors banged at that very spot as Myers fired again and again into their faces. They were screaming at the white men, with Myers hollering back at them.

Three others hurried over, ramming their muzzles through the flimsy chinking, firing as soon as they found a target. There was, for the moment, no problem of that. There seemed to be more than enough targets at the walls as the warriors hurled themselves against the sturdy pickets with unrestrained fury, only an arm's length from the defenders.

Seamus watched one attacker bend over and brazenly peer between the pickets into the interior. The Irishman jammed his pistol into the loophole and watched the enemy's face disappear in a spray of gun smoke and crimson as the warrior brought his hands to his eyes, turned and stumbled off. He crumpled to the ground a few yards from the store, dead before he hit the grass.

"I need one or two of you sonsabitches over here with me!" Keeler growled like a buffalo bull with his bangers caught on some cat-claw brush.

Seamus rose and in a crouch scurried to the west wall of the store where the old cook was busy having a private duel of it with some warriors swarming over the stockade wall. Every last animal in the corral was already down, bleeding and screaming, thrashing in pain. Or already lying still in silent, sudden death.

"That goddamned corral is proving to be more cover to them red bastirds than it helps us," Donegan commented as he shoved another sixteen rounds in the Henry's loading tube, then suspended another four more between the fingers of his left hand like long brass pods.

"We gotta try to get to that bastion at the northwest corner!" Leonard hollered through the smoke and heat-haze and clamor. "Who'll try with me?"

"I'll go!" declared Billy Tyler, a young hunter.

Leonard looked at Donegan and Keeler hunkered at the wall. "Cover us, boys!"

Then the clerk was gone out the west door into the stockade, on his heels the young buffalo hunter with his brand new Sharps .40.

"You heard the man," Keeler snapped, putting his Remington pistol to use.

Seamus covered them as best he could, glancing once then a second time to see the two men dancing across the open ground, small eruptions of dirt kicked up around their boots. A bullet smacked into the north wall inches from Leonard's nose. In less time than it would take to light a damp cigar, the clerk suddenly turned about-face and bumped into Tyler as he scurried back to the store. Behind the pair, coming over the west wall, a warrior dropped to the ground with a screeching war cry. More shots came whining past, fired from the direction of the nearby corral.

Tyler wheeled, trying to find Leonard, who was sprinting like a hellion for the store. He wheeled about in time to find the warrior dashing for him, arm cocked, a pistol held at ready. Tyler fired, then fired a second time. Each of the bullets collided with the brown body, the first stopping the warrior in his tracks, the second knocking him back a step. He looked down at his chest, then crumpled.

The young hunter darted for the body, grabbing the warrior by the long hair gathered at the nape of the dead man's neck. Setting off for the store, Tyler was lunging forward as fast as he could in a crouch, dragging the bloody warrior like a prize he would not relinquish, when he reached the doorway. He straightened of a sudden, arched back with a face gone white . . . then crumpled to his knees, swiping at his back with his left hand as he fell forward across the sandy threshold.

Seamus dropped the Henry and pulled the second of his .44s. He had it barking the moment it hit his palm while he settled over Tyler, grabbing the back of the hunter's belt to drag the wounded man inside the store.

"Goddamn! Goddamn!" Keeler muttered, pulling his knife from his belt and stabbing a long slit in Tyler's shirt.

"That shot came from your corral, Leonard," Donegan said, turning to glare at the clerk as the old salt sting of temper passed over him. He glanced down at Tyler for a moment, then over the others. "I don't know how—but before this morning's done, we've got to get that corral cleaned out. That—or we'll bloody well be cleaned out ourselves."

"They got 'im in the lights," Keeler said. He was a frosty-browed man who in his long life had likely seen his share of death already.

"Likely he'll be drowning in his own juices soon," Leonard groaned, his eyes going from man to man.

"No," Donegan said quietly. "Get 'im sitting up—so his chest don't fill so fast. He might last."

The young hunter's eyes fluttered open a moment, and although glazed, they found and held on the Irishman as Seamus pulled the body upright against the mud wall.

"Thanks . . ." Tyler murmured, pink froth seeping from his lips. "Tell . . . tell Bat for me—"

Then Tyler seized up with a coughing spasm that brought up more fluid and a chunk of lung. His head rolled to the side as he fought for air. Donegan turned away.

He had watched enough men die. In that bloody war of rebellion fought from the valleys of Virginia to the ridges and forests of Pennsylvania. Seamus knew that look, the pasty feel of a man's skin when the body is down to its last few minutes. Tyler didn't have a chance.

And for a moment as he rose, hurrying for the east wall, Donegan wondered if any of them had a chance.

"That'un Billy killed," Keeler said to them as he peered through one of the Comanche slots he had poked through the wall, "damn sight looks like Stone Calf's son."

"The Cheyenne chief?" asked Henry Born, his voice filled with wonder. "I figured him for a peace chief."

"Not no more." Keeler nodded, wiping some blood from Tyler's chin. "Sumbitch—but don't you know his son getting killed gonna make them Cheyenne brownskins fight hard now."

16

Moon of Fat Horses, 1874

Quanah glanced over his shoulder now, finding Isatai still sitting upon his horse atop the hill, out of range of the taibos' far-shooting guns.

He swore at the shaman. Just as he had cursed Isatai throughout the first hours of that long, long morning. Painted all in yellow, with his sacred war bonnet of sage sprigs tied around his head, Isatai had never charged down on the white man's earth lodges. Instead, he had ridden into the meadow at the far right side of the line, then quickly made his way to the crest of that nearby knoll.

At the first of the white man's earth lodges they came upon, Quanah and many others reined off from the main sweep of the charge. Timbo continued on with the rest.

Furiously driving his heels into the gray horse's flanks, the Kwahadi whirled the animal savagely just before he collided with the plank door. Obediently, the horse backed again and again, hurling itself against the door as Quanah attempted to drive it in on the defenders. The door held.

His blood hot in failure, the Kwahadi reluctantly galloped away from the walls of the earth lodge, emptying his pistol into a nearby window. He joined those forming a tight, red noose circling the building where the hated tai-

156

bos cowered out of sight. Only sporadically did the white men fire back at Quanah's screaming warriors.

Having a sudden inspiration, he called out to another Kwahadi to follow him in tearing away from the maddening, noisy whirl. Quanah led Wolf Tongue to the wall of that first earth lodge, climbed to the back of the tall gray horse and pulled himself atop the grassy dirt the white man had spread over the roof of his building.

As he and Wolf Tongue reached the middle of the roof, Quanah heard another blast of the mulatto's horn. He did not know what the call meant—and he figured few of the hundreds did either. But for some reason the whirling ring of horsemen racing flank to flank around and around the building broke off their circle and rode back across the meadow.

He did not care. There was the hot, mean, sweaty work of war to be done. "Esa-Que, we dig the tai-bos out!"

Wolf Tongue nodded, grinning. "Like the wolf will dig out his prey!"

Using their knives and hands, all that they had, the two warriors were nonetheless unable to burrow through the thick layer of prairie sod so encrusted with the tangled roots of buffalo grass and bluestem. Furious enough that his eyes misted in fury, Quanah rose to his feet and shouted his curses on the white men cowering only inches below his moccasins.

With a brassy, summer's day blare, the Negro deserter's bugle blew again on the hot wind as Quanah darted to the southern edge of the roof. With that shrieking horn's notes rising beneath the pale, cornflower-blue sky, close to two hundred warriors reined once more for the Rath store. Upon its roof stood the Kwahadi chief, his arms outstretched, silhouetted against the sky, screaming his call for death.

Quanah waved the horsemen on, shouting encouragement to the riders as they neared the store. A few sporadic shots erupted from the building. As if yanked by strings, all but one of the warriors dropped to the far side of the ponies and circled the earth lodge. The solitary warrior raised his arm in greeting to his chief on the roof.

"Horse Chief!" Quanah bellowed in reply. "Come—together we will dig out the prairie rats and kill them one by one!"

Many times since childhood had they ridden together. Now the Comanche warrior savagely brought his pony around near the door to the Rath & Company store as he dismounted on a dead run, a pistol in one hand, his huge war axe in the other. A puff of dust spurted behind him as Quanah watched the young warrior cross the last few yards to the wall of the white man's earth lodge—

—where Horse Chief suddenly skidded to a stop only a matter of feet from the wood door, gazing down at his chest. Across it opened a second blossom of red that drove Horse Chief to stumble back a step. He fought forward again, lowering his head like a bull in rut, but as Quanah watched, the warrior's feet suddenly gave out beneath him as a third bullet hit Horse Chief, spinning him about violently. He pitched backward and moved no more.

Wolf Tongue was the first off the roof, leaping atop his pony a moment before Quanah dropped to the back of the big gray. The war chief sawed the rein around in a tight circle, racing the horse back along the earth lodge, a matter of an arm's length from the wall.

Quanah heard the angry snarl of the guns as he raced along the east wall, heard the bitter whine of the white man's bullets as he leaned off the horse. Yet this time he could not hide behind the horse as the others were. This time Quanah had to hang on with a hand tangled in the gray's mane, a heel locked over the gray's huge flank as he leaned toward the wall, toward the windows and doors, toward the spitting muzzles of the tai-bos' guns, reaching down and with inhuman strength grabbing the back of Horse Chief's belt. Unable to lift the dead warrior to his lap, Quanah reined the gray horse away from the earth building as the white man's lead wasps followed him into the meadow.

"He is dead," said Wild Mustang, another Comanche warrior after Quanah had gently lowered the body of Horse Chief, then leaped to the grass himself.

"He was the bravest of us, Cobay," Quanah said, kneeling.

The Kwahadi war chief gently laid his hand on the breast of his old friend, his palm coming away with Horse Chief's warm, sticky blood. Quanah slapped the blood upon his own breast, over his heart, mixing it with the earth paint and grease, the sweat and the dust furring every inch of his bare skin.

"Years ago, your blood became mine. And mine became yours, Horse Chief. Know now that your death will not be in vain. Isatai lied to us—"

"Quanah!" Rag Full of Holes said, shocked.

"He did lie!" Quanah snapped back, rising suddenly, glaring at Full of Holes's face. He turned to glance at the ongoing battle as more and more warriors left the circle and dismounted, choosing to fight behind wagons or the tall, wide stacks the tai-bos had made of their dried buffalo hides, most as big as a small earth lodge.

"We have two scalps," Wild Mustang told him.

"How?"

"Timbo and the others found two white men hiding beneath the canvas covering their wagon."

He squinted into the new sunlight, shading his eyes with one hand to find Isatai still atop a nearby hill, his ocher-painted body glorious in the yellow light. "Only two? Any of ours?"

"Stone Calf's son, a Cheyenne, was killed. Now Horse Chief—a Kwahadi. Another Cheyenne, named Spots on the Feathers."

"Three?" Quanah shrieked in a rage. "And we were supposed to club the white man in his sleep?"

"Quanah, we are gratified to have the two scalps now. There will be more soon. It is only the beginning of the fight."

He whirled on Wild Mustang. "This fight was supposed to be over by now!"

"Things have gone well enough, Quanah. Do not be mad at Isatai because the white man was not asleep. We have the scalps, and some wagons to pilfer through already.

Surely, I agree that we did not club the white man in his blankets—but the day is young."

For some reason, Quanah did not like the feel of this morning. His sense of things was not right. And now a good friend was dead while the rest were giving up the close fighting.

"No!" he shouted, waving angrily at the hundreds as they dismounted and slapped the rumps of their ponies to send the animals off. "We cannot fight these white men like this! Their guns shoot harder, their bullets go farther! We cannot defeat the white man like this!"

"Leave them fight," Full of Holes said. "We will ferret the tai-bos out soon enough. They will run out of those far-shooting bullets—"

Quanah whirled on him, nearly knocking Full of Holes off his feet as he swept past, leaping to the back of the gray horse again. He stopped momentarily beside Wild Mustang, tearing the long, fourteen-foot lance from his friend's grasp. "If no other will fight like a Comanche—let it be told down to our grandchildren's grandchildren that Quanah Pah-kuh was the last Kwahadi warrior!"

He dug heels into the gray's ribs as the animal burst into a run. Straight for the door he raced, that long buffalo lance held parallel to the dry breast of the ground, he swept over the stunted grass, drawing closer still to the Rath store where Horse Chief had fallen. Quanah grieved. In his own way, the Kwahadi chief grieved.

Just as he neared the earth wall, the east door cracked open slightly, a muzzle appearing. Quanah was there with the lance, jabbing it into the black strip where the white rifleman must be standing. Shouts burst from the darkness as the weight of the door slammed on the lance. Fighting furiously, reining the gray back, Quanah struggled to free the lance. A bullet snarled past his braid. A second almost burned his nostrils.

With a final, mighty pull, Quanah broke the buffalo lance in half and wheeled the gray about, reining the horse for the meadow once more, where the huge stacks of buffalo hides hid Comanche and Kiowa snipers. Of a sudden he was airborne, vaulting over the neck of the great horse as it went down, pitching its rider forward into the dry, drought-ravaged grass.

For a moment he felt the blackness pulling him down like the shifting sands of the river sucked the unwary. Then Quanah shook his head to pull himself out of the quagmire. His mind exploded with shooting stars. And he realized his right arm and shoulder were not responding. His back felt as if it had been split in two. Slowly he raised his left arm and he rolled over off the numb right shoulder. It was then he saw the last thrashing of the big gray horse.

A funnel of dirt exploded near his useless right hand. Another showered a moccasin with earth. The tai-bos knew he was down and in the grass. Lying here still many yards from that stack of hides.

Quanah Parker crawled for his life. It seemed of a circle in some way: the white man had taken back his great, gray horse.

But too, the white man had taken the life of a good friend.

As the dirt erupted around him, angry bullets whistling past his ears, Quanah remembered their first horse raid into Texas together as mere boys, remembered how they both had come of age in the battle of Antelope Hills. How they had sworn to protect one another with their lives.

First his mother and then his father. Followed by one friend after another.

So now Quanah Parker cursed again, because the white man was taking everything from him. Everything.

Everything had moved so quickly for Billy in those next few minutes. Someone who sounded like Fred Leonard had hollered from the Myers store for Bat.

Over the diminishing thunder of hooves as the warriors broke off their circling attack, Masterson had hollered back from the east doorway that he was in the saloon.

Leonard had roared that Billy Tyler was hit and wanted Bat.

"You don't stand a chance of making it between hell and breakfast, Bat," Billy tried to tell him.

Masterson's face had gone as dark as a square of trade

plug. "Like you, he's my friend, Billy. If it were you—I'd come." He rose and stood hunched at the door. "Cover me —all of you!"

Perhaps it had been the hand of God Himself that had shielded Masterson in that spirited race from the saloon to the Myers stockade. Billy was sure nothing else short of divine intervention could have kept Bat from running smack into a bullet in those few seconds it took the youngest of the hunters to sprint clear to the east wall of the stockade and dive inside the crack of a door opened for him.

Later in the fighting and sniping, near ten o'clock, Dixon moved to the west wall and poked a new hole through the pickets so he could look in the direction of the Rath store. Some seventy-five yards off stood one of the tall hide ricks, every bit as big as O'Keefe's blacksmith shop itself. Then something caught his eye. At the corner of the stack fluttered some black feathers. Billy crouched, held his breath and aimed. Fired.

The feathers disappeared as the warrior backed anxiously to the far side of the hide rick. Putting himself in view of the riflemen inside the Rath store. Now they fired upon him, driving the warrior back into Dixon's sights. Nearby stood the Indian's gaily-painted pony, nervously cropping at the grass.

Billy tried again. His bullet knocked dust off the corner of the hide rick. Back and forth the warrior danced behind the stack of dried hides for the next ten minutes. Tiring of the do-si-do with the Indian, Dixon laid his front blade on the warrior's pony, deciding to aim for the colorful calico ribbons braided in the pony's mane. The animal dropped immediately, a bullet through its head.

Without the cover of his pony, the warrior made a much better target. Dixon drove home another cartridge into the .50-caliber Sharps he had switched with Oscar Sheppard, took deliberate aim at what little he could see—nothing more than some feathers fluttering at the corner of the hide rick—and fired.

The warrior bolted from hiding, sprinting toward the cottonwoods for about fifteen yards, then suddenly spilled in the brittle grass. He was down only a moment before he bolted onto his feet again with the yip of a coyote pup and sprinted off a little farther when he dropped again. Up again, yipping at the top of his lungs, zigging and zagging until he reached the cover of the trees while Dixon watched, more amused than amazed.

A noisy crow fluttered in through the solitary window of Hanrahan's saloon and perched on a shelf where broken crockery littered the floor below. *"Kraw! Kerr-raawww!"* it called.

"Get outta here!" Dixon shouted at the bird roosting just over his shoulder.

"He got you scared?" Bermuda Carlisle asked.

"You know well as I crows don't mean anything good," Dixon replied. He looked at the old buffalo man smiling at him. There was still a lot of fire in Bermuda's eye, steel in the old man's lean belly. Carlisle knew as well as any, for he had long proved himself out here in this country, a plainsman with saddle calluses clear up to his elbows.

"Don't claim to be superstitious about death, are you?"

Outside in the meadow the naked horsemen sounded like a roving pack of mountain cats, all filled with a painful dose of porcupine quills in their jaws.

"Look out yonder—and you tell me, Bermuda," Billy snarled, turning back to his loophole, a cold drop of sweat shinnying down his backbone.

Crows meant no good. They carried news of death. Dixon wondered who it was, and why the crow had come to tell him—perched right over his shoulder, cawing away. Was it Masterson? Had Bat made it to Myers's place all right? Or could it be Tyler? It had to be Tyler the crow was cawing about. Or maybe—would it be the Irishman?

"G'won now!" He swung the muzzle of the big .50 at the crow angrily. Scared more of the supernatural than he was of anything he could see. No matter what color the man's skin, Billy Dixon weren't afraid of nothing he could see.

"Too bad, boys," Carlisle commiserated with a grin on his face as he swiped beads of sweat off his brow. "A damned shame that Injuns don't have pelts half as good as buffler—so the sonsabitches'd be worth something in the shooting."

Some of the others laughed as Hanrahan inched his way out of a squat and crabbed over to Dixon.

"We're in a bad way," Hanrahan said as he settled beside the young hunter.

With the sun noon high, sulled in the sky and refusing to move like a lazy mule, they had been under siege for better than six hours now. Dry as chalk itself, the air tasted like it had been fried in sulfurous tar.

"We got a better chance than Dudley and Wallace had," Billy whispered. "I saw 'em, Jim—least what was left of 'em." And that sight had been enough to shove what he had left of his breakfast that day clear up around his tonsils. He swallowed hard against the bad taste in his mouth. "I'll bet the bastards what killed 'em are right out there, been shooting at us all morning."

"Weren't a pretty sight to see, I heard."

"The red bastards propped their heads up," Billy snarled.

Hanrahan squinted, as if imagining it. "What the hell for?"

"For 'em to watch their own torture. Cut 'em from upstream gullet to downcreek gut-end."

"They sliced 'em open . . . and c-cut their pizzer and balls off?"

Dixon nodded. "Then burned 'em. Set a fire down there."

With a pale-eyed, loafer wolf of a look in his well-seamed eyes, Hanrahan glanced at his groin and shuddered involuntarily. "Where was their goddamned bites?"

Billy shrugged a shoulder, glancing back out the loophole.

A "bite" was what the veterans of buffalo country carried in a pocket, always handy in the event of attack. No man wanted to be captured alive by the red raiders of the Staked Plain. Their bites were made from wolf poison—strychnine mostly—rolled into a paper cartridge. Ready for a man to shove between his teeth and bite if he found himself hopelessly surrounded and about to be taken.

."Jesus, Mary and Joseph—I don't know where they was. Maybe they didn't even carry one."

"You got yours?"

Dixon patted a pocket. "My mama didn't waste her cooking on no feebleminded children." He sighed, wiping his sweating palms off on the fronts of his britches. "We'll know next time to listen to that shit about the Injuns coming—won't we, Jimmy?"

"Damn if I didn't try to get everyone up."

Dixon nodded, a grim look to his dark eyes. "That business with the ridgepole was a good'un, Jimmy. So, you doing any good with that Sharps I gave you?"

Hanrahan gazed at it. "Everyone else has a rifle now but Sheppard. Still, the worse thing is we're running out of ammunition for what guns we do have. Scarcer than a harpsichord playing choir music in a Dodge City whorehouse."

Dixon nodded without humor, grim-lipped as he said, "My cartridges left over at Rath's store."

The saloonkeeper grinned. "So—where you figure the odds are in us making it, Billy? Over to Myers's? Or run for Rath's?"

He bit softly on the inside of his cheek, wishing he had another slice of chew right now to nestle beside his tongue. He was hot and thirsty and . . .

"Rath's. 'Sides, that's where the most ammunition is right now—just come down from Dodge. You fixing on coming, Jimmy?"

He nodded. "You and I see things through the same keyhole, my friend. I figure there's gotta be at least two of us go. Carry back enough ammunition to make that run worthwhile."

The far side of the room erupted with cheers.

Hiram Watson turned to yell over to them, "Billy Ogg just dropped one of the sonsabitches. Shot his pony clean out from under 'im."

At that same wall James McKinley announced that another warrior was racing in for a rescue on a white pony. Dixon got to the east wall just as the rider swept by the unhorsed warrior, heaving him up behind him. They wheeled about in a spray of dust as Ogg and McKinley trained their rifles on the pair. Ogg's gun roared first, the bullet striking a rear leg of the white pony.

It faltered, nearly spilling the rump rider desperately clutching the first warrior. They both began to frantically whip the pony toward the far meadow and safety atop the staggering three-legged animal.

"You ready?" Hanrahan asked.

Billy sucked a hot, bitter breath down his throat. The acrid taste of burnt gunpowder choked him. "Ready. Go out the door—or the window?"

Hanrahan shrugged, figuring it on his own. "I allow as how we can be at a full run better coming out that door." He motioned to the west.

Dixon considered. "I'll take the window. It's a straight shot to Rath's."

"All right, we'll do it," Hanrahan agreed. "After you, young'un."

"I'm taking odds on ol' Hanrahan beating Dixon to Rath's store!" shouted Bermuda Carlisle, stirring up the rest.

"Hah! He'll hoof about as awkward as a bear in a bramble patch!" Billy Ogg replied with a snort. "I'll take some of that! Twenty dollars says Dixon beats Hanrahan!"

"Fifty says Dixon don't!" Oscar Sheppard piped up.

"Shit, you're crazy!" McKinley chimed in. "Another twenty on Billy. Sometimes a man just don't know what another can do until it comes down to the nut-cutting."

Dixon didn't listen to the rest of the wagering. He had himself pressed against the earth wall beside the wide window . . . then flung himself through it and was on the ground, hitting the dirt at a dead run, trying hard to remember if he had even touched the windowsill on his way out and down.

It did not matter now, for he could hear the pounding of his own heart. No—it was the hammering of Hanrahan's boots right behind him. The older man was huffing like a steam locomotive. And the raspy howl of his own breath as he closed on the Rath store reminded Billy of a buffalo bull bellowing in the rut.

With some surprise he realized he really was hollering, his throat burning from the torture. And Hanrahan was yelling right at Dixon's shoulder.

Lord, that old man has long legs, Billy thought as Hanrahan surged ahead.

"Open the goddamned door!" shrieked the saloon-keeper as the air around them whistled and whined, snarling bullets beginning to smack the earth wall ahead of them like hands slapping wet clay.

"Jesus, Mary and Joseph—Hanrahan!" Billy crowed as the doorway ahead of them opened like a blessing from St. Peter and God Himself. "Can you ever run for a old man!"

17

June 27, 1874

If nothing else, Masterson had sand.

Donegan had been the one to hold the door ready to open as the young hunter sprinted across the open ground from Hanrahan's saloon.

"He's my best friend in Dodge," Bat huffed, still breathless as he knelt to cradle Billy Tyler's head in his lap, wiping some blood from Tyler's lips with the sleeve of his grimy long-handles.

"He called for you special," said the oldest man there, Billy Keeler. "Times like this for a man, he wants his friends around."

Masterson eased some of Tyler's long hair out of the youth's eyes. "I'm here now, Billy. 'm here."

Seamus thought he saw some real gratitude there in Tyler's eyes—Masterson's only reply.

With the sun rising ever higher in the midsummer sky, the morning had dragged on and on interminably. With the doors closed and not a breeze stirring, the men in the Myers store began to suffer, most in stony silence. To Seamus, it felt hot enough to render a panful of lard from a single flea, as if every pore in his body were opened and leaching. Even on that stinking island six summers back, Forsyth's men had themselves a breeze, he recalled. Then he remembered how the flies and beetles and spiders had found the dead horses and the oozy wounds of the men. And then evening came with its blessing of sundown, substituting the noise of Cheyenne gunfire for the buzzing curse of winged torment. Mosquitoes.*

But right now, he'd take those mosquitoes—if he could only have the cool, have that breeze moving down into the valley of the Arickaree even with the noisy torment on wing.

"Hot as a Dutch oven with my baking-powder biscuits burning," Keeler muttered on the far side of Masterson.

"He could use some water," Bat said, running a fingertip over Tyler's slack, parched lips.

"Wounded man always needs more water'n the rest," Seamus said, remembering how the wounded hollered or whimpered from those rifle pits, stretched out beneath a relentless sun that baked Beecher Island.

"Billy needs some water," Masterson said again, a little more anxious this time.

He pulled himself out from under the wounded hunter and crabbed over to a wooden bucket. He looked in to find it all but empty. In a crouch he scurried for the west door.

"B-Bat?"

"Hold up, Masterson," Donegan ordered.

Keeler stopped the young hunter at the same time. "Tyler wants you."

"Don't go, Bat," Tyler implored his friend. "I took it in the lights out there . . . the stockade."

"I gotta, Billy," Masterson replied, filled with youthful bravado. "You need water."

Keeler wrenched the bucket's rope handle from Masterson. "You're staying with Tyler."

"No I ain't—"

Donegan pulled Masterson back down. "Do as Keeler tells you, Bat. No man gonna think less of you for staying with Tyler. Besides, we'll tell you if you're standing a little short around here."

"Don't you see—them Cheyenne know me, Bat," Keeler

* The Plainsmen Series, vol. 3, *The Stalkers*

tried to explain. "They might'n give me a break—but none to a dad-blamed stranger to 'em like you."

The old cook creaked to his feet, leaned against the door a moment, gazing through a bullet-splintered hole in the planks, then pushed the door open just as Keeler's black dog dove out between its owner's legs. The cook stumbled, nearly sprawling, but caught himself as the bucket went tumbling and the west wall of the stockade erupted in a fury of gunfire.

As Donegan watched and the dog whimpered in its death throes, Keeler picked himself up and dashed for the well, threw the bucket in and hauled it back out as the top of the stockade wall continued to spit fire and belch a gray pall of smoke. The bullets sang around the lithe old man as he sprinted back to the store. Earth erupted in tiny volcanoes, slapped the earth wall ahead of him, splattered against the plank door that Donegan thrust open to admit Keeler.

Then the old man handed the bucket to Masterson and collapsed against the wall. He began to laugh.

"Son of a whore," he exclaimed, his brown tongue licking at the graying beard and mustache that was tobacco-stained yellow around his thin-lipped mouth. "Them bastards hauled Hell out of its shuck . . . but I made it whole. By God—I'm still whole, ain't I?"

"That's right, you bone-rack crowbait," growled Dutch Born. "Cain't believe you made it back."

Donegan was chuckling with him. "No one else as lucky as you, Keeler. No one else would ever made it to the well —and you come humping back here without spilling a bleeming drop!"

"Should've been whiskey, by God!" Mike McCabe growled.

"Been whiskey I was bringing back, them Injun's aim been a lot better, I'd wager!" Keeler bellowed. He wagged his head, as if still stunned that he had made it.

"Don't be so damned surprised," Seamus told him.

He looked up at the Irishman, his eyes alive and sparkling, more young than the wrinkled flesh around them. "Shit, son—it's just that I couldn't *not* go. Don't you see?

I've lived many a year and I've come to know most men are often betrayed by their weaknesses."

"No man would've thought less of you if you hadn't gone, Keeler," Born said.

The old cook smiled at them, seeing their new respect in those eyes. But what was more, Donegan figured, was the new respect Keeler had for himself.

"I know what you mean about a man doing what he fears most doing," Donegan replied quietly, patting the old man's knee and then moving away to rump back against the wall.

"Here, Billy," Masterson said to Tyler as he dragged a greasy bandanna from his neck, dipped it in the cool water and bathed the wounded man's face.

"Gimme a drink—wouldya, Bat?"

Keeler handed Masterson a cup, and Bat propped Tyler's head up as he drank. When Billy had enough, he gazed up into Masterson's eyes and sputtered away from the cup.

"Thankee, Bat. You been the best friend I ever had."

Then ever so slowly as they all watched, Billy Tyler's eyes rolled back and closed, his head collapsing against Bat Masterson's shoulder.

After a few minutes Donegan inched closer. "He's dead, Bat."

Masterson was some time in answering as the nearby rattle of gunfire continued, unabated, rising then falling. "I know." He sighed, touching his friend's gray, waxy face. "I . . . I just wanna sit here with him for a while."

Donegan patted the young hunter on the shoulder before he moved off again. He felt like he might cry if he didn't. As hard as he was having to fight off screaming Comanche and the rest, Seamus was also having to fight off crying. Young men dying on damn fool errands. If it weren't some young soldier riding off on an Indian campaign, then it was a young buffalo hunter come to make his fortune in hides.

He choked on the gall of that. Remembering he had come to this valley to find his own fortune. And it would likely mean his life. What did he have to show for these years?

Times such as these always nudged a remembrance in him that he had again stretched his good fortune about as thin as spider silk.

Then Seamus tried squeezing that dark brooding from the front of his mind. He had been through all of this before—and what it always forced him to think on. But after all this time and all these years and battles and blood and scars, he still didn't have any better an answer. How many times had he gallantly or reluctantly bellied up to stare death in the eye—so many times a naive young soldier blue charging forward through smoke thicker than a hickory ham shed in Virginia's Shenandoah Valley, bellowing at the top of his lungs and waving cold steel at the end of his arm, ordered forward whenever the Confederate artillery had paused to cool its sooty throats?

It was times like this that such fears gathered back around the Irishman, in gentle wind whispers of a moment when he was forced once more to soberly betake his innermost doubts on those yesterday trails not put beneath the heels of his big boots, forced to consider the sour forks of the road not taken, and the path that had brought him here.

Why, oh why hadn't he chosen the simple path that Uncle Ian had taken? It was a life he had watched others earn, the life he himself probably wanted as much as any down in the core of him, a life that had so far eluded him—

"Listen!" Ed Trevor shouted above the clamor in the store.

"Sounds like someone chopping wood," said James Campbell.

"Coming from the Scheidler wagon, boys," Charley Armitage said. "That'un them bastards tipped over for a barricade."

"Chopping through the bottom, I'll bet," Frenchy put in.

"You figure they're making loopholes to shoot at us?" asked Seth Hathaway.

"Naw. Them red devils is pilfering through the

171

Scheidlers' plunder. Kinda like them—rather steal than fight," answered Dutch Born.

"Lookee," said Fred Leonard. "C'mere—you can see 'em hacking on it with their tomahawks. Five of 'em."

Several of the others huddled at Leonard's loophole.

"Let's give 'em a greeting," Leonard suggested.

Armitage and Born stuffed their barrels through the pickets with Leonard, then Fred counted.

"One, two, three—fire!"

Each bullet hit a target, sending splinters and a spray of flour into the air, along with one cry of pain. Two warriors burst onto their feet and sprinted a retreat.

"Lookit them run, will you?" exclaimed Keeler as the riflemen reloaded.

Suddenly a sixth figure arose from the bullet-riddled wagon and took off in a crouch.

"It's a goddamned nigger!" yelled Trevor.

"Nigger's painted up just like a Comanche, he is!" Hathaway said.

"That's the sonofabitch blowing the goddanged bugle!" shouted Born. "Shoot him, Fred!"

Leonard shoved his rifle into Armitage's hands. "You're a better shot—take him!"

Charley did not wait to be nudged into it. He stuffed the loaded .40-caliber Sharps through the wall, drew his bead down on the coffee-skinned back and glittering trumpet slung over the runner's shoulder, and squeezed back on the trigger.

The Sharps roared, belching smoke as the white men set up a cheer. The renegade pitched forward as if hammered by a mule hoof, spilling a tin cup filled with sugar and another filled with coffee that he had tried to carry away in each hand.

"You drilled him clean through the lights!" McCabe hollered, dancing a bit of a jig, his long red hair flying.

"That'll end his damned music," Born sighed. "Hate bugle music, I do. Always did, matter of fact."

Another darky, Seamus thought grimly. What was it that led men like them to abandon the life they had and go over to the blanket? What made a former soldier for the Negro

172

Cavalry join up with the Comanche? Was life so bad for a darky on this southern frontier that he'd just up and go over to the h'athens that way, given the chance? And as that thought rambled through Donegan, it pricked a memory he had long held buried below the surface of many fears.

Jack O'Neill—the mulatto who had tracked Donegan for the better part of a year, so the story was told years ago in those forts of western Kansas. O'Neill, who had become a Cheyenne Dog Soldier and run with Roman Nose, until Forsyth dogged their backtrail long enough that the Cheyenne and Brule Sioux were forced to turn around and fight.* The mulatto who had come closer to killing Donegan than any man before him—with the exception of that smooth-faced Confederate officer who had carved a long slice along the Irishman's back with Toledo steel. Had it not been for Bill Cody taking care of that giant Jack O'Neill,† Seamus knew he would not be hunkered here in this hot, stinking hellhole, fighting off the Comanches.

How many times had he promised himself to get away from putting his life on the line as it was at this moment? How many more times would it come down to the nut-cutting—them or he?

"Lookee here now," Frenchy said from his loophole. "One brave bastard riding in close to count his coup on this here building."

Seamus stirred, thankful to have his thoughts yanked from O'Neill and that brush with his own mortality. Perhaps it was time to do more than think about making a change in his life. To consider settling down with a woman who could keep him pleased. Someone who would take his mind off chasing this pot of gold. Just like Sharp Grover himself had said before: true wealth is found in a man's own happiness, not in the depth of his pockets.

Her vision swam before him, looking willing and warmer and all the softer than spring wind. Samantha even loved poetry. How many women had ever asked him to recite

* The Plainsmen Series, vol. 3, *The Stalkers*
† The Plainsmen Series, vol. 4, *Black Sun*

some for them? Not one since Boston Towne, where as a youngster he first memorized what was in the books on that shelf in the tawdry house men visited after dark. Samantha Pike had listened to his words as if they were songs of love between only them. And he remembered how she had seemed to touch something deep and long submerged within him as she rocked atop his rigid manhood.

No, it wasn't only the all-consuming physical draining she took of him—she had looked down at him with those moist lips and teal eyes of hers and a smile that would crack glacial rock, moving atop him as he caressed and kissed her suspended breasts—begging him to whisper more poetry to her. Faith, but she had touched a part of him not touched before.

Few men could walk away from a woman like that. And he had. But had he come away whole? A man was bound to leave something of themselves behind with a woman like Samantha Pike. Maybe he had left something with Jennifer Wheatley as well. Maybe his willingness to trust, to have faith in another. If not a willingness to trust Samantha, then perhaps he had sacrificed his willingness to trust in himself. But she had been willing to heal him, to allow him time to let the poison seep out of the wound caused by another. She had trusted in him. He had felt it from the first. Samantha Pike had completely, irrevocably, and irretrievably trusted in him.

As he joined the rest peering through the loopholes, they watched a lone warrior loping his pony in a weaving pattern, heading straight for the Myers store. He carried a shield near the top of his left arm, and in his right hand, a huge Walker Colt.

No one thought to shoot at the solitary warrior as the horseman approached, likely stunned at this show of courage. But when the Indian made it to the southeast corner of the wall, he promptly and without ceremony shoved his pistol through an opening in the mud chinking and emptied the Walker Colt.

The store filled with noise and more blinding gun smoke from the Walker Colt, bullets rattling off tables and clanging against tin plates, crashing through expensive bone china that tinkled over tin cups and broken glass oil-lamp globes. But not one of the six bullets hit its mark—none of the white men were hit.

"Don't let that one ride off!" Born shouted, drawing a bead on the horseman. "The rest will get their balls swolled up to come in and try that shit too."

At twenty yards from the store Born's shot knocked the warrior off his pony. As the animal pranced away, the courageous Indian struggled to his feet and began walking—calmly, deliberately, for the hide ricks not far away.

"Die, you red bastard!" Fred Myers growled as his bullet hit the warrior.

"Right through his bellows!" Armitage cheered.

This time the Indian fell to his knees, collapsing onto his side. Pulling another pistol from his breechclout belt, he pressed it into his mouth. Yanked back on the trigger. A spray of gore and blood splattered the grass as the brave warrior convulsed, then lay still.

Things got quiet for a while as the white men settled back against their grain sacks and barrels of trade goods, each of them considering that singular act of bravery. Outside, the warriors would yelp and holler, firing occasionally as the afternoon wore on. With hot breeze hissing past his face, Donegan wondered if he would have the nerve to put a pistol in his own mouth when the time came. Nerve enough when the warriors swept over the walls. Nerve enough to pull the trigger and blow his own brains out.

And all of this doubt come now, regretting that not once had he given Samantha any idea how deeply she had touched him. That was the worst part of his curse and this fear he felt—unable to tell a woman just how vulnerable he was to her. How many times had drink been nothing more than something to kill the despair he felt for not being able to talk of what lay in his heart? How many times had whiskey been something to dull the sadness and loneliness never far from haunting him in those sober moments?

"Wish we knew how things was with the others," McCabe said absently.

"I figure they're holding out," Donegan replied, glad once more not to be alone with his thoughts. "Hear gunfire still coming from the direction of the saloon. And some gunfire beyond it. Who was over there in Rath's last night, besides Olds and his wife?"

"Langton and Eddy, no doubt," said Leonard. Then he growled, "They work for Rath. Son of a bitch, Rath is—running out and knowing about this attack coming."

"Anyone else with 'em?" asked Trevor.

"Probably Andy Johnson and Sam Smith. They been working for Rath," Hathaway commented.

Donegan looked around. "Where's O'Keefe? You figure the Injins got him? He wasn't over to the saloon when the first dance of the grand ball was called."

Masterson shook his head. "No, he weren't at Hanrahan's. But I remember seeing him hotfooting it to Rath's when the whole shebang got started."

Donegan sighed, chuckling a bit. "Been quite a dance, ain't it, boys?" Then he clucked, eyes narrowing. "Shame, it is. Over there at Rath's—they're poor on riflemen right now. By the saints, I do pray they'll fare well."

No one said anything for a long time after that. And Seamus figured they were doing some praying like he was, each man in his own way.

He laid his head back against the sod and closed his red, smoke-burned eyes for a moment. Outside, for that moment, the sounds faded, thankfully. He thought again of Samantha, easily—then grew irritated again as the memory of her got all jumbled up like snarled latigo with the memory of another who had come through his life before—the woman who had promised, then withdrawn her love and left him high on the Bozeman Road. Jennifer Wheatley.*

A man wasn't supposed to be ruined by love. A man was just expected to find it easy mending a broken heart. And still no one would ever know how long and hard he had despaired of vanished dreams. Unable to free himself of her memory—of Jennifer Wheatley's wild sort of softness that day as she bathed in the waters of Piney Creek, the sun shimmering off her auburn hair like red fire. A vision

* The Plainsmen Series, vol. 2, *Red Cloud's Revenge*

of her beauty that for all the intervening years had grown to become more and more unsettling and unnerving.

He squeezed his eyes tightly. It helped some of the burning. Hid a few of the silent tears. One day, should he make it out of this bloody meadow, he would tell Samantha. Some way to find the words to tell her of the others. And then his need for her swelled in him like a tangible thing.

Damn, but one of them had to be the answer.

Then the noisy crow was back at the doorway, cawing loudly. He smiled. And it felt good. How that huge black bird had survived the long and bloody morning, he had no idea.

There's been plenty of death for you already, he thought. Go now. Why don't you fly far away now and be satisfied?

It made Donegan's stomach go cold, looking at that big, sleek, black bird nestled on a wooden shelf, cocking its head as it stared directly at him. And he remembered Reuben Waller telling him about crows. How the black bird was a harbinger of death.

So why does this black bastard keep coming back to stare at me?

18

June 27, 1874

Dixon watched Hanrahan go, bolting through the door and sprinting across the open, dusty ground as fast as a man could who was carrying two burlap sacks of cartridges for the riflemen over in the saloon. Billy was staying put.

As soon as the two had flung themselves into Charley Rath's store, the defenders had begun begging one or both of them to stay. None of the six already there was that good a shot. Besides, they pleaded with Dixon, there was Hannah to think of. Billy had gazed a moment over at the old woman's prairie-wrinkled face as she knelt beside her husband, and decided then and there he would stay.

Billy vowed that if the warriors overran the store, he would be the one to kill the woman rather than allow her to fall into the hands of those warriors. Hannah Olds could have been his mother.

As soon as the spouts of dirt were no longer kicked up around Hanrahan's boots, and the saloonkeeper lunged through the door opened to welcome his return to the soddy saloon, Billy turned back to gaze around the store and its defenses. The others had done a good job of it, piling sacks of grain and beans, along with a few kegs along the walls. In those furious first minutes, someone had kicked over the slop pail that had been sitting next to Hannah's stove. Sometimes now, when the breeze might move just right, the air stunk of old grease gone rancid. From a far-off corner came a whiff of something thick and oily— the smell of kerosene pitch. Likely spilled or bullet-riddled.

For now it seemed like a long-distance waiting game. With the warriors abandoning their horses and taking up positions to snipe at the three buildings while the hunters and skinners and cooks and clerks hid in the shadows, every man jack of them growing hotter and hotter still as the summer sun climbed relentlessly into a pale Panhandle sky.

From time to time the warriors seemed to act in concert, firing heavy volleys that proved to be the signal for their wounded among the grass and brush to retreat. Then the air would grow still again for a long while and Billy could hear the arrival of another horse from the meadow. He wagged his head sadly. Horses being the gregarious sort of creature they were, any company was better than none whatsoever. So it was that the animals belonging to the hide men had been wandering back to the buildings all morning, most of them already seriously wounded, yet returning to the sod walls knowing this was where they would find a master, perhaps in some dull-witted way hoping for someone to relieve their suffering. Some of the horses and mules whinnied or hawed in their pain. Others had fallen and thrashed more quietly near the sod walls.

From time to time Billy could hear the warrior bullets hit the big animals, smacking like sodden putty. Breath driven out of him with every wound until the screeching animal fell. Until there were no more animals left standing outside those three earth buildings. The Indians had seen to it there would be no chance of escape come nightfall.

"What time you figure, Billy?" asked Andy Johnson quietly.

Time had clearly stiffened that afternoon, sun sulled like it was in the sky. Dixon studied the quality of light coming through the window and over the transom just above the place where he lay. "Figure it's getting on to four o'clock, Swede."

"I reckon you're right as tits on a sow's belly," Johnson replied. "Makes me spooky, this quiet."

With that reminder, Dixon realized the firing from the meadow had slackened considerably. For so long the guns had rattled incessantly that he had grown numb to it.

"You figure they're up to something?" asked Tom O'Keefe, the blacksmith.

"Do turkey buzzards eat strange meat?" Billy answered with a shrug, the cold sweat down his backbone finally starting to dry. "I think they've learned the hard way about our guns. They know that we hit what we aim for."

"That, and our guns shoot far," Johnson added. "We been shooting the billy-be-hell out of 'em, and I haven't seen any gun smoke from their side except a long ways off. Looks to me like them red devils is pulling back a ways and staying quiet as hay-bale mice."

"Got out from under our goddamned guns is what they're doing," Sam Smith exclaimed, one man as homely as blue sin.

"I'll get me a good look," Dixon said, craning his neck to look up the stack of feed sacks the others had piled near the door at the north end of the west wall of the store. It was there that construction supervisor Andy Johnson had cut a crude transom over the door. As there was no glass for it, the transom had remained open.

Sack by sack, with the borrowed .50-caliber Sharps in hand, Billy made his way to the top of the door and peered out, squinting into the late afternoon light, still brilliant at this time of year. From south to north he screwed his eyes across the western extent of the meadow that stretched toward a line of low, rugged, buzzard-bone bluffs. Across the flat ground lay a litter of wagons, hide ricks, dead horses, mules and ponies. Besides a few of the dozen or so brown bodies that Dixon could see from his wobbly perch. Those, the warriors abandoned where they fell, too close to the white man's guns.

As his eyes slowly crawled back from north to west, Billy vowed he wanted to remember this scene well, to mark it in his heart, if not sear it in his memory—

He saw something stir in the tall grass . . . eight hundred yards off toward those low ridges. Eight hundred at least. He squinted, shading his eyes with one hand. Sure enough, something was moving through the grass out there. About all there *was* moving out there for the time being.

Carefully, he dragged the Sharps up from under his leg and poked the barrel through the transom.

"You see something?" O'Keefe asked.

"Maybe so."

"Shoot the red bastard where he looks the biggest," said old man Olds.

Feeling uneasy about his wobbly perch, Dixon brought up the rear sight and quickly gauged his windage. Then squeezed back on the trigger.

He was abruptly shoved backward with a grunt, toppled by the recoil of the powerful weapon. He came down in a clatter of washtubs, tin cups, china dishes and a shower of dust.

"Oh, God—Dixon's shot!" George Eddy shouted to the others as he rushed over to the young buffalo hunter.

"I ain't hurt, dammit!"

"You shot, Billy?" asked James Langton as the rest hurried around him, looking down as Dixon lay in a heap at the bottom of the pile of grain and flour sacks.

"Nothing hurt but my pride," Billy snorted. "Got knocked off my set is all."

O'Keefe and Johnson helped him up, dusted Dixon off.

"There's something out there I need to find out about," Billy said as he turned to make his way back to the top of the stacks.

At the transom, this time he carefully adjusted the top

two sacks, eased down among them so that when the recoil hit his shoulder, he would not lose his balance. Finding his far-off target still crawling through the tall grass, making for the distant trees, Dixon took his sight picture, held, and pulled the trigger.

"Jesus, Mary and Joseph," he muttered.

"You hit it?" O'Keefe asked.

"No, dammit," Dixon growled. "Saw where my bullet went, though. Held a hair too high on the bastard."

"In a pig's eye—you'll get 'im this time," cheered Sam Smith.

Dixon loaded again, then nestled his cheek along the stock a third time. When the pungent smoke again drifted from the transom, he stared at the far grass, eight hundred yards distant. Nothing moved. He waited the longest time, watching, thinking his eyes might be playing tricks on him. Still nothing moved.

"S'pose I got 'im," Dixon said.

There was a sudden cheer from the rest. He turned and grinned down at them, watching the dance of William Olds's Adam's apple up and down the thin cords of his wrinkled neck. Ex-Confederate Sam Smith, who had fought with Hood, was he-coon yelling, ki-yipping and slapping his leg.

It was something short-lived, but joyous just the same. For too long that day they had been without reason to celebrate.

In the shade of a plum thicket, Quanah Parker had laid out of the sun for the middle of the day. Now the great orb had slipped from mid-sky and was halfway on its journey toward its nightly rest.

Over the hours, feeling had returned to his shoulder and arm. Each time he had put his hand back to touch the shoulder blade, his fingers had come away with very little blood. So it had made him wonder—so much pain, this wound that took away the use of his arm . . . yet no great flow of blood.

But, that wondering was nothing compared to his anger and confusion, thinking how it was that he had been shot.

Over and over he had attempted to put the pieces of it together, like the cleaning of each piece to the Walker Colt his father gave him as a youth. The horse had been shot out from under him, and when Quanah had taken refuge behind an old buffalo carcass that wood rats had nested high with weeds, it was there the bullet had struck him.

By the time a half-dozen young Kwahadis had come to rescue him from the plum thicket where he had crawled, the war chief was convinced one of the Indians had tried to kill him.

So with his piece of red blanket, Quanah had called back his warriors, assembling the war chiefs for an immediate council. He demanded of his lieutenants to know who would be courageous enough to confess their poor marksmanship, if not their dark intent. With mutual distrust, every man there denied shooting the Kwahadi chief.

"This is a day for evil medicine," Isatai declared, quick in his attempt to make up for the failure of his prophecy. "The white man makes evil medicine over his guns."

In that anxious, frustrated circle of war chiefs gathered in safety behind the crest of a low hill, that explanation made as much sense as anything. Not able to understand anything having to do with ballistics and ricocheting bullets, the Indian grasped onto what he could fathom: the evil ways of the white man and what dark spells the buffalo hunters could put upon their weapons.

"Perhaps," Quanah said finally, seeing all eyes on him as he carefully volved the wounded, prickly-numb shoulder. "It is as I thought while I waited in the plum brush. Perhaps the white man has made him a fearful new weapon that fires bullets that can circle around and shoot a man in the back."

Then he glanced at Isatai, finding on the young shaman's yellow face something new. No longer was there the face of haughty arrogance staring back at him. Isatai realized his claim of power had been found to be impotent.

. "The Cheyenne," Isatai grumbled, his eyes gone wild and feral as they dodged from chief to chief. "They have ruined my medicine!"

"You are no shaman! You no longer have the special

skunk medicine to make bullets into water!" retorted Hippy, a Cheyenne war chief. "There are many good men dead because of your foolishness!"

"Yes!" shouted Elk Shoulder, another Cheyenne. "We should kill you ourselves, rather than let the white man do it for us!"

"You Cheyenne are to blame," Isatai argued. "One of you . . . yes—you," he pointed. "It was you who killed the skunk on the way here. I ordered you not to."

"You are without courage!" Elk Shoulder shouted. "My own son is killed. Down in that meadow. Will your medicine protect you, Isatai? Will you go recover his body?"

"You Cheyenne ruined my medicine!"

Elk Shoulder spat on Isatai's bare, ocher-painted leg, which hung off the side of the yellow pony. The shaman stared a moment at the spittle as it slowly oozed down his flesh.

The Cheyenne's voice rumbled with foreboding as he inched toward the Comanche shaman. "If you are truly powerful, go down to that meadow and bring me the body of my son. Then I will believe the words of your mouth."

"Will you Cheyenne not listen?" Isatai roared, stunning them all. "When you killed the skunk, you destroyed my personal medicine with the Spirit Above. I am not to blame—"

With a loud splat and a muffled scream of surprise and pain, a bullet hit the yellow painted pony Isatai sat upon, squarely in the head.

Backing away suddenly, several of the war chiefs clamped hands over their mouths while Isatai scrambled from his pony as it crumpled to the ground.

"Aiyeee!"

"The white man shoots us when we cannot see him!"

Now even Quanah was frightened. This was the second time this day that he had experienced such evil from the white man's guns. First he was hit by a bullet than skulked around behind him and struck from the back. And now, as they sat talking behind a hill, a bullet came out of nowhere and killed Isatai's pony. This was truly powerful magic. And he loathed his white blood all the more for it.

Hippy had his elk-antler quirt swinging at the end of his arm as he closed on Isatai, his eyes filled with hate, his face as black as a coming thunderstorm. "What's the matter with your medicine now, shaman? It cannot save you from white man's bullets—nor will it save you from the beating I'm going to deliver!"

Quanah and two of the older Cheyenne chiefs stepped in front of Hippy and Elk Shoulder as more of the young warriors surged forward to give Isatai the beating they all felt the shaman deserved.

"Look before you!" Quanah ordered them. "See how he is already shamed. His medicine is like water now. His shame is enough. Let it be enough that Isatai will have to live out all his days with this disgrace."

"The little ones will know of his shame!" Hippy vowed.

"Yes, long will the little ones know of the mistakes made this day," Quanah agreed.

More than two dozen warriors lay dead—half of them right under the muzzles of the white man's guns where the Kwahadi could not rescue the bodies. Twice that many were wounded, already dragged from the meadow to the safety of the timber where the women could nurse the wounds, or there await the certain death that would greet some before night fell this long, bloody day.

"Quanah!"

He turned, finding the face of his young friend, Timbo. Halting close, Timbo dismounted. The four warriors with him reined up but did not dismount.

"We have another dead friend, Quanah," Timbo said.

"You rescued his body from the white man's—"

"No," Timbo interrupted, his eyes frightened like a small animal's. Those eyes glanced quickly to the others, then came back to rest on the war chief. "Quanah, he was not killed attacking the earth lodges. The six of us, we were there," he said, pointing a little to the north. "Behind those hills. Sitting in a circle, talking of our plans—how to rescue the bodies of our friends. When we had decided on a plan, we leaped atop our ponies . . . and that is when the bullet struck. We did not hear it, Quanah! These bul-

184

ets from the white man's guns come and we do not hear them! This bullet killed—"

Quanah embraced the trembling young warrior suddenly, silencing him. "There is evil in the tai-bos' guns. That they can shoot bullets we do not hear coming. That these guns kill us behind trees and hills . . . no man is safe from such evil."

Timbo struggled a moment with himself, then appeared to regain his composure. "We will take my friend to the women."

"This is all you can do now," Quanah replied quietly. "Perhaps it is all any of us can do now—to mourn our dead."

Those rifles of the white man had proved potent. Far more powerful than the strength of Isatai's medicine, stronger even than the will of the young Kwahadi war chief to drive the tai-bos from this land. Yes, he was angry—but not only angry at the white man. There was little to celebrate. Two scalps and a little food found among the wagons they had looted. A few horses had been captured, but far too many had been killed during the first few fiery minutes of battle at dawn. And now the brown grass in that meadow was littered not only with the carcasses of animals, but far too many puddles of crimson stained the trampled bluestem and bunchweed of this evil place.

Not that long ago the hundreds of horsemen had been filled with heart to overrun this place of the hide men. But now, having found the white men awake and not to be clubbed in their sleep, finding the guns far-shooting, finding the white men unwilling to come out of their earth-walled burrows . . . all the fight had seeped out of the warriors like milk from a cracked bowl Quanah had discovered inside a settler's soddy two summers before. Never had any fight gone this badly, for this long.

As if the white man's hand had cruelly ripped it from his breast, Quanah sensed the heart had clearly gone out of his people.

19

June 27, 1874

"It's over," Donegan said quietly.

He rose to his feet, his hung-over head throbbing as he peered through a loophole in the pickets where that morning they had knocked loose the dried mud. Clearly, it appeared the warriors had disappeared like rain splatter fallen into deep and thirsty dust.

"I think the Irishman may be right," Dutch Born agreed. "Listen."

"I don't hear a thing," replied Charley Armitage.

"That's just what I mean," Born said.

"Ain't been much shooting to speak of for some time," added the old man, Keeler.

"Don't see much moving around out there," Fred Leonard said from his post at the wall.

"Only Injuns I seen for better'n a hour," said Mike McCabe, "is them dead'uns spraddled on the grass."

"You fought with the Yankees, didn't you, Irishman?" asked Keeler, his top lip serrated with deep wrinkles as he tongued his brown cud of tobacco.

Seamus grinned. "It shows, does it?"

"I can tell you been under fire a whole danged lot, Irishman. And top of that, I never knowed a Irishman what fought for the Confederacy. S'pose I can add as good as the next fella."

"Second Cavalry."

"Sheridan's Army of the Potomac," Keeler replied, then let go with a low whistle. "Damn if a strange dog don't get his ass sniffed. You was with Little Phil in the Shenandoah too, weren't you?"

Donegan nodded. "Never figured out why the last fighting in a war like that is always the bloodiest."

"Same in a scrap with Injuns," added Armitage as he strode to the west door. He cracked it cautiously, setting one eye into the opening.

"See anything?" Born asked.

"Just this dead Injun Tyler was dragging back."

"Cheyenne," Donegan told them.

"So you know he's Cheyenne, do you?" McCabe growled. "How's it you so sure?"

"Fought enough of 'em. From the Bozeman Road down to the Arickaree and on to Summit Springs. I know Cheyenne, McCabe."

"Whooooeee, fellas!" cried Keeler. "This Irishman's the genuwine article—one hell of a man come fit with hair on his brisket clean down to his hobbles!"

"Shit," growled the always irritated McCabe, "that don't mean he knows Cheyenne from—"

"There's Bermuda!" Frenchy hollered, keeping watch through the pickets on the south wall.

Some of the others rushed to look too. Another three of them ventured cautiously into the corral, their rifles at ready.

Donegan and Armitage raised the bolt on the huge double doors facing the bare western hills, then slowly drew both doors back into the store, allowing a great, warm wash of the settling light into the building. He breathed deep of the quiet.

"Smells pretty good, don't it?" Armitage asked.

"It will for a while yet," Seamus replied. "We don't do something about these Injin bodies . . . them horse carcasses—before you know it, this place will be stinking like that island where Roman Nose had us pinned down for nine days."

The meadow was littered with the carcasses of fifty-six enemy ponies and ten of the hide men's horses, besides a dozen mules and more than twenty-eight oxen belonging to the Scheidlers—each animal already starting to bloat beneath the summer sun. If a man listened intently enough, he could hear the buzzing and the scritch-scritching of the little things at work already: those flying, crawling, wriggling creatures drawn to the stench of the blood and the gore and the decaying flesh.

Eventually the rest of the defenders at Hanrahan's saloon emerged into the sunlight, following Bermuda Carlisle—the first to bravely make the venture. Some of them turned to holler for Dixon and the rest in Charley Rath's store, urging them out.

"Someone ought'n count the dead Injuns, I s'pose," Keeler suggested as he strode off, appointing himself.

"Only those what's wanting some of the plunder," Armitage replied gruffly. "I figure first off we ought to look to Ike and Shorty." Charlie had known Ike and Shorty for some time and took no small offense that the rest did not concern themselves over their proper and immediate burying.

Donegan, along with James Campbell and Ed Trevor, followed Armitage to the overturned wagons behind which they found the stripped, mutilated bodies of the Scheidler brothers. For the better part of the morning and into the early afternoon, the warriors had flaunted the scalps of the two white men, hoping to enrage the hunters, provoking them into something foolish.

"Lookit that—the red bastards even scalped Shorty's dog," Armitage whimpered as he knelt beside the animal.

"Put up one helluva fight when the Injins found the boys hid under the wagon covers," Donegan said, remembering how the Scheidlers had concealed themselves in those early minutes of the fight as the warriors swarmed into the wagon yard outside Myers's stockade.

Only when two dozen of the horsemen dismounted to pilfer through the wagons did the unsuspecting warriors pull back one of the canvas covers—and were greeted by a blast from Shorty's gun. Ike had bolted from his wagon, sprinting for the stockade, but had not made it far before he was shot, then dragged back to be butchered beside his brother. As the warriors began their mutilation of the warm bodies, the huge, black-furred Newfoundland had done its best to guard the earthly remains of its masters, grittily attacking the butchers. With a pitiful whimper, the Comanche had clubbed the four-legged defender, then scalped it as well as the men. The hound had proved itself a worthy enemy, brave in battle.

Donegan found himself understanding. Then wondered if he had been out here on this mapless frontier a bit too long—if he were now beginning to savvy these first inklings of the Indian mind.

"I'll go fetch us up some shovels," Armitage said before he turned back to the stockade, ashen-faced.

Donegan nodded without a word, then strode off for the open meadow where stood the huge ricks of dried flint hides. The huge gray horse had drawn his attention during the middle of the morning's fight, the way its rider had whirled and dared and taunted the white riflemen. Making of his broad back as much a target as any brave man would in the face of so many muzzles and marksmen. And an animal as big as the gray horse had made itself a dandy target.

As he stood over the carcass, staring down at the green-backed flies buzzing in and out of the ears, eyes and along the open mouth, not to mention how the insects collected among the drying blood, Donegan counted seven bullet wounds in the animal's sides and flanks. Which brought him to remembering The General's last, valiant race that hot summer dawn on the high plains of Colorado Territory before the renegade Bob North brought the great animal down and sent the Irishman sprawling onto a sandy scut of island in the middle of a nameless river where he and Forsyth's scouts fought for their lives across the next nine days.

"You coming to help me?" Armitage shouted from the wagons.

Donegan turned, dragging a hand beneath his dribbling nose, and blinked his stinging eyes. It was all right—this mourning still. A good animal should be remembered and grieved like he would any friend.

Not quite halfway along the north wall of the Myers stockade, Armitage stopped and planted his shovel in the ground. There, working together at the same time, both he and Donegan began digging. From time to time others showed up to relieve them. Small celebrations erupted as the defenders from the saloon and Rath's store eventually wandered over—replete with back-slapping and congratulations. Then the occasion grew sober once more as the somber task of digging a grave for the three men continued into the first deepening hints of early dusk.

As the huge black crow settled silently atop the stockade pickets nearby, cocking its head as if to listen in respectfully, Fred Leonard spoke some words over the graves where they had laid the three bodies side by side in their blankets, shoulder to shoulder. Then James Langton recited some scripture from memory and Sam Smith brought out his mouth harp, knocked it against his palm to clear it of dust from the pocket in his filthy britches, and blew a mournful dirge over that pit yawning now to claim three of their own.

For a few moments the two dozen stood in silence at the edge of the grave, each in his own thoughts. Then the crow grew noisy once more, calling out raucously as it took to flight in a great flapping of its black wings. The men stirred.

"Black bastard," muttered Carlisle as he shoved his felt hat back on his head.

"How many the sonsabitches you count, Bermuda?" Donegan asked the veteran hunter who had been the first to venture from the saloon and claim some of the plunder from the warrior dead.

"We got thirteen of 'em good Injuns now," Carlisle answered. "No telling how many got dragged off or crawled off and died out there in the brush. But, great God in Beulah, we did get thirteen—against these three friends of ours."

"I say the score ain't even then," McCabe growled his protest. "Them thirteen for these three good men. In a way, I hope those sonsabitches do come back tomorrow."

"So let's use what light we got left to make this place tight afore morning," Hanrahan suggested as three men began humping sod back into the grave.

"You raised that black flag over your place, I see," Leonard said to Hanrahan.

"Maybe anyone coming in will see it—figure that we've had trouble."

"If they didn't hear the noise of all these guns," added Seth Hathaway.

"Not a man inside of twenty miles couldn't hear what went on here today," snorted Hiram Watson.

"Let's do as Jimmy says," Dixon told them. "Get water pulled and repairs made before morning."

"And any man needing to reload cartridges better be at it before it gets too dark," Hanrahan warned, glancing at the sun easing down on the western hills. "I don't cotton to the idea of having lamps lit and making targets for ourselves. We ain't got much daylight left."

Dixon came up and stopped beside the Irishman, saying quietly, "I'm worried about Fannie."

Donegan peered around. "She ain't with you all day?"

"She run off when the shooting started. We was there together, me scratching her ears—"

"Come to think of it, I ain't seen any of the other dogs been hanging around here either," Donegan replied, trying to offer hope. "I suppose they ran off for cover." He clamped a hand on the young hunter's shoulder. "She'll come back, Fannie will."

"Found this on a Injun bridle," Dixon said, pulling a scalp from his belt.

"You plundered the bodies too, did you?" Donegan asked as he took the long scalp and held it up to the fading light. Brown, and of a fine texture. "This is a white woman's hair."

Dixon nodded. "The rest got kerchiefs and silver armbands and belt pouches and shields and quirts. All sorts of souvenirs."

"Something for your grandchildren, Billy," Seamus said, handing the scalp back to Dixon.

"Nothing for yours, Irishman?"

He sighed. Then shook his head, thin-lipped. "No. Not this time."

"Dixon made a long shot this afternoon," said Tom O'Keefe as he came up to the pair. "Least eight hundred yards. You ever go out to see about the Injun crawling through that grass, Billy?"

Dixon nodded. "He must've crawled for at least a quarter mile with a busted knee where I shot him. I could follow the blood through the grass from where he was hit until I found his body where I finally killed him."

"Eight hundred yards? That's some shooting," Donegan said.

"Not for Dixon," O'Keefe bragged. "He's one of the best I've seen or even heard tell of in buffalo country."

"That warrior was packed for bear, Seamus," Dixon replied. "I found a pistol in his belt, a bow and quiver of arrows on his shoulder, and in arm's reach I found his shot pouch with fifteen army cartridges in it, along with a powder horn. And I claimed his .50-caliber needle gun, a Springfield—army, it was."

In addition to the thirteen enemy dead, George Eddy tallied the dead horses, mules and oxen stiffening in the fading light. Near the Rath store lay the carcass of the young colt the men had presented to Hannah Olds weeks before, wrapped in the blanket the old woman had sewn to protect her pet from the rapacious mosquitoes. Another victim of the morning's brutal attack.

"How 'bout a whiskey, Irishman?" Dixon asked.

"Not in the mood for drinking like I done last night," Seamus replied, a hint of a grin crossing his smoke-blackened face. "But a whiskey or two would go a long way to smoothing out the wrinkles right now."

"One or two will do nicely, then we'll get settled for the night," Dixon replied as they started for Hanrahan's saloon. The rest were breaking up and heading for one or another of the three buildings. He shuddered noticeably. "I feel like they're watching us."

Donegan stopped and turned, his eyes slowly scanning the western hills. "No doubt of that, Billy. When you don't see the red divils—that's when you know they're watching."

"One horse, just one horse. And I'd ride north for help," Dixon declared as they reached the saloon.

"We'll work on that tomorrow," Donegan replied, knowing the unrelenting tension would be eating at most of the rest come nightfall. Here, in the middle of a great wilderness. Without any way to get word out. But for him, it wasn't the first time. How was he to assure that it would be the last?

"Right now, Billy—let's wash down the dust with this saddle varnish Hanrahan calls whiskey."

It had been a day when their medicine went sour in their mouths.

Lone Wolf had seen enough victories in his life, but lately he had witnessed far too many defeats. Still, there was one day darker than this had been—the morning the Yellow Hair Custer had put the rope around the necks of Satanta and Lone Wolf, threatening to hang the Kiowa chiefs if they did not bring their people in to the reservation at old Fort Cobb.

The old fort was no longer there, in ruins now. Replaced by the soldier camp called Sill. And the Yellow Hair was somewhere on the northern plains now, Lone Wolf was told—harassing and killing the Sioux and Northern Cheyenne.

This was a dark day indeed for the hopes and prayers of the Kiowa. Darker than the day he had learned of the deaths of a son and a nephew. Darker still than the day he and Red Otter had been forced to abandon the two bodies among the rocks as they were pursued by the yellowleg soldiers.

Here in his later years, the old chief felt like a sucked-on plum, no longer with much to celebrate. There were too few horses to steal, and the white man's cattle were too skinny. Besides, there never were enough scalps. And with today's fight, all they had to show for their trouble was a little coffee and sugar, the scalps of two white men and a long strip of fur from a snarling, black dog that had torn up three Kwahadis before it was killed.

The Cheyenne had to be kept from striking Isatai by the Comanche chiefs. They were furious, these Cheyenne. And were saying they were going north on their own to wreak their vengeance on the settlements just beyond their reservation.

It was better, Lone Wolf thought. Find the white man's settlements instead of fighting these hunters burrowed in the shadows of their earth lodges. These men had evil weapons that they fired today and killed tomorrow. Weapons that fired without sound or that shot bullets good at circling behind an enemy. To fight an enemy such as this was a foolish undertaking. Two scalps and the fur of a dog was not enough to make an old warrior like Lone Wolf foolish enough to stay around and try again tomorrow.

True, some of his warriors had the scalps of four of the buffalo hunters they had killed on the way to the earth lodge settlement. The Kiowa had discovered the camp of two men they promptly captured and tortured, tying them down then propping their heads up so the white hide men could watch as they were opened up then had their manhood cut off and stuffed in their lying mouths while burning embers were dropped on their bellies. The next day, his warriors found a camp with two more hunters.

With a snort, Lone Wolf glanced over at the shamed Isatai.

Alone, the Kiowa chief and his warriors had accounted for more scalps than all these hundreds of warriors had taken, with all the powerful medicine and incantations of this yellow-smeared shaman. Were it to do any good, to avenge the deaths of good Comanche and Cheyenne warriors killed this day, Lone Wolf hungered to kill Isatai with his own bare hands. Slowly, slowly choking the life out of the shaman.

The way the white man was slowly, slowly choking the life out of Lone Wolf's people.

20

June 28–29, 1874

More times than he wanted to count, Billy had awakened during that short, summer night, sweating like a lemonade jug in July from the frightening, nightmarish visions he suffered, more than from the sultry heat.

Time and again he had bolted upright, drenched, remembering what had slapped him awake: those dreams of charging horsemen racing toward him across the valley as the first rays of light broke the horizon like bloody, sparkling lances fanning into the sky; the booming of the hunters' guns and the cracks of the Indian weapons; the screams of horses and terrified cries of men; along with the persistent smell of burnt powder and drying blood on the breeze as the day grew old.

And every time he blinked his eyes clear, realizing it was the middle of the night and he was still lying on the dirt floor of Hanrahan's saloon, Dixon found the black silhouette of the long-haired Irishman leaning back against the doorframe, his Henry across his curled legs, a pipe curling shadowy smoke about his head.

Each man to his own thoughts, Dixon brooded as he again found a place for his cheek on a curled arm. Each man, his own demons.

The graying of the sky in the east came sooner than any of them wanted. Billy was the first to stir from his bedroll, awakening Donegan at the doorway where the Irishman had kept his silent vigil through that first dark night.

"Fix us some coffee, Billy," Seamus said, hawking up some night-gather in his throat.

The rest were not long in rising, one by one coming to the loopholes in the walls to have themselves a look at the sky slowly draining of black. A few quickly wandered out into the faint coolness of the predawn to relieve themselves on the dusty, hoof-hammered ground.

"You see anything through the night, Irishman?" Hanrahan asked as he passed Donegan at the door.

"Nor heard a sound."

Hanrahan sighed as Dixon buttoned his britches and came back to join them. The noisy crow fluttered past them, swooping like a bat out of the blackness of night, coming to rest on the carcass of an Indian pony.

"There's not a thing out there alive," Dixon replied quietly. " 'Cept that damned crow."

"It's going to have the feast of its life this day," Donegan said as he set the Henry against the wall and unbuttoned his britches.

"Yeah, that sun comes up—this place is going to stink something fierce," Dixon complained.

After breakfast of hot coffee, pan biscuits and fried meat, the men formed themselves into work details. The greatest problem was in moving the huge carcasses of horse and oxen. Without teams and tackle to perform this heavy work, the men had to improvise sleds from dried hides rigged with ropes, moved with man's muscle. Beneath the rising, relentless sun, they began to roll the bloating carcasses onto the flint hides, then dragged them downwind and as far as possible from the buildings. Three to four men could move a horse or oxen in that manner. But when they began work on a dozen ponies and horses that lay clustered between Rath's store and the saloon, the hide men decided to dig a shallow pit and bury the carcasses right where they were found.

Without any ceremony or sign of joy, the thirteen warrior bodies were dragged off onto the prairie to the west of the buildings and left to the predators that were already being drawn to the feast.

At mid-morning one of the men hollered out, pointing to the bluffs to the east where sat a band of feathered horsemen. While most stood watching, curious and speculating, a few snatched up their heavy rifles and attempted the long-range shot. After the warriors returned some of the desultory fire, they disappeared beyond the top of the ridge.

"We'll show 'em we still got plenty of fight in us," Dixon explained as he brought the big fifty down from his shoulder, watching the last of the horsemen disappear from the distant skyline. The warriors would not be seen for the rest of the day.

"What I wouldn't give for a horse right now," Charlie Armitage sighed.

"Even a old mule," Mike McCabe echoed the lament.

Dixon chuckled. "Anything so you could ride on out of here, eh?"

"Something, anything—to ride, so to get word out," Billy Ogg agreed with the general sentiment.

Despite the fact that they had scared off that last bunch of horsemen, and despite the fact that there had been no renewal of attack at dawn, Dixon realized there hung a specter of gloom over the settlement nonetheless. The men went back to work on the bloating carcasses. It was, after all, something to do. And something to do just might keep their minds off their desperate situation for the moment.

"Riders coming in!"

At the warning from a sentry posted on the roof of Rath's store, Dixon and the rest turned, snatching up their weapons as the first horsemen appeared from the southern treeline. Then a wagon rumbled out of the shadows, and shortly a second wagon materialized out of the shimmering waves of heat rising from the sun-baked prairie. Billy swiped his greasy sleeve across his eyes, clearing them of the stinging sweat.

George Bellfield reined up before the gathering. A German immigrant and Union veteran of the Civil War, he looked over them all, then found Hanrahan among the crowd.

"I tink you play fun on Bellfield," he said in his broken English, tapping a thick finger against his chest.

"Why you say that, George?" Hanrahan asked, inching up.

Bellfield pointed at the top of the saloon as his two skinners brought their wagons to a halt nearby. "We see flag. Black says trouble. Bellfield did not know what trouble you be in, Jimmy."

"Injuns."

Bellfield sniffed the air. He grinned, grimly. "Lots of dead Injuns, eh, fellas?"

"Thank God you're here now," gushed William Olds as he stopped beside Bellfield's mount. "I can get my Hannah out of here on one of your horses."

"We'll figure some way to get her out, Bill," Hanrahan replied, stepping closer to Bellfield.

"You have a goot fight of it, Jimmy?" the German asked.

"Yes."

Bellfield leaned back in the saddle, pulled his hat off and swiped a finger around inside the band. "I see that flag first —say to my boys, 'Dem fellers think dey's damn smart alretty.' But you fellers do all right fighting, eh?"

Hanrahan answered, "Three of us is all they got."

"You see any sign of feather coming in?" Dutch Born asked.

Bellfield wagged his head, then eased out of the saddle. "Notting out there. Can't smell them."

While Bellfield and his skinner set about unhitching their animals and making camp for their outfit, the rest returned to their grisly labors. However, it wasn't long before another crew rolled in from the north—the English brothers, Jim and Bob Cator.

"No, we didn't hear a damn thing," Jim Cator explained.

"Not a shot," agreed Bob Cator.

"How far were you camped from us?" Dixon asked.

"Couldn't been more than twenty, maybe twenty-five miles," answered Jim Cator.

"I don't believe this," Bob Cator sighed. "How do you figure they would have the balls to attack this stronghold— with all of you armed and ready?"

"Armed maybe," Donegan replied. "But we were far from ready, boys."

"I been thinking we ought to send a few of us out to warn some of the other hunting camps in the nearby countryside—let 'em know what the red bastards done here," Hanrahan suggested.

"Spread word that the sumbitches let the wolf out and are coming for scalps," growled Billy Keeler.

Two men volunteered to ride, one east, the other west, both circling back to the north carrying word of the fight. No one dared ride south for the time being.

Dixon cleared his throat as he wiped sweat from his face with a bandanna. "Any way you cut the deck, at least now we got us some horses so we can send for help."

"I'm wanting to go," Henry Lease volunteered as he stepped to the front of the group. One of Bellfield's skinners, Lease had just ridden in. "I'll make the ride north. What you fellas think it's worth?"

"Anyone against Henry going?" asked Jim Hanrahan, peering around the group.

When no one opposed Lease, Dixon replied, "I figure that ride oughta pay you at least a hundred dollars, Henry. I'll pass the hat for you. A man got balls enough to volunteer—no man's about to stand in your way."

Lease grinned. "I'll get ready to ride out at sundown.

Leave when it gets slap dark." He strode away from Bellfield's wagons purposefully.

"You figure he'll make it all the way to Dodge City, Irishman?" Dixon asked.

Seamus shook his head slightly as the rest of the men scattered on other business. "I don't figure we'll ever see Henry Lease again."

Early that evening in the saloon, the hunters took up a collection of $250 to pay Henry Lease for his courageous ride. Blinking back some salty tears, his voice husky with appreciation, Lease climbed aboard George Bellfield's strongest horse and reined north past the Myers & Leonard compound, quickly swallowed by the inky darkness.

The rest went back to cleaning their guns, trying their best to wait out another short, sultry night. To Dixon it seemed the weather grew all the hotter that first day after the battle, and sundown brought little in the way of relief from the mean, muggy temperatures. By day they had baked beneath a brassy, domed sky. And this second night found the settlement's defenders once more broiling in their own juices.

Again Dixon tried sleeping. Still the nightmares haunted him. He decided not to chance it. Pulling on his boots, he quietly moved over to the dark figure crouched in the doorway.

"What's a man like you think about all night, sitting up like this, Irishman?" he asked as he settled against the outside of the wall near the doorjamb where Donegan sat his post.

"Women."

The answer came so quickly, so decisively, that it caught Dixon off guard.

"Bet you've had a lot of women in your time. So, it stands to reason you've got a lot to think about."

In the darkness, Donegan nodded. "Lot of women perhaps, Billy. But only two . . . maybe three, worth remembering—worth thinking this hard about."

* * *

199

Already the full moon under which Quanah Parker's warriors attacked two days ago was waning. It was now the Moon of Black Cherries.

With each new night to come on this long trail, the moon above would shrink until it was but a sliver of its previous grandeur when he had allowed himself to believe in the shaman, allowed himself once more to hope. With each succeeding winter since the battle of Antelope Hills, when the white man had recaptured his mother, Quanah felt a little more of his hope die inside him like a puffball shriveling as the season aged.

But this past spring he had at last allowed himself to believe.

Having watched his warriors hurl themselves against the might of the buffalo hunters' guns would prove a cruel memory he would have to suffer for the rest of his life.

A new moon always gave the dreamers among the Kwahadi cause to hope. But they were the dreamers after all, not the warriors. Not the chiefs charged with the welfare of the bands. But if he would allow himself to believe one more time, perhaps this new moon was an omen that he must return to his people, to gather them about him once more, doing his best to forget the shame and humiliation heaped upon the Kwahadi by the grave mistakes of Isatai.

Perhaps . . . the Kwahadi were never meant to hold a sun dance.

Yes, he decided. That had been their sin, their transgression. Whereas the other tribes held their annual sun-gazing dances, the Comanche had never celebrated in that fashion. Perhaps, Quanah thought, the Spirit Above was telling the Comanche to return to their old ways, the trusted path.

Do not follow the ways of the Shahiyena or the Kiowa. Trust only in the path walked by the ancient ones.

So now Quanah Parker would go. Reluctantly turning his back on the meadow where the tai-bos raised their earth lodges, Quanah led most of his Kwahadi away from that evil place, leaving behind only a dozen warriors to keep an eye on the hide hunters for a few days, then turn about and ride quickly to catch up to the main column, bringing their intelligence with them when they too put the meadow behind them.

Once again he would counsel that his people avoid the white man, as they had attempted to do for far back in the generations. Only when it proved wise for the young men to attack outlying settlements for horses and scalps and plunder had Quanah approved of such violent contact with the tai-bos. In just the past generation, after all, such raids on the white settlers had come to mean that the yellowlegs would come chasing after the warriors who always disappeared onto the Staked Plain like breathsmoke gone in a winter gale.

What bothered Quanah most, like a wolf spider incessantly crawling about in the pit of him, was that the yellowlegs appeared to have given up on chasing the fleeing warriors. Now the tai-bo and buffalo soldiers preferred to track the villages of women and children and old ones, especially while the warriors were off hunting buffalo or raiding for ponies and scalps. Whenever the soldiers went in search for the villages, they always found what they were looking for. Especially when the eyes and ears for the yellowlegs were those hated Tonkawas—the Indians who ate the flesh of other people. With the Tonkawas leading the yellowlegs, more women and children and the old ones would soon be killed or captured.

How best to walk this road? Quanah wondered. A road between raiding the settlements, as they had always done far back into any man's memory, and keeping the hated Tonkawa trackers from finding the villages filled with their families.

His thoughts flowed as quick as a prairie stream after a spring rain, flowed back to Tonarcy and their three children in the village nestled among the trees, in the sheltering shadows of a deep canyon far out on the Staked Plain.

How he wanted to cup his hands about her small, firm breasts and suckle at them now. Feeling her hands roaming up and down the length of his brown body, then taking his rigid flesh in her palms and kneading it insistently until he could stand the torture no longer and drove himself furiously within her.

Tonarcy would arch her back, thrusting her lithe body up at him, the way this great stretch of prairie thrust itself against the endless horizon. And as surely as that horizon of brown earth was forever locked to the pale blue of the summer sky, Tonarcy would lock her legs about him, pulling him ever deeper into the heated moistness of her.

How he loved the way her fingernails raked the great muscles of his back as he rocked above her, watching those breasts quiver with the driving power of each thrust. How he loved the way she pulled on his hair, yanking his head down to her lips so she could bite his neck, down his shoulder, across his chest—leaving bruises that marked him for many suns.

The last bruises she had left him with were long gone now.

Quanah needed to be home in their lodge, to hear their children snoring softly beneath the stars of a prairie night. To once more taste the stale flavor of buffalo and prairie onions on Tonarcy's breath as his mouth sought hers in those cold, delicious moments just before the first streaks of dawn burst out of the bowels of the earth.

The way the explosions erupted from deep inside him as he burst inside his woman.

Then slowed his mighty, bull-like thrusts and lay with his woman cuddled within the shelter of his arms and legs, protecting her as she returned to sleep.

Quanah prayed nothing would steal her from him. How he needed the shelter of her arms and legs and mouth and moist heat right now.

Quanah prayed.

21

Late June–Early July, 1874

In a grove of trees less than three miles from the meadow, Donegan, Dixon and Hanrahan made a startling discovery the third day after the attack. Leggings and moccasins and blankets had been cut to ribbons and left behind. Much of it bloodied.

The ground around the area had been trampled by many feet, many hooves. Dark stains dotted the hammered grass and dust. The sight of so much of it soaking into the thirsty soil reminded Seamus of the fire and thunder of long-forgotten battlefields—of peach-faced boys calling for their mothers, of old men crying out like babies, and not enough unwounded to hold the hands of all the dying.

"Why they cut up their clothes like that?" asked Jim Hanrahan. "Get to the bullet wounds?"

Seamus shook his head. "I figure it's like Jim Bridger told me: when a warrior dies, the rest divide up what he has worth keeping. And the rest they just cut up because he won't be needing it where he's going."

"We gave 'em billy-be-hell, looks to be," Dixon said.

To look at the place where the wounded had undoubtedly been brought was enough to give a man pause, and reason to wonder.

"As many of 'em as they were," Seamus said, "still they didn't stand a chance against the big guns."

"If they'd found us asleep," Hanrahan sighed with that sheepish, boyish grin of his, "we'd all be wolf bait by now. Had 'em a easy time of it running us over."

"But you saw to it that enough of us was awake," Dixon replied, also grinning. "I s'pose me and the rest owe you our lives, Jim."

Hanrahan appeared genuinely embarrassed. "With Rath and Myers and the Mooar brothers skeedaddling north to Dodge when they found out—I had a choice to make. Everything I owned was there in that saloon. I wasn't about to turn my back on it. If I saved the lives of most every man there—they helped save all that my life's worth too. I figure we're all even, in my account."

Dixon gazed off. "Our guns did make the day, boys."

"Like yours did yesterday," Donegan reminded them. "If one shot put a end to that red siege at Adobe Walls, it was yours, Billy."

"Wasn't nothing, Irishman," Dixon replied, wagging it off. "Just a scratch shot."

Not long past sunup the day before, the third of the bloody siege, more than a dozen feathered horsemen had appeared in the east, on a high, red butte a little less than a mile away from the meadow.

"You figure they're up to something? After all this time?" Billy Ogg had asked as more of the white men gathered outside the saloon.

"Naw, I doubt they'll be riding down on us any more—after the drubbing we give 'em," Donegan had replied.

"Just the same—I'm getting mighty sore at seeing the red devils come and go as they wish," Dixon had growled, "while we're holed up here like field mice." He then turned and snatched up the .50-caliber Sharps.

"You look mad as a spit-on sowbug, Billy. What you fixing to do?" Ogg had asked as he and a good number of the hunters traipsed after Dixon to a bullet-splintered wagon.

"Don't any of you figure I can shoot one of them red bastards from here?" Dixon had asked the group.

Most of them shrugged, unsure.

"I'll put ten dollars on Dixon," Seamus told them. "Ten dollars says Billy can hit one of the horsemen."

Some had anteed up their bets, but most had stayed neutral as Dixon loaded the big .50 and made himself a rest right where he stood against the wagon sidewall. Dixon raised the rear sight after he had tossed a handful of dust in the air. When his calculations were complete, the hunter asked for quiet. After a few moments he pulled his cheek from the butt stock and rubbed his eyes.

"Lot of trouble seeing that far," he said.

"That's more'n half a mile, Billy," Hanrahan said. "Far more."

Donegan nodded, himself aware of the trouble Dixon was having with the heat waves shimmering in all that distance between the Sharps's sights and the targets on the far bluff.

Dixon once more nestled his cheek against the stock, took a deep breath, then let most of it out while he slowly squeezed the trigger.

With a roar, the gun had belched smoke and shoved Dixon's shoulder from his rest. He backed from the wagon's sidewall as the booming echo disappeared across the valley as if it were swallowed by the great distance. When the sound had all but gone . . . the white hunters watched one of the horsemen suddenly twist atop his pony and spin to the ground.

As the rest of the warriors hurriedly wheeled their mounts and disappeared from the top of the bluff, the white men ripped their hats off and cheered, pounding Dixon heartily on the back, marveling at the distance of his shot. Donegan had stood back, collecting his bets—nonetheless in awe himself at not only the miraculous shot, but that these men who were all proven marksmen at great distances would be found congratulating one of their own on such a remarkable feat.

"Lookee there!" Ogg had called out as they danced and jigged their joy.

Atop the far bluff two of the horsemen reappeared, this time on foot. They quickly scooped up the fallen warrior and dragged him off, disappearing from sight once more.

Ever since the day of the fight, the weather had grown more miserably hot. No longer merely sultry. The prairie was baking and drying, withering grass and drying ponds where the game struggled to breathe in the oppressive oven of the southern plains.

That third day more hunters had come into the settlement, brought in by the news carried through the surrounding countryside. With more proven marksmen arriving daily, the hide men began fortifying the buildings in fear of a renewed attack. With their only water supply outside the protection of their earth walls, Swede Johnson dug a well inside the Rath store so they would not suffer for want of water with a renewed attack. More mud was chinked between the pickets, and the bastions were reinforced. Actual loopholes for firing rifles were now gouged through the walls of all three buildings. The most difficult addition was in fashioning a small lookout post atop both the Rath and Myers buildings. By climbing up a ladder to the small, sod-walled bastion through a hole cut in the roof, a constant and rotating watch could be maintained by the growing population at the settlement. They consoled themselves that they would be even more ready when the naked, screaming horsemen returned to the meadow.

During that midday ride the fourth day, Donegan, Dixon and Hanrahan found the ruins of the warriors' hospital. That trampled, bloodstained grass was a more sobering reminder of the power of the white man's guns than all the windy tales of those who told and retold the stories of their individual exploits during those terrifying first hours of the attack on Adobe Walls.

By afternoon of the fifth day, Donegan counted close to a hundred men come in and camped at the settlement. Between clerks and stock tenders, cooks and skinners and hunters, they now formed a small, resolute army of white men here far to the south of the dead line. Plunked down in the heart of Indian country, but with none of them having any particular stomach of late to go wandering about in search of the herds.

The sun had begun to settle toward the west that first day of July when a sharp cry was raised from the lookout post atop the Myers store.

"Injuns! Injuns coming!"

From the sentry perch atop the Rath store, William Olds shouted frantically. "I see 'em! Injuns coming!"

Clambering to his feet beside Dixon at the east wall of the Rath store, Donegan whirled, sweeping up the Henry repeater. After they hurriedly dragged their animals into the two corrals, the white men sprinted into each of the three buildings, everyone hollering orders to one another. A single gunshot split the noisy, sultry air of the Rath & Company store.

Whirling, Seamus watched the body of William Olds fall from the ladder, the back of his head a bloody, pulpy stew.

"What the hell happened?" demanded James Langton as Dixon knelt over the Rath employee at the foot of the ladder.

"Somebody shoot him?" Donegan asked.

"Billy!" shrieked Hannah Olds as she crumpled beside her husband, scooping his bloody head onto her flour-crusted apron. She was quickly covered with a seeping slick of crimson. "Oh, God—Billy!"

"Are the red bastards back?" someone asked.

"Who shot him?" asked another.

"His gun went off somehow," Dixon explained, wagging his head.

"Must've snagged on something as he was coming down," replied Sam Smith.

Dixon rose from the old couple and pulled Donegan away. "The bullet went right up through his chin and out the back of the old man's head."

Donegan nodded. "That's number four."

"Number four?"

"First Ike and Shorty Scheidler. Then Billy Tyler. Now those Injins they spotted just killed their fourth victim."

Outside, men on the ground were clamoring for news from the lookout atop the Myers store.

"They're up the valley a ways," the guard shouted, pointing up Adobe Walls Creek. "Moving off slow. To the east."

"How many?"

"Twenty-five. Maybeso, thirty."

"You see any more?"

"No—not what I can see from here."

For a few anxious minutes every man of them waited, fearing this news signaled a renewed attack. But as the afternoon wore long and the shadows lengthened ever onward to the east where the thirty horsemen had disappeared, it became clear no attack would be forthcoming.

"She sat at his side through it all," Billy said quietly, of a sudden and out of the blue that evening as the light eased out of the sky after they had buried William Olds in a solitary grave southeast of the Rath store.

"Hannah?" asked Donegan.

He nodded. "Reloading guns for the old man, wiping sweat out of his eyes. Like . . . like she really loved that old wolf."

Donegan cleared his throat. It was hard, what with the sudden, hot lump clogging it. "I . . . I suppose she did love him, Billy."

"I was there in Rath's with 'em for part of the fight, Seamus," Billy tried to explain. "The rest, they asked me to stay—'cause of her. Being a woman and all."

"I remember you telling about it."

"But there wasn't a one of us there what wouldn't've fought tooth and toenail for her, if'n it'd come down to them red savages getting in the door and it being hand-to-hand. It was like . . . well, some of the boys say she's been like a mother to a lot of us. A fine woman—what didn't deserve this happening to her."

"No woman would, Billy. To have her man come through a bloody fight the likes of what we got through—then to shoot himself by accident three days later. Makes a man wonder on the time he's got left him on earth, it does," Donegan replied thoughtfully, his voice gone wistful as the first stars came out, one by one.

In those few hours following the senseless death of William Olds, if not the past few days since the dawn attack, Seamus found himself brooding more and more on that fragrant woman he had left behind at Sharp Grover's place outside of Jacksboro, Texas. She had done all that was in her power to make him know just how truly pleased and content she was to be around him.

Was she truly happiness? Or was his thinking now ruled only by the excruciating loneliness he felt holding his life prisoner. At times of late he had forced himself to stare down into his soul and come away with the feeling like it was looking down into a black, seemingly bottomless cavern. Empty. And utterly cold.

Ultimately and desperately in need of a woman's love to fill that gaping chasm. This wandering and liquoring and whoring was all right for a younger man. And he had been a younger man of a bygone day. But these feelings of unsettled yearning were still new and he wanted to be certain. Sure and certain before he rode back to Jacksboro. Back to Samantha Pike.

"You riding with us to Dodge, Seamus?" asked Dixon.

He nodded. "Fixing to light out soon, ain't you?"

"Whole caboodle of us packing up and heading north. The partnership with me and Hanrahan still good—you want to throw in with us, Irishman? Maybeso, I'll go back to hunting buff one day soon."

"Don't figure I'll throw in with you now, Billy."

"Hunting still good someplace else," Dixon explained. "We'll let this country cool off for a while. Find where the herds gone and shoot our way through 'em."

"No, Billy. I will ride north with the lot of you, then cut back south through the Territories, down through Camp Supply and Sill."

"What's there in Injun Territory has you going after it?"

"Nothing in Injin country," he said. "Going down to Texas."

Dixon turned to look more fully at the Irishman now. Slowly, a smile took root across the young hunter's face. "Jesus, Mary and Joseph! If I don't figure but what you got woman troubles on your mind, Donegan. That's it—ain't it?"

He shook his head, shrugging self-consciously.

"Yes, it is! Ain't much else make a man ride hundreds of miles out of his way, and through Injun Territory to boot."

"I just figure to settle down with Sharp like he's wanted me to—like I should've to begin with last summer."

"Stillwell told me Sharp's sister-in-law took a real shine to you, Seamus."

"He did, did he?"

Dixon nodded. "Before Jack took off north to go sign up to scout for Colonel Miles." The young hide man fell quiet for a time, digging a stick into the dry, flaky soil.

That gap in conversation as the light eased out of the sky put Donegan's thoughts back to wandering. And when his thoughts wandered, chances were awfully good that they would lead him south of the Red River.

Easily remembering the bold tilt to her chin when she grew set in her mind on something. Or the full cut of those ripe, moist lips when she pouted to convince him otherwise. She was very much a real live and warmed-up woman with a wanton mold to her body. Again he recalled how her pale hair captured light just the way a mirror captured the flicker of a candle's flame. Wasn't easy to squeeze her out of his mind anymore, burned as she was into his deepest memory. At times it seemed almost as if she were to remain forever on his skin, where she had touched his flesh, just the way he reflected time and again on her flesh,

209

on the tangle of freckles that spilled into that great cleft between her breasts.

Perhaps it was time to settle into a routine with Sharp Grover, both of them to walk off early of a morning into the frost-tattled forest surrounding the old man's place and supply meat for Samantha's rich squirrel stew so crowded with tiny morsels of tender, red meat and those big, softened chunks of white potatoes—

"You figure it's coming to a all-out war, Seamus?"

Dixon's voice interrupted the warmth in his breast and the flavor on his tongue.

"These warrior bands keep at it this way," Donegan replied, "yes—it will, for certain."

Dixon stretched his back, gazing into the distance. "Then, I figure my hunting days are numbered."

"Too dangerous to be a buffalo man now, Billy?"

"Naw. Just that I'm set on following after Sharp Grover's footsteps some, I s'pose. Wander on up to Larned myself and sign up with Stillwell and the rest. Ride for Colonel Nelson A. Miles since this war's a'coming."

Seamus looked at the handsome face framed by the long, dark hair. "So you set your sights on becoming an army scout now, Billy Dixon?"

"I s'pose I have at that, Seamus," he answered. "Same as you've set your sights on that woman who I'm told is waiting for you back down there in Texas."

22

Moon of Black Cherries, 1874

In the two weeks that had passed following the disastrous attack on the buffalo hunters at Adobe Walls, Lone Wolf and his warriors had slipped back onto their reservation near Fort Sill, where Kicking Bird's Kiowa were just getting their annual sun dance underway.

On the other hand, the Cheyenne war bands had refused to return to Darlington. Instead, Stone Calf, Medicine Water and the other war chiefs had marched north to attack a wagon train bound for Fort Supply and killed four teamsters before the warriors rode northwest into Colorado Territory, where they raided outlying settlements, killing an estimated sixty men, women and children as a general alarm spread through a growing section of the central and southern plains.

During the daily council gatherings of the Kiowa head men, the coming war was debated, hotly at times. The visiting Comanche delegates, anxious to have the matter settled then be off on their raids, claimed the Kiowas "talked too much." In return, the Kiowas huffed that the Comanche were as impetuous as children. As the hours and days of deliberation droned on, one chief after another sided with Kicking Bird's peace faction. First to declare his adherence to the white man's road was Dangerous Eagle, brother of Big Tree, the same war chief who with Satanta had spent time in the white man's prison down in Tehas. Next to choose the road of peace was Stumbling Bear, a great warrior of many winters. Then came Chief Sun Boy, named for the long-ago founder of the Kiowa tribe.

Yet most electrifying was the decision of Napawat, the tribe's most powerful shaman. Without his spiritual sanction, most warriors would never dare ride off to make war.

Things did not bode well, but through an intensive emotional appeal, Lone Wolf was able to finally convince the great war chief and shaman, Mamanti, to again lead a revenge raid into Tehas. Ever since that day Lone Wolf had been forced to ride off without the bones of his son and nephew, leaving the remains in the land south of the Red River, the Kiowa war chief had carried a smoldering desire for revenge. Now, before the great council of chiefs and warriors, Lone Wolf clearly challenged the manhood of the others, saying that the soldiers would not have killed Tauankia and Guitain if the other warriors had shown more bravery in battle.

Mamanti was a huge man supported by massive bones that seemed far too thick to ever be broken. Known as the Swan, he was not only the logical choice to lead a revenge raid, but the popular choice as well: he had led the successful raid on the Warren wagon train three winters before. More so, the shaman was one of the few in many generations of Kiowa tradition to possess owl medicine that could foretell the future.

In a momentous ceremony that last day of those deliberations, the aging Satanta not only gave up his role as leader in the tribe, handing his long, red medicine lance over to White Cowbird, but also renounced his membership in the Koitsenko, the highest Kiowa warrior society—in which members vow to stake themselves to the ground and die rather than retreat in battle. That time suffered in the white man's prisons had mellowed the old warrior—Satanta simply stated to his old companions of the war path that it was now time for him to return to the reservation and the white man's road.

On the final evening of the sun-dance celebration, messengers from Mamanti circulated among the faithful, telling the young warriors to meet at the shaman's lodge when darkness fell. There, on a separate hill overlooking the sundance arbor, more than four dozen gathered as the sun sat scarlet and gold in the west, seated before the shaman's lodge door as the last shafts of light faded from the sky. When all was dark, and quiet had descended upon the gathering, they were greeted with a rustle of huge wings beating the air, and the faint hooting of an owl, both sounds coming from within the wizard's lodge. Lone Wolf himself was eager to hear the words of the shaman after the all-seeing owl spirit had looked into the future.

"Our raid will be successful," Mamanti declared after he had emerged and walked to the center of the hushed gathering.

The warriors hooted triumphantly themselves, their blood growing hotter. Older men thumped on rawhide drums while the women trilled in joyous anticipation.

"We will take only one scalp—yet not one of us will fall," continued the shaman. "But," and Mamanti paused, stroking the feathers of his stuffed owl while the rest grew hushed, "we must not wait until morning to leave. We must ride tonight!"

Without hesitation the warriors and their women spun into action, gathering weapons and dried meat for the trail, bringing into camp the pampered and adorned war ponies, packing extra moccasins and earth paint and medicine objects. Beneath a nibbled moon late that night, July tenth, Mamanti and his owl medicine led a bitter, unhappy Lone Wolf, along with Red Otter and better than fifty scalp-hungry warriors, away from the sun-dance camp on the North Fork of the Red River, their noses pointed south for the land of the Tehannos.

The day following the conclusion of the Kiowa sun dance, Kicking Bird lost no time taking his reservation band, which easily accounted for three-fourths of the tribe, back to their Cache Creek camp. The peace chief had grown frightened for his people with all the renewed talk of raids and war.

By the time the sun had reached mid-sky that first day, Lone Wolf's raiders had reached the Prairie Dog Fork of the Red River and discovered a small herd of buffalo. Here they butchered meat for the trail, then crossed into Tehas near the Panhandle meridian, establishing their base camp some ten miles south of the Red River on a hill populated by a prairie-dog town. Here they hobbled and picketed the trail horses while their war ponies were painted and prepared for the hunt. When the buffalo-hair cinches on their pad saddles were tightened, Mamanti led the fighting men south by east across the Pease and Wichita rivers, where some scouts discovered a few head of the white man's spotted buffalo. Three of the cattle were butchered then barbecued whole atop a mesquite blaze before the war party pushed on until sundown overtook them, having marched another thirty miles into the land of the white settlers.

"Tomorrow we will find the ones we will fight," Mamanti promised them that night after he had consulted his feathered spirit helper. "One scalp—perhaps two. But I am sure of one. And the warriors who will count coup will be riding on gray horses." Then, to the surprise of the rest, the shaman strode over to Tsentonkee, the youngest of them all, and coming on his first raid.

"This youngster has the heart of an old warrior," Mamanti declared. "He will count coup tomorrow and win a bay horse to show off when we return north. Put on your paint and sleep lightly. We will ride out before dawn."

As Lone Wolf moved among the young warriors decorating themselves according to family tradition or spiritual guidance, the revenge fever burned within him as never before. This he would do for the blood of his blood—avenge the deaths of his own family. His loose hair hung in clumps where Lone Wolf had chopped it off in mourning. And both he and Red Otter were forbidden by tribal tradition from wearing paint until the deaths of their sons had been avenged. Just before dawn Mamanti ordered the war party off once again.

Not long after sunrise they came to the Salt Prairie, where the shaman had led the Kiowa on a successful attack against the Warren wagon train. It was a spartan land, broken by outcroppings of rock and hills dotted with mesquite. Lone Wolf pointed out the sandstone hill atop which they had buried a casualty of the skirmish with the white men. As was their custom, the warriors rolled back the stones from the cairn and with prayers looked upon the bones of Ordlee, one of the few Comanches along on that raid three winters gone.

Although it was nearing midday, an unexpected and sudden gust of cold wind snaked its way up the hill as the warriors prayed over the bones, asking their spirit helpers for success that day. As most wandered back toward their ponies, the warriors quietly muttered that they wished to be gone from this evil place.

"Aiyeee!" yipped one of the guards left with the ponies. He pointed down the far, eastern slope of the hill.

There, among the brush and trees at the base of the slope, rode four white horsemen, as yet unaware of the warriors on the hill above them.

"It is a good day!" shouted Lone Wolf, sprinting to his pony with the others.

With a whoop, the fifty galloped off the hill after their quarry. The four could not fail to hear the noisy charge and immediately put spurs to their horses, reining to the east for Cox Mountain. On the rugged slopes, the white men crossed a section of broken, rocky ground where it would prove harder for the warriors to track them.

Moments after the Kiowas entered the area, their unshod ponies began to suffer. It wasn't long before Mamanti was compelled to call off the chase, realizing hooves were being shredded on the rocky ground. Their fever still worked up, three warriors then shot calves they discovered in the area. With pieces of the green hides secured around the wounded hooves, the war party backtracked to the east, where they headed for a saddle between two low peaks, hoping there to spot some new prey.

It was not long after they had climbed that high ground dividing the drainage of the Brazos from the West Fork of the Trinity that the advance scouts returned with good news.

"How many?" Lone Wolf asked.

"More than twenty," answered Hunting Horse. "All wear white hats."

Not sure what that sign meant, Lone Wolf nonetheless smiled at Mamanti. "This is the fight you have seen with your medicine, Swan."

"Are they coming this way?" asked Mamanti.

Hunting Horse nodded. "Their eyes are on the ground —they are following our trail, here."

Mamanti nodded. "Then we will give them a surprise."

The war chief and shaman gave the orders for the rest to split up and disperse their trail, doubling back quickly to wait in ambush for the white men. With the rest waiting anxiously in hiding, Mamanti and Loud Talker rode out and dismounted in plain view, acting as if their ponies were totally broken down, hoping to lure the white men into their trap.

Waiting among those anxious to close the trap, Lone Wolf's heart beat furiously within his chest. It had not pounded this loudly in many a summer. This was to be a glorious day of avenging the blood of his family.

A major by appointment from the governor of Texas, selected to command the Texas Frontier Battalion of Rangers, John B. Jones led twenty-five of his own men and ten more from Captain G. W. Stephens's company into Lost Valley. Since first light they had been dogging a hot trail of a large war party on its way east.

Jones hoped it was the Comanches he had been trying to corner for the past two days, following their attack on the nearby ranch of famous Texas cattleman, Oliver Loving. The war party had killed a cowboy before escaping with a half-dozen horses. This was to be the major's first action, and more than almost anything, he wanted to make a name for himself.

Only two months before, Jones had received his commission. Immediately he had begun to tour the settlements of northwestern Texas, forming six companies of Texas Rangers. Many of the men who rode with the major were young, without experience in border warfare, men who grew clearly agitated as the trail warmed this second morning of the chase. Jones worried that they would not hold under fire.

Just last night, after a quick supper of beans and hard bread, Major Jones had told the assembled group, "We Rangers, as well as the Indians we'll be running across, will fight under the black flag. We ask no quarter, and will give none. When we fall into their hands, they will scalp us and frightfully mutilate our bodies, cutting and hacking us to pieces. We likely won't do as bad as they will to us, but we'll scalp them just the same. That says a lot to these redskinned raiders. Indian scalps in a Ranger camp is going to become as common a sight as pony tracks."

Ever since first light this morning, Jones had been pushing the men hard. Twice they had come across places where the Indians had watered their ponies. At both places the Rangers had found chunks of charred meat left behind by the war party.

Despite the freshening trail they had been following all morning from the Salt Prairie, the major was nonetheless struck by the solitary beauty of Lost Valley. From side to side his eyes scanned slowly, back and forth across the almost level floor ringed by rugged, timbered ridges. At the far northern end of the valley lay the Loving spread.

Now the unshod tracks grew so fresh that the hot, persistent breeze hadn't yet had a chance to stir the dust. Around him the young recruits grew more excited, working each other up for the coming fight. A few galloped on ahead despite stern warnings from both Jones and Captain Stephens. The major was clearly nettled. This was his chance to shine, and he wasn't about to let these greenhorns snuff it for him. A small man in build, only some five feet eight inches tall and weighing only 140 pounds, but nonetheless a man of dynamic will, Jones had, after all, been handpicked by Richard Coke, the politically powerful governor of Texas.

Two months back Coke had seized the political reins of Texas with the support of his newly-formed Ranger units, acting for the time being as the governor's private militia in throwing out the carpetbaggers and their Republican cronies, to restore the Democratic party's rule to the state. In decline for the past fifteen years, the revamped Rangers proved to be the military muscle in Coke's coup d'état. The new governor vowed to protect the settlements and put an end to the Indian problem once and for all.

"If the army isn't able to protect Texans—then, by God, Texans will protect Texans!" he promised when sworn in.

Back in April the Texas legislature had responded to Coke's call to arms and once more gave the breath of life to the famed Texas Rangers. Two fighting units were installed. Major John B. Jones commanded the Frontier Battalion, whose job it was to patrol and protect life and property along the four-hundred-mile-long border between Texas settlers and the hostiles raiding off the Staked Plain. While it was said that the U.S. Army was to keep the Indians on the reservations and drive the hostiles back to the reservation, the six companies organized by Jones clearly had one purpose in mind: they were to serve as "Indian exterminators."

Instead of herding the bands back to the Territories, the Rangers were commissioned to engage the warriors when and where found. And kill them.

"That's why we'll give no quarter, and can expect none," Jones told his scouting party. "The only thing an Indian understands is force and fearlessness, and striking hard. We will strike them hard and kill as many as we can."

Once the Indian trail had freshened, Jones pressed ahead with two dozen of his best. The rest, some ten of the Rangers, were to follow along as they could, held in reserve. Almost single-handedly now, the major commanded some forty thousand square miles of Texas wilderness, with 450 Rangers answering his call to arms. Beneath his long, drooping, black mustache, Jones smiled. Although it might give most men pause before riding into action against proven warriors, the fact that he alone among his men had ever been under fire did not deter the major. He would make Governor Coke proud—perhaps this very day, the twelfth of July, as they entered Lost Valley, a few miles northwest of Jacksboro.

"They're breaking up, Major," announced the young outrider, Ed Carnal, as he reined up in front of Jones and Stephens.

"That's just what I feared," replied the major grittily. "We'll break off here, Captain."

Then Jones did the unthinkable act of a man unaccustomed to fighting Indians: he divided his forces, hoping to follow all the tracks back to where they again gathered.

23

July 12, 1874

Lone Wolf watched expectantly, his heart pounding in his ears as the twenty-five white men entered the mouth of the valley. One of them waved his arm and yelled something to the others.

He figured this was the white man's chief, the way he was giving orders to the other riders. Two men broke off from the main group and reined over to ride the flanks, each on a course that would take him toward the warriors waiting in ambush among the timbered hills rimming the valley.

The closest rider, all alone now, reined his horse toward the timber where Lone Wolf, Red Otter and four others sat in a loose knot back in the shadows of the timber. With his eyes constantly moving, the white man scanned the hillside, then for a few moments studied the ground for some trail sign, then went back to searching over the timber above him.

Behind Lone Wolf the chief heard the quiet approach of more ponies. Glancing over his shoulder, he saw Lone Young Man leading a dozen other warriors down the slope through the mesquite trees. They came to a halt behind Lone Wolf and the others, waiting. Together they watched the solitary white man headed their way, slowly, slowly.

The Kiowa made no move, becoming part of the landscape, their ponies still in the midday heat, heads hung in respite from the rigors of the trail. As well, the warriors themselves sat motionless, their lances, rifles and bows ready. Only the air hummed with activity as deerflies buzzed and bees droned, busy in the heat.

Of a sudden, the white rider savagely reined his horse up at a hundred yards. Its neck wrenched back, the animal almost went down with the white man. For a few heartbeats the horseman sat like a stone, able to do nothing but stare at Lone Wolf and the rest—as they sat glaring back at the white man.

What made the lone horseman do what he did next, Lone Wolf would never be able to say. But at a distance of a hundred yards, the white man pulled out his pistol and began popping off shots at the eighteen warriors. With the first puff of smoke, Lone Wolf knew the man was an utter fool. There followed the distant sound of that shot a heartbeat later. Another puff and its distant pop.

As the rest of the warriors poured off the hillside toward the lone horseman, Lone Wolf remembered thinking how stupid the white man was to think he could hit anything at that distance.

Of a sudden the horseman reined about, ramming heels into the ribs of his big horse, and lit out for the rest of his group as it progressed slowly up the valley, dogging the war party's tracks.

To a man, the white horsemen were turning about on the trail, having heard the shots, perhaps even now hearing the warning shouts coming from the solitary tracker. And in that next instant, Lone Wolf watched Mamanti's plan brought to play. Down from both hillsides rushed the rest of the warriors, more than thirty in all. As the white men whirled, ready to retreat out of the valley, the warriors who had come down the slope with Lone Young Man closed the trap.

Lone Wolf yelped as he pushed his pony into action. It was good!

There would be blood on the ground this day.

John B. Jones cursed as he watched the warriors pouring down on his men. The oldest trick in the book—those two decoys up ahead—and he had fallen for it.

Ed Carnal was riding in, hell-bent for election from the right flank, his mouth like a huge O as he hollered something.

Jones looked off to the left flank and found Lee Corn riding in. Except Corn wasn't hollering, nor was he shooting. He was holding his right arm, swaying in the saddle.

"Form up! Form up, goddammit!" Jones bellowed, rising in his stirrups. "Meet 'em head on!"

He was throwing his arms this way then that—adding emphasis to his orders as he spread out his raw recruits in a broad line. At this exact moment he had a little less than twenty to meet the charge. The other four were still up ahead, racing back to the main body.

Damn them, Jones thought. "Green as grass," he muttered under his breath. They were so damned anxious at the bit to follow that trail—look what it's got 'em now. Look what it's got us all.

"Fellas, we'll fire in volley upon my order!" he directed. "Maybe we can turn 'em, at best. Keep 'em at bay, at the worst. Now, *fire!*"

All along that line of young horsemen the guns erupted. Jones swore it was like the valley itself had exploded, smoke billowing in gray shards above them in the stifling, hot breeze coming down Cameron Creek. The last four rode in, as did Lee Corn, clearly wounded.

"Stephens, get Corn some help!" Jones hollered at his captain.

"I'm all right, Major," Corn growled back, clutching his arm. "I'll live—don't waste time on me for now."

Jones turned and ordered, *"Fire!"*

The valley exploded again just as the warriors regrouped and were about to begin another charge.

"We'll hold 'em at bay, by God!" Jones yelled as a bullet whistled by his ear. It was a sound once heard, always remembered. Those years back in Tennessee and Virginia, fighting the Yankees. Jones doubted he would ever forget the sound of a bullet whining past his ear.

"Major—we don't stand a chance out here in the open!" shouted Captain Stephens. "We don't find cover—we won't have the chance of a fart in a whirlwind!"

Jones had to agree. Looking around, he saw that his men stood their ground on grit only, in the middle of that open, flat valley. The only cover was offered by the timber on the sides of the hills. And there just might be more of that on up the valley where it dog-legged to the northeast, following the narrow creek into the hazy distance. The only ground he knew for sure was back the way they came, what they had just crossed from the south.

An arroyo he remembered. Little better than a hundred yards long, maybe all of five feet deep. They could get the horses down there, dismount and make a stand of it.

"Back to the south, Captain! The arroyo!"

But as he gave the order, the warriors swarmed around to the south, as if sensing the attempt at escape.

Stephens's horse was fighting its bit as the captain came up beside Jones. "We been siwashed, Major! We'll just have to fight our way through the red bastards!"

"Have at 'em, men—leg up and lay flat along the withers, boys . . . follow me!" Jones shouted, waving his pistol arm for the rest to follow.

In a mad, noisy dash, the Rangers made good their bluster, riding straight for the warriors who stood between them and the arroyo. Like demonic eagle-eyed hell-winds, they drove the Kiowa back in a frantic retreat, the Indians finally taking momentary refuge behind a low ridge. Then of a sudden, the warriors regrouped and whirled back on the white men.

Making it back to the ravine was not without cost to the Rangers. As the Kiowa regained their senses after falling back, and surged toward those white horsemen bringing up the rear, two more Rangers were wounded. Yet by some hand other than their own, most of the green recruits managed to stay in the saddle until they reached the edge of the arroyo.

George Moore was one of the first to dismount on a run, whacking his horse on the flank with the flat of his pistol barrel, driving it down into the arroyo as he turned to cover the rest arriving on his heels. He knelt and fired, his bullet striking Red Otter's horse squarely in the chest. As the animal keeled over to the side, Moore began to rise, covering the last of those who would make it to the ravine. A Kiowa bullet cut him off at mid-leg, shattering a knee and leaving him with a wound that would cripple the Ranger for the rest of his life.

Jones was firing and counting, then fired again and counted more of those who dug in at the side of the arroyo with him. The major was still missing two . . . no, three of his own escort. Lee Corn and the man named Richard Wheeler. Along with Billy Glass.

As a gust of hot breeze stirred some of the biting, gray gun smoke on his left, Jones caught sight of Corn and Wheeler making it into the timber more than eighty yards away, short of the arroyo and now on their own.

Turning back to his right, Jones spotted the last Ranger. Several yards short of the ravine lay Billy Glass, stretched on his side. As Jones watched, some of the warriors dared rush in to raise the white man's scalp, but gunfire from the arroyo turned them and put them to flight more than once.

Glass seemed to come to, looking down at his shirt slicked with blood, bright in the afternoon light. With one arm that barely moved, Glass reached around his belt and pulled out his skinning knife. Afraid the young man was about to kill himself rather than fall into the hands of the Indians, Jones shouted, his words blown back at him on a hot, stifling gust of wind.

Glass shoved the bone handle of his knife between his teeth and bit down as he lay among the dry stalks of buffalo grass.

Jones felt his eyes sting for a moment. "By Jupiter, that boy's got huevos the size of turkey eggs. Whatever you do, fellas—don't let 'em near Billy," he ordered.

The rest nodded their heads. Without a word, they reloaded pistols and carbines, an assortment of Starrs and Sharps and Spencers among them as they held their ground and pushed back the warriors trying again for Glass's scalp.

In his breast, Jones felt his heart swell with pride as he tore his eyes away from the wounded Ranger with Stephens's call.

"Major! Them slippery bastards're setting up behind that ridge," said the captain, pointing to a nearby ridge at the right side of the valley.

From there, the major knew, the Indians could pour down a heavy fire on the ravine—keeping his men pinned down as long as they wanted. Time—and they really didn't have much to spare. That and water. Jones scuffed his boot into the dry, flaky bottom of the arroyo, hoping it would give him hope. Nothing but a gauzy dust. No chance of burrowing for water here.

"Are these Comanches, Captain?" asked Jones. He knew Stephens would know—this was his territory, and these were his Indians.

The captain wagged his head. "Look like Kiowa. Probably jumped the river for a little raiding. Still—I don't figure it can be the same bunch hit Loving's ranch."

"Right now, I suppose it doesn't matter much a damn who they are, does it? Just, well—a man likes to know what red bastards got him pinned down under this sun with no shade."

"Major!"

Jones and the rest heard Wheeler's call from the brush off to their left. The warning was enough to catch the flicker of movement among the timber. Two warriors were coming, darting from tree to tree, heading for Glass.

"They want Billy's scalp mighty bad," Jones said. "Keep 'em back, boys!"

By some power other than his own, Glass became aware of his danger in that next moment. Dragging himself along with one arm, he began crawling toward the arroyo, kicking up tufts of dry grass and spraying dust with his boots as he inched pitiably toward his comrades.

"Don't let 'em get me!" he whimpered as he struggled through the brittle grass. "My God—don't let 'em get me!"

Stephens yelled, "Major Jones! That's—"

"I see him, dammit," Jones growled, whirling away from his captain. He crabbed down the dusty arroyo as he shouted above the racket of gunfire. "I want three volunteers," he asked them. "One to go get Glass. The other two will cover the first. Who will go?"

A dozen hands shot up, then more. Jones took the first three he had seen volunteer. He wanted them out of the arroyo and moving before they had a chance to think about what they had just agreed to do.

"From here we'll keep those two by the trees at bay—now, go!"

Ordering the rest to lay down a covering fire that would hold the two warriors behind their trees, Jones turned back to watch the rescue of Billy Glass. All three reached the wounded Ranger, one man immediately grabbing Glass's arms while the other two flanked him, slowly, calmly firing toward the trees.

After what seemed like a month of Sundays, the Rangers had Glass over the lip of the arroyo and down into the dust of the bottom.

As soon as he knelt over Glass, Jones knew the youth had received a death wound.

"I'm gonna be all right, ain't I, Major?"

He nodded, working his words past the sour ball at the back of his throat. He patted Glass's shoulder gently. "You lay here till we get these red bastards drove off. Then we'll get you saddled up and off to a doctor."

"I'll be all right—you just get me a drink of water, sir."

With his eyes, Jones told another Ranger he was to see to Glass's thirst. Then he scooted back through the dust to the side of the ravine where the scared and inexperienced gunmen were nonetheless holding the Kiowas back. What they needed more than anything at this moment was encouragement. Pulling himself up the back wall of the ravine, Jones brazenly exposed himself to Indian fire as he strode up and down the length of the arroyo, cheering the young recruits, ordering them to spread out, keeping them from bunching themselves too closely out of fear.

"They can't overwhelm us, boys," he told them. "Not if we stay spread out. Just think about what you're doing each time you take a shot—and they damned well won't chance overrunning us."

As the bullets rattled and ricocheted around him, the major pressed his field glasses against an oak tree to steady his view of the distance. Watching as best he could every action of his enemy.

When the Kiowa gunfire increased, Jones was immediately suspicious. In minutes he realized the reason for the covering fire. The warriors were circling back behind the arroyo. They had gained the timbered slopes behind his men, where they began to open up on the exposed Rangers. Unless he did something now, the warriors were likely to take the day.

"You—Lewis and Robertson. Come with me!" he hollered at two of the Rangers. Although none of them had been under any enemy fire until this day, Jones figured William Lewis and Walter Robertson might just do because they were a bit older than the rest. He led them scrambling up a bare knoll where stood a scrawny scrub oak tree about 150 yards from the arroyo.

"There," he said, pointing to the Indians' newly-won position as they fired down into the arroyo. "You two stay here . . . until they get you or the fight's over."

Both nodded wordlessly before Jones turned and scurried back down the bald hill.

"Major Jones," called Lieutenant Hiram Wilson as Jones returned to the arroyo. "It's Glass."

Jones came down the length of the ravine and knelt over the body. The eyes were closed. There was a look of peace on the face.

"He's dead, isn't he?"

Wilson nodded.

"At least he's out of pain now," Jones said. "God bless his soul."

"God bless us all, Major," whispered the young lieutenant.

As the long summer afternoon dragged on, the heat began to do terrible things to those Rangers exposed beneath the midsummer ravages of the sun. Their eyes stung with sweat, objects in the distance swimming. Their lips cracked and mouths grew parched until Jones showed them how to take a small pebble and put it in their mouths to stimulate some saliva. One young Ranger, no more than eighteen at most, refused to give up on finding water and dug a hole in the floor of the ravine, as deep as his arm. At the bottom of the hole he pressed his swollen, bloody lips to the moist sand, hoping for some relief.

Soon, Jones knew they would need water. Cameron Creek, with its cool trickle and beckoning pool, lay so close, yet so far.

After better than two more hours of fighting, two of Captain Stephens's company announced they were going for water. Jones stood before the pair, Mel Porter and David Bailey, unable to come up with one good reason to try stopping the men as Porter and Bailey scooped up empty canteens and climbed into their saddles.

"You remember seeing that pool?" Jones asked them, grabbing Porter's bridle. When the young Ranger nodded, Jones continued, "About a half mile, to the north."

"We'll be back, Major," Porter replied. "Cover us best you can."

He watched the tired horses claw their way up the side of the ravine with dust flying in clouds from every hoof. Then Jones turned back to cover the two. And started to wonder why there wasn't much gunfire coming from the Indian positions.

24

July 12, 1874

Across the time it would take the sun to travel from mid-sky to halfway toward the western horizon, the Kiowas had attempted to pick off the white men in the arroyo and on the hillside. But they weren't having much luck.

Then Lone Wolf suggested something to Mamanti: the white man would soon be in great need of water. The tai-bos were not like Indians who could endure long periods of thirst. And, if the Kiowas were to slow their riflefire, it might appear to the white men that the Indians were retiring from the fight, giving the white men a chance at making it to the inviting pool in the nearby creek.

Mamanti smiled. "Then we will attack, and put the fear of the rabbit in their hearts! It is a good plan, Lone Wolf."

The old chief knew Mamanti would like it. After all, Mamanti liked laying traps. More than that, he liked springing the traps. It did not take long for them to pass the word to the rest. Mamanti took about a dozen of the warriors to the west with him in a wide, circling movement that brought them to the top of a ridge northwest of the cool, beckoning pool formed by Cameron Creek. Lone Wolf led another two dozen warriors and hid in the thick brush and mesquite above the creek bank itself. When Mamanti's warriors struck, Lone Wolf's group would close the trap and prevent any escape. But for the time being, some of the warriors armed with far-shooting guns began aiming at the horses the white man had tied in the brush. Every now and then one of the animals would fall, thrashing and screaming out in pain until it died. The thrashing frightened the other animals. At this rate there soon would be no more horses for the white man to ride away from this place.

His heart was again in his throat, waiting. His belly wriggled with the anxious flutter of unseen insects. Lone Wolf did not like this waiting. Even though it had been many, many moons, he had been patient, eager to avenge the death of his son and nephew. His chance would soon arrive.

It wasn't long before the white men grew daring and two of them mounted up, sprinting for the creek bank.

The first rider, ahead by more than fifty yards, dismounted and waded into the cool pond, gulping frantically as he pulled the stoppers from two canteens and plunged them beneath the rippling surface while his chin lapped hungrily at the water. After several moments crawled by, the white man whirled at a sound come from behind him. Instead of finding the second rider, the white man saw more than twenty painted warriors bearing down on him—screaming their war cries, weapons raised in the still, hot air.

Major John Jones had watched Mel Porter sprint into the pool and guzzle water, knowing any second the attack was sure to come. When it did, David Bailey was just reining up, entering the brush along the creek bank. At the first war cry and gunshots, Bailey sawed the reins about savagely, kicking his horse into a blur of motion.

But instead of circling a little east of the arroyo, Bailey aimed directly for the ravine, galloping south. Which is why he ran right into Mamanti's warriors.

Jones watched more than ten of them suddenly appear from the brush and frighten Bailey's horse. The Ranger halted in a spray of dust, attempting to turn around, but he was surrounded. Able to fire only two shots before he was impaled on a fourteen-foot buffalo lance and dragged from his horse, Bailey tumbled to the ground beneath the onslaught as the men in the ravine watched helplessly, able to do nothing but fire at that feverish knot of screaming, victorious warriors.

His Rangers were shouting too—in anger, disgust, frustration, perhaps some swallowed-down fear that the very same fate awaited them. Jones turned to find Mel Porter had dropped the canteens and leaped to his saddle. Kicking his horse furiously, Porter galloped north as two Kiowa warriors on fresh ponies broke from the brush on the creek bank, hot in pursuit. The ponies gained steadily on the Ranger's fatigued mount. As the pair of warriors neared their quarry, they whooped their joy, ready to count coup. Porter emptied his pistol at them, then flung the weapon at the closest warrior in sheer rage.

Just as the warrior was swinging his long lance down, Porter turned in the saddle, slipping off the horse and spilling into the brush and grass near the edge of the creek. As the warriors argued momentarily over the possession of the white man's bay horse, Porter dove through the brush, his arms churning like the wings of a prairie swift, and jumped into the creek and swam downstream, careful to stay beneath the surface for as long as he could.

When he poked his head up to suck in a breath, the water around Porter came alive with bullets smacking the surface. Behind him the pair of warriors turned to flee at the gunfire. Confused and bewildered, Porter turned back to face downstream again and realized he had discovered the hiding place of Lee Corn and Richard Wheeler—beneath some overhanging brush at the creek bank. He was staring point-blank into the muzzles of their pistols.

"By God—it's me: Porter. Mel Porter!" he shrieked at them.

"Get on in here," Wheeler growled. "We thought you was a Injun coming for us."

As far as Major Jones knew, his command had been whittled down through the afternoon: Corn, Moore and Glass. And now Porter and Bailey gone. The odds weren't in their favor, but those odds didn't appear to be any the worse than they had been when the afternoon skirmish had begun.

They could wait out the warriors. And with all but three of the horses run off or shot, there was little choice but to wait out the siege.

John B. Jones had never liked being forced into a corner.

Lone Wolf quickly slid from the back of his pony and strode triumphantly to stand over the white man who had been captured by the Kiowas. His eyes had grown as dark as the sap that leaks from hillside pine each spring. For so long he could not utter the names of the dead. But now, in sudden triumph, he shrieked to the sky, raising the brass pipe-tomahawk he held glinting against the sun, shouting the names of his son and nephew.

"Tauankia! Guitain!"

When he peered down at the white man's face, he saw nothing but fear. Surely his manhood was shrunk up to the size of rabbit berries. Such fear disgusted Lone Wolf.

With a mighty heave, the Kiowa chief brought the toma-hawk blade down into that face. The blood and gore that splattered him only fed his rage as he yanked against the resistance to free the tomahawk. The white man was still alive, screaming, thrashing, blinded and struggling with bloody hands to pull the weapon from his tormentor.

Lone Wolf hurled the tomahawk down again. And again. And one last time before the enemy's body ceased all movement. He wiped the brass blade across the white man's splattered britches then shoved it in his belt, where he pulled free a curved skinning knife. Its blade he plunged into the enemy's bowels below the ribs on one side of the body, then yanked across the entire width of the abdomen. With the tip of the blade he pulled some of the greasy purple gut-coil from the long slit. Then more and more, until a mound of it lay quivering in the hot dust.

Once more wiping a bloody weapon across the dead man's britches, dark now with glistening blood, Lone Wolf turned to the rest, many of whom were young warriors yet to earn their first coup.

"Thank you, Spirit Above," he prayed. "Oh, thank you —for what has been done today. My poor son, Tauankia, has been paid back. His spirit is satisfied. Now listen! It was Mamay-day-te who made the first coup on this enemy by touching the white man with his hand. Because of this, and because Mamay-day-te loved my son, I am going to honor him today. I am going to give him my name. Every-body, listen! Let the name of Mamay-day-te remain here on this battleground. Let the name of Mamay-day-te be forgotten. From now on—call this warrior Lone Wolf!"

The young warrior, a boyhood friend of Lone Wolf's son, knelt down and ripped off the scalp of the enemy. When Mamay-day-te finished, the hot-blooded warriors poked the body with their lances, filled it with arrows and bullets, hacked at the limbs and fingers and manhood parts while Lone Wolf sang his old victory song.

> "I have seen my enemy, Spirit Helper.
> He is over the hill.
> I have seen my enemy, Spirit Helper—
> And death is his companion!"

Mamanti, the war party leader, stepped beside Lone Wolf. "The death of your son is avenged. None of us are hurt."

Lone Wolf nodded, looking over the group of young warriors butchering the white man's body. "Yes, and we captured the gray horse you saw in your vision. This was a good day!"

Turning from the chief, Mamanti gave his orders. "Mount, all of you. We are returning home . . . in victory!"

They waited until dark was swallowing the valley before moving out on the major's orders.

At dusk, Lieutenant Hiram Wilson found a pony that had been abandoned by the war party. With some struggle, the Rangers hoisted the body of Billy Glass across the pony's back, lashing wrists to ankles so it would not fall during their march through the dark. Then Jones pulled out, marching his men north for the Loving ranch.

Thirst was still as much a problem as it had been when Bailey and Porter had galloped off and disappeared. So after traveling some two miles before one of the men discovered moonlight reflecting from a small pool among the mesquite, the Rangers greedily hurried forward and surrounded the pool on their knees. Jones did not like the brackish taste of the water. Too, they had to scoop aside inches of scum to get down to something drinkable. But it nonetheless satisfied a day-long suffering in most. The Rangers pressed on to the north, refreshed.

Still, Jones had four men unaccounted for and needed to get word out on the attack. Such was all the major thought about during that long march.

It was close to midnight when the Rangers reached the Loving ranch, less than five miles from the Lost Valley fight. While some of his men ripped boards from the smokehouse to build a crude box for Billy Glass, John Jones sat down to pen his plea.

July 12th

To the Commanding Officer of U.S. Troops at
Ft. Richardson,

Sir,
I was attacked today four miles South of Lovings Ranch by about one hundred well-armed Indians. Had only thirty-five men and lost one man killed, one wounded and five missing. Fought them three hours and drove them off, but have not force enough to attack them. Can you send me assistance to Lovings. The Indians are still in the valley. Lost twelve horses.

Jno. B. Jones
Maj. Comdg. Frontier Battalion

Knowing that Jacksboro and the army post were less than twenty miles to the southeast, Jones wanted most to send Lee Corn out with the message. He was his best rider. But while Corn was still among the missing, Corn's horse had been one of the three to survive the Kiowas' onslaught. Again Jones called for volunteers to carry his plea. He chose the first man to raise his arm.

"After you get out about five miles," Jones explained to the Ranger mounting up on Lee Corn's horse, "give the animal his head. He ought to know his way back home, even in the dark. Let him take you in."

Young John Holmes nodded, his eyes bright in the moonlight. "I'll make it, Major." He saluted and reined out of the yard, gone in the darkness.

Just before dawn, the three missing Rangers hobbled in to the Loving ranch. Corn, Wheeler and Porter were accounted for, making their way north on foot after darkness fell. It had been a harrowing journey, one in which they described stopping every few yards to listen to the sounds of the night, sure the warriors had left behind sentries and were ready to pounce on them at any moment.

After sunrise that morning, the Rangers and Loving's ranch hands held a short burial service for Billy Glass. His grave was dug next to that of the cowboy killed by Comanches two days before.

It wasn't long before a rustle of excitement shot through the ranch. Two companies of brunettes, I and L of the Tenth U.S. Negro Cavalry from Richardson, marched into the yard. Jones mounted as many of his Rangers as he could atop Loving's stock and rode south to Lost Valley, accompanied by Captain T. A. Baldwin's soldiers.

There, between the arroyo and Cameron Creek, the Rangers located the butchered remains of young David Bailey. His head was gone, severed from the body then likely dragged off by a predator, Jones told the rest. While Baldwin divided his troops and sent them out to scour the valley for trail sign of the hostiles, Jones called his Rangers together.

"Dig him a grave and be quick about it," the major ordered.

Then Jones pulled off six of those who were having the most trouble looking at the naked, bloody remains.

This half-dozen he spread out to act as guards while they buried what was left of Bailey where the Ranger had fallen. His final resting place little more than a shallow trench the men had dug out of the flaky soil with their knives and tin cups, anything they could use to bury one of their own.

"Not a sign of them anywhere, Major," admitted Captain Baldwin when he dismounted upon returning later that morning.

"I feared they would escape," Jones replied, clearly bitter.

"Where to from here for you?"

"We'll ride in to Jacksboro with you, Captain. It's there we'll reoutfit and push on."

"Push on, Major Jones? Hunting Indians?"

The small, lithe dynamo nodded, his lips a thin line of determination for a moment. "Yes, Captain. That's my job, don't you see? I hunt Indians."

25

Late July–August, 1874

"How is it you know Sharp Grover?" asked Colonel Ranald Slidell Mackenzie.

Tearing his eyes from the soldiers, Seamus Donegan glanced at the older scout, grinning. "You mean Abner, Colonel?"

Mackenzie smiled, winking at Grover. "Well enough to call him by his Christian name . . . and not get a broken nose for it, I see."

This young commander of the Fourth Cavalry turned and settled into his simple ladder-backed chair. He was not the sort who cottoned to the amenities of fort duty, Seamus figured. Mackenzie was a man who preferred the world of campaign and action to this fort duty. The colonel's office here at Fort Concho was spare, just like the man himself: here one found very little that did not serve a purpose. Mackenzie had devoted his life to this army. But for all those years chasing after the raiders of the Texas Panhandle country, the colonel had little to show for all his time except a single arrow wound in the leg.

From time to time the Tonkawa trackers, perhaps the Lipans or Seminole guides the army would hire, would cross the trail of a raiding party, follow it and bring Mackenzie's troops to a small village—but had yet to bring the colonel to the village where Mackenzie could finally prove that all his chasing up and down the length of the Staked Plain had been of real purpose and worth after all. For all the prisoners taken, for all the Indian ponies captured, for all the lodges and blankets and robes and winter meat burned to blackened ash—Ranald Slidell Mackenzie yearned for something more.

He wanted Quanah Parker.

And, Seamus Donegan knew, Mackenzie would hire on anyone who could shoot and ride and track as well as Sharp Grover said the Irishman could.

"Very well then—you're hired, Mr. Donegan. A dollar a

day and found. You'll feed your horse like we will most of the time: off the land," he told Seamus, his fingers forming a steeple in front of his narrow chin. "Sharp, get this new scout squared away. I'm putting him in your care, and we don't have much time left before we'll be ordered out."

Grover slapped Seamus on the back, nudging Donegan toward the door. "So I've got to nursemaid you again, is it, Irishman? Lordee, if you aren't like a stubborn tick on a old bull's hide—hard to get rid of."

Outside Seamus stopped and said, "You wanting to get rid of me, is it?"

"Hell now, Seamus," Grover replied. "That was just joking. Not grown to be thin-skinned, have you?"

"Naw," he answered, shoving a fist in Grover's direction.

"Good. Why, Becky and Samantha both would have my hide nailed to the barn wall if I let you get away."

Donegan drank deep of the hot, late-summer air. It reminded him of another summer campaign, that one spent following Major Sandy Forsyth with fifty ragtag civilians hoping to snip long enough at Roman Nose's ass that the Cheyenne would turn and fight. Turn and fight they had. But it was more. Here again his nose brought the smells of gun oil and soaped leather, the fragrances of chewing tobacco and pipe smoke and cheap whiskey, the heady aromas of potent coffee and of urine-stained britches and the stench of men too long in the saddle for too damned many days without rest.

His mind grew a'swirl of campaigns wherein he had worn Union blue, a gold slash down his leg, and a few chevrons hurriedly sewn at his arms in those later years. Campaigns east and campaigns west: the white man doing his damnedest to wrench this land from the squatters who had roamed and ruled it for generations, and drawn from it their life force. Their culture. Their spirit.

Across the parade some officer bawled out a command and a mounted company put their horses into motion. The army had to be like that, he mused. On a campaign, someone had to give orders. The rest had to take them. Here at Concho, Mackenzie was gathering six hundred different men—each a different mind and soul and character in six hundred different bodies. But out on the coming campaign, Mackenzie had to see to it that things were put in order. On a march like this after the Kwahadi and the Kiowa Koitsenko and the Cheyenne Dog Soldiers all rolled into one nasty, dirty little war of it—Seamus understood that Ranald Slidell Mackenzie had to weld them all into one.

If they were to survive, much less be victorious, out there on the Staked Plain where the brown horsemen had ruled for centuries, Mackenzie had to fuse the six hundred into one.

"Man needs something to do with his time, I suppose, Sharp."

"Yes. A man does," and suddenly Grover grew morose as they set off across the sun-baked parade of Fort Concho. "This damned drought all but made a beggar out of me, Irishman. What crops didn't burn in the field aren't worth my time harvesting. And the stock isn't coming along like it should. I'll need another year, maybe two, before I can afford to buy the kind of breeding mares it will take to make horse-raising pay."

"You'll do it," Seamus said with an air of confident certainty. "If anyone can make a go of it in this country, Sharp Grover sure as blazes can."

Seamus admired the older man more than he could ever begin to tell Grover. And one thing the Irishman doubted he could ever bring himself to telling Sharp was that Grover had become like an uncle to him. Hardly knowing either Liam or Ian since the time they had shipped to Amerikay when he was but a small lad, Seamus had come to know Grover far better: as a trusted friend, and the closest thing to family he had left. There were brothers and sisters back in Eire. But their faces were the faces of children—what he could remember of them standing alongside his mother at that dock the gray day his ship set off from the green isle in search of those two uncles disappeared across the ocean in Amerikay.* Brothers and sisters, likely cousins and aunts and uncles back there in

* The Plainsmen Series, vol. 1, *Sioux Dawn*

County Kilkenney and County Tyrone too. But they, yes, they might as well be strangers to him for all it was worth. It was a far different life from theirs that he chose to live. With people who became family by choice, not by chance.

Across the years he had wandered the west, Seamus had surrounded himself with family of choice.

So it was with some real joy that Donegan had marched south to Jacksboro the day after he and Billy Dixon and all the rest had made it back to Dodge City without spotting another brown horseman wearing paint or sprouting feathers. As soon as he bailed out of Dixon's light wagon, which had carried him north from Adobe Walls, Donegan pulled both pistols and checked the loads, a gesture sure not to escape Dixon's keen eye.

"Where you headed that you'll need all that lead and powder, Seamus?" Dixon had asked there in the dust of Dodge City's Front Street.

"Going to look up Louis Abragon," he said quietly. "Figure he was the one who wants to see me rubbed out. I'll oblige him and show up on his doorstep."

Dixon leaped down from the front of his huge freight wagon and called Frenchy and Masterson over. "You finish up here for us, fellas. I'll be back in a while. Me and the Irishman going to call on an old friend."

"I can do this myself," Donegan had protested.

"I know you can. Just want to see for myself what you do."

"You need help?" asked young Masterson.

Dixon shook his head, his eyes finally leaving Donegan's face. "No. Thanks all the same, Bat. The Irishman's just got some business to take care of."

"You need help, Donegan," Masterson said, catching hold of the Irishman's sleeve, "you just call it. I'll be there. I figure someway I owe you—what you tried to do saving Billy Tyler back there at the Walls."

"I'll remember, Bat."

"Don't you ever forget—I owe you," Masterson repeated as the pair walked away from the long train of wagons.

But as things turned out, Abragon wasn't around so that

the Irishman could throttle him, choke the breath out of him and beat him until the Mexican was ready to talk about what precious secrets the map hid that would make the saloon owner want to kill Donegan for them.

"He's . . . he's dead?" Seamus shrieked at the bartender in Abragon's place who had just informed them of Abragon's demise.

"Yep. Got hisself killed. Uh, almost three weeks ago now."

"Killed? Someone shoot him?" Dixon asked.

"No," and he wagged his head. "One of the girls, fact be —we all think it was Kate 'cause Abragon was especially hard on her. Think he was more'n just sweet on her. Kept too much the eye on her, you see—well, rest of us figure it was her poisoned Abragon. Seems reasonable she got ahold of some wolfer's strychnine and dumped it in Abragon's food, maybe in his drink. Anyway—strychnine ain't a pretty death, fellas. And the old Mex went kicking all the way till he just lay still. Right over there," and the bartender pointed in the direction of Abragon's private table in a smoky corner.

"He's dead and buried?" Seamus asked, his voice rising in frustration and disbelief.

"Saw him choke down his last breath for myself. Lord how Kate laughed and laughed as Abragon was foaming at the mouth, his tongue swelling, struggling to get a breath. She stood over him and laughed and laughed." He wiped the inside of a dirty glass with a greasy towel. "Women do have a strange sense of humor, don't they, fellas?"

Donegan and Dixon had looked at one another. Dixon rolled his eyes as he turned from the bar. Seamus laid down his money and swept up the bottle of whiskey they had been served. He had paused a moment over the spot where the bartender said Abragon had died. Donegan couldn't help it—he was bitter. Bitter that he had been robbed of another chance to exact some revenge on the Mexican.

"Women do have a strange sense of humor," Billy Dixon said, repeating the bartender's words as Donegan settled in the rickety chair at an empty table. His eyes were going over the girls in the smoky room, noisy with the hurrah and celebration of incoming buffalo men just up from the notorious fight at Adobe Walls.

"Problem is," Donegan replied as he poured them each a drink, "we men don't know for sure just when the women are being humorous, or being downright serious."

"Here's to women," Dixon proposed the toast, lofting his glass in the air. "What we don't know about 'em can downright kill a man."

"Amen to that," Donegan said, his mind beginning to slip back down to Texas and a certain woman said to be waiting for him there.

He remembered the smell of her, the full fleshiness of her as he gripped her tight, pinning her down in that hay inside Grover's fragrant barn. Remembered too the taste of her now, even as the whiskey burned a big, raw hole straight down to his belly. He licked his lips, recalling the earthy flavor of her sweaty skin as she writhed beneath him.

It was their first night together in the barn that he had remembered, sitting there in Dodge City that hot July day. But something inside him told Seamus it was not to be their last.

From Dodge City the very next morning Seamus had ridden out on a new horse purchased with a stake given him by Billy Dixon. With a promise to repay the money before another winter passed, the Irishman had hurried to put Kansas behind him, pushing south by east through the Territories. If he keep his eyes and ears open, Seamus figured, a wary man could avoid any young coup-hungry bucks wandering back and forth between the reservations and the Staked Plain. Too, he had learned he had to be watchful of any white men he happened across. There was a hard breed of man making a life for himself on the fringes of the reservations—outside of any white settlement, outside the law and army justice. And just because their skin was pink did not cancel out the very real chance they wouldn't love to knock Donegan in the head and steal his horse, his guns and everything he carried. Maybe even put a bullet in his head. Just so to simplify things.

It was a relief when Seamus had finally laid eyes on that dirt-colored Red River at last, knowing he was come to Texas. The river meant Fort Richardson and the thriving settlement of Jacksboro weren't far—a little less than 150 miles left to ride. His ass had been scrubbing leather since the early days of the Civil War, and a few more days and a few more miles meant little when she was waiting at the end of the line for him.

Gone since last winter, that first night after Seamus rode into Sharp Grover's yard was one the Irishman was not likely to soon forget. The way Rebecca and Samantha fried up a plump chicken, with white gravy and biscuits as big as his fist, along with some of Rebecca's garden onions mixed in the greens she served on the side, not to mention Grover's special fruit brandy brought out for only the most special of occasions.

The way Samantha had kept turning to look at him that evening as she moved from stove to fireplace, table and back again, rarely taking her eyes off him, reaching out to touch him from time to time—why, Seamus knew that surely was a most special occasion. And when it came time that Rebecca shuffled a drunk and grumpy Sharp off to bed, with a wink to a clearly blushing Samantha that neither of the women suspected Donegan had seen—Seamus was as ready for her as she was hungry for him.

Now he stood at Fort Concho with Sharp Grover, hired on as a civilian scout for Mackenzie's push against the nomadic red raiders of the Staked Plain. Word around the post was that there would be columns marching against the hostiles from five directions. Those bands they did not drive back to the reservation were to be destroyed. To Seamus it sounded every bit like his old commanders, "Uncle Billy" Sherman and "Little Phil" Sheridan, had at last taken all they were going to take of bloodshed on the southern plains. They had conceived of a plan that would get about this business of ending once and for all the Indian problem from the Arkansas clear down to the Rio Grande.

"If need be," one old Fourth Cavalry sergeant said that evening as Seamus was drawing extra shoes and nails for his mount in the stables, "we'll just have to rub the red bastards off the face of the earth."

It was work, he told himself. Something he could readily do: this hunt and track and stalk and fight. And there was little doubt Seamus needed the money. With what he owed Billy Dixon for the horse and other plunder to stake him back south to Texas, with what he owed Sharp Grover to get him from Jacksboro to Fort Concho—he needed the work.

And when this bloody little war was done, he'd likely ride back to that shady horse ranch outside of Jacksboro, Texas, with his friend, Abner Grover, sure of finding someone waiting there for him. It was like that in the army, or just working for a campaign outfit: all some men wanted was a woman who wouldn't cry when it came time for him to ride off leaving her behind while he marched away, following a man called Mackenzie.

Samantha was that sort. He had seen it in her red-rimmed eyes that morning he and Grover left. She had been crying but had washed and splashed cold water on her face and done her best to make it seem it didn't cut her deep that he was leaving her again. But she bit her lip every time it threatened to betray her, and he was certain she had held him tight enough that he wouldn't feel her trembling in his arms.

She was the sort of woman a man could leave behind and go marching off to war. Yet, to him now, Samantha Pike was the sort of woman he wanted to come home to. A woman who had filled a few of his nights with such splendid memories. Memories enough to last him many a cold night to come sleeping on the hard ground of the Staked Plain.

Still, it was not merely the intangible vision of her and the remembrance of the fevered coupling they had shared. He had something more now, something he could touch in the dark of prairie night that would make their separation that much more difficult to bear.

Seamus would carry a small, lace, ladies' handkerchief scented with the lilac smell of her. Carry it into the coming war with the red lords of the Staked Plain.

26

August 22–23, 1874

Reuben Waller had no idea what they would find when Captain Louis Carpenter's H Company got north to the Wichita Agency at Anadarko.

Following the electrifying news that a massive war party had attacked buffalo hunters at Adobe Walls then followed up that siege with other sporadic attacks on settlers and settlements from Kansas down to Texas, the War Department and the Indian Bureau finally agreed on a common policy to get tough. And part of that new posture was to separate the peaceful Indians from those who were inclined to take to the warpath.

On 21 July, General William Tecumseh Sherman telegraphed General Philip H. Sheridan that henceforth reservation boundaries were to be disregarded by the army, that hostile war parties were to be pursued and chastised wherever those warriors were to be found. In an effort to separate the wheat from chaff among the many bands of Cheyenne, Kiowa and Comanche, an immediate enrollment was decided upon. Those on the reservation by a specified closing date, answering the enrollment and submitting to a daily roll call, were to be considered peaceful. The rest were hostile and would be subject to annihilation.

Meanwhile, in Indian Territory itself, the warrior bands were doing their worst: they struck Signal Hill a few miles east of Fort Sill, killing one civilian; the next day some of Satanta's own warriors brazenly rode out of their camp, marching downriver, where they captured and killed two more civilians; the next afternoon, only eight miles south of Fort Sill, a war party shot and butchered two cowboys riding north from their Texas ranch.

And as each week passed, it became more and more clear to both Agent James Haworth and Colonel "Black Jack" Davidson that neither of them was getting the response from the tribes that both had hoped they would. By the end of the first week in August, only 173 of the Kiowas had come in to be enrolled; only 108 Apaches and 83 Comanches under Horseback, Cheevers and Quirts Quip. The bulk of the Kiowas, in fact, had abandoned Kicking Bird's band and gone north with some of their old war chiefs to the Wichita Agency at Anadarko.

The pressure on the agents to supply the needs of these bands increased tenfold when some sixty lodges of Nocona Comanches under chief Big Red Meat came in to enroll and receive their allotments. They and a Kiowa band under Lone Wolf had long been belligerent and refused the agent's request to give up their ponies and weapons. In addition, these warrior bands had been plundering the field crops of the agency's "civilized" Indians, Wichitas and Caddos. On top of it all, strong rumors had it that both Big Red Meat and Lone Wolf had taken part in the attack on Adobe Walls and were to be considered very dangerous.

On 21 August, Haworth's man on the scene, acting agent J. Connell, sent a frightened messenger to Colonel Davidson with word that things had grown ugly there at Anadarko and that he expected trouble any day. Besides the surly mood the warriors were in, there simply wasn't enough rations to go around—and now the white man was demanding that each warrior give his name up so the agent could write it down on a page in his book. His name, the names of his wives and children. To the Indian mind, this giving away of his name was surely not a good thing.

Besides Carpenter's H Company, Davidson would also lead companies C, E and L on that march north the thirty-seven miles from Fort Sill to the scene at Anadarko. Upon his arrival at noon on Saturday, the twenty-second, ration day for the Wichitas, Caddos, Pawnees and Penateka Comanche, the colonel immediately demanded his first audience with chief Big Red Meat, whose warriors were clearly on hand, making a nuisance of themselves with the beef allotment being rationed to the peaceful bands. Evidently the Comanche and Kiowa men were expecting trouble and had grown agitated, sending their women and children over the hills as soon as they received word Davidson's soldiers were drawing near. Big Red Meat and Lone Wolf were clearly anticipating a fight.

"You and your people must surrender," Davidson reminded Big Red Meat through interpreter Horace Jones in the heart of the Comanche camp. "Since you did not register with the agent soon enough, I have no choice but to consider you as hostile. Besides, I am told you and your warriors took part in the fight at Adobe Walls. Now you must give up your weapons, hand them over to my soldiers and return to your own agency at Fort Sill as prisoners of war. Then your people will be given something to eat."

It was a tense scene, with Big Red Meat sternly disagreeing until two of his head men convinced the chief that it would be all right to hand over their weapons. But then Davidson had Horace Jones tell the chief that they expected not just the rifles and pistols, but all weapons—including bows and arrows.

To Reuben Waller it seemed that this demand for total surrender of all weapons had suddenly become a sticky point of pride with the Comanche chief. Never before had any of the bands been required to give up their bows. It was at that crucial moment when a large number of Lone Wolf's Kiowas showed up on the outskirts of the Comanche village and began taunting Big Red Meat's warriors.

"What are they saying to the chief?" Davidson asked, turning to Jones.

"The Kiowas are saying all the Comanche warriors are women. Saying they are afraid of your few buffalo soldiers. Hold it," Jones said, cocking his head to listen to more of the increasing fervor of the rabble.

He bent his head low. "Colonel—we might have trouble here."

"Why do you say that, Jones?"

"The Kiowas just told the Comanches to fight us, to start things—that they would help the Comanches to kill us all."

That look on Davidson's face was the whitest Reuben Waller had ever seen a white man get. But as quickly, the shock of the interpreter's words faded beneath the sudden whoop of warriors crying out their war songs. Chief Big Red Meat cried the loudest as he leaped from his pony, shaking his blanket to frighten the soldier horses, then wheeled and dashed for the thick brush.

"Stop him!" Davidson cried out. "Shoot him if you have to—but stop him now!"

A half-dozen soldiers fired their Springfields. Big Red Meat was still running: not a bullet touched him before he reached the blackjack oaks for cover. But those shots were as quickly returned in spades as the Kiowas and Comanches tore off their blankets, exposing rifles and pistols—firing point-blank into the ranks of the buffalo soldiers, then turning to flee back in the thick timber.

"Dammit, Colonel! There's friendly Penatekas over there! Your men are firing into their camp," shouted the interpreter.

In frustration Colonel Davidson jabbed a fist into the air as the Kiowas and Big Red Meat's Comanches mingled among the friendly Comanche village. "Do your best to separate the hostiles before you shoot—but shoot, by God!"

Quickly the anxious troops were brought to order as snipers began to chip away at them from the surrounding woods.

"First platoon ready!" Waller was hollering above the bedlam, trying to maintain control over his squad. "Fire!"

Nearby, Carpenter was commanding the second platoon. The red-faced captain shouted his own orders now. "Fire!"

"Reload, men. Reload!" Waller demanded of them in the lull while Carpenter's squad volley-fired into the brush where the warriors had disappeared.

After about ten minutes the fighting died off and Davidson called for a report of casualties.

"Not a man was hit—wounded or killed?" asked the colonel, shaking his head in disbelief as he received the news. "How many of the enemy can we account for?"

His adjutant, Sam Woodward, shifted his feet nervously. "None of the companies can account for any enemy casualties, Colonel."

To Waller it was next to impossible for all that lead to be hurled back and forth between the soldiers and warriors for more than ten minutes, not to have any wounded on either side of the skirmish.

"All right, dammit," Davidson growled. "We'll try to

245

drive the hostiles off so we don't harm the peaceful bands. Company L—you will dismount and go on foot to clear the commissary and the corral of those Kiowa snipers who are giving my rear and right flank the fits."

As L Company held down Lone Wolf's snipers, Carpenter's men remounted and followed their white captain into the teeth of the Indian's weapons—succeeding in driving the Comanche and Kiowa backward, but scattering the warriors in all directions across the Washita River, where they began plundering the cabins of a friendly Delaware named Black Beaver, along with looting trader William Shirley's store, where the warriors unfurled bolts of colorful cloth as they rode across the yard, slit open grain sacks and smashed every piece of china and crockery. Carpenter pursued, pushing his mounts across the Washita into the timber where the warriors whirled to fight, but only momentarily.

Waller heard the hiss of the bullet, felt the burn along his side, sensing the warmth and wetness more than the coming of any pain. He looked down as his horse fought the bit, its screams filling the air as Waller dabbed his fingers at the flesh wound.

After all these years, he thought, to finally feel a warrior's bullet after all these years. He swallowed down the pain and rode on, encouraging his men as the icy sting washed over him in hot, blue waves that threatened to pull him from his saddle.

With the hostiles scattered and running, Davidson recalled his troops as the shooting died off. The colonel directed his companies to secure the agency and then ordered the destruction of the Noconas' lodges and property as the summer sun sank like an angry red protest in the west.

From time to time through the dark of that night, snipers crept back close to the soldier lines on the south side of the Washita, succeeding in keeping Davidson's troops awake and watchful. Behind Waller and his men rose the glow of those great bonfires as the people of Big Red Meat's band watched their lives go up in smoke, everything they owned turned to ash.

Reports trickled in of casualties: no soldiers killed, with four wounded, but the warriors had murdered trader Shirley's Negro houseboy, who had gone running for help when the trading house was attacked, in addition to the murder of three white civilians working in their fields a few miles downriver and two Delaware employees of the chief named Black Beaver.

Beneath the first gray light of dawn the following morning, 23 August, the warriors resumed their sniping as they attempted to keep the soldiers at bay while some three hundred warriors worked their way into position on some high ground overlooking the Wichita Agency.

"Captain Carpenter," Davidson ordered, "I am placing E and L at your disposal. Take them and your H—and drive the enemy from that ridge."

In a brief but furious battle that required the three companies to skirmish for every foot of ground from the bottom of the slope all the way to the crest of the hill, the warriors ultimately gave way and fell back, some running upriver, the rest disappearing down the Washita. Despite the uneasy calm that came over the battlefield, something nagged at Reuben Waller while the rest of the three companies celebrated their victory there on the hilltop.

He had smelled that odor before, and not all that long ago either.

"Fire, Captain," he explained to Carpenter moments later after riding down to the agency grounds. "Look yonder through the trees there. The smoke. The Injuns set it to drive us off."

"And the wind is most definitely coming our way, Sergeant," Carpenter said, sensing the seriousness of the threat. "Take your squad and set some backfires before the wind drives those flames onto the agency grounds."

While Waller and his men did as Carpenter had ordered, the wind itself was far from cooperating with the puny efforts of humankind. It shifted out of the north, immediately causing the brunettes' backfires to roar out of control, rampaging in sheets of flame licking right in the direction of the agency buildings. What should have been a temporary maneuver turned out to be a dirty, smoky, stinking fatigue duty that lasted all afternoon before the soldiers got control of the fire lines and managed to save the saw-mill, school and offices of the Anadarko Agency.

"The bastards're probably laughing up their sleeves at us, Sergeant," growled a disgusted Carpenter.

"Might be—but I figure the army's going to get the last laugh on them, Captain," Waller replied, his smoke-black-ened face gleaming in the afternoon light. "Come a day real soon, we'll be the ones to call the last dance of the night."

27

Late August 1874

As far as things went in the military scheme of things, that brief skirmish at Anadarko down in Indian Territory really settled very little.

Yet it did have one lasting effect on the rest of the forth-coming campaign. Davidson's four companies of buffalo soldiers had once and for all cut the deck: separating the peaceful reservation Indians from those bands that were clearly hostile. Only those who had not answered the daily roll call at Sill, Anadarko, and the Cheyenne Agency up at Darlington, were now fleeing west toward the headwaters of the Red and Brazos rivers on the Staked Plain. These were the bands the army wanted to crush.

And the army now had a clearly drawn line between those who walked the white man's road and those who would fight to the end.

Already Sherman's and Sheridan's campaign to bring peace to the southern plains was in motion: five columns were converging on the Panhandle at last.

Up and down the rungs of echelon, the army was so sure of its impending victory and in the cunning cleverness of its five-pronged attack that when a party of government sur-veyors requested a detail of troops to accompany them through southern Kansas, the army refused.

"Not only am I without men to spare you—what with the strength General Miles has taken from us for his campaign

—but there are simply no hostile Indians in this area where you are headed," explained the officer, jabbing his finger at his map, that finger landing in Kansas, just north of Indian Territory.

Captain Oliver Francis Short had to swallow down his anger and leave before he grew any more furious with the soldier. It was something he had had to learn to do in his forty-one years. His was one of eight teams completing the survey of public lands in Kansas for the government. Born and raised back east in Ohio, Short had been a resident of Leavenworth for the past twenty years. In fact, he had been a member of the original survey party platting Kansas Territory in the fifties.

Short ofttimes joked about having his scalp taken by Indians, telling friends and coworkers, "As many times as those proslavers out of Missouri wanted to deprive me of my hair—I don't think there's an Injun who can separate this scalp from me!"

The leader of the second group to travel with Short was Captain Luther A. Thrasher. Also forty-one and a veteran of pro-Union, abolitionist forces in Kansas during the rebellion, Thrasher got along well with Short.

Oliver liked the men he worked with this trip out, despite any rumbles of anxiety over the recent Indian scares. And besides, Short really did love the outdoors more than most men. It was there he truly felt in his element. It was with his normal enthusiasm that he gathered his crew at Dodge City that first week in August: his assistant, a Captain Abram Cutler; his two sons, Harry and Daniel; another assistant named James Shaw; along with several assistants who were students at Kansas University. Joining forces with Thrasher's team, the twenty-two men marched southwest for Meade County on the border of the Territories, where they were contracted to survey some two thousand miles of section lines.

In a broad, beautiful valley, Short and Thrasher established their base camp beside a spring where a single large cottonwood flourished, giving the local name to the place: Lone Tree Valley. Here the grass was good for the stock, with clean, sweet water. Besides, the surveyors discovered rocks aplenty to use as corner markers as they worked their way from section to section, platting the land for the claims of future settlers. Even Oliver's pet dog liked the place, chasing after rabbits and field mice from sunup to sundown.

Although he was aware of recent disturbances caused by the Indians, Captain Short found himself agreeing that there really was little cause for alarm. However, both he and Thrasher nonetheless agreed that should either party fall under attack, they were to set fire to the summer-dried grass as a means to signal the others. With plans for their departure made that Saturday upon arriving at Lone Tree Valley, both teams set about readying their tools and stowing gear in the wagons. Sunday saw the men attend a short worship service, after which Captain Short spent the shank of the afternoon reading in his bible after he had washed clothes.

As they were cleaning up from breakfast on Monday morning, 24 August, a group of three buffalo hunters stopped in camp and shared a cup of coffee before moving on north, agreeing to carry Short's letter to his wife, Francis, on to Dodge where it would be forwarded back to Leavenworth. Then the group hitched up their teams and separated for the day's labors.

"You'll take care, won't you, Pa?" asked Harry Short.

Oliver gazed at his eldest son, who he was leaving in camp to oversee the repair of some equipment that morning. "Do your work and keep your hands busy, Harry. The day will pass quickly enough." He urged the oxen away from the spring.

"Keep your eyes along the horizon, Oliver!" hollered Luther Thrasher as the Short wagons pulled away to the south.

"We'll see nothing but blue sky today, Luther," Short replied, his pet dog seated beside him as he waved. "Until suppertime."

Short's group waved farewell to the others and was quickly swallowed by the tall, waving grass and rolling hills of the central plains, like an ocean swallows a dinghy.

* * *

Medicine Water knew he wasn't the smartest Cheyenne war chief that ever sat a buffalo pony. But he had been smart enough to slip his war party north between three marching columns of soldiers.

The armies of Miles and Buell and Price were all behind him now, converging on the Staked Plain to make war. Medicine Water's brown horsemen had southern Kansas all to themselves.

For most of his life the war chief had been less than successful as a raider. There were other war chiefs far better at planning than he. But Medicine Water had two things on his side. First of all, he was as primitive a predator as was a prairie wolf—and that made for a fierce reputation among his people. And secondly, Medicine Water was married to Buffalo Calf Woman—a full-fledged warrior in her own right, one who had drawn blood and counted many a coup in numerous raids as she rode along on her husband's sorties. In her breast beat a heart as cold as that of Medicine Water, and for white folks she felt nothing but hatred and fury.

Ten years before, Buffalo Calf Woman had lost her first husband to Colonel John M. Chivington at the Sand Creek Massacre, along with their three children. Let no warrior make a mistake: she was clearly second-in-command of this war party, some twenty-five strong. They each had their reasons for following Medicine Water and Buffalo Calf Woman north following the poor showing at Adobe Walls, but one thing each warrior held in common: where this predatory husband and his wife went, there was sure to be blood and plunder and ponies. Never any lack of excitement.

Their fourth day across the medicine line, that northern boundary marking the extent of the Cheyenne Reservation, young Yellow Horse rode back to report that he had discovered some wagon tracks plowing the tall grass. Medicine Water and the rest dismounted to inspect the ground.

"They are traveling south," Buffalo Calf Woman said, looking to the southeast.

"Perhaps they are supply wagons, going to Camp Supply," Yellow Horse suggested.

"Yes," Medicine Water replied, his wolfish grin slashing his fleshy, bronze face. His eyes had gone the color of dark underbellies of thunderclouds rolling across the prairie. "Those wagons will carry much plunder."

With Yellow Horse leading the rest by a hundred yards, the war party set off once more at a lively pace, riding south by southeast along the fresh wagon tracks made through the tall bluestem grass just that morning, now in the summer days of the Moon When Geese Shed Their Feathers.

Besides the blankets and flour and coffee and sugar, there might also be a few guns they could steal from the white men who were driving the wagons. A wagon meant that they would steal some of the white man's horses as well. It would be good. Horses to replace those ponies white horse thieves had been stealing right off the Cheyenne Reservation.

And there would surely be a scalp or two to make the others happy. Medicine Water had enough scalps. He hoped the wagons carried some of the burning water that made his eyes sting and his head feel light, like down from a goose. Able to float away after he had swallowed enough. It was at times like that when Medicine Water most enjoyed rutting with Buffalo Calf Woman. When she had enough of the burning water, she would strip off her clothing and chase him unashamedly through camp, then drop to her hands and knees, wagging her ample rump provocatively until Medicine Water plunged himself into her, just to listen to her grunt, enjoying herself with such abandon.

With the burning water in their bellies, they were like two insatiable animals enjoying one another's flesh.

Yes, Medicine Water hoped he would find some whiskey in the white man's wagons.

"Pa, look over there," said fourteen-year-old Daniel Short, pointing at the summer-smudged skyline, hazed with shimmering mirages.

Oliver gazed over his shoulder at the northern horizon. It was just after midday, the sun hung high in a pale blue sky. The glare often hurt his eyes anymore. They swam with the distance and the grass waving beneath a persistent hot breeze.

"Can you see them, Oliver?" asked Abram Cutler.

"I think so," and he really did believe he saw the horsemen fanning out on the horizon to the northeast now.

"What are they?"

"Oh, God—they're Indians!" Cutler suddenly shouted.

Short was in motion that next heartbeat. "Everyone in the wagon. Quickly!"

Oliver had the plodding oxen turning as soon as he had slapped their backsides with leather. He thought he heard one of the young men whimpering in the back, and prayed it was not Daniel. No, not his own son crying in fear and panic and—

He bit off the thought the way he would bite off a dark corner of a plug. Just keep these oxen moving. Maybe they could get close enough to their camp that the others would hear the gunshots. Yes, there would be gunfire, Oliver thought. Those Indian ponies are far faster than these hulking oxen pulling this wagon with all of us and our gear in it.

He turned slightly, flinging his voice over his shoulder. "Abram! See what you can do to lighten the load!"

"You want me to throw our instruments out?"

"We can't go fast enough with all of us and the weight too. Throw the blessed instruments out!"

The other five men promptly obeyed, heaving boxes and tripods and leather cases over the sidewalls as the wagon lurched and rumbled over the uneven prairie. He figured they had been running over a mile already. Perhaps close to two miles . . .

"Is that all?" Short demanded.

"Everything but our guns." Cutler's face was white, pasty.

"Then get ready to use them," Short told them. "These oxen have about had it."

A moment later a dozen warriors had swept along each side of the wagon. Most were hollering, crying out their pagan chants and those war songs Oliver had heard so much about. It made his throat seize to hear them now for himself, slapping again and again the thick latigo reins down on the rumps of the oxen. Then the grinning warriors began firing their weapons, bullets slapping the side of the wagon. One of the four oxen grunted, throwing its head about before it went down in a tumble of traces.

"Jump!" he hollered at the rest the instant before the wagon began to keel over on the double-tree.

The warriors swept in then, firing at the three remaining, snorting oxen. It was as if they were putting off bringing the pitiful little skirmish to an end too quickly.

One by one the surveyors went down. Oliver watched his Daniel fall. Then Shaw's son Allen. And finally two of the young students from the university, Harry Jones and John Keuchler, crumpled, lifeless. As he turned to find himself a better position behind one of the downed oxen, a bullet struck Short.

He grunted, surprised. He had always thought you weren't supposed to hear the bullet that got you. That's what they had said during the war: that you never heard one. But by damned, he had heard that one.

"James," he whispered, his mouth filling with blood, hot and sticky like warm syrup.

"Oh, Jesus," James Shaw said as he turned and found Oliver sinking.

Oliver wanted to cry out in pain. Maybe even rage. He had never done anything to these people . . . then he remembered his bible, thought of nothing else and began crawling for it . . . somewhere here in all of this jumble of gear.

He quickly gave up. Oliver simply didn't have the strength. Looking up into the sun and sky where Shaw crouched over him, Short said, "Make a run for it. Run." He could barely hand his pistol over to the older man. He was panting for breath now, so hard to breathe. It felt as if his lungs were full of hot coals.

The fifty-one-year-old Shaw stared down into the captain's face, taking the pistol. "I suppose I could run. Chances are as good as staying here."

Shaw dragged Short's hand away from Oliver's chest and shook it, with a look in his eyes that Oliver did not like. It was a look that said they were parting for the last time. And Oliver sure as hell did not like that.

He wanted to growl something angry, but said only, "Now—go!"

Short watched Shaw scramble to his feet and vault a dead ox, firing two shots as he leaped through the tall grass.

With renewed whoops and screeching calls, the warriors swarmed toward Shaw. Then the scene was all gone from Oliver's vision. But he could still hear the pounding of hoofbeats somewhere behind him now. James was running, hard. And he could almost hear Shaw's rapid breathing, his thundering boots.

He must be trying to make it to the top of that hill behind . .

There was a flurry of shots. A pause. Then another flurry of shots that gave Oliver some hope.

Then all was quiet. And the sun beat down on him while his breathing grew harder and harder. After a long time, the glaring, blinding sun was blotted out.

Oliver blinked, barely able now even to move his eyes. Seeing and not believing as he gazed upward into the face of an incredibly ugly Indian woman. In her hand she held a limp scalp, dripping with blood. In the other, a huge butcher knife, slick with crimson. He could see the dirt under her fingernails, the blood crusted in dark half-moons back of the nails.

Short watched her face, hypnotized as she gripped his hair, yanked his head back, and brutally dragged the butcher knife across his throat.

Gurgling with that last, wheezing breath, Oliver called his wife's name.

"F-Francis . . ."

Medicine Water saw that his warriors were satisfied, not only with the white men they had killed and had just finished mutilating, but also with the shiny objects of great curiosity they had found among the enemy's belongings.

Yellow Horse called frantically, his voice filled with fear. Stepping over the body of the man whose throat Buffalo

Calf Woman had slit, the war chief found the others staring like frightened children at a round object lying on the ground at the center of their ring of dusty moccasins.

When he picked it up, the others drew back suddenly. "You see this before?" he demanded of Yellow Horse.

The young warrior nodded, wide-eyed. "I dropped it . . . it frightened me."

Medicine Water looked it over suspiciously, top and bottom, then held the round object, about the size of his palm, against his ear. He had long ago learned that some white men carried magical objects that made soft noises. But this made no noise. He shook it, then brought it to his ear once more. Still no noise.

"Perhaps it is not magical," he admitted with a shrug, trying to hand it back to Yellow Horse.

But the young warrior shrank from the object. The others jerked back from it as well.

"It is evil, Medicine Water!" Yellow Horse explained, fear in his voice.

"Evil?"

"Turn . . . turn it, and watch," Yellow Horse pantomimed with his hands, not wishing to get any closer to the object.

Medicine Water turned it in his outstretched palm. Then jerked his hand away. The object spun to the dust.

It was truly evil.

The long black arrow inside the object always pointed in the direction the white men came from: the north. This was truly evil medicine. Although the long black arrow danced and bobbed a bit, it had still pointed toward the white man's settlements in the land called Kansas.

This could only mean that it was some powerful divining object the white man used to bring other white men, perhaps even yellowleg soldiers, after the Indian.

He kicked it with his toe. It lay there, the black arrow trembling. Then coming to a rest.

Abruptly, Medicine Water grabbed the evil thing and smashed it violently into the dead white man's forehead with all his strength.

Evil for evil, Medicine Water thought, gratified as he

gazed down at the dead man, the front of his sweat-stained shirt now drying with dull-brown blood from the gaping neck wound. The white man's features sagged after Buffalo Calf Woman had scalped him. Yet he had smashed the object into the man's head with such force that it clung there, embedded into the skull and blood and lacerated flesh.

Evil for evil.

No white man would ever again use that evil object to divine anything. And these white men would never again bring their evil to the doorstep of Indian ground.

"We ride," he growled at them.

He wanted to be away from there before the evil spirits began to rise from these lifeless bodies. This was truly a bad place. And it made the powerful, thick-witted Medicine Water more than a little frightened.

He punished his pony making his escape from that place of the white man's demons.

"Captain Thrasher! Captain Thrasher!"

Luther Thrasher stood from the noon fire where he had set a pot of water to boil coffee and watched one of his workers riding in.

"What is it, Crist? You look like you've seen a ghost."

S. B. Crist licked his dry lips as he dismounted. "I got a feeling something's wrong. I seen the Short wagon."

As Thrasher glanced over his shoulder, he saw Harry Short stepping up.

"Pa's wagon?"

Crist nodded.

"You see anyone around it?" Thrasher asked, a sinking feeling going cold in his gut like a stone.

"No. No stock."

"Did you go to the wagon? Was their gear in it?" Harry Short demanded, his voice rising with fear.

"I didn't go there. Just watched it long enough to know it was deserted."

"Where?"

He pointed. "About three miles that way. Over by Crooked Creek."

"Let's go." Then, in afterthought, Thrasher turned to Short. "Why don't you do as your father asked you, Harry: stay here and tend to camp while we go. There's likely nothing wrong—they just wandered off from the wagon working."

"But where are the oxen?" Harry asked, shrieking. "I'm going with you!"

Thrasher caught him roughly. "You'll stay here. Until your father returns, I'm in charge—and that's an order, Harry. Stay . . . here."

After he had designated two of his men to stay behind with the teenaged Harry Short, Thrasher took Crist and two others with him, each man heavily armed as a precaution, and headed for Crooked Creek, herding a pair of plodding oxen with them to hitch to the disembodied wagon.

They came across the first of the toolboxes pitched from the wagon. Then more and more of the surveyors' tools were found scattered in a rough line that led them to the scene. For better than three miles, over the rolling hills and across Crooked Creek itself, the six men had been chased as they pitched everything from the wagon, fighting off their attackers. There were emptied cartridges and shell cases all along the last two miles of the chase. Eventually, the captain figured, the seven men had been overwhelmed.

As Luther Thrasher slowly walked around the scene, a bandanna covering his mouth and nose, he knew he would not soon forget this sight. Much less the sickeningly sweet odor of decaying, bloated flesh. It had been two days since he had seen these men.

All seven were laid out in a row, facing the sky, horribly mutilated. Thrasher had never seen anything like this. Oh, he had heard stories told. But never actually laid his own eyes on anything so savagely gruesome.

Piled in the tall, dry grass, still hitched to the wagon, lay the four oxen, their sides bristling with arrows or pocked with bullet holes infested now with flies and beetles. Rear haunches had been sliced off and carried away as food by the raiders.

It made Thrasher aware of the noise here in the awe-
258

some silence of this grassy swale near the creek. The noise of the huge deerflies crawling over and in and through the blood and gore of the men and their terrible wounds.

Young John Keuchler's skull was caved in, as were the skulls of both James Shaw and his son Allen. Harry Jones, along with both Oliver Short and young Daniel Short, had been entirely scalped, from brow to nape of the neck, taking off the tops of the ears with the scalp. All were still fully clothed, their garments ripped where the warriors had slashed the victims, pockets turned inside out looking for something to steal.

But most horrific was the condition of Oliver Short—that compass smashed into his forehead, blood pooled and dried now in the corners of his wide-open eyes. Staring back at Luther Thrasher.

"Captain."

He welcomed the diversion, walking over to where Crist was pointing at the ground.

"Look at the boot prints," Crist suggested. "They run off this way—and I mean he was running."

Thrasher nodded. "Yes, those are Shaw's prints. The old man was running when they got him."

"Dragged him back here to the others. Think he was the last?" Crist asked.

Then Luther nodded. "God bless his soul—but if he were the last, and had to watch what happened to the rest of these . . . to his son as well . . . then, God bless James Shaw's soul."

28

Moon of Plums Ripening, 1874

Lone Wolf and Mamanti had hurried their people west on the trail to Palo Duro Canyon after those two days of fighting at the Anadarko Agency had driven off not only Big Red Meat's band of Comanches, but the hostile Kiowa bands as well. Davidson's buffalo soldiers had seen to that.

Now, along with the Comanches, the Kiowa were fleeing almost due west, across Rainy Mountain Creek and Elk

Creek, striking for both the North and Salt forks of the Red River before they would arrive at the Prairie Dog Fork which would lead them to the deep red hues of that deep canyon slashed into the flat, forbidding desert face of the Staked Plain. It was there in the Palo Duro that Lone Wolf would make plans with Mamanti to lead more raids south of the Red River, into the land of the white man's ranches and settlements.

At Lost Valley, Lone Wolf had claimed revenge on the young white man for the death of Tauankia. Now he could get on with this business of making war.

Almost single-handedly Lone Wolf had irritated the pride of Big Red Meat and pricked the manhood feelings of the chief's Comanche warriors—stirring up the two-day skirmish at the Wichita Agency.

And yet Lone Wolf knew it was but the beginning.

This was to be a glorious war, he thought as he watched the other head men of the Kiowa bands gather in a large circle beneath the mesquite trees along a narrow stream here west of the North Fork of the Red River. It had been a brutally hot summer, hotter than any summer the old men in the tribe could remember in their long lifetimes, in the stories of the ones gone before. So it was they gathered at twilight as the weary village on the move quieted for the night and the men could talk about the route they would take over the next few days. More especially, they were gathering to talk about the news brought in by scouts that afternoon: a long supply train of wagons had been spotted to the north of the Washita, in the direction of the Antelope Hills and moving south. It was within easy striking distance. A brief skirmish would be all that was needed, and Lone Wolf's people would have not only the supplies captured, but a resounding victory under their belts. Lone Wolf was filled with happy anticipation.

Still, even with as much success as his war band had enjoyed in the last two moons, Lone Wolf did not like the looks on some of the faces as the old men and warriors settled to the ground on pieces of buffalo robe and blanket for this council.

Mamanti called for a burning brand. It was hurried from

the fire by a young student of the shaman. Mamanti stoked the great pipe, then offered his prayer to the four winds and the sky, finally praying to the Earth Mother to protect them as the Kiowa people walked across her breast in peace, raced their ponies across her breast in war.

As the pipe made its slow, deliberate path around the great circle of their council ring, Lone Wolf angrily sensed that the atmosphere had become grave, when it should have been much more joyous. And after Mamanti had discussed his opinion on the route to take over the next few days, Lone Wolf knew why so many of the others wore such dark, morose masks of doubt and defeat on their faces. It was even more plain to see as one after another of the Kiowa head men spoke that they had lost their militant fervor—while that same fever still burned in Lone Wolf's breast.

"But our women and children grow very hungry," Woman's Heart complained.

"We can feed them on the juicy hump of the buffalo when we have gone a little farther," Mamanti reminded them. "They have only to wait."

"They are hungry now," Big Tree said, then his eyes touched each one of the militant ones. "Each of us knows the white hunters have been there before us. Not one among you can guarantee there will be buffalo when we reach the Staked Plain."

"This is true," Woman's Heart agreed. "The buffalo hunters—they have killed most of the great herds already. And we cannot find the buffalo that remain."

"We have not looked hard enough," Lone Wolf said, growing disgusted with the direction this talk was taking. He never would have thought—

"I must go back," Satanta said suddenly, stunning the entire assembly.

"Go? Go back?" Lone Wolf asked his old friend, the cold catching in his chest like a winter storm.

Satanta nodded. "If the soldiers catch me making war again, catch me even roaming with a war band . . . they will put the iron bracelets on my hands and feet. Carry me back to Tehas where they will work me on the tracks for the smoking horse again. I could not take that, old friend."

For the moment Lone Wolf was confused. He felt sympathy for his longtime friend. They had fought the white man, gone on raids together as young men, held out together as long as they could—even been threatened with hanging death at the end of Yellow Hair Custer's rope. Yet Satanta had remained strong, resolved.

And now . . .

"You will go back too, Big Tree?" Lone Wolf turned to ask of the other war chief, who with Satanta had been imprisoned in Tehas.

Big Tree nodded. Only that.

"So. This is what we come to?" Lone Wolf asked as the others averted their eyes from him. "I now see Kicking Bird is not the only one who likes the taste of the white man's greasy bacon, the texture of the white man's worm-infested flour, eh?"

Woman's Heart stood, haughty and furious at the affront, ready to leave the council. "No, I do not like the taste of the white man's food. But when it is all I have to feed my children, I will take it. No longer can I feed them on your promises, Lone Wolf. Their little bellies grow emptier with every day. Your promises don't even fill our hearts any longer."

"I make no promises that are not true!" Lone Wolf snapped. "We will find the buffalo. We will unite with all the Comanche and Cheyenne who wish to live free. We will live as our fathers did—and drive the white man out of this land. And we will attack that wagon train near the Washita, wipe it out—"

"No!" Woman's Heart shouted, pointing, his hand trembling. "No more can we allow the Tonkawas and Delawares and Pawnee trackers to lead the yellowleg soldiers to our villages and kill our families. The buffalo are going, Lone Wolf! Listen! Can you hear the great herds moving north? See there—along the skyline to the west? There are no buffalo out there. And soon there will be no free Indians there either. Not Cheyenne. Not Comanche." His throat seized a moment. "And not Kiowa."

"I will be there," Mamanti said harshly, holding up his sacred stuffed owl—a symbol of not only his office, but his occult power as well. "And so will my people."

"You will be dead, Mamanti," Big Tree said suddenly, a sad, bitter tone to his voice. "And there will be no one to grieve for you. The Tonkawas will see that your families are killed by the same soldiers that will harry and hunt and track you down. Until the only Kiowa left are those of us who will return to the reservation."

For long moments it was quiet, until Satanta said, "I go now." He arose slowly, his huge bulk still a powerful image in the life of his people. "Tomorrow, we start back to the reservation."

"You will beg the agent to let you live beside the stinking camp of Kicking Bird, where his people grow ill?" Lone Wolf asked.

Satanta nodded, his face almost impassive. "Yes, if we must, we will live in that camp beside the stinking water filled with human offal. Where the air is filled with the stench and the sickness of the soldier fort. At least there we will know that the soldiers will not attack at dawn, will not murder our women and children and the old ones."

"It is for the old ones that I keep fighting," Lone Wolf said as he stood. "It is for the little ones too."

Surprising most in that circle, Lone Wolf suddenly crossed the council ring and embraced his old friend of long-ago days.

"I will always remember the Satanta I grew up with," he said, tears moistening his eyes. "The Satanta who carried his red lance into battle, wetting it with the blood of many an enemy—Tonkawa, Pawnee, Caddo and white man. That is the Satanta who will always live in here." A finger tapped against his heart.

For a moment the White Bear could not speak, and when he did, Satanta was still reluctant to bring his eyes to Lone Wolf's. But slowly he brought Lone Wolf's hand to his breast, laying it over his heart.

"And it is here in the heart of Satanta, that you shall always live, my friend. For you are the last of the mighty Kiowa."

The ninth of September, he thought, rocking on the seat of the high-walled Pittsburgh freight wagon.

James McKinley had himself enough of buffalo hunting for now. Across two seasons he had hunted the great beasts south of the Arkansas, then pushed south of the Cimarron. And then he had gone even farther with the others last spring, all the way to the Canadian and the settlement that came to be known as Adobe Walls. McKinley had been there in Jimmy Hanrahan's saloon the morning those screaming brown horsemen raced out of the sun and almost battered in the doors before he and the rest could throw tables down for barricades and start returning gunfire at the hundreds and hundreds streaming into the meadow.

McKinley shuddered involuntarily now—as yet unable to shake the vision of that day-long siege, still troubled by it all the more at nights. He awoke sweating at times, even though the season was slowly turning. A brief, noisy, crackling thundershower came across this land most every day now. Turning the air damp and chill. Yet he still awoke sweating, afraid. Knowing how lucky he and the rest had been.

Even with those brief daily thunderstorms, the drought continued. The ground only drank up each brief cloudburst, without becoming so much as muddy.

Giving up on the idea of hunting buffalo until the Indian war was settled, McKinley had hired out to wagonmaster Jacob Sandford as a contract teamster once the government got its southern campaign rolling. He was employed to haul freight from Fort Dodge to Camp Supply, and from there on south as Colonel Nelson A. Miles marched steadfastly into Indian country. By now, the ninth, Miles had established a cantonment on the banks of the North Fork of the Red River, near the caprock of the Staked Plain. From there he was already striking out at the infernal warrior bands who had attacked Adobe Walls, who were continuing to murder and plunder and burn up and down the entire length of the Panhandle of Texas.

With the sway and rock of the big wagons pulled by a six-hitch of mule, McKinley could let his eyes droop against the warm autumn sun and doze a bit. His team obediently followed the wagon before them, forever plodding south-west out of Fort Supply for the base camp established by Miles. There were thirty-six wagons, most covered by dingy canvas. Strung up and down the trail on either side of the column were some fifty soldiers, I Company of the Fifth Infantry. And out in the van as skirmishers sent ahead of them all rode Lieutenant Frank West and a dozen troopers from the Sixth Cavalry. In command of these men and the train was Captain Wyllys Lyman of the Fifth Infantry, widely known as an officer Miles himself trusted highly.

They had begun this long, circuitous march back at Miles's base camp. With empty wagons Lyman had led the escort northeast to the Canadian, where they were to have met a wagon train due out of Camp Supply on 5 September. For two anxious days Lyman had waited while his teamsters languished in camp before the captain sent out six of his own men under Lieutenant Frank West to find out what had become of the train from Fort Supply. The following day an alarm was raised when a teamster named Moore was found murdered and scalped not far from camp. Every man was put on alert.

Late on the eighth, the wagons from Camp Supply showed up at Lyman's camp on Commission Creek—a full four days late. The campaign supplies were off-loaded into the captain's wagons for the return trip. Plans were to heave about at sunrise the next morning, laden with what fodder an army on the move badly needed.

Then sometime in the early morning hours of the ninth, a ripple of excitement shot through the sleeping encampment. Four men had found their way into camp, leading not only four weary, muddy horses, but a teenaged captive. He was a red-haired herd guard who the four white men had taken prisoner on their frightening trip north. Yet they had discovered this pony guard was actually a white boy. Evidently taken captive as a small child, the youth called himself Tehan, for the land where he had been taken by the Kiowa, his adopted people.

Around the fires the grimy, muddy four gathered, hunger and trial written on their gaunt faces. Lieutenant Frank Baldwin, Miles's own chief of scouts, was accompanied by three civilian buffalo hunters known to McKinley: Ira Wing, Lem Wilson and William Schmalsle. The four greedily gulped at half-boiled coffee and stuffed their mouths with hardtack and raw bacon, grease dripping off their whiskered chins as they told of their harrowing trip north to locate the overdue Lyman.

"Miles was goddamned worried about you, Captain," declared Baldwin. "Especially when he got word that some of the hostiles slipped around behind his column and might be between Kansas and him. He was afeared for you and your train."

"Who are these hostiles?" Lyman had asked.

"Two hundred Cheyenne, we're told. Got reports on 'em making trouble," Baldwin said between gulps of coffee.

"Eat up, men," Lyman told the four. "Then you can tell us of your journey here."

When they did, Baldwin told a tale of three days of running into war parties time and again, of being forced to escape for their lives in the dark up sheer canyon walls, of running smack into an Indian village, mistaking the lodges for what they thought were the army's conical Sibley tents.

Just this morning at their breakfast fires, Lyman had confided in Sandford's civilian teamsters what he would not share with his own soldiers: that in the report from Miles brought them by Baldwin, the colonel had expressed worry that some of the hostiles had slipped around behind his own column as they had marched south. Lyman strongly suggested that the drivers keep their eyes moving from here on out, searching the distant hills along the road. He wanted no surprise if indeed the warrior bands had slipped behind the Miles command—chopping the colonel's supply line as neatly as they would with a scalping knife.

That morning as the sun poked its head over the blackjack oaks in the east, Baldwin saluted and bid the wagon train farewell. The lieutenant was continuing on to Fort Supply with Miles's dispatches and two of his civilian scouts, Wilson and Wing. William Schmalsle had been selected to ride back with Lyman's train, placed in charge of the redheaded Kiowa captive Baldwin was sending back for Miles himself to interrogate.

The autumn sun on its morning climb was finally beginning to warm the air a little this ninth day of September. To James McKinley, it damn well promised to be a beautiful day.

Then the air resounded with gunfire and the screams of warriors.

McKinley's heart shot to his throat as men began shouting up and down the long column of thirty-six wagons. Unlike most of the others, civilian and teamster, this survivor of Adobe Walls knew what it meant to be under attack.

29

September 9–11, 1874

Lone Wolf had watched the progressive battle all morning. From the first moment of attack, the Kiowa and Comanche warriors had harassed the white men and the soldiers up and down both sides of their long column. Horsemen darted back and forth, sniping here and there, looking for a soft spot to attack, hungry for coup counting.

If the days were numbered that a young man could make a name for himself earning scalps and ponies, then this might surely be one of the last great battles for these young warriors. It was a glorious day to fight, Lone Wolf thought through the long morning as the wagon train ground slowly toward the Washita.

From hill to hill he and Mamanti rode as the morning progressed, stopping from time to time to watch the fighting as the wagons and their soldier escort plodded forward, for the most part keeping the brown horsemen at bay. Now as the sun hung just past mid-sky, Big Red Meat rode up and halted beside the two Kiowa chiefs.

"I am tiring of this fight," the Comanche growled.

"Me too," replied Mamanti, glancing at Lone Wolf.

He nodded. "If we keep fighting like this—there will be no scalps for the young men. No presents for the women."

Mamanti laughed. "We dare not go back to camp without presents."

Lone Wolf chuckled along with Big Red Meat. "That is right," the Kiowa said. "The women already know about this wagon train and they will not be denied their presents!"

"I think we should make the wagon train stop so we can fight this out," Big Red Meat suggested.

"Yes," Mamanti agreed.

Lone Wolf considered, his eyes scanning the countryside ahead of the white man's long train of wagons. "There," and he pointed. "The trail they are on will take them to that creek. The banks are steep. The wagons and their mules will be slow in crossing. It is there our warriors must press our all-out attack."

Normally the wagons on the trail were kept some twenty yards apart. But now every driver's team was nosing the rear of the wagon in front of him.

All morning long, almost from those first shots, the Indians had been racing up and down the column, pushing here and there against Lieutenant West's cavalry, troopers doing a splendid job of keeping the van cleared for the first wagon. And now, with the sun at mid-heaven, James McKinley wondered if Captain Lyman intended on making this a running fight for the rest of the day. While the screeching voices fell about them like hammer strikes on an iron tire, the soldiers kept firing, marching, reloading and firing again when they had a target—although most of the time the brown, painted riders galloped by in nothing more threatening than a grand display of their horsemanship. Some hung from the far sides of their ponies, others sat erect, daring the soldiers to shoot them from their animals. And a courageous few actually stood atop the backs of the lunging, leaping ponies that raced up and down the length of the caravan, lending a touch of the traveling circus to their wild display of horsemanship.

All these young, green soldiers, thought McKinley as he watched the skirmish progress through the day—young soldiers, each one dreaming of smooth-skinned bodies, and until this morning counting down the hours of march until beans for supper. How well McKinley knew that soldiers dream of only three things: grub, whiskey when they could afford it, and women when they could find them. But always a soldier thought of whiskey and women. Not such bad things for a man to dwell on . . .

Up ahead in the broken, austere country, McKinley caught a glimpse of the beckoning line of green that signaled they were coming to a creek. And there, would be forced to make a crossing. Forced to slow their pace for the teams ahead descending the sharp creek banks with brakes set and teams grunting against their loads, the teamsters would become more of a target. But there at the creekbank was just where Captain Lyman was, swirling 'round and 'round on his horse, shouting orders and encouragement as the first team with wagonmaster Sandford nosed warily down to the ford, trace chains jangling, axles squealing, accompanied by snorts and hoof thuds from the team, whipcracks and a fair measure of curses from Sandford himself.

A second, then a third rumbled down the steep bank as the first team began its climb up the far side of Gageby Creek. The Washita itself could not be far now.

Of a sudden the air erupted with even more wild screeching and gunfire, sounds so hot McKinley believed those war whoops could have burned a man's ears off. On three sides the warriors charged in now, catching most of the wagons bunched as the teamsters were forced to grind to a halt for the crossing. An advantage worth pressing.

"First and second squads—left oblique!" Lyman shouted, his voice cracking like a quirt on still air as he waved an arm wildly at the brown horsemen racing for them.

In a whirl of dust the captain wheeled his frightened mount and shouted to the far side of the train. "Sergeant deArmond! Third and fourth squads—right oblique!"

With only a salute, the trail-worn veteran sergeant prodded his well-trained troops into a defensive formation.

With orders barked up and down both columns of infantry, I Company hurried forward, the two wings spreading like the sides of an arrow point, slowly, gradually, noisily and not without casualties, pushing the charging, screaming warriors back, foot by foot, then yard by yard, from the crossing.

Their grit held fast that day.

One after another the wagons rumbled down the bank, through the water then up again to cross Gageby Creek as the air grew hotter still, filled with the angry, snarling wasps of lead and iron-tipped arrows. In amazement, James McKinley watched the young, mustached Lyman on the far side of the creek, sitting tall in the saddle, his service revolver in hand, signaling, prodding, urging the teamsters across the ford, forming those who made the climb up the dusty rise into a corral of their wagons.

McKinley was in the creek and driving his mules up the slippery side slashed by many an iron wagon tire when he heard the pleas for help behind him. He turned to see a young teamster grow petrified when his own team balked at the edge of the water, whipping their heads and fighting the reins.

Sergeant Nicholas deArmond spun toward the creek on foot, splashing past McKinley, bellering for a couple of men to come with him. The old sergeant never made it to the wagon.

As James watched, deArmond stopped suddenly in midstream, as if he had been brought upright by a bolt of lightning. He began to clutch at his back, then fell facedown, arms akimbo, into the shallow stream.

Right behind the sergeant, the two privates were scooping deArmond's body out of the summertime flow of Gageby Creek with that next breath, dragging him toward the faltering team. Together they hoisted the sergeant's soggy body into the back of the freight wagon then splashed to the front pair of mules. There they whipped and prodded and beat and cursed the animals across as more lead slapped the water around them.

In a matter of minutes the last of the thirty-six wagons made the crossing and closed Lyman's corral on the far side of Gageby Creek.

The siege began.

This kind of warfare would take longer for his young men to win, Lone Wolf realized. But at least the wagons were no longer moving. The white man and his plunder were going nowhere now.

One great charge, then another, the warriors made on that wagon corral. The fighting became furious as the hundreds of warriors then attempted to draw closer and closer still on foot. It was a time of great glory for the young ones: to perform brave deeds and earn many coups.

But to Lone Wolf's consternation, the white men held the warriors off. Time and again, charge after charge, the warriors fell back, unable to breech that ring of wagons and mules and flaming muzzles.

"We will have to wait them out," Lone Wolf told Mamanti and Big Red Meat.

The other two regarded the sky.

"The sun has made half its journey already," Big Red Meat said, sounding dissatisfied with what Lone Wolf had suggested.

He would not let the Comanche's doubt nettle him. "There is always tomorrow, when the sun will rise again. We can wait."

"But the white man will try to make it to water," Mamanti said.

"We both remember the fight where I avenged the death of my son." He watched Mamanti nod with a smile. "Be assured there will be a few mice that flee the den to go for water," he told them. "All we have to do . . . is wait."

In the first of those wild, screaming, noisy charges, Lieutenant Granville Lewis was knocked from his perch atop a wagon seat, shot through the knee and crying in agony. Two soldiers near Lewis dragged him out of the wagon and onto the ground, where one of them ripped off a belt and tried to stop the flow of blood. The Indian bullet had clipped a big artery in the back of the lieutenant's knee. In moments Lewis fell quiet, no longer thrashing about, his face ashen. Any man who looked at the lieutenant knew he had quickly plummeted into shock and likely was close to death already from loss of blood.

"Make him as comfortable as you can," Wyllys Lyman told the soldiers, then turned away, his eyes momentarily touching James McKinley.

"You've been under fire before, haven't you? Fight in the rebellion?" Lyman asked.

McKinley shook his head. "Not old enough."

"Where then?"

"Adobe Walls."

Lyman smiled. "By blue Jesus, I'm glad to have you here with me today, Mister . . . ?"

"McKinley. James."

Lyman nodded thoughtfully, then was gone suddenly, trotting off to the far side of the corral, where they were hollering for him from the low depression of an old buffalo wallow.

Hell, McKinley thought, these red bastards got us so far over the barrel at this crossing that our asses are pointing sun-high. James swallowed hard, watching Lyman go, then replied in a low whisper, "I ain't so damned glad to be here with you today, Lieutenant."

For the rest of the afternoon and on into the first streaks of twilight coming down on the prairie, the warriors fired sniping shots at the soldiers and civilians taking shelter behind the wagons. When they could, the warriors tried to hit the mules. For the most part they were making more of a nuisance of themselves than posing a serious threat, now that they had ceased mounting their concerted charges.

Without so much as a word of it being spoken, every man in that corral knew what their situation was: halfway between the Miles cantonment and Fort Supply. And what water they had was in their canteens and water barrels, along with a little murky, scum-covered rainwater slowly drying in that old buffalo wallow on the far side of the corral.

How many days would it be before Miles realized the wagon train was late? How many more days would it take for the relief Miles would send to make it here, scare off the warriors and lift the siege and save their hash?

272

From time to time the bullets flew past his ear and over his head like angry hornets. Sometimes they struck something more than the canvas tops on some of the wagons, smacking into the iron bows, or slamming into the oak and ash barrels of flour and sugar and coffee. In the center of the corral the soldiers had stacked the precious boxes of ammunition. One thing was certain, this bunch wasn't going to run out of ammunition, McKinley chided himself. Water might become a real problem—but they had enough cartridges to hold off every warrior on the entire southern plains if they had to.

Beneath the purple glow of twilight, Lyman ordered his soldiers to begin work on rifle pits that would completely surround the wagon corral. With their bayonets, their pocketknives, tin cups and plates and lengths of board torn from opened ammunition crates, the infantry and cavalry alike began to dig in.

No one had to ask the captain why. Every man jack of them knew this was a siege.

Between Mamanti and himself, Lone Wolf chose groups of warriors to sleep and eat, while others they put to work digging pits to fight from, trenches dug in the ground as close to the white man's wagons as the warriors dared go under cover of darkness.

From time to time one of the warriors would grow tired of digging with his hands and his knife, for such was woman's work. Fighting was a task for a man. And a warrior here or there would resume shooting in the dark, aiming in the general direction of the wagon corral. It wasn't a lot of shooting, Lone Wolf mused. Just enough to remain almost constant. Enough that he knew he would not get much sleep this night before the sky in the east turned the color of old ash in a fire pit back in his lodge.

He wanted his wife's warmth right now, thinking about her plump body heat. Especially as cold as the nights were getting now. After the sun went down in the west, the ground gave up its heat quickly this season of the year. He shivered, feeling very old at this moment. Wishing he again had the hot blood of a young man.

Then he cursed himself for being so foolish. Perhaps he did not have the hot blood of a young man for coupling with women, but Lone Wolf knew he still possessed the hot blood of a young man for making war on the whites.

His hatred would keep him warm this night. Until dawn his hatred of the pale-skinned ones would keep Lone Wolf warm.

In the murky light of sundown, some of the warriors had again mounted their ponies and circled the corral, again showing off their horsemanship and acrobatics, noisily crying out and firing beneath the animals' necks at the wagons, but doing little damage.

Once the dark had clotted around them blacker than the unopened paunch of a buffalo calf, McKinley tried dozing. But he was too uncomfortable sitting up behind the wagon wheel in his rifle pit. Besides, every time he started to nod off, another rattle of gunfire would startle everyone away, men start yelling, warriors whooping for a few moments until things quieted down. It was that way all night. Enough to put a man's teeth on edge and get his nerves scraped raw by the time the sun was crawling out of the east.

"My God," he whispered, nudging the young infantryman beside him. "Look."

The soldier rubbed the sleep-grit from his eyes and blinked into the gray light. "Red bastards dug pits too."

"Sure as hell did," McKinley answered.

From the front lines of both sides the riflefire erupted as soon as it was light enough to make out a target. And the sporadic duel continued throughout the morning and into the late afternoon. More noise than damage done.

By twilight of that second day the water situation had become a genuine concern. The sun had seen to it that the rainwater caught at the bottom of the scummy buffalo wallow had all but dried. And throughout two days of fighting beneath that same sun, the soldiers had drained their canteens. Any water kegs lashed to the far sides of the wagons were riddled with holes already, drained of their precious contents.

Those kegs lashed to the near sides of the wagons were nearly empty as the men refilled their canteens periodically beneath an unmerciful brassy globe suspended like an unmoving orb. Yet the sun did fall, despite predictions that it wouldn't from the hot, thirsty, swollen-tongued soldiers.

Sometime after dark but before moonrise, McKinley learned that some of the soldiers had gone out to find water at a pool where Gageby Creek eddied against the bank less than a quarter mile away. They had taken the Kiowa captive along when he had expressed a desire to help them fetch the water. Word passed around the ring now beneath the stars had it that the young red-haired captive had made good his escape from the soldiers, who brought back a scanty supply of water for all their trouble.

McKinley turned at the sound of the horse's snort and the low voices coming near. He watched Lyman hand the buffalo hunter, William F. Schmalsle, an official note.

> In the field near Washita River
> 3 o'clock, P.M., Sept. 10th, 1874

Commanding Officer
Camp Supply

Sir:

I have the honor to report that I am corralled by Comanches, two miles north of the Washita, on Gen'l Miles' trail. We have been engaged since yesterday morning, having moved since first firing, about 12 miles. I consider it injudicious to attempt to proceed further, in view of the importance of my train, and the broken ground ahead. It was nearly stampeded yesterday. Communication with Gen'l. Miles is closed. My scout very properly will not return.

Lt. Lewis is dangerously wounded through the knee and I think he will die if he has no medical assistance. The Assistant Wagoner McCoy is mortally wounded, I fear. Sergeant DeArmon, Co. I, 5th Infantry is killed, a dozen mules disabled.

I think I may properly ask quick aid especially for

Lieut. Lewis, a most valuable officer. I have only a small pool of rain water for the men which will dry up today.

I estimate the number of Indians vaguely at several hundred (as Lieut. Baldwin did), whom we have punished somewhat.

Scout Marshall, who left Camp Supply, I am told, has not reached me.

I have but twelve mounted men—West made a pretty charge with them yesterday.

> Very respectfully
> Your obedient servant,
>   (s) W. Lyman
> Capt. 5th Infantry
> Commdg. Train Guard

When Schmalsle had stuffed the note inside his greasy shirt, he shook hands with the captain. Then turned to James and held out his hand. The front of his bib shirt was stained with brown-black tobacco-juice dribble, standing out beneath the starshine.

"You gonna wish me luck too, McKinley? Say a prayer that them Injuns don't eat my testicles off?" he asked.

They shook. "You acting cockier than a sassback jaybird. What you fixing on doing, Bill?"

Self-conscious, he checked the near stirrup. "Riding out of here, see."

"Are you, now?"

"As sure as buffler pies draw flies." His face went a little more serious, furrows raised between his brows. "I volunteered to go, Jimmy—don't like the company in these parts." He turned to Lyman of a sudden, with a quick grin. "Not your soldiers, Captain. I was meaning these infernal redskins."

"God go with you, Mr. Schmalsle," Lyman said quietly, then saluted the civilian as he climbed aboard the horse.

Struck dumb of a sudden, McKinley didn't know what to say. He had always taken Schmalsle as a soft sort, not the kind would volunteer to ride into the dark through that red gauntlet. McKinley had been through the fire of Adobe

Walls and knew the others would long be considered heroes. But this—this ride Schmalsle was about to make—was something altogether different, a unique sort of sand and tallow required. Why, the idea of leading a horse single-handed out into that darkness was enough to curdle a man's blood to fly pepper. And here, this quiet Billy Schmalsle was about to go with a grin on his face—

"Pull that tongue back!" Lyman shouted to a knot of a half-dozen soldiers.

In the darkness, they muscled the freight wagon back far enough for the horseman to slip into the night, and Schmalsle was gone.

"I hope he makes it," McKinley said, standing there beside Wyllys Lyman, drenched in autumn starshine.

The officer only nodded, dragged a hand beneath one eye before he strode off toward the far side of the corral, clearing his throat.

30

September 11–13, 1874

Lone Wolf had to laugh. And it felt good.

When the young red-haired Kiowa escaped his captors and slipped back to the Kiowa lines with his story of the white men wandering around in the dark, frightened by every sound as they looked for a water hole that wasn't there and allowed the boy to disappear unnoticed, Lone Wolf found that very funny. Along with the fact that Tehan told them the white men were growing most desperate for water.

Their siege was working.

"And you got some new clothes for all your time and trouble among the soldiers, eh?" Lone Wolf asked the youth.

Tehan twirled around, showing off his baggy soldier britches, cuffed at the ankles above his moccasins, proud of his baggy soldier tunic, also rolled up to the wrists. The brass buttons shone brightly beneath the starshine. "You do not mind if I keep them?"

Lone Wolf laughed again, rubbing the youth's head. "No, I do not mind. These soldier clothes you won in battle —the same as any weapon or clothing taken from enemy dead. You were brave and cagey like a fox—waiting for your chance to escape. Yes, I am proud of you, young one: convincing the soldiers you were glad to be back among your own kind."

Tehan beamed proudly, straightening his back. "I did not want to go back to live among the white men. My father would beat me again, and besides—I like eating raw liver."

"Go now. Get yourself something to eat at one of the fires, Tehan," the Kiowa chief told him.

After finding a quiet place where he could lean against a mesquite tree, Lone Wolf smoked his small pipe, finding that he was getting low on tobacco. Perhaps those wagons carried some of the white man's tobacco cubes, he thought as he drew the heady smoke deep into his lungs, holding it there as he felt it seep into every corner and crevice of his chest, then slowly released its powerful aroma through his nose. This was one thing the white man was good for—he made good tobacco, Lone Wolf mused.

And guns. The white man made guns and powder and bullets.

Good for guns and tobacco. And little else, he brooded, his forehead wrinkling.

The next thing he remembered was the cold breeze nuzzling the braid at the side of his cheek. Opening his eyes, Lone Wolf found the sky graying with dawn. He closed his eyes again until the first shots were fired, opening the third day of the siege.

That morning the Kiowa and Comanche warriors again fought from their rifle pits, the white man from his. Then early in the afternoon as the sun slid out of mid-sky, a pair of Comanche scouts came riding out of the south and reined up before Big Red Meat.

In a matter of minutes the Comanche chief strode over to Lone Wolf and Mamanti.

"I am curious to know what your scouts have found out," Lone Wolf told the Comanche.

"They say there are two groups of soldiers nearing us now," Big Red Meat informed them.

"Where?" Mamanti asked.

"North. And northwest."

Lone Wolf sighed. "Perhaps we have had all our fun for now?"

Mamanti strode off to the shade of a mesquite tree, where he once more unwrapped the coyote bundle and brought out the stuffed owl. In a few minutes he was back with Lone Wolf and Big Red Meat.

"Yes. The spirits say we should go before those soldiers get here to rescue the white men in the wagons."

Lone Wolf looked at the Comanche. "Your scouts found the soldiers. My war chief with the owl medicine tells me it is time to leave. Shall we ride away together?"

Big Red Meat considered. "I am wanting to go to the pretty canyon where the water is sweet and the air cool in the day."

"Palo Duro?" Mamanti asked.

"Yes."

Lone Wolf smiled. "It is a good place. Plenty of wood and grass. And we can be safe there. Yes."

The Comanche grinned. "Then we will ride there together?"

The Kiowa smiled at the Comanche chief. "We are together in this war, are we not?"

"Lone Wolf! Mamanti—you must stop Yellow Wolf!"

They turned to find a warrior hurrying in their direction, shouting. Lone Wolf asked, "What is it I must stop him from?"

The warrior was breathless, pointing to a group of others struggling to keep young Yellow Wolf from climbing atop his pony. "He wants to ride alone and attack the wagons. We have learned the news from the Comanche scout that more soldiers are coming—and Yellow Wolf wants to earn his glory before we leave."

"Tell his brother to keep him from leaving."

As Lone Wolf was turning away from the scene, he saw a lone, young half-breed warrior preparing his bonnet with earth paint, tying a white sash about his waist. Motioning

279

the shaman to join him, Lone Wolf strode over to Mamanti's nephew. "This one, he is your brother's son?"

"Yes," Mamanti answered. "His mother is Mexican. A captive who is a good woman."

"Will you let him ride into the face of the soldier guns, Swan?"

Mamanti nodded. "He started life with a curse against him—his Mexican blood. If today he makes a name for himself by bravely riding . . . perhaps dying . . . then that curse will be lifted."

Botalye stopped his pony by the war leaders. "They stopped Yellow Wolf. But I am going. I am going to see how much power these rifles of the white men have. Wish me well, Uncle?"

Mamanti held his hand up. They clasped wrists. "I wish you all the power I have to give."

"*Keee-yiii!*" the youth shouted. "Then I will be successful!"

He reined away, pounding his heels into the pony's ribs, racing out of the trees straight for the rifle pits, intending to ride right over the white men burrowed like rabbits in their holes. As he left the brush, the Kiowas and Comanches opened up on the wagon corral to cover his approach.

The white men, soldiers and civilians, returned the fire, a few of them realizing that a solitary warrior was racing their way, carrying nothing more than a long wand in one hand, a rawhide circle suspended at its apex where was tied a long, brown scalp. No weapons, only that sacred rawhide medicine wheel as the young Botalye came screeching at the top of his lungs, his face contorted in both fear and excitement.

In three leaps he cleared the trenches, bullets whistling all about him. Frightened that his pony had been hit, Botalye brought the animal about in a broad circle, patting its neck, cooing to it as the pony snorted and stamped, nostrils flaring. On the far side of the corral the Kiowa and Comanche were standing, jumping, cheering his success. On this side too the rest of the warriors were hollering at him—singing of his bravery.

But Botalye was not yet done. Again he hammered the

pony's ribs. For an instant the animal fought the single rein, then leaped away again, once more racing straight for the black muzzles of the white man's rifles, which began to spit more orange and yellow flame as he vaulted over their crude trenches.

After that second charge, the warriors on all sides of the wagon corral were growing wild with celebration. Mamanti was running toward him, holding his powerful owl medicine aloft, yelling something. Botalye could not understand, could not hear for all the noise of cheering pounding his ears.

Yet it was not only the loud voices singing in his ears. As his heart throbbed in his throat, the youth only knew he had this act of bravery to complete.

As Mamanti lunged for his nephew's rein, Botalye pulled away, lunging along the neck of the pony.

"Come back, nephew! Do not do this!" Mamanti shouted.

This time the youth watched the eyes of the soldiers as he rode over them. He was not sure, but on some of the young, pink faces he thought he read some envy, perhaps something akin to admiration.

The warriors on the far side of the corral were around him now, touching his leg, his arm, singing his praises. This was an unheard of thing: to charge into the white man's guns unarmed. Only one other Kiowa in the entire oral history of the tribe had ever done it three times before. And that was long before any man now alive could remember.

Tilting his chin to the sky, Botalye said his prayer, urging his pony out of the crowd.

They grabbed for his rein. Lunged for his foot, grabbed for an ankle.

"Come back—no one has ever attempted four charges!" they yelled at him. "No one!"

This time the white men were standing, throwing their rifles to their shoulders. They would not make it easy for him, his mind raced. Botalye would have to part them the way a fighting fish parts fast water to swim upstream.

A bullet clipped the single feather he wore tied at his

scalp lock. A second burned a furrow along his flesh as it sang past. Another struck his hand gripping the rein close to the powerful pony's neck. But the animal did not falter. A final bullet whined past, clipping the knot tied in the white sash at his waist.

And then Botalye was among the enemy—through them —and clearing the far side of the trenches.

Mamanti was grabbing at the bridle, Lone Wolf was pulling, urging him off the pony. There was singing and dancing. Somewhere the old men were pounding drums. A few women were coming forward and trilling their tongues in ancient praise-giving. All were singing of his unheard of courage. His name would go down in the legends of their people.

"Are you hurt, young one?" asked the oldest chief among them, Poor Buffalo.

Botalye looked down at his body, smeared with sweat and furred with dust, searching for wounds. But he was not hurt. Still, his heart would not get out of his throat to allow him to speak.

Poor Buffalo cried out. Lone Wolf answered with a victorious cry of his own. The whole valley rocked with the raucous cheer of hundreds of throats.

"No more are you the Mexican half-breed called Botalye," declared Poor Buffalo. "I give you a new name. From this day forward, you will be known as 'He Wouldn't Listen to Them'!"

Yesterday, the eleventh of September, not long before the lone warrior rode back and forth over the rifle pits, the men had greedily broken into the supplies they were hauling to General Miles. Not only were the wounded moaning pitiably for water—every man inside that wagon corral was in a bad way because of thirst.

James McKinley couldn't remember who came up with the idea, but it had been one of Lyman's men. God bless him, McKinley thought again now. Those cans of fruit they opened, hungrily, thirstily sucking down the juice, licking the inner crevices of each can opened—that had saved Lyman's little command.

Today at dawn the sun never rose in the sky.

It was funny for McKinley to think of it like that, but it seemed it happened just that way. Heavy banks of clouds had gathered themselves overhead sometime overnight, obscuring the rising of the sun.

"Looks like they're pulling back!" someone shouted from the far side of the corral in that diffuse, gray light of predawn.

And as soon as he had said it, gunfire erupted from the Indian positions ringing the wagon train.

But despite the fact that a few warriors were left behind to keep the white men occupied, it wasn't long before it became apparent that the majority of the horsemen had pulled off. Where they had gone and if they would stay gone were the two main subjects of whispered discussion that morning until Lyman called an officers' conference to decide on a plan of action.

Lieutenant Frank West volunteered to take his dozen cavalry, riding out to clear what warriors still remained to harass them. It was another pretty show, filled with flurries of gunfire and wheeling about into line for another wild charge echoed by war whoops and more gunfire, so that eventually it truly seemed the white men were alone here by Gageby Creek.

Lyman immediately ordered half of the able-bodied to rush to the nearby pool a quarter mile away and fill canteens and mess kettles with fresh water. Everyone celebrated in his own way, blessing the water—finally, plenty of it.

"Damn, but that do taste good " muttered the soldier down on his hands and knees beside James McKinley.

"Don't it?" McKinley said, the precious moisture dripping like dew off his ragged chin whiskers.

"We got 'em now, don't we, mister?" asked the soldier. "Got them red sonsabitches four ways of Sunday."

Then not long after the darkness of night's retreat had spread itself into a pasty, gray light, the undergut of the sky split itself, opening on the white men and soldiers huddled in their rifle pits. Whereas yesterday and the day before had been unmercifully hot, with little breeze stirring—this day proved to be even more miserable as the men sat in the puddles found gathering at the bottom of every pit. They shivered with every gust of wind that shouldered out of the northwest, reminding them autumn was clearly on its way.

Some of the men even lapped at the muddy rainwater collecting around them in depressions in the red-tinged, sandy soil, scooping with their hands in futile attempts to empty their pits. Others sat stoically in the water, knowing at least that they could warm it with their own body heat while they waited out these final hours of the siege.

No one really doubted that the Indians were only pulling back to regroup. No man there within that miserable wagon corral dared allow himself to think they had driven the warriors off.

That same morning, buffalo hunter Schmalsle reached Fort Supply not long after the gray rising of the sun behind the thunderclouds. Minutes before noon Lieutenant Henry Kingsbury loped away to the southwest, leading forty-five troopers, seven scouts and the post surgeon to attend to Lyman's wounded.

In the afternoon mist and murky haze left in the wake of the bone-numbing storm, some of the men on the west side of the corral believed they saw objects moving in the distance. The alarm went up and the corral prepared for a renewed attack. With the rainstorm rumbling on east, they were certain the Indians had returned.

"No Injun likes the rain," McKinley told the young soldier in the pit beside him.

"Shit. I don't like the rain," growled the trooper, his lips blue with cold, his clothing soaked as he shifted in the puddle where he sat, shivering uncontrollably. "Just a fire. Just a little, goddamned fire is all I want right now."

For some time Lyman watched the distant objects himself through field glasses and determined those riders marching in from the west might be some relief. To attract the rescue party, he ordered three volleys fired by ten of his infantry while he sent another group to a nearby hill to watch the strangers' movement. After less than thirty minutes it appeared the distant column was veering off sharply to the north for some reason, refusing to investigate Lyman's volleys.

The soldiers fired another succession of volleys, but the marching column disappeared beyond the far horizon that much quicker. Some palpable despair settled over the cold wagon corral that afternoon as the sun slipped momentarily beneath the far western clouds, making quite a brilliant show of itself before twilight swallowed the day and night descended on the Texas Panhandle. Except for the moaning of the wounded and the officers constantly moving about checking on the men keeping watch at every side of the corral, there wasn't much noise, and even less talk. Wasn't much use in talking, and nothing else to do but for a man to brood on their condition here halfway between Fort Supply and Colonel Miles's base camp. Besides, there were two dead and three wounded. McKinley knew if two of those wounded soldiers didn't get attention soon, there'd be two more bodies to wrap in blankets.

Without much trouble, McKinley remembered that first night at Adobe Walls. How Jimmy Hanrahan had opened up his best stuff for those in the saloon and let them all have a taste of good whiskey, chased by a little sweet brandy. They had saluted one another, and roundly toasted their holding the day against the horde of horsemen. That had been a shining time, that night—yes, it surely had.

It made McKinley wish all the more that he were someplace else, anyplace with some of those buffalo hunters.

From time to time he slept, awakening to the sound of thundering hoofbeats, only to find it had been his own snoring, or that of the young soldier shivering beside him that had snapped him to. James fell back into a fitful sleep again and again until the moon sank a couple hours after midnight. He was trying to make a soft place for his shoulder against the side of the rifle pit when he heard what he took to be the faint chink of a bit chain.

With the hair rising on the back of his neck, McKinley pulled up his Sharps and pointed it at the inky, starlit darkness, searching the east side of the corral. Something stirred out there across that open ground—something back in the trees. He made a rest for the rifle, boring his elbow into the sodden soil, ready—

"Ho! The train!"

A voice hollered from the northeast, back in those inky trees.

"Captain!" shouted some soldier in a pit not far from McKinley's.

"Captain Lyman? You there, Captain?" a voice called from the dark treeline.

James couldn't be sure, but it sort of sounded like that voice belonged to Billy Schmalsle, a fellow buffalo hunter. The one who had balls enough to slip away into the darkness and ride alone through the red gauntlet to—

"I brought the help you wanted, Captain Lyman!"

James turned as the rustle of men and motion swelled like a living thing all around him of a sudden. Soldiers and civilians crowding to the east side of the corral now. More noise a'rustle from the timber.

"Is that you, Schmalsle?" Lyman asked, his voice booming into the night.

"Damned if it ain't, Captain!" Schmalsle replied. Then it sounded like he flung his voice behind him. "Y'all c'mon now, Lieutenant. I told you I'd get your men here in the dark, by damned. I told you I could do it."

"Yes—please. Come on in, f-fellas." Lyman's strong voice cracked now. "We'd . . . we'd sure appreciate the company."

31

Moon of Scarlet Plums, 1874

Despite the miles traveled and the days put behind him, Medicine Water was still suspicious of some of the strange things the wagon men had been carrying with them when his Cheyenne warriors had attacked the whites three weeks before. One after another, his war party had discarded the papers and poles, chains, corner markers, leather and wooden boxes, and all the rest of those shiny objects, coming to believe that these too might prove to be evil.

Just as evil as was the shiny disk with its dancing needle before he smashed it into the white man's forehead.

In the days since that attack, he had been leading the war party north by west in a rambling course across the open, rolling countryside without seeing as much as a sign of any more white men. These were good days, with little to concern them, for the soldiers had all marched south of them now, he supposed, sorting through it in his dull way like a bear scratching at a rotten tree stump, clawing away at the ants and bees and grubs he brought to his pink tongue. But those soldiers were chasing after Stone Calf and the rest, trying to herd the slippery Kwahadis onto the reservation. Perhaps, Medicine Water told himself repeatedly, he could even lead his little war party far enough north now to reach their cousins among the Northern Cheyenne: Lame Deer and Little Bear and Two Moons. From the land, they would take what they needed in the way of food. There were antelope and deer aplenty.

And if they ran across any white men, travelers or settlers, then his warriors would take what they wanted.

It seemed very simple in his untroubled equation of life.

"Medicine Water!"

He was shaken from his lazy reverie atop the back of his rocking pony by the shouts coming from one of the young scouts racing back to the war party.

"A wagon!"

"Only one?" he asked, sneering with disappointment.

The young scout nodded. "Moving west. Not far."

"How many men?"

"One riding. Another walking beside the wagon."

"Only two white men?" asked Buffalo Calf Woman, her tongue flicking across her dry lips, dark eyes searching her husband's.

This time the scout shook his head. "No, there are others."

Medicine Water grinned. "Women?" Then he *felt* his wife's eyes on him.

"Yes," and he held up the fingers on his grimy hand. "At least that many. Two walking. The rest riding in the wagon."

"Do they have a lot for us to steal?" Buffalo Calf Woman inquired, her eyes brightened by the prospect.

The scout's head bobbed eagerly.

"Two men . . . and five women," and with the way his mouth watered, and the manner in which he said it, Medicine Water knew immediately he had made his wife angry.

Buffalo Calf Woman was glowering at him. Then she smiled, playing with a long, greasy sprig of her own hair, an evil glint come to her eye. "Scalps are scalps, my husband. If they are a man's . . . even if they are a woman's."

She still looked at the world through a child's eyes. Yet this was to be the fourth month she would again expect the "woman's surprise," as her mother called it.

Four months ago Sophia German had started bleeding. She was becoming a woman—so said her mother and three older sisters. Sophia wasn't sure she was ready for that just yet. She wasn't yet ready to let go being a child.

This great, rolling land offered so much play beneath the deep late-summer blue canopy arching over them day after long, long day of marching west, following Papa's dream of reaching the Rockies of Colorado. The fifth of seven children born to John and Lydia German, Sophia still looked at things through a child's eyes. Even this work of coming west, and work it had been.

She had been born in the spring, thirteen years before on the family farm back in the Blue Ridge Mountain country of northwestern Georgia. And almost as far back as Sophia could remember, Papa had talked about Colorado: the great, yawning, untouched valleys waiting for his plow, a grand land draped endlessly as far as the eye could see below the immeasurable bulk of mountains that ran from horizon to distant horizon, each one still capped with snow in these late days of summer heat. He always told them these wistful tales of that Garden of Eden around the family table, and now at every evening fire—explaining again how he had begun dreaming of this far land back during the war when he had been a prisoner of the Yankees, listening to another Confederate who spoke longingly of the glowing letters he had received from a friend gone to the

288

goldfields in the Rockies two years before the war. Cherry Creek. Cripple Creek. Why, even Denver City itself . . .

When German limped home from that filthy, typhus-ridden prison at Rock Island, Illinois, Colorado had already become his obsession. There was nothing left in Georgia—the farm burned and ravaged by Sherman's troops. So in some way, it seemed to John and Lydia that God had taken away just about everything so that He could make them ready to receive His blessed bounty in the west. The family prepared to make their way across the plains to the seductive lure of the Rockies.

Starting with little, John German ran out of money after getting only as far as Sparta, Tennessee. By hiring out, doing what he could to feed his family for some time, the farmer was finally able to set aside enough so they could press on to Howell County, Missouri, where some of Lydia's family lived. There they traded their wagon and ox team for a shabby cabin on 160 swampy acres of ground capable of growing little but mosquitoes and ague. For more than two years John German stuck it out and tried his best, watching his children grow sicker with tuberculosis from both the climate and the continued hunger.

He was determined to move on and seize his dream.

In Stone County, Missouri, German worked for his uncle across some four months so he could earn enough to reoutfit for the trip he vowed his family would finally make. From there the Germans moved west to Elgin County, Kansas, where both John and son Stephen, eighteen years old, hired out to work the fields on the Osage Reservation.

After ten months of laboring for other people among the Osage, John German declared he would not be denied his dream of the Rockies. Lydia protested, as did the older children. Sophia herself recalled hearing the angry voices of her father and mother, along with sister Rebecca, who was twenty, and Stephen—the three of them bickering with Papa that they did not want to move on.

On August 15, a day Sophia noted in her small journal, the Germans pulled away for the distant mountains with what little they owned tucked in a squeaky, much-used wagon.

"We'll head northwest from here," John German had declared to them that morning before he slapped leather down on the backs of the oxen, his eyes afire with the promise close at hand. "When we strike the Union Pacific tracks on the Federal Road, we'll follow them west. That Smoky Hill Road will get us where we want to go."

Sophia remembered looking at the faces of the others almost a month ago now, realizing that for her mother, brother and oldest sister, the Rockies were not where they wanted to go. Still, there had been happiness in last night's camp among these rolling hills. Yesterday they had met an eastbound party who had informed them that with only another day's travel they should reach Fort Wallace on the Smoky Hill Route. That meant two days from now they'd be in Colorado Territory. But while it would be many, many miles before they came across a settler's cabin, they were nonetheless advised to stay close by the river, where they would be assured of plenty of water. Traveling alongside the railroad tracks, on the other hand, while it meant running across more people, also made for a much drier journey.

Such excitement she had seen written on her papa's face. Such celebration he made of that twilight campfire, speaking with so much accomplishment of the last nine years and the hard work of all to arrive at this threshold. Then John German had sent his family to bed early so that they could get an early start this morning.

The dew had lasted longer than normal, so most of the younger ones had been riding, up and out of the tall, damp grass that soaked dry-split boots and knee stockings and dresses. Stephen was walking beside the plodding team, urging them from time to time with some persuasion from his willow switch.

"Look, Pa," he called back to his father on the wagon seat next to his mother. "Antelope."

John German nodded. "You do have the eyes of a hunter, Stephen."

"May I go try my hand, Pa?" Stephen asked eagerly. "Bring back something for Mama's kettle tonight."

"Yes—go ahead," John German replied with a smile.

"In fact, I'll go with you. Here, Lydia." He handed his wife the reins and jumped to the ground, bounding up beside his son as they took off toward a saddle between two low hills.

Rebecca and Catherine were both walking beside the wagon, driving the few plodding milk-cows along and wagering who would attract the first soldier to talk with her that afternoon when they arrived at Fort Wallace.

Sophia laughed behind her hand at that, sneaking a listen to that silly talk of the older girls. Such discussions of young men always made Sophia laugh. She did not know why her older sisters got all cow-eyed when they talked of men, much less why Rebecca and Catherine got all spindly-kneed whenever a young man came around and started paying attention to one or the other of them.

The air suddenly split with shrieks. Some from her older sisters. Distant warning carried across the waving grass.

As she poked her head out the front of the wagon over her mother's shoulder, she heard Lydia say something she knew she would never forget.

"Dear merciful God in Heaven—deliver us!"

What Sophia saw next she knew would stay just behind her eyes for as long as she would live.

John German had yanked Stephen around, lunging at the youth. Then her brother showed he was more fleet, running faster, her papa lagging quickly behind, big-boned and heavyset as he was. Abruptly, he stopped, turning slowly to look back at his pursuers, more than twenty-five in all, now pouring through the saddle between those two low hills. Then Papa turned back to look at the wagon, waving his arms wildly, his chest suddenly a blossom of bright red staining that greasy shirt Mama washed and rewashed each week until it was ready to fall apart.

A warrior, his long, loose hair lifting in the hot breeze that had dried the dew gathered on the tall, brittle stalks of buffalo grass, swept up behind her papa and drove an ugly, nail-studded club into the back of John German's head as the white man slowed, the hole in his lungs taking its toll. Sophia saw part of the scalp and skull come away with that ugly club, caught among the long nails the way her little hand had looked just last winter, pulling at the bloody placental sacks when their old hound had shed her last litter in the tinderbox beside the cookstove.

"John!" Lydia shrieked as she bolted down off the front of the wagon, hands drawing up her dress as she raced over the uneven ground.

A trio of warriors reined up around her, laughing, preventing her from escaping the tight noose of their ponies as she shoved and fought against the animals, fists flailing in desperation and rage. Suddenly Lydia yanked on the bare, dirty leg of one of the warriors, attempting to shove her way to her husband.

In a flash of glinting sunlight Sophia saw the warrior's arm piston down against a background of pale blue sky, in his hand a tomahawk. A spray of blood shot from her mother's head as Lydia collapsed to the grass, the lower half of her face gone, cleaved as horribly as Sophia remembered they would butcher a hog strung up behind the barn back home in Georgia so many years ago.

Sophia was screaming along with the other girls, listening to their mother gurgle her last protests, then through her tears Sophia watched a grotesque figure rise from the grass behind the horse-mounted warriors. At first she wasn't sure, blinking her hot eyes—then could tell from the bloodstained, greasy shirt. It was her father. He clambered to his feet, wobbly, the top of his head gone in a dark, shiny pulp. But somehow he stumbled forward two steps, lurched to a halt, then stumbled forward a bit more, one arm reaching out as if he meant to defend his wife and family from these naked, brown attackers.

Approaching behind him, Sophia finally noticed the last rider, sitting wide and squat atop his pony, kicking the animal forward until the warrior reached her father. The Indian drove his tomahawk down into the back of her father's head, leaving it there as John German slowly sank to his knees, then collapsed onto his face, disappearing into the grass.

Rebecca's terrified screams pulled Sophia around. She dove beneath the wagon bed, banging her head on the possumbelly where they carried extra firewood. A half-dozen warriors had Rebecca surrounded, laughing, playfully lunging at her, then retreating as she swung the firewood axe at her tormentors. Tears tracked the dust on her face as one finally swept in behind her and wrenched the axe free. A second lunged in and with both hands grabbed the collar of her long dress, ripping it downward in a loud rending, so that it hung at her waist.

A third was there suddenly, his hands pulling and twisting at Rebecca's breasts, another warrior ripping the dress off the young woman from behind her. Together four of them pushed her to the ground, each holding a leg or arm while a fifth pulled aside his breechclout, holding his stiffened manhood in his hand.

At that moment Sophia knew she would never forget the sight of that—a man's privates. She had seen horses and cattle, pigs and dogs and other male animals . . . but never a man's. Gulping, wide-eyed and terrified, she watched as the warrior knelt between Rebecca's outstretched legs and drove that stiffened flesh into her sister's belly.

Rebecca was struggling against the four who held her spread and the one who pinned her to the ground, shrieking as the first finished and a second exposed himself, plopping down atop the young woman when a hand suddenly yanked on Sophia's hair, savagely dragging her from the shadows beneath the wagon.

Yanked around like a child's toy top, Sophia immediately recognized her tormentor as the large, fleshy warrior who had driven the tomahawk into her papa's head, leaving it there as John German fell into the dusty, brittle grass. The warrior was laughing, a huge, stinking hole opened in the Indian's face. Then something seemed wrong, out of place to the girl.

This one was not dressed like the others. This warrior was not naked on legs and chest as were the rest. No—this one was not a warrior at all, but a woman. Her large, unbound breasts heaving as she laughed, that stench coming from her mouth as she dragged Sophia close, locking an arm cruelly around her neck.

Elsewhere nearby, the other four sisters were by now

captured, each held by a pair of warriors, forced to watch the brutal gang rape of Rebecca, made to listen to Rebecca's screams, her begging the others to help.

Sophia turned away, refusing to watch, seeing then the patch of browning blood high on Catherine's left thigh. Her sister's dress was torn around the leg wound, the broken, splintered shaft of an arrow still embedded in the girl's thigh.

Around Rebecca the brown-skinned men laughed, jumping and cavorting about, each taking their quick turns atop her naked, white body, her legs trembling now from pain and rage and terror, the creamy inside of her thighs flecked with blood from the manhood parts of the warriors, blood collected beneath in the thirsty soil. Yet something told Sophia some of that blood came from Rebecca's own insides.

At last it looked as if the brutalizing was over when one of the older warriors strode up, growling something to the others. They were done with Rebecca—done with their fun as the older one shooed the rest away. The eldest daughter was sobbing, rolling onto her hands and knees, calling out to her sisters as she clawed through the grass to retrieve the shreds of her clothing when the older warrior suddenly wheeled, pointed his pistol at her head, and pulled the trigger.

The grass beneath Rebecca splattered with blood and brain as the naked white body collapsed, quivered, then lay still.

The other five girls screeched in terror, having watched Rebecca's fate as the older warrior walked up to them all, one by one fingering their hair, walking slowly from girl to girl, as if assessing the color and length.

Sophia lunged for Joanna as her fifteen-year-old sister was pulled away from the others, led to the far side of the wagon. When other warriors were dragging Sophia and the rest of her sisters to the front of the wagon, she jerked to hear a single gunshot.

Wildly kicking, Sophia tore away from her captors and rushed to the back of the wagon. The older warrior who had killed Rebecca stood hunched over Joanna, his knife slicing off her long chestnut hair. It's because her hair is the longest, Sophia thought—because Joanna's hair is the longest.

Then the warrior woman yanked Sophia off her feet, pulling her own hair, swinging the girl around to slap her brutally across the mouth. She collapsed, sobbing, near Joanna's bloodied head as the warriors clambered into the wagon for the first time, tossing out boxes and crates and satchels and bedding. Clanking and banging and thudding, everything went onto the ground. These few possessions her father and mother had accumulated in their life together lay scattered on the prairie in a matter of seconds.

Sophia smelled something burning, and turned to find two warriors had started a fire in the foot well of the wagon. Another four or five cut the team loose and drove the lumbering animals some distance from the wagon before they brought them down, yelling and yipping as if it were great sport to run down the slow, plodding oxen.

"Oh, dear God—"

Catherine's quiet expression caused Sophia to turn back to the wagon where the bodies of her mother and father were being dragged up by their ankles, plopped into line with those of Rebecca, Joanna and finally Stephen's. Sophia grew sickened as they scalped the last four, then a warrior went through her brother's pockets, and finding nothing, slashed open his pants, cutting off Stephen's manhood and jabbing the bloody flesh into her brother's slack, gaping mouth.

Sophia collapsed to her knees, retching, at long last loosing the biscuits and salt-pork they had eaten that morning for breakfast at dawn, her father excited to get on the trail to Fort Wallace.

The back of Sophia's head cried out in pain as the warrior woman yanked her to her feet, yellow vomit dribbling down the front of Sophia's dress as she fought to get her legs beneath her and struggled not to look at the butchered, bloodied, defiled bodies of her family. Instead, she forced herself to look at the face of the Indian woman, studying the dirt caked in the deep crevices of her face. Then Sophia shuddered as she finally gazed into the woman's eyes. She had never seen human eyes shine the light back at her quite like that. Only animal eyes.

They were pushing her away, shoving Sophia off with her three sisters. She turned to look back at the wagon, now in a full blaze. The warrior woman drove a foot into her back, causing the white girl to stumble and grunt in pain as she fell.

Little seven-year-old Julie and young Addie, who was only five, helped pull her up from the dust and trampled grass. They were crying. Quiet tears seeping down their young, ruddy cheeks.

"Don't look," little Addie told her older sister. "Just don't look."

32

September 12, 1874

Billy Dixon was certain of it. As much as the soldier might try to pass it off, Colonel Nelson A. Miles was worried about that ammunition and food getting down to him from Camp Supply. Lyman's wagon train should have made it back long ago.

From his camp on McClellan Creek in the eastern extreme of the Texas Panhandle, Miles had dispatched Dixon and the half-breed Amos Chapman to ride northwest on the Fort Supply Road and find out what they could.

"You can take as many soldiers as you want, Dixon," the colonel had explained in firelit darkness two nights before.

Billy had glanced at Chapman. The interpreter from Camp Supply had merely shrugged.

"It's better we don't go with a whole passel of soldiers," Dixon replied. "Gimme four."

Miles shook his head. "That's all?"

Dixon had only nodded.

The colonel selected four veterans of the Sixth Cavalry to go along with the two scouts. Besides hurrying along the Lyman supply train, the colonel wanted the six to carry some urgent dispatches on to Camp Supply. The six had plunged into the prairie darkness the night of 10 September, two days back.

True to his vow of last July, Dixon had left Dodge City and volunteered his services to Miles not long after the wagon train of buffalo hunters made it north to the Arkansas River settlement. Since then Billy had been scouting for one of the five columns the army and Indian Department hoped would end this outbreak once and for all.

Back on 26 July, Bill Sherman had talked his old friend Sam Grant into ending civilian control of the agencies. By the time Sherman got through, Grant's "Quaker Peace Policy" was nothing more than an abandoned memory for the history books. Immediately word went out from Washington City to all posts and agencies: the army was assuming control; all friendly Indians were to come in and enroll with the agents by 3 August; those bands who did not report for enrollment by the closing date would be chased, harassed, captured, dismounted and disarmed, becoming prisoners of war. If they were not killed.

By the second week of August the battle lines had been drawn. Those on the reservation were considered peaceful. Those bands who had fled to the ancient security of the Staked Plain were hostile. It was to be a classic Sherman campaign: five columns would converge from different directions to effect the final clean-up before winter set in. Major William R. Price was marching east along the Canadian River from Fort Union, New Mexico, with eight companies of the Eighth Cavalry to effect a junction with Miles.

Lieutenant Colonel George P. Buell, leading four troops of the Ninth U.S. Negro Cavalry and two from the Tenth, along with two companies of the Eleventh Infantry and thirty scouts, was moving northwest across the Brazos from Fort Griffin, Texas.

Lieutenant Colonel John W. "Black Jack" Davidson was leading six troops of Tenth U.S. Negro Cavalry, three companies of the Eleventh Infantry and forty-four scouts west from Fort Sill, I.T.

Due south of the caprock and Staked Plain, Colonel Ranald S. Mackenzie was probing north out of Fort Concho at the head of a column comprised of the largest prong of the attack: eight companies of his famous Fourth Cavalry, four more of the Tenth Cavalry, one from the Eleventh Infantry along with some thirty scouts.

And Nelson A. Miles himself, marching at the van of eight troops of the Sixth Cavalry, four companies of the colonel's own Fifth Infantry, along with one Parrot ten-pounder and two Gatling guns.

That made for more than three thousand soldiers converging on the ancient buffalo ground of the Kiowa and Comanche—with orders from Washington City to disregard the various army departmental lines, not to mention disregarding reservations. As Major General C. C. Augur wrote to Mackenzie on 28 August, "You are at liberty to follow the Indians wherever they go, even to the Agencies."

The war was on.

On 11 August, Billy Dixon left Fort Dodge with the Miles column. He was headed back to Indian country. But this time he wouldn't be hunting buffalo. This time he would be looking for what Miles was hunting: Indians to fight.

His eyes searched the land to the east this second predawn morning. Already the horizon had turned gray. To the west what he could see of the sky was a jumble of black-bellied storm clouds. They'd be wet before the day was out, Billy figured. But if he and Chapman could find them a dry place to wait out the day, they'd do just fine.

It had been that way for the last two nights. Moving by feel as much as by moonlight and starshine across the countryside, picking their way north by northeast as they went. Come sunrise yesterday, they had hidden and slept and kept watch in rotation throughout the day. They would do the same today. And in a couple more sunrises, this bunch could be in sight of the flagpole at Camp Supply.

From the looks of the country, Billy figured he was ascending the divide between Gageby Creek and the Washita River. Perhaps they should stop here on this side of the divide and go into hiding, he argued with himself as he glanced over his right shoulder once more, watching the gray go to a thin red line that reminded him of the bloody phlegm dribbling from a bull's nostrils when he had drilled him in the lights. The sky was going red. Maybe, just maybe, they could push it a little and cover a bit more ground before they had to find some cover.

Besides, he really couldn't see anything here on the Gageby Creek side of the divide that would do if the sky opened up on them the way it was threatening to do. Already the coming dawn seemed to be ripping back more and more of the land, exposing more and more of the ominous, roiling western horizon. The rain would be just fine, just fine, he figured. They had been without fresh water to fill their empty canteens in more than a day now. This ride was turning into a real badlands doings, and things appeared to be getting worse with every mile—until the sky lit enough to expose that faraway promise of rain.

Anxious to get over the divide and into cover as the sky paled, Billy nudged his horse into a trot. Behind him the others followed and picked up the pace, Chapman closing the file.

As he crested the rise, Dixon could not believe his eyes. He blinked them, his heart shooting into this throat.

"Jesus, Mary and Joseph!" he cried, sawing the reins about, nearly bringing his horse down as he did so.

Sergeant Z. T. Woodall cried out, "What the hell are you—"

Then it seemed the whole of the northern extent of the divide erupted in a bright show of feathered horsemen who had suddenly spotted the half-dozen white men in the gray light of dawn. Without a moment's delay, they were racing for their quarry, screeching, hammering their ponies into a gallop. So close were they to Dixon's party when Billy bumped into them that the warriors were able to surge around the white men on three sides. In a matter of seconds they closed the circle.

Dixon had his pistol out, his eyes frantically searching for a place to make a stand of it. Not that he was anything new to fighting Indians—it was just that a fella had to have him a proper place to do it.

"Dismount!" he shouted to the four soldiers.

"Stay in the saddle!" countermanded Sergeant Woodall, his black mustache quivering with anger. "We can make a run for it!"

Dixon yanked on the sergeant's bridle, staring up at the older man. "We run, we'll get cut off one at a time in a running fight. Now, get down and fight!"

Woodall muttered as the bullets began to whine overhead and the sun's rays lanced out of the east in a brilliant crimson. "A good cavalryman—forced to fight on foot! Arrggg!" he swore. "Smith—you're horse holder!"

Dixon turned away as the others were dropping to the ground, opening fire with his pistol as the air buzzed around him. He recognized that first unforgettable sound of lead smacking into flesh. Private George W. Smith, designated to be horse holder for the rest, crumpled in half with a cry of desperate pain. He stretched out slowly like a dying man will, clawing the ground for the pistol he had dropped, just out of reach. Then Smith quit moving.

One of the mounts the private had been holding screamed as it was hit and began kicking its rear legs, 'round and 'round in a frantic circle before it tore off through the closing red noose.

Dixon pulled his second pistol as Chapman went down with a grunt, holding his leg below the knee.

"Billy! I'm hit!" Chapman groaned as he squatted there in the new light of day, bright darkness seeping between his copper fingers.

The half-breed tried to hold his own as Private John Harrington was winged in the left arm. The soldier cried out for help.

Woodall started for Harrington as the ground around the sergeant began to erupt with dirt funnels. Just as he reached the private, Woodall's face went white. He put his hand to his belly and brought it away, dampened with crimson.

"Jesus . . ." Billy growled when he saw Woodall blanch.

Already four of the six were wounded. Their horses with extra ammunition in the saddlebags had been driven off. And all of that inside the first two minutes.

Worse still, the way the warriors were pressing in on

them was proving a closer fight than anything Dixon had been in—closer even than having the damned Comanches battering at the very doors of Jimmy Hanrahan's saloon with their pony hooves and rifle butts and fourteen-foot lances draped with scalps.

Maybe this was it, something suddenly cold in his belly told him. Today was Billy Dixon's last stand.

He decided then and there in the space of one heartbeat that if this sunrise were to be his last, he would do his best work with his gun this day, making every shot count, and giving back hurt for hurt, blazing away at this war party as much as he could before they overwhelmed his wounded, whittled-down party.

Of the six men—Smith dead and three more wounded . . . against more than 125 warriors already painted, their ponies decked for battle.

How had he been so damned stupid to walk right into them in the dark?

Then, by some miracle, the warriors were pushed back momentarily. The screaming faded. Dixon caught his breath, trying to make sense of it. The five of them, most wounded like they were, had nonetheless turned that first frightening charge come so close Billy swore he could almost smell the buffalo jerky on the warriors' hot breath. If he and the rest were to survive another five minutes, ten or more, they needed to find some cover.

But without the horses to shoot and barricade behind . . . Billy grew desperate, his eyes searching this way then that across the heaving ground . . . there! That old depression atop a low rise on the open, rolling land dotted with mesquite. Several hundred yards away to the south—a long-abandoned buffalo wallow, where the great bulls had come during the rut of a bygone day, horning the ground, tossing dust over their heads then rolling in the depression they had formed to relieve some of the itching from the ticks and fleas and mosquitoes and buffalo gnats that tormented the shaggy beasts. A few inches deep, and less than a dozen feet across . . .

What that wallow offered wasn't much. But it was a damned sight better than anything else they had on this bald, sandy knob of ground. And it beckoned to Billy Dixon like a hearth in a prairie storm.

"C'mon, fellas!" Dixon shouted, pointing his pistol. "To the wallow—let's make our stand there!"

Private Peter Rath was at Woodall's side, and with the help of the wounded Harrington, the two privates got the wobbly sergeant to his feet and started with Dixon.

"Anything's better'n dying out here," Woodall barked, forcing a smile onto his well-seamed face, which was a war map of his Civil War battles. "Get me there, soldiers. Just get me to that goddamned hole."

Dixon saw them beginning their charge, coming in again, then the racket grew thunderous in his ears once more as the two soldiers took off together, scurrying across the dusty slope, half dragging the third. Billy sprinted past them, running like sunlight on creek water, reaching the wallow where he whirled and flopped to his belly, firing at the incoming horsemen as the air around him grew suddenly light with the emergence of the orange globe at the edge of the earth.

"Amos!" Dixon shouted, seeing Chapman had not moved across the slope.

"G'won, B-Billy," he hollered.

"C'mon, goddammit! Hurry!" Dixon screeched at the trio of soldiers, wagging a pistol arm. Then he was clambering out of the wallow and running toward Chapman as the keening war cries grew deafening. But of a sudden all he could hear was the huffing of his own breath and the pounding of his boots across the sandy soil.

Chapman saw, heard him coming. "I can't, Billy—"

He fired his pistol once, aimed and fired a second time. "Jesus, Amos—I'm coming for you!"

Chapman growled forcefully, his face gone white with pain, "Stay back, you skittle-minded fool!"

Then the enemy fire grew too hot and Dixon did something he was ashamed of as soon as he whirled and lunged back toward the wallow. The bullet wound burned through the calf of his leg as his throat went dry as sand. The ground around him snarled as lead ricocheted from the rocks, rattling the mesquite brush angrily. On grit alone

Billy clawed back onto his feet, limping . . . hobbling away from the open ground where the half-breed lay on his belly, plugging away as best a man can when his lower leg is broken.

Dixon slid into the wallow behind the others, the wave of pain passing over him, threatening to engulf him like the rain-swollen Canadian River had earlier that spring. He finally caught his breath and bellied over to fire the pistol, emptying it before the second charge was turned in a noisy, profane show of the warriors' disappointment. He glanced over the rest of them, wondering how these young soldiers were holding up. Likely one or two would wet their britches from belt to brisket with each new assault now.

" 'Bout as noisy as a Gypsy tinker's cart, don't you think?" asked the sergeant, grinning crookedly beneath that bent horseshoe of a mustache.

"Start digging, fellas," Dixon told them as he shoved a cartridge in the Sharps then dragged out both pistols to reload.

"Dig?" Harrington asked as he gazed down at his own wounded arm.

"Damn right. Get digging," he snarled at the soldiers. "Make this deeper. Throw your dirt up here on the lip. Now—do it!"

Rath and Harrington looked at Woodall for confirmation. The sergeant did not hesitate. He nodded, then painfully dragged his own belt knife out of its scabbard and went to work at his corner of the buffalo wallow. Using knives if they had them, only hands if they didn't, the four were like prairie rats, badgers and wolf spiders spraying sand from their excavations as fast as they could dig, shoring up the rim of this long-abandoned buffalo wallow. Making it just a little tougher for those brown-skinned horsemen to find a target down in this dusty pit scraped out of a hillside in the middle of nowhere.

"We'll damn well sell our lives dearly," Dixon told them.

Woodall's eyes were the first to tell Billy that the veteran sergeant agreed. Beneath that bulb of a nose, Woodall's mustache was a well-waxed affair, bent like a gleaming black horseshoe over his mouth as he said, "The scout's right, boys. Give 'em hell to the last man."

"Lemme wrap your arm, Harrington," Rath offered, jabbing his knife into the tail of his own tunic and sawing off a dirty bandage he secured around the wounded soldier.

"Do anything for you, Sergeant?" Dixon asked.

Woodall swallowed hard, gritting behind his grin. He glanced briefly down at his bloody hand. "Just keep me sitting up, boys. Gut wound can be nasty."

"Dixon . . . look," Harrington said, wagging his service revolver across the slope:

He was afraid it was another charge, but what he saw was only Amos Chapman, slowly dragging himself along through the brush, pushing with one leg, pulling with one arm. Inch by inch, foot by foot across the sandy ground as bullets spun and whined about him.

"They'll get him! God, they'll get him for sure!" Harrington squealed.

"Shuddup," Woodall growled, yanking Harrington back against the side of the pit. "Stay down and you'll stay alive."

It was more than Billy could take. No man who wanted to live that much should have to fight alone, out there, making an easy target of himself with hundreds of red-skinned marksmen making sport of him.

No man who wanted to live that much should have to die alone.

With the protests of the soldiers in his ears, Billy was out of the wallow, over the sandy rim, sprinting as he had sprinted only once before in his life: racing alongside Seamus Donegan and Billy Ogg when they had run for Jimmy Hanrahan's saloon of another sunrise on these Panhandle plains.

Chapman growled, a grin forced in the thin line of his lips, "Glad to see you, Billy."

"Shuddup and grab a'holt of me, Amos," he snapped, stuffing one of the pistols in his wide belt. "Sling you on my back."

Raising himself on his good knee, Chapman heaved himself up and slung his arms around Dixon's neck as the shorter man struggled to rise, clearly straining. Chapman let go.

"You can't make it with both of us—"

Dixon whirled on the half-breed. "Goddammit—you hold onto me, or I'm gonna drag you there by myself!"

Chapman swallowed down his pain and nodded, circling Dixon's neck again as the warriors kicked their ponies back up the sandy slope dotted with mesquite brush.

With a grunt, Billy finally got his legs under him and started forward. The wounded calf cried out . . . but once he was moving, he was not about to stop. Moving this fast, under the head of steam, he was like the pistons of a locomotive and would have fallen if he had stopped. His momentum and the greater weight of Amos Chapman carried him along that hillside toward the buffalo wallow.

The screams of the soldiers rang in his ears, accompanying the painful grunts of Chapman clung like a swollen tick to his back as each ramming footstep in that race shot pain through the half-breed's broken leg. Billy collapsed at the edge of the wallow, flinging Chapman past him, over the scooped-up sand and into the bottom as the screeching warriors came within range and the soldiers opened up, letting fly what they could.

Dixon wished he had something in his stomach to puke up as the pain in his leg sent cold shards of ice to his brain. But there was nothing left in his belly but a little water and some yellow bile. His leg was oozing more blood now as he tore his canvas britches away from the wound.

He yanked the greasy bandanna from around his neck and knotted it around the calf. Then looked up at Amos Chapman lying across the dusty buffalo wallow from him.

The half-breed swiped sand from the side of his face with a grimy hand. "Thank you, Billy Dixon. I owe you my life."

He knew that was a tough thing for a man like Chapman to bring himself to say. So Dixon smiled as he dragged his Sharps into his shoulder, ready to pass it off.

"By damn, you better help hold these bastards off, Amos. I didn't come all the way out there to drag your brown ass in here for nothing. I brung you here to work."

33

"Amos! Heya, heya! We got you now, Amos!"

The slope rang with the warriors' taunts after Dixon's rescue of Chapman had driven the brown-skinned horsemen into a fury. They charged again, circling the buffalo wallow for a few frantic minutes, then rode out of rifle range once more. Then they began to taunt the half-breed they knew.

"Good to have friends, ain't it?" Billy Dixon asked, half a grin on his face, gritting as he tightened the bandanna around his calf.

"Yep—you are that: a friend what saved me," Chapman agreed.

Billy chuckled. "Naw, Amos. I was talking about them redskins. Friends like that—them knowing your name: Chapman."

The half-breed nodded. "Yeah. Them knowing me just makes 'em want my scalp more'n yours, Billy."

"Damn shame," Dixon replied. " 'Cause mine's sure a lot prettier'n yours, Amos."

For the next several hours as the sun made its brief appearance that morning, climbing into the growing overcast of the autumn sky, those Kiowa and Comanche warriors who had just abandoned their siege of Captain Wyllys Lyman's wagon train when they unexpectedly bumped into the six white men attempted to draw their red noose all the tighter around the enemy bellied down in that shallow buffalo wallow. True to the season, it did grow warm for a time. But hotter still were the white man's guns each trip the warriors chose to burst from the brush atop their paint-smeared, feather-bedecked ponies, spurring the animals around and around the wallow, firing when they could, each young warrior screeching out his war song, intent on counting coup on this miserable handful of white men.

Of a sudden Harrington raised himself up against his side of the wallow, desperation etched on his young face, and yelled, "It's no use, boys. No use. We might as well give up!"

A bullet stung the side of the wallow where they had scooped up the dirt, spraying sand into Harrington's mouth, gagging the soldier.

"Damn you!" Woodall growled. "Get down, Private!"

"Giddown," Chapman ordered.

Dixon dragged the soldier down to the center of the pit, holding the young private there as the bullets sang overhead. "It ain't no use, true enough, soldier—if you go and give up. But we got us a chance: we keep our heads, and make our guns answer them Kiowa bastards."

It got quiet a few moments as Harrington settled, still trembling like a wet hound shaking himself from muzzle to tail root. Dixon eventually took his hand off the soldier's chest and dragged his wounded leg back to the edge of the rifle pit as the charge dissipated and the warriors rode back to confer at the edge of the mesquite.

"Wish we had that gun," Sergeant Woodall said absently, gazing across the slope at the body.

"Smith's?" asked Private Rath.

"Yeah," Woodall replied. "Ain't seen him move a bit."

"He's gone. Sure as hell, we could use that gun of his," Dixon agreed. "Suicide to try it, though. For now, anyway. Besides, as long as Amos keeps shooting center, you soldiers got two of the finest marksmen on the high plains right here, don't you know?"

"That a fact?" Woodall said, starting to chuckle, then wincing when it caused him pain.

"A damn undisputed, bald-face fact," Chapman said, winking at Dixon. "Why, Billy's handier with that Sharps than a Comanche with a new knife."

"You boys just be sure to make every bullet count," Billy told them. "Don't waste ammunition. Make sure you hit something you pull the trigger."

"Here they come!" Chapman roared.

This time there appeared a dozen warriors carrying their long buffalo lances riding in the vanguard. From the fourteen-foot spears dangled scalps of different colors tied amid a flurry of feathers fluttering on the hot wind.

"Amos—take the one on the right," Dixon ordered as his cheek nestled against the stock.

They fired almost together, the two leaders of the lance charge pitching backward into the sand and mesquite. Harrington and Rath cheered as the charge broke up with the fall of the leaders.

"Them two had more brass than a saloon monkey's butt," Chapman hissed.

"You know, Amos—they could've had us in that first charge," Dixon said as he shoved another cartridge in the Sharps.

Chapman nodded. "Stupid Injuns. Brave, but stupid."

Dixon winked. "Then I suppose that only makes you half smart, right?"

"Smart enough to get a feather-headed runt like you to come do a damn fool stunt like dragging me back in here, Billy. Now, you tell me who's more stupid: you, or me?"

"Chapman makes a good point," Woodall said at the far side of the wallow. "Can't blame him for being stupid if he got you to run that lead gauntlet for him."

Dixon smiled, turning back to look down the slope where the warriors were gathered. "Needed the exercise, don't you know."

As the morning dragged closer and closer to noon, with the sun rising higher and higher, the heat increasing while the boiling black thunderheads continued to roll their way out of the west with the swiftness of spilled coffee staining a freshly laundered blue tablecloth, the men alternately dug their rifle pit deeper and fired with each renewed attack. With each successive charge, more ponies fell, more warriors dragged off by other horsemen, and more shields and lances and tomahawks and rifles littered the sandy soil of this lonely little battlefield.

"Hot enough to boil gravy in here," Woodall commented sourly, then grinned that crooked smile of his.

"Injuns call it, *sam-ya ceze-t'e,*" said Chapman. "The time of blackened tongues, boys. The thirst devil."

Dixon gazed into the brassy, breathless sky, squinting beneath a shading hand. Wondering if the Indians didn't get him, then that goddamned sun sure would. Maybe, just maybe, he was already laying in the sand of his own bury-ing box. He swallowed it down and looked back over the fear-pinched faces of the soldiers.

"By the way, boys," Billy said offhandedly, as cool as he could make it, "just so you'll remember: always keep a last bullet in your pistol. Never go empty."

"You want us to always have one of us with a gun loaded, that it?" asked the sergeant.

"No," Dixon said eventually, looking at Woodall squarely. "Keep the last bullet for yourself."

From the expressions on every soldier's face following his statement, Dixon knew they understood the heavy stakes they were playing. These soldiers realized that they could not take the chance of falling into the hands of the warriors. Billy himself had heard enough of the old-timers' talk, besides seeing with his own eyes too many stripped and butchered stark white bodies staked out on the prairie, tortured with fire or sliced limb from limb with slow, metic-ulous precision. He would just have to keep their juices up, their fighting spirit aroused, to have half a chance to come out of this alive. And to do all that, Billy Dixon would have to be as determined to live as dog salmon fighting fast water.

"None of you happen to have a flask along, would you?" asked Sergeant Woodall as the bright sun began its slow descent from mid-sky.

The heat had turned brutal.

At the moment of attack when they were dismounting, Billy had tossed off his wide-brimmed slouch hat, as it made him too fine of a target. Now he cursed himself for pitching it as far from him as he could. Dixon felt as if the wallow were no better place than a cast-iron skillet in which the five of them were simmering slowly, slowly broil-ing in their own juices by some devilish design.

"Sorry, Sergeant," Billy replied. "Know how you feel. We're about as scant of water as whiskey is at a Shouting Baptist prayer-tent meeting, aren't we?"

They laughed a little as Dixon ran his tongue around inside his mouth, sensing it gone pasty. Reaching inside his shirt, he pulled out a small plug of dark tobacco, sliced a chew off of it and tossed it across to Woodall and Harrington.

"Go ahead and share what's left there among the rest of you. Might keep your mouth wet."

Rath choked on the tobacco and spit his out a few minutes later, preferring to dream of water, he said, rather than have to swallow that tobacco juice.

"Listen to that, will you?" Chapman said after the first distant clap of thunder rolled in from the west.

"You don't suppose we'd be lucky enough to get some of that rain, do you?" asked Rath.

"Looks like we might," Dixon assured him as another thunder roll rattled like dried buffalo bones across the sandy hills. "The way these goddamned flies been biting, it's a sure sign of rain coming."

Billy twisted slightly to gaze down the slope, watching the warriors. They too were glancing now and then at the onrushing storm, listening to the distant rattle of thunder on the open land. "Them red bastards been playing with us, ain't they, Amos?"

Chapman nodded. "Yep."

"What do you mean, playing with us?" asked the sergeant.

Dixon chewed on it, selecting his words. "They could've had us first off, run us right into the ground. This bunch is wanting to make some sport of this—this is big medicine to them, riding up close to this wallow, daring us. They want to count as much coup as they can before they figure to wipe us out."

"That coming?" Rath asked sourly.

"Could be. If the rain don't get here first," Dixon replied. "I figure they'll make as much sport of it for as long as they can drag it out."

By the middle of the afternoon the five had been pinned down in the bottom of their simmering skillet for more than nine hours. Dixon watched the others between each wild circling charge the warriors made, while he reloaded his guns and those of the others from time to time. Studying these men whose lives and whose deaths had suddenly been thrown together with his.

The sergeant was likely the worst off. It seemed he could barely move. Chapman wasn't all that much better, though. Amos winced in pain each time he tried shifting his position. Not only did he have a broken leg, but he was continuing to lose blood just like Woodall was. At the same time, Harrington was growing more and more useless with every hour as his wounded arm made it increasingly difficult for him to hold a rifle.

Looking down at the warriors conferring in the mesquite, then glancing at the dark thunderheads rolling all the nearer, Dixon realized that if those Kiowas and Comanches realized just what straits the white men were in, they would charge up here and be done with it in one fell swoop. Somehow, he had to keep the others sitting up, conscious, and returning the Indians' fire, bullet for bullet . . . if only to fool the redskins and hold them at bay.

Suddenly the ground shook, making Dixon jump—as if it was the thunder of nearby hooves. But instead of warrior ponies, this was a nearby jolt of lightning so close it seemed day ballooned all around them, followed immediately by a tremendous clap of thunder. As if on cue, the sky began to dribble loose a few drops, causing a sensation among the warriors down in the mesquite. After a moment it seemed someone had slit open the underbelly of the sky. The torrent fell in slate-colored sheets, driving the warriors back among the trees, where they attempted to find as much cover as possible.

But up the sandy slope in the buffalo wallow, there was an immediate cry of relief as the men stuck their tongues out, licked the driving rain off their hands, raised their chins skyward, eyes closed, drinking in every precious drop they could. Billy said a quiet little prayer, remembering how his departed mother had taught him to pray at her knee. He swallowed hard, a sudden overwhelming emptiness pummeling his gut. His mother . . .

For years he had carried a picture of her. The only tangible thing he had of her, of his entire family. For all these years of growing up and roaming the prairies, that faded chromo had been his only link with family, with something that wasn't transitory and temporal. But now it was gone. In the saddlebags on that horse the warriors had run off at dawn at the moment of attack. Then for a moment he was thankful to God for the blessing of this rain for an altogether different reason. The others would not be able to see how the hot moisture rolled from his eyes, and the dribble from his nose would not betray his pain.

The rain was a blessing.

Yet then the wind caught up with those black-bellied clouds, sending silver tongues of fire shooting to the ground, rumbling, brass bellows echoing across the parched land. Where before they had been broiling beneath the brassy sky, now the five were drenched, squatting like five mud toads in their gray, blood-tinged pond. The wind grew to be a troublesome enemy, robbing Dixon and the others of every residue of body heat they could produce. Weakened already by loss of blood and the extremities of pitched battle, the pitiful heroes of the buffalo wallow began to wonder what more could conspire against them than the weather and the red horsemen of these plains.

"Damn, if it don't seem heaven's belly been knifed from breechclout to breastbone," Dixon sputtered into the driving rain that stung their sunburned, rawhided faces.

More lightning slashed the side of their hill, like ragged platinum chains flung out of the dark clouds directly overhead.

Their coats, extra clothing, their very life line had been run off with the horses. Even the hats of most had been lost in the first panic-filled minutes of attack. Woodall wore Harrington's hat, now a soppy, shapeless shelter atop the sergeant's head.

Billy thought once more about his coat—gone now, tied behind his saddle. Yet most important was what had been in the pocket of that coat, what he had carried all these years. The chromo of his mother.

Billy sniffled, angry at himself for it, and turned back to look at how the others were holding up as the rain softened, pattering the cold inches of water gathering around their legs.

"Help me sit him up," Dixon asked Private Rath, crawling through the bloody water.

Together they struggled to prop Sergeant Woodall against the side of the pit. The soldier was freezing, being robbed of all body heat, trembling like leaf shadows hung over still water. Although Woodall's condition was worsening, Dixon and the rest realized they all must give the appearance of being able-bodied and ready to fight off any resumed charge from their enemies.

"I . . . I'm sorry," Woodall groaned, fighting to come to, his lips quivering.

"It's all right," Billy said softly as they propped the sergeant upright. "Just try to stay awake. Your life . . . our lives may depend on you too, Sergeant."

He dragged his wounded leg back across the bottom of the wallow. By now several inches of muddy, cold water had collected, mixing with the defenders' blood in an evil concoction that continued to drain them of strength, suck out their resolve, sap the very fiber that until now had been what demanded they hold out against great odds.

When the thunderstorm had relinquished its fury, rolling on to the east, Dixon studied the mesquite flats for signs that the warriors would resume their wild, suicidal charges. But for the moment, at least, it appeared to the young scout that the cold wind and numbing rain had done much to destroy the martial ardor of the war party. As their ponies grazed on the brittle, sun-cured grass, recouping their strength, the warriors argued and debated with one another, their blankets drawn tightly, almost forlornly, about them.

"I'm going after the gun," Dixon announced to the others.

"S-Smith's?" chattered Private Rath, his teeth rattling like a box of dominoes spilled across an oak table. His lips were blue and quivering as he bit down on them, hair stringing in his eyes.

"Yes. We need the gun, bullets too," Billy explained.

"Y-You're no shape to go: your leg," Rath said, raising himself off the side of the pit. "Stay and c-cover me."

Dixon was stunned, stunned enough to sit there in awe

as the older soldier crawled past him, sloshing through the bloody mud and up the sandy side of the wallow, bellying across the parched slope toward Private George W. Smith's body.

He watched Rath reach Smith, where he gently rolled the body onto its side, intending to loosen the buckle on the gun belt. Of a sudden Rath let the body slump back onto its belly, then turned and quickly crabbed back to the wallow.

Dixon was angry, watching the soldier approach. Rath had volunteered, after all. "Why the hell didn't you—"

"He's alive!" Rath sputtered.

"Alive?" Woodall asked, appearing to perk up with the news.

Rath nodded. "I can't get him myself." He looked squarely into Dixon's eyes. "Help me drag him in here."

"You goddamned right I will," Billy replied.

Together they hurried on their hands and knees to Smith's side, where Dixon found the private shot through the left lung. Across the greasy undershirt he was wearing spread a great splatter of stain that looked like molasses. His skin the color and texture of old honeycomb, Billy realized the soldier was likely drowning in his own blood. The wound quietly wheezed, whistling with each shallow, labored breath.

"Get him atween us," he told Rath. "Can you help us, Smith? Help us by standing some?"

The private groaned his answer, struggling on wobbly legs to rise. It had been hours that he had been unconscious, losing blood beneath the unrelenting sun, loosing body heat before the driving thunderstorm.

Across the soggy, rain-cut sandy slope Rath and Dixon dragged a stumbling, dying George Smith, into the mud of the buffalo wallow, where they laid him a few feet from Woodall.

"Good to see you reporting for duty, Private," said the sergeant, his voice cracking.

Smith's eyes did the talking for him, buried like darkened twelve-hour coals in his ashen face.

Dixon knew the private didn't have long.

Strong pulled up his pistol and fired, dropping the Comanche.

Donegan whirled on Strong, bringing his Henry up.

"You got something to say to me, Irishman?"

Seamus felt Grover's hand on his arm. He slowly lowered the repeater. "We could use him, Strong."

The interpreter laughed. "You stupid mick. He'd be no good to us alive. A Comanche never talks. The only good one's a dead one." He nudged his horse over to the bloodied Tonkawa. "The scalp's yours, Henry. Be sure to take the goddamned ears with it." Strong glanced over his shoulder at Donegan with a smile as he urged his horse off toward Boehm's main flank.

"You no help Henry," growled the Tonkawa as he pranced past Donegan and Sharp with the full scalp, complete with dangling ears and silver earrings. "Maybe Comanche get you—you no help Henry."

"You should've let me put a bullet through him, Sharp," Donegan hissed.

Sharp shook his head. "More trouble for you than one Comanche's worth. Strong's a bad number, likely a backshooter too. That's his sort of work: back-shooting. 'Cause his kind's so weak he needs a brass rail under his boot and a bar to rest his elbows on. A genuine hairless Mexican pup—"

"Grover!"

They both looked up, finding Thompson and Strong on the ridge above them. The lieutenant was waving them on. "C'mon, boys. Boehm's got 'em on the run and they're fanning out. I've got my orders to follow their trail so we can report back to Mackenzie, where the sonsabitches are heading."

Seamus watched the pair disappear over the lip of the ridge. "Those Comanche are scattering—just like the Cheyenne did to Carr in 'sixty-nine."*

Grover wearily hoisted himself aboard his horse. "But the general damn well found those Dog Soldiers at Summit Springs, didn't he?"

* The Plainsmen Series, vol. 4, *Black Sun*

"You might say," Seamus recalled as they pushed their mounts up the loose, red-hued talus after the rest. "It was Bill Cody found Tall Bull's village for Carr." He spit out what he had left of a chew. "Now it looks like it's up to us to see if we can keep any of these sonsabitches from getting away from Mackenzie."

Grover wagged his head, urging his horse up the rocky scree of the slope. "I'm getting too damned old to be doing this much more."

"Sounds like you've decided to make this your last trip courtesy of the U.S. Army?"

The older man scowled. "Let's just say I been doing a lot of praying that I go home forked on a horse, Irishman . . . and not laid flat in a pine box."

36

September 27–28, 1874

It was as evident to Mackenzie as it was to any Indian fighter then on the plains that in retreating to the east, the warriors who had attacked and harried his column were doing their best to draw the soldiers away from their villages filled with women and children.

No one needed to explain that old ruse to the colonel. Mackenzie had fought these very same warriors again and again in previous campaigns. And this time he was not to be deterred. Three-Finger Kinzie had a surprise for the Comanche and Kiowa and Cheyenne.

But to make his enemies believe he had been fooled, throughout the entire day of the twenty-seventh Mackenzie marched his column to the northeast, following the freshest Indian trail. Still, while his troops were marching northeast, Mackenzie's scouts were slipping around to sniff over the country to the northwest.

Soon enough it became evident to Seamus Donegan that the warriors who had been keeping an eye on the soldier columns had grown satisfied enough that the army was marching out of danger that they could abandon their spying on the soldiers. Despite all that consoling talk he gave

"We need your gun, Smith," Dixon said as his trembling, numbed fingers fought the buckle on the private's gun belt.

The soldier nodded dumbly. He tried to say something, but the air only wheezed from the bullet wound.

That's when Billy remembered the willow switch dropped by one of the wounded warriors not far from the wallow earlier that morning. He scrambled to the edge of the pit, spotting it where he had remembered it would be, then clambered out of the mud once more. Back in the wallow he used his knife to hack a swatch from the silk bandanna he had tied around his leg wound earlier—then knelt over Smith, pulling the private against him as he worked below the soldier's left shoulder blade. Dixon gently, yet persistently, inserted a portion of the silk bandanna into the bullet wound, using the thin willow switch as a probe. The wheezing stopped as Dixon laid the private back against the side of the wallow.

And of a sudden his belly felt hungry for the first time in hours. Something so strong that it began chewing in his gut like a wolf. He had to get his mind off that pinched belly—

"You been shot up pretty good yourself," Rath commented, a look of real admiration in his eyes as Dixon dragged himself away from Smith.

"What?" he started to ask, then looked over his shoulder at the blousy, cashmere shirt he was wearing. "Oh, yeah. Looks like they damned well tried their best, didn't they?"

"You're a lucky man, Dixon," Woodall said.

Billy nodded, realizing the warriors had fairly peppered his shirt with bullet holes. Then he gazed at Smith as he said, "We're all damned lucky, fellas. Every last one of us."

34

September 13, 1874

As the sun sank yesterday, so did the spirits of those men huddled in the buffalo wallow.

The stars came out to twinkle overhead like mica chips as wisps of clouds on the tail end of the electrifying thunderstorm danced across a thumbnail sliver of a moon. At night this rolling land was whittled down to shards and remnants, streaked of starlight and shadow.

The wind came up, carrying on its brutal chill the songs of nearby prairie wolves. Billy Dixon shivered with every gust whipping through the bullet holes in his shirt. He pushed some of the long hair out of his face and kept his eyes moving. He reminded himself again: keep your eyes moving.

Just because they had seen the warriors turning away at sundown and riding off to the north did not mean the Indians wouldn't try something sneaky. Like coming back and making a rush at the wallow in the dark. Billy was experienced enough a plainsmen not to believe that horseshit about Indians never attacking at night. If the red bastards figured they could overrun the white men without the loss of their lives in doing it under the cover of darkness, then the Kiowa and Cheyenne surely were the sort to give it a try.

Best he could, Billy kept his eyes moving throughout that night. A couple times he caught himself jerking awake —cursing himself that he had dozed off. In the dim moonshine he would turn, finding the five other dark shapes huddled at the sides of the wallow. From time to time he heard someone turn atop the huge tumbleweeds the size of bushel baskets he and Rath had slipped out and gathered after sundown. By crushing the weeds down somewhat, they kept the men out of the muddy, blood-tinged soup at the bottom of the wallow, serving much like a nest of comfortless bedsprings. Throughout that long night, the others turned and tossed, huddled as best they could out of the wind that came to rob them of what little heat their bodies could produce.

Bone-numbing cold hurried along on the hoary fingers of that wind shuffling out of the north.

Not too long before slap-dark, while Billy had begun cleaning every gun one by one with a scrap of his shirt and that willow twig he had used to plug the hole in Private Smith's chest, they had begun talking. All of them except Smith, that is. The private was in a delirium, for the most

himself, this ride was proving to be every bit as spooky as any night he had spent in the darkness on Beecher Island. He didn't need reminding to keep his eyes moving now across the vast, muddy expanse of the Staked Plain. But not one of the trackers had found a single feather, pony or war lance. Lots of tracks. But no warriors. And certainly no villages. The Indians had simply disappeared, as if swallowed by the earth.

Sergeant John B. Charlton, second-in-command with Lieutenant Thompson's scouts, pressed forward with Donegan and a handful of Tonkawa trackers. Other groups were pushing across the wilderness in different directions. Mackenzie demanded answers, demanded to know how the enemy could simply vanish into the rarefied air of the southern plains. More to the point, Mackenzie demanded to know where the hell his quarry had gone.

Mile after mile they rode, eyes sweeping over the endless inland sea of summer-burned buffalo grass until suddenly the Lipan and Tonkawa riding ahead halted. One threw up an arm, alerting Sergeant Charlton and the others.

"They found something," said the sergeant who owned a narrow, over-long face.

"And I doubt it's pony tracks," Seamus replied.

Catching up with Johnson and Job, the latter a Tonkawa tracker, Charlton dismounted with Donegan and moved forward on foot. After another twenty yards Johnson stopped, signing that they should leave their horses with the others. Only then could Charlton and Donegan proceed through the wind-shorn grass with the two trackers.

Charlton's eyes narrowed, his mouth working a moment before he spoke, that brindle mustache of his extending over his upper lip like a shake awning over a mercantile's front porch. "Just keep our heads up and our peckers down and do what we're told to do, I s'pose. Figure this is a mite important."

Leaving their animals with the rest of the Tonkawas, the pair of white men followed Johnson and Job forward, quietly and slowly.

In moments a great crevasse in the prairie opened up before them.

As Seamus crawled on his belly to the lip of the ravine, it became clear that this was no small arroyo. The bottom of this canyon lay more than a thousand feet below them. As the sun climbed toward mid-sky it began to illuminate the lush stands of cedar and cottonwood and mesquite down below along the Prairie Dog Fork of the Red River. The changing quality of light brought to play the changing hues of ocher and pinks, yellows and white striated through the millennia of erosion carving this wonder of nature out of the austere severity of the Staked Plain.

Donegan lay there with the others in silence, every one of them clearly in awe of this wonder of nature.

"Injun," Johnson whispered finally, pointing for Charlton, who lay beside him at the lip of the crevasse. "Much Injun."

As more clouds moved off the face of the sun, they could begin to make out the shadowy movement of a horse herd far below, feeding in the luxurious grasses along the stream.

"Don't that break a tooth, Irishman? You're an old cavalryman. How many you figure?" asked the sergeant in a harsh whisper.

Seamus shook his head, unable to estimate at first. "Fifteen hundred. No more than two thousand."

"And that's about what we see," Charlton replied. "Look there."

Down the canyon from where they lay, the shafts of sunlight were beginning to play on the blue-gray wisps of morning wood smoke rising from hundreds of lodges. While he could not make out most of the lodges themselves for the trees and the twisting course of the canyon, Seamus nonetheless could recognize the clear evidence of camp smoke. They had found the enemy.

Charlton slid backward on his belly a few yards before he rose, dusting himself as Donegan stood. He appeared anxious as a church mouse as he said, "Let's go tell Mackenzie he's got 'em cornered."

During that kidney-hammering ride back to rejoin the

main command, Donegan found himself turning in the saddle to look over their backtrail, finding it hard to believe they had not been discovered. Every bit as hard to believe that the Indians had watched Mackenzie's troops march off to the northeast then abandoned their surveillance. Yet it was a fact: Charlton's scouts were not followed.

Back with the slow-moving column just past midday, the sergeant lost no time reporting the momentous news to Mackenzie.

With his eyes probing the distance, the colonel declared, "Not that I give a shake in hell for it, but on the outside chance we are being watched, I won't give the enemy any reason to suspect that we've found their villages. I'll only slow the order of march for the rest of the afternoon."

In late afternoon a halt was ordered and the entire command went about as if they were making camp for the night near the headwaters of Tule Creek.

But as soon as dark descended upon the land, orders were passed up and down the valley. This time there would be no wagons along, no brake-blocks snarling against their creaking wheels. Mackenzie was traveling light and lean. With the regimental pack mules burdened with twelve days' rations, Mackenzie remounted his cavalry beneath the stars, turned about at the head of Tule Canyon and pointed them northwest under the cover of night. The Fourth Cavalry was no longer stalking elusive warriors. They were closing the jaws of their trap around the enemy's villages.

Beneath rose-tinted gold light of dawn on the high plains that Monday morning, after covering some twenty-five miles in light marching order from Tule Canyon, Thompson's Tonkawa trackers again stopped the command, this time only yards from the crimson-tinged crevice of the Palo Duro.

Once more Seamus was struck by the sudden, raw beauty of this canyon—like a deep, bloody laceration of a fissure cracking the deadly monotony of the Staked Plain. All lay quiet below them in the cold, chill shadows of dawn.

And for a moment he knew how it must feel to be a

prairie wolf crouched, its prey within reach, ready to spring.

It was called the Place of the Chinaberry Trees.

Here his Kwahadi Comanches had been joined by the Cheyenne of Stone Calf, then the Kiowa of Lone Wolf and Mamanti and Poor Buffalo camped farther upstream. A few lodges of Arapaho had been raised among the Comanches. Three separate villages, three separate pony herds.

He was tired, every muscle in his lithe body tested in the past few days of fighting, feinting, drawing off the yellowlegs who had continued to march despite the bad weather. With every mile the soldiers put behind them, Quanah Parker grew more convinced these yellowlegs were commanded by the obsessed Three-Finger Kinzie.

A resolute enemy, this Kinzie. One who would not give up easily, nor one who would not turn about unless convinced to do so by defeat or by the weather. Still, Quanah knew he had come up against Three-Finger Kinzie twice before. Perhaps more. Yet Quanah still rode at the van of his people. His Kwahadi still free to roam the southern plains.

He had awakened not long ago, finding the delicious, warm dampness of her flesh against his beneath the buffalo robes. Last night when he had returned at last, staking his pony out beside the lodge before he ducked through the doorway, Quanah had been too weary to do more than gulp down a few mouthfuls of antelope before his head sank to the furry mat of their bed clothing at the rear of their lodge. But when he had slept a few hours, awakening in the cold stillness of early morning, Quanah's loins stirred with desire as he ran his hands over the firm fullness of Tonarcy's small breasts, sensing how the nipples grew rigid beneath his touch.

Her hands had urgently sought out his flesh, her lips and tongue sought out his mouth as she guided him toward her waiting heat.

Now she was snoring softly beside him as sparks leaped from the kindling he set on the coals of last night's fire, tiny dancing fireflies that climbed ever upward toward the dark-

part, and there wasn't a damned thing any of them could do. So while Dixon swabbed a scrap of his cashmere shirt in and out of every pistol and down the long barrels of their carbines, the men discussed the fact that they would live only by getting help. Then talked about just how they were to get help. Every man jack of them realized what it would mean to walk away from this wallow alone, to plunge into the unknown out there, with more than a hundred warriors all worked up by their failure to overrun the wallow and likely still lurking nearby. A most dangerous proposition—something akin to taking one's life like a handful of puffball dust and tossing it into the cold wind that caressed this high land of the Texas Panhandle.

"I'll go," Dixon volunteered, knowing there was only one other physically able to make the journey. "I figure I know the way better'n Rath, and how to get through to Camp Supply."

The others wrangled over it.

Then Rath himself abruptly interrupted the argument. "It really doesn't matter much what you decide. 'Cause there's only two of us can go. Dixon and me. And I should go—"

"You don't know where you're headed," Dixon said.

"I don't, for now." Rath nodded in the starshine darkness, his lips a thin line of determination. He was some older than the young Dixon, a soldier who had marched for the Union army through the last fourteen months of the rebellion. "You tell me how I ought to go, where—and I'll do it."

"No," Dixon replied quietly. "You ought not take the chance of getting lost and running smack into them red bastards."

"No," Rath said even more firmly. "The others—they need you here. Can't you see that? You mean more to them here, where you can handle a gun—than out there. No, you stay, Dixon. Just tell me how to go, show me how to follow the stars or something," and he shrugged, pointing at the night sky. "I'll find my way. You're needed here, watching over the others. And when those Indians come back, they'll need you even more."

317

It was finally decided. Rath listened intently to Dixon explain that they should be close to the Camp Supply Road, absorbing the scout's explaining of how to lay east of the tail on the Big Dipper and keep the north star off like thus. Dixon figured Rath could feel the well-cleaved ruts of the wagon road, even if the soldier couldn't see them beneath the pale moonlight.

Sergeant Woodall shook hands with, then saluted Private Peter Rath, then they all fell quiet as the soldier bellied over the side of the buffalo wallow and was as quickly gulped by the immense, cold darkness of that endless prairie.

"Will he make it?" Woodall asked in a whisper sometime later as Dixon sloshed through the freezing, muddy water to check on George Smith.

Dixon stopped, measuring his response carefully. "If it's God's will, Sergeant, he'll make it."

The moon was sinking in the west on its quick autumnal ride across the night sky, more than two hours after Rath had left, when the darkness brought a change in the night sounds to Dixon's ear. Slowly he rolled onto his belly, attempting to make sense of the change between the rumbling, labored breathing of the men in the wallow. He wasn't sure, but it sounded to be as if someone were sneaking up to the edge of the wallow.

Perhaps a scout, maybe more than one. Come out of the darkness to determine the condition of the white men.

Billy couldn't gamble that the Kiowa or Comanche scout would return with news of how bad off they were. He had to get to that redskin and gut him before he could get back to the war party.

Dixon dragged himself over the side of the sandy pit.

Woodall turned. "Where you—"

"Shhh," he warned harshly. "I'll be back."

Into the darkness he crabbed, his pistol in his left hand just in case. But he intended to do it with his right. With the bone-handled knife he held there. It had gutted and skinned its share of buffalo in his time, honed and sharpened around many a night fire, until the blade was but a

ness of the smokehole at the top of the lodge where the great spiral of poles met, then spread once more.

Such was the seasonal fate of his people, this coming together from afar, meeting in this Place of the Chinaberry Trees—bound together as the lodgepoles were bound one to another with that thick rope, then parting once more, each band to make its own way on the prairie. Without the white man. Without the settlers. Without the railroads. And without the buffalo hunters come to slaughter and leave in ruin all that the Kwahadi had been before the white man had come to this high land the Comanche called home.

For many lifetimes the Kwahadi had been coming to this Place of the Chinaberry Trees. He remembered many trips here: as a young child carried in the arms of his blond-haired mother, later following his father, Nocona, after Quanah had learned to ride. A great, cool place this was in the summer. A safe place this was, warm and out of the cruel wind when the winter blizzards ravaged the prairie overhead. The last few days that wind of a changing season had grown ugly and carried with it the hint of cold spit.

Cut down through the heart of the Llano Estacado by the Prairie Dog Town Fork until the canyon lay more than forty miles in length, stretching from one to six miles of torturous, winding width. Here Quanah's people had always found the rich grasses to fatten their great herds, plenty of firewood to warm their lodges, and safety while the women scraped and cured the hides of the brother buffalo.

But of late every thought of the buffalo brought a gnawing twinge of pain to the young war chief. More than once he had seen with his own eyes the litter of rotting carcasses stretching mile after mile after mile across the killing ground. Still Quanah held out some hope that the red man could hold back the white, despite the fact that to the north and south of this canyon the tai-bos had scratched at the earth and raised his earth lodges and were killing off the buffalo. East of here the enemy was laying the great iron tracks for his smoking horse. Perhaps the white man would be satisfied, Quanah prayed—be finally sated and leave this last best place to the Kwahadi for all time to come, as they had lived for all time gone before.

Up there on the prairie itself across the past several moons, the streams had dried like a newborn's birthcord cut from their tiny belly, dried and shriveled. Grasshoppers and locusts and winged insects of all nature had descended from the pale skies to seize dominion over the hot expanse of the summer-ravaged buffalo grass. Normally high enough to brush the soles of his moccasins as he rode across this inland kingdom, this past summer had seen the grass stunted, yellowed early.

Had such a drought come to this land in summers gone by, the great herds of buffalo would have starved to death without the rich grass to survive on; would have stampeded in thirst as the creeks and streams and rivers slowly dried and turned to choking dust beneath the relentless sun.

But now there were few buffalo left to feed on the inland grasses any more. Few left to wander in search of the ancient watering holes.

Perhaps it all had something to do with Isatai and his failed medicine.

Perhaps, Quanah feared with some of the serpent's wisdom he had acquired, it had more to do with their failure to defeat the white hide men at the settlement of earth lodges.

Instead of the great herds slowly migrating before the shifting winds of the ever-changing seasons, now there were only the great piles of bones and skulls and stinking carcasses reaching ever onward toward the horizon as far as any man could see. Those bleaching bones, along with the coming of the wolves and buzzards and all manner of carrion eaters.

Yes, he had seen the killing grounds with his own eyes. And would never forget. How could a man, he asked himself, forget those places where the tai-bo hide men made their stand, the ground littered with brass casings like so many flecks of gold among the stalks of grass, lying there used up and abandoned against the gray dust of the prairie, the gold slowly turning green with the seasons?

How would he ever be able to forget? Was he to forget?

But here his people and the other tribes could try to forget the tragedy visited upon them by the buffalo hunters —here in this beautiful place of color carved by the spirits, dotted with cool springs, draped with gurgling waterfalls. It was spoken of by the old ones around the fires that the pale-skinned warriors who wore the strange metal heads had marched out of the south and visited this very place in their wanderings. Before they had retreated once more to the south, never to return to the land of the Comanche.

At times a thought nagged him, the way a gnat would at times buzz persistent at Quanah's eyelid. Perhaps, he brooded, he ought to take his people south where the pale-skinned metal-head soldiers had disappeared centuries before. Many times had he led the young warriors to that land of the dark-skinned Mexican Indians to raid for horses and cattle and other plunder. Perhaps there the yellowlegs would not dare to follow.

And every time he worried on this, another voice from within told Quanah he had time enough to decide on moving his people south, far away from the reach of Three-Finger Kinzie and his soldiers. He had enough time to decide on moving south beyond the coming cold reach of winter's icy winds.

Quanah left his hand on her small, firm breast as he watched the fireflies spiral to the darkened smokehole above him. Once again he marveled that her skin was as soft as the belly of a newborn puppy. Perhaps later he would suckle milk from the breast. Perhaps.

Here to the peace of this quiet canyon valley his people had gathered to begin preparations for the coming winter. Every lodge was filled with meat dried to last until those first hunts of the spring that would always follow the time of great cold. Food and shelter and wood here to last them through the time of great cold. It was enough, if only the soldiers would leave be the women and children of these wandering bands—women who daily hung the meat out to dry, pegged out the hides to be fleshed, children who ran and laughed and played along the dancing waters of the sparkling creek gurgling through the floor of the canyon where Quanah's people once more retreated to hide from the yellowlegs.

Closing his eyes to sleep, he drank in the fragrant air touched by the perfume of the mesquite wood burning in his fire.

Here once more his people would be safe.

37

September 28, 1874

He couldn't remember the last time he slept. But right now, outside of feeling Samantha's warm, willing flesh beneath his, sleep would be the most delicious thing Seamus could imagine.

Here he was, inching his way down this narrow foot trail, leading his horse, clinging almost by hope and a prayer alone to the bloodred vertical cliff of Palo Duro Canyon with the rest of Lieutenant Thompson's scouts. The first men Mackenzie had ordered over the side, down to the valley floor where the colonel would engage the enemy.

It was just past four o'clock in the morning, a few stars still out in that crooked strip of sky above him.

"Mr. Thompson," an anxious, pacing Mackenzie had told them minutes before as the rose light of dawn was shot through with golden lances along the eastern edge of the whole world, "take your men into the canyon and open the fight."

Almost an hour ago the scouts had brought the colonel and his troops to the edge of the Palo Duro—yet there was no apparent way down. But by marching northwest for more than a mile along the canyon rim, the Tonkawas finally located this narrow goat trail.

Donegan had charged headlong into a solid phalanx of Confederate infantry; galloped hale and hearty into the teeth of row upon row of Confederate artillery, each black throat spewing grapeshot and canister and bone-shredding death; and he had held men together under the best the Sioux and Cheyenne could throw at them. But this, this

fraction of its original width. But Billy Dixon figured it could do the job on one or more red niggers.

Circling slowly, he got behind the sounds of the man, then slowly made his way in until he was close enough to make his lunge—sweeping his arm around the enemy's throat, yanking him back, ready to plunge the knife—

"Oh, God—don't kill me!"

"Rath?"

Dixon virtually hurled the private away from him, shaking—his blood hot for the killing. Suddenly interrupting that bloodlust left him trembling like an aspen leaf in a winter gale.

"I . . . I couldn't find the road, Dixon," Rath started to explain in a whisper, the look of shame evident on his face beneath the dim starshine. "I been wandering about."

Billy could tell the man was close to sobbing. "Why didn't you say something?"

"I didn't know where I was," Rath said, his lower lip thrust out like a raw slice of deer liver. Then he was sobbing, with what seemed to be some relief. "I was afraid from the sounds of it, I had bumped into some of that war party. And when you grabbed me—I was certain of it. I was afraid I would . . . was gonna die."

Billy grabbed the soldier's sleeve. "C'mon. Let's go before we do get caught out here. The others—they'll be glad to see you. 'Specially the sergeant. I think he was worried 'bout you."

By the time the two made it back to the wallow, they found Woodall and Harrington at Smith's side, Chapman watching the far approach.

"He wants us to kill him," Harrington explained as Dixon sloshed over to them.

"You find the road?" Woodall asked Rath.

The private shook his head.

"Is Smith getting worse?" Dixon asked.

"Put me out of my pain, please," Smith gurgled, his speech laden with phlegm as his chest filled with blood, slowly suffocating himself.

"None of us can do that," Dixon explained.

"Gimme gun," Smith said, one hand weakly imploring the rest. "I do it."

Billy gazed a long time at Smith, the soldier's face gone as pale as a limestone bluff. Then he looked at Harrington and at Rath. "You two stay with him. Keep him from doing himself harm. Make him comfortable as you can—maybe he'll sleep."

Then Dixon dragged himself across the swampy wallow. "How's the leg, Amos?"

Chapman snorted, dragging a hand beneath his runny nose. "Still broke, Billy. How's yours?"

"Still got a hole in it. We're a pair, ain't we, Amos?"

"As poor a pair as I'd ever hope to draw from the deck, I'll tell you."

Dixon sighed, staring up at the Big Dipper. "I'm going in the morning."

Chapman nodded eventually, gazing back out on the starlit slope, the hulking mesquite seeming all the larger beneath, with the play of silver light. He didn't say anything, as if Dixon's declaration didn't need his approval. What Billy had said was not up for discussion. More a statement of cold fact.

"Likely you're right, Dixon."

"You in shape to watch over things here?"

"As good as any the rest," Chapman replied.

"Get some sleep while you can, Amos. I'll wake you afore sunup."

An hour later, when the wind died and the last of the clouds had swept across the dusting of stars pricking the prairie blackness overhead, sounds seemed more clear. And then Billy noticed that something else had changed. Quietly he crawled through the bloody slush slicking the bottom of the wallow, put out his hand and held it an inch from Smith's face. Nothing.

His fingers laid on the private's skin. He took them away after a minute. The flesh gone cold. Dixon slowly pulled down the two eyelids and dragged himself back across the wallow to wait out the coming dawn.

When it came time for Billy to go, he and Rath gently took the dead soldier's body and laid it out just beyond the lip of the wallow. Sergeant Woodall handed Rath a silk handkerchief he carried inside his shirt.

"Put this over Private Smith's face," Woodall said.

Rath did so. Everyone knew it was all they had to serve as a decent shroud for the dead.

Shaking hands with the three soldiers, then wordlessly embracing Amos, Dixon rolled out of the muddy wallow onto the prairie in the gray light of predawn and pointed his nose north by northeast, feeling his way up the gentle rise of the divide that rose between Gageby Creek and the Washita River here in the uncharted wilderness west of Indian Territory.

In something less than a mile he struck the wagon ruts of the Camp Supply Road, pointing like a beacon to the northeast, both deep creases in the prairie eventually converging far off at the gray edge of the horizon. As the sky grew ever more light, he hurried along, until he was almost loping. Having found his wind, Dixon figured he could keep up the pace all day if he had to: running some, then walking, then running a bit more. He had to hurry. There were others back there who were waiting, depending on him. Their time was running out.

He had covered a little more than two miles, the eastern side of the world caressed now with a brightening crimson-tinged orange presaging the coming sun, when he made out a moving, throbbing mass of horsemen coming in his direction. The bunch grew and grew in size until the entire caravan covered more than an acre in size.

Frightened, Dixon plunged into the brush, then crabbed to the top of a small knoll where he lay among the mesquite, watching the distant horsemen approach. Perhaps the warriors had worked themselves into another fighting frenzy and were returning at dawn, just as they had attacked the six yesterday.

With his heart in his throat, trying his best to make out the throbbing shapes coming out of the newborn daylight to the east, Billy finally stood, waving his Sharps at the end of his arm. The horsemen were moving in columns of fours, not in single file, as warriors would ride across the plains.

Quickly Dixon fired a shot from his rifle. Then reloaded and fired a second shot on down the hillside. Then he stumbled down the slope of the hill, still waving, his mouth moving, almost unable to utter a sound, tears streaming unashamedly down his mud-crusted cheeks, softening the mud crusted in his mustache and beard.

A blue-clad flanker reined up before him. "Who the hell are you?"

"Billy Dixon," he answered, finding his voice a strange thing there in the gray light of day-coming on the Camp Supply Road. "Courier for Miles."

"General Nelson A. Miles?" another soldier asked, urging his horse forward from the ranks of the horsemen, stopping before the civilian.

"Yessir."

"I'm Major William R. Price, Eighth Cavalry—out of Fort Bascomb," the man boomed. "Yesterday we ran onto Captain Lyman's wagon train. He was hit a few days back by a large war party." Price flung a thumb back along his column. "Lyman's right behind us with the general's supplies and forage. By God—we're looking for Miles ourselves. Where the devil is he?"

Dixon pointed. "We was carrying dispatches bound for Camp Supply, Major. Me and another scout and four of the general's soldiers got ambushed by Injuns yesterday. We're shot up pretty bad. Not far back there—in the mud of a buffalo wallow."

"You held them off?"

"Yes, Major."

Price pushed his slouch hat back, regarding the civilian.

"You suppose it was that same bunch we skirted around, Major?" asked one of the soldiers at Price's side.

Then Dixon saw the major shoot the officer a disapproving glance. Price had evidently been doing his best to avoid conflict with the huge war party, and by doing so had instead stumbled right into Dixon's half-dozen couriers.

"You got a surgeon along, Major?"

"I do," Price replied, the look in his eyes almost thankful for Dixon taking him off the hook. He turned in the saddle. "Bring Surgeon Fouts up."

When the physician had reached the major's side, Price said, "This courier has some wounded I want you to examine, Surgeon. Take your two stewards and determine the nature of their wounds."

"All right," Fouts said, sounding almost bored. "Show us to your couriers."

Dixon pointed down the road. "Just keep going over in that direction, not by the road. Bear hard to the south, sir. You want me to show you?"

Fouts shook his head. "No, son. You stay with the major. We'll find it."

He watched the surgeon and his two stewards ride off as Price began asking him questions regarding the fight at the buffalo wallow. Glancing over his shoulder minutes later, Dixon realized the surgeon was bearing too far to the north. He tried yelling at them but they had gone too far away to hear his voice. Dixon instead fired his rifle, getting the surgeon's attention. He waved them to the left, pointing them more to the south. In a matter of moments they would be within rifle range of the wallow. Dixon turned back to Price as the major resumed his questioning.

"You have one dead?"

"When I left, sir. Three of the other four was shot up. Some worse'n others—"

The roar of Chapman's buffalo gun cut off the rest of Dixon's words. Billy recognized the sound of that gun, as any good hide man learned to recognize the sound of another hunter's loads. In the distance, halfway between where he stood and the wallow, one of the steward's horses was keeling over to the ground.

"Jesus, Mary and Joseph!" Dixon muttered as he tore off running. He was heaving, his chest burning before he knew it. How his legs were staying under him, he had no idea—just that they were pumping across the heaving land. Without anything to eat in two days, with that bullet wound in his calf that still seeped, without any sleep in more than twenty-four hours, he ran.

"Amos! Amos! It's me!" he hollered, thundering past the frightened surgeon and his two stewards, who were cowering among the mesquite brush.

Chapman was struggling to elbow his way above the lip of the wallow as Dixon approached.

"Goddamn you, Dixon!"

"Amos—why in hell you shooting at the doctor?"

"Doctor?" Woodall asked, his voice catching in his throat.

"I brung you a surgeon, boys," Dixon replied, grinning.

"Shit, Billy," Amos growled, looking sheepish. "Don't you go blaming me for not knowing. I heard two shots a while back, then another one not long ago, and then made out them three on horseback coming our way. I just figured they'd made quick work of you and was coming up to do in the rest of us."

Grumbling about how ungrateful the men in the wallow were, Surgeon Fouts crawled around the edge of the pit, examining the wounds of all, including Dixon. The stewards stood nearby, nervously glancing at the body on the ground.

"This one's dead?"

"Smith. Private," Woodall said. "Killed in action, Surgeon."

Standing and straightening his coat, Fouts again glanced over the scene perfunctorily. "I see. For this motley band of couriers, you almost cost the life of one of my stewards. Hell, you might damn well have shot me."

Dixon watched him turn and mount up, ordering his stewards to ride double.

"Doctor? Ain't . . . ain't you gonna tend to these men?"

"Not a one of you are going to die," he hurled his words over his shoulder. "I must report the unfortunate loss of government property to Major Price. A horse is a costly piece of equipment."

"That son of a bitch," growled Woodall. He started to rise, wincing as he struggled up. Harrington and Rath held him down.

"You stay put. I don't want you bleeding no more," Dixon told him.

Such was Price's determination when the major rode up with the rest of his command. He looked with disdain upon the muddy buffalo wallow, more so at the poor condition of its defenders, yet did not order the surgeon to attend to their wounds. Instead, Major William R. Price chastised the defenders for their destruction of government property in killing a fine horse, which he was now going to have to account for in a report that would reflect on his campaign record.

"Where you going, Major?" Dixon asked as Price gave the orders for his column to move out.

"To escort Captain Lyman's supply train to General Miles's base camp."

Dixon was fast growing furious. "You ain't leaving anyone with us?"

Price looked them over. "You held them off once, Dixon. I don't have any doubt you can again, if need be. Besides, we're sweeping the country clear of hostiles as we go."

Billy was sputtering mad, his rage burning with more fire than had that Kiowa bullet when it burrowed through his leg. "How 'bout some doctoring supplies."

Price snorted. "If the surgeon ascertained that you needed medical attention, he would have left them." The major started to rein away.

Dixon grabbed the officer's bridle. "What about ammunition? We're low, goddammit. If those red bastards do come back—we don't stand a lick of a chance, Major!"

"Release my horse," Price hissed. When Dixon had done so, Price went on. "I do not feel compelled by your situation here to leave you any arms or ammunition. We have driven the warriors before us and you should not have any need for resupply from us."

"For God sake—leave these men some food, Major," Dixon pleaded, shaking his head in disbelief. His hand shook as he pointed to the wounded in the buffalo wallow. "These men . . . none of 'em et in more'n a day and a half."

"I have nothing, sir."

"You got a whole goddamned supply train!"

"Step back, Dixon—or I will have you placed under arrest!" Price snarled, then kicked his horse savagely and loped away from the wallow.

As the major rode on down the slope, a few soldiers who had been within earshot eased out of column and scurried past the muddy depression, handing the five survivors what they could of their rations of dried beef and hardtack, quickly glancing at the muddy, bloodied body of Private Smith, then hurrying back into formation.

"God bless you," Woodall told them, each and every one, as they gave what they could in the way of rations, a few cartridges for the defenders' army carbines before they marched out of sight, moving south for Miles's cantonment.

"The general will send someone back for us soon as he hears," the sergeant reminded the men left behind at the wallow. "Miles won't let that strutting peacock of a major get away with this, he won't."

The sun rose that day, climbed to mid-sky then fell into the far west, eventually drying the muddy soup at the bottom of the buffalo wallow before twilight descended for a second time on the five defenders. Stars came out and an autumn moon rose in the southeastern sky, slowly, hour by hour climbing past mid-heaven.

Billy could not quite force his eyes to stay open, nor keep his ears alert for all his fatigue. He knew it must be some time past midnight as his eyelids drooped, heavier and heavier—

The distant blare of a bugle brought them all alert.

"That wasn't—" Woodall began in a hopeful gush.

Then it was there again, a little more clear this time.

"By damn—it's out of the south!" Dixon roared. He was swallowing the lump in his throat, biting his lip as Rath and Harrington hugged one another, then pounded Woodall on the back.

Dixon fired his Sharps. Chapman raised his and fired as well. Now the bugler blew a different call, and then the men in the wallow made out the sound of voices coming toward them out of the night-black. White voices calling for direction.

"This way!" Dixon yelled, his voice seizing in his throat. "We're . . . we're over here!"

Billy held his hand out to Amos Chapman as the sound of the mounted horse soldiers drew closer and closer. They shook in silence, neither one having to speak what was in their hearts.

35

Late September 1874

For seven days that last week of August, Colonel Ranald Slidell Mackenzie marched his 640 men north from Fort Concho toward the caprock of the Staked Plain, where he would engage the red lords of the southern prairie.

Never before had the Army of the West ordered into the field an expedition of comparable battle experience, readiness and downright grit. Both the geography and the climate would soon do their best to crack the colonel's resolve. It had already proved to be the hottest summer in any man's memory, an excruciating torture of dry water holes found by the advance scouts, stifling clouds of dust raised by wagon tires and horse hooves, as well as nothing but sun-withered grass to feed the animals following each day's punishing march, any of it cruel enough for man and horse alike as Mackenzie demanded more and more of his "Southern Column" with each subsequent day.

But already Seamus had realized this was a real fighting unit, filled up and down the ranks, tunic, stripe and braid, with men who would take their due and not grumble about the heat and food, the saddle galls and the bad water. On that tough ride north, it didn't take long for the Irishman to realize the Fourth Cavalry was the one outfit Sherman and Sheridan had to send out to crush these tribes of the southern plains. Mackenzie's men would do it, by damn— these soldiers who would follow their colonel not only to Hell and back, but twice around the Devil on the way.

Then on 30 August, Sharp Grover, Seamus Donegan, the Fort Richardson post guide named Henry W. Strong and three of Grover's Seminoles found enough graze along with enough water in both Catfish Creek and the nearby Freshwater Fork of the Brazos River to satisfy the colonel's requirement for a supply camp. Mackenzie halted his columns just south of the majestic caprock, allowing his troops to recoup themselves and their animals after the brutalizing march. Here stood a massive series of hulking buttes and rocky cliffs rising at times more than a thousand feet over the surrounding prairie noted for its stark, naked austerity. Those cliffs supported juniper and cottonwood and mesquite of the famed Llano Estacado. Ancient home to the Kwahadi Comanche.

Here were given rise the four tongues of the Red River, each racing turbulent and earth-colored to the east, each cutting across the centuries its own meandering canyons into the ocher and red, yellow and pink escarpments of this no-man's land. With each spring came the runoff, with each autumn more thunderstorms, swelling each trickle to overflowing, slashing away at the loose, sandy soil, water careening down every dangerous scree-covered slope to create a broken maze of cliff and canyon spiderwebbing the southern reaches of the Texas Panhandle.

This was to be the third campaign in four years for Mackenzie's famous Fourth. And would prove to be the singular career effort that would finally win a reputation for the ambitious, nervous-ridden, harsh and eccentric colonel who would again drive his men to the point of breaking in his search for Quanah Parker's Kwahadis. In addition to eight companies of his own Fourth Cavalry, four companies of the Tenth Infantry and one company of the Eleventh Infantry marched under Mackenzie. His scouts were organized under Lieutenant William A. Thompson and Sergeant John B. Charlton, the same soldier who was credited for firing the fatal shot into the breast of Kiowa chief Satank three years before. These soldier scouts were joined by Grover and Donegan, a dozen Tonkawas, a handful of Lipan-Apaches and thirteen coffee-skinned Seminoles.

One of the Lipans, Seamus had recently learned, was actually a Mexican half-breed named Johnson who had for many years operated out of the Rio Grande country as a

was something different, teetering on the brink of a sheer, precipitous drop.

Most of all Seamus was afraid of letting any of the others know just how scared he was at this moment. An enemy he could see, dodge, avoid, fire back at . . . that was something he could deal with. But his descent into the shadowy, murky, mist-shrouded bowels of this canyon was moment by moment becoming the most harrowing experience of his life. And for one of the few times in his life, he had to suffer with that fear rather than fighting it off through nerve-numbing action—tasting his fear there on the back of his tongue, like sucking on an old brass cartridge.

Donegan was near the front, sliding along as slowly as he could between Sharp Grover and Sergeant John Charlton. Behind them came the Tonkawas and Seminoles, most painted enough to satisfy their personal spirits, yet still dressed in blue tunics to accommodate their fears of being taken for the enemy in the heat of the coming fray. Horses snorted up and down the canyon wall as the scouts slowly worked their way down the narrow switchback trail that clung like a dark ribbon in the shadows of dawn to the crimson rock. Overhead Seamus made out the muffled voices of officers and enlisted as Mackenzie's troops followed the scouts into the darkness of this great laceration gouged out of the Staked Plain.

They had a thousand feet to go, down into darkness all the way. And this last thousand feet of Mackenzie's campaign would take a cold, cast-iron, double-riveted kind of nerve to get them all down to the fighting ground.

Troop A, under the capable Captain Eugene B. Beaumont, had been selected to lead the attack with Thompson's scouts, who would be allowed to break off and capture the enemy's pony herd. Mackenzie knew as well as any commander on the plains what it would mean to his enemy to lose those ponies.

The chill rising from the canyon this dawn was almost ghostly, climbing on the shoulders of the mist and remnants of last night's fires. Seamus caught the first whiff of cedar smoke carried on the breeze that nudged the hair at his shoulder. The air grew colder as they dropped farther and farther into the shadows of the canyon. From time to time as he inched his way down, he dared look below to the valley floor—and for but a glance he allowed himself, Seamus saw the forest of buffalo-hide lodges mingled in among the cedar and mesquite and cottonwood and chinaberry, pale as a white man's sun-cured skin against the darker green of the luxurious grasses. Smoke laid against those dark-leafed, shadowy trees like a gauzy veil upon an Irish bride's dark hair.

"Lor', feddas," one of the black-skinned Seminoles exclaimed behind Donegan as the mists parted and the scouts caught a momentary glimpse of the immense herds, "lookit all the sheep an' goats grezzin' down there."

Just behind him, Seamus heard Charlton reply, "For sure we got a big surprise coming for those red-bellies."

For these gut-wrenching moments, the great, grazing herds were the farthest thing from Donegan's mind. He slid along the red wall a step at a time, obsessed with his fear that the warriors below were only waiting for them, knowing the army was coming. Any moment now, he was certain as his heart pounded in his ears, the Kiowa and Comanche and all the rest would begin to pick off the enemy—Thompson's scouts and Mackenzie's troops—trapped like fish in a barrel, pinned helplessly like clay targets against the crimson canyon wall, listening to the rasp of saddle leather and the jingle of bit-chains, and the pounding of his own heart.

This descent was truly as the anxious colonel had characterized it when he had turned from Thompson's scouts to begin explaining the trail to his officers. Words that faded behind Seamus as he had started down the trail, straight down into Ranald Slidell Mackenzie's "jaws of death."

Captain Napoleon McLaughlin was ordered to hold his battalion in reserve at the top of the trail while Mackenzie joined Captain Beaumont's men at the point of attack. These and other things Seamus tried desperately to work over in his mind as he slid along the trail, keeping his back brushing along the sandy wall step by step. Seamus didn't know how long they had been inching their way down. It

Comanchero gun-runner to the Comanche, trading in captives and cattle and horses stolen from the settlements and reservations. When the half-breed had seen the writing on the wall and presented himself to Mackenzie, offering his services as a guide to the trackless expanse of the Llano Estacado, the colonel snatched Johnson up without hesitation. While the soldiers established the base camp, Johnson was directed to take the Seminoles north to begin scouring the country, looking for trails, sign, smoke—anything that might lead Mackenzie to the enemy.

Johnson's trackers returned to tell the colonel they had cut three separate trails.

Leaving three of his infantry companies behind on Catfish Creek to garrison his supply base on 20 September, Mackenzie immediately pushed his column north—450 men, twenty-one commissioned officers, three surgeons, both white and Indian scouts along with Lieutenant H. W. Lawton's supply train and its infantry escort. His cavalry Mackenzie divided into two battalions: the first, Troops D, F, I and K under Captain Napoleon B. McLaughlin, who had attained a credible Civil War record and been the virtual hero of Mackenzie's attack on the Kickapoo village at Remolino, Mexico, in 1873; the second composed of A, E, H and L under Captain Eugene B. Beaumont, blooded at Gettysburg and a genuine hero in Sherman's siege at Atlanta, under whose command Mackenzie's forces had attacked the expansive Comanche camp on the North Fork of the Red River in 1872.

After two days' travel, the horrid drought that had wreaked its vengeance on the southern plains finally broke. Whereas before the men and horses had to march through stifling dust raised by thousands of hooves and iron tires, now the soldiers and their mounts were forced to muck through thick, red gumbo, sleep in the cold mud like homeless litters of shoats, and grow accustomed to living day and night soaked to the skin beneath a relentlessly gray autumn sky.

Mackenzie drove his cavalry hard. The supply train struggled to keep up as the colonel's scouts sniffed and probed here then there, feeling their way north along the face of the caprock, trying to sense where the warriors and their villages would be found. Knowing, as they talked about every night over smoky fires of wet wood when wood could be found, that the enemy was slowly being squeezed between five columns. One day soon the fight would come —when the Kiowa and Comanche and Cheyenne no longer had anyplace to turn, to escape. One day . . . soon.

For two days, the twenty-second and twenty-third, Mackenzie called a halt on colorful Quitaque Creek, hoping his outfit could dry out and ready itself to move on into the broken country formed centuries before by the tributaries of the Red River. The next day his command was again battered by a horrific thunderstorm that sent lightning crashing against the pink and white buttes, torrents of swollen creeks rushing past his huddled forces who cowed before the brutal winds whipped out of the north. After nearly three days of intermittent northers, the weather eventually cleared on the twenty-fifth.

As quickly Mackenzie was among them, whipping his men into formation, bawling orders. He was late, and impatient for it.

They made twenty grueling miles that day, only the Fourth Cavalry able to reach Tule Canyon, leaving his infantry and supply train to muck along through the mire and mud as well as they could far to the rear. During that grueling day, even the cavalry were ordered to intermittently walk as a means of preserving their mounts.

At dusk a bone-weary Seamus Donegan followed the rest of the scouts back into that canyon to find Mackenzie's troops making camp.

"You crossed a fresh trail, I understand," Mackenzie demanded without ceremony as he hurried up to his chief of scouts.

Lieutenant Thompson nodded.

Sharp Grover moved up to talk. "Maybe as many as fifteen hundred ponies."

"Where's it headed?" the colonel inquired, his eyes alive with keen interest.

"East," answered Henry Strong.

"But it is my estimation they are drawing us off, Mr. Strong," said the colonel. "A village that big can't be moving east—toward the reservations. We've flushed them and they're fleeing *north!*"

Mackenzie was a whirl of motion, turning to holler into the twilight illuminated with a hundred fires. "Beaumont! Get me Captain Beaumont!"

While McLaughlin's First Battalion was allowed to recoup in the canyon, Mackenzie ordered Beaumont's Second Battalion to follow the trail. Gratified that he wasn't needed to ride along with the Seminoles to show Beaumont the way, Donegan tore at some dried beef and soaked his hardtack in a steaming cup of coffee that night before he collapsed in his bedroll, the fragrant wisp of a lace handkerchief under his cheek.

Mackenzie found nothing that night, for all his trouble groping around in the dark.

At dawn the colonel moved another five miles down the Tule Canyon, still probing, most every man among them watching the scouts who, to the trailwise, had grown all the more wary. Sign was to be found everywhere a man cared to look. At sundown Thompson's scouts returned to the new camp with reports of warrior activity in the entire area.

"They'll hit us tonight for sure, Seamus."

"These Comanche like that?" Donegan asked, glancing at the sky as he asked.

Grover looked up at the coming full moon as well. "It's another Comanche moon, Irishman. The third since they hit you at Adobe Walls. Damn right these bastards attack at night. Mackenzie knows that as well as any man."

Donegan nodded. "Aye, I forgot you rode with the colonel—fighting these same bloody h'athens a few winters ago."

Hoofbeats hammered through the rocky canyon. Voices called out greeting as the solitary horseman rode past. The Comanchero stopped for a moment, his horse lathered, speaking in broken Kiowa with Henry Strong.

"What's Johnson say?" Donegan asked Grover, knowing

Sharp understood some of the Kiowa tongue, the universal language of the southern plains.

"Said he saw some buffalo running northwest of us, almost due north in fact."

"What's up there?"

Grover shrugged as Johnson pulled away from the white scouts, intent on searching out Mackenzie in the camp stretched like a rawhide thong alongside Tule Creek. "Don't rightly know, Seamus. But if the buffalo are running, it's likely someone's running 'em."

It wasn't long before criers were coming through camp, with orders to prepare for an expected attack from the hostiles. As Donegan and Grover picketed their horses, then hobbled the animals' forelegs, the older scout suggested "cross-lining": with a length of rope tying a forehoof to the opposite hind leg.

"You act like these Comanche gonna run off with the horses," Seamus said as he tightened the last knot on his horse.

"Damn right I do," Grover replied. "When I last rode with Mackenzie, the bloody Kwahadi did just that: run off the regiment's horses—including the colonel's personal mount. Damn, was he mad. I doubt a man ever forgets something like that."

"Mackenzie been waiting for a crack at these bastirds, is it?"

"Look around you, Seamus," Grover said, pointing out the colonel's preparations. Squads of skirmishers, what the soldiers called "sleeping parties" of a dozen to fifteen men, were placed out among the rocks around the entire herd. Every man was on alert, pickets placed every twenty feet along the length of the perimeter. "Mackenzie may've been beat once. But he learned his lesson well. And the colonel ain't a man to be beat a second time. He's come here to this country to win this ride out. Mark my word—Mackenzie's gonna win."

Three hours after sunset, the Comanche came.

More than 250 horsemen tore in among the regiment's herd where Beaumont's A Company held their ground, driving back the baffled raiders. But instead of being

seemed like at least twenty minutes, perhaps longer. And they were only halfway to the valley floor. His horse snorted, yanking its head back suddenly at it lost a foreleg. Loose rocks tumbled.

"Easy, son. Easy," Grover whispered back to him.

Donegan drew down on the reins gently, rubbing the animal's muzzle, then put his reluctant feet in motion once more. The animal's fear made him feel better about his own. But now he became sure the warriors below could hear his heart pounding in his chest like a huge, rawhide-headed war drum. Little else could he make out but the surging of his own heart as foot by foot, yard by yard, Thompson led his scouts, Mackenzie and eight companies of the Fourth Cavalry into the sleepy maw of the Palo Duro.

"Great jumping thunder!" a voice cried up ahead. Thompson's.

As suddenly, Seamus was craning his neck, finding the dim form of a warrior not far below them, perched among the rocks near the bottom, waving his red blanket. Dropping it in a flutter of shadowy movement, the warrior swept up his rifle.

"Get that sonofabitch!" Grover hollered at Thompson, yanking his pistol from his belt.

Donegan gulped, hurling his body against the canyon wall while the two guns roared as if one. He watched the warrior hurtled backward against the pale rocks and crumple.

As quickly, there came other sounds down to his right, among the trees and mesquite brush and willow clustered along a narrow ribbon of creek glowing silver in the coming light of day. Another warrior suddenly appeared out of the shadows and timber. He cried out his war song, his head thrown back and voice shrill in echo, beating his chest with a hand before he turned and disappeared.

"Get moving, men!" Thompson shouted at the top of his lungs. "Get down as fast as you can and form up!"

Then the lieutenant and Grover were gone in the murky gray light. Donegan peered up the canyon wall, the far extent grown bright red now as the rising sun lanced its beams halfway down to the valley floor. Along that narrow thread of trail were strung the buglike shapes of man and horse, sliding, slipping, hurrying as best they could now that they had been discovered. Orders barked up and down the canyon, echoing over the report of those two simultaneous shots disappearing up the canyon, swallowed by the sheer immensity of this valley.

Another gun roared off to his right. The warrior who had cried out his war song had returned, thrown his rifle to his shoulder and fired his shot. Seamus stumbled onto the short, steep slope that would take him another twenty feet to the valley floor as the Indian fired his second shot.

There was no way Thompson could have enough men down to enjoin the fight before the warriors would engage them. For what few were there with Donegan now, it was like dropping a raw buffalo hump tenderloin into a pack of hungry wolves.

"Sonofabitch!" Grover was yelling somewhere to his right.

Then in a blur of motion at his left, Donegan saw the older man, his pistol drawn, firing two times, then a third as the warrior catapulted backwards, his bare chest smeared rosy in the coming light of day.

Quanah was just then emerging from his lodge into the chill shadows of dawn. The Kwahadi camp was the last of five circles clustered along the twisting creek.

The first, faint gunshot rumbled from up the canyon, farther north.

He pulled his breechclout aside, shivering as he wet the ground. A hunter already busy this morning, he thought. Likely far up by the Kiowa camp of Red Warbonnet, near the mouth of Blanca Cita Creek.

Peering up at the distant lip of the canyon wall some thousand feet above him, Quanah marveled once more at the colors of this special, sacred place. A breeze noisily raised itself through the dry leaves of the cottonwood about him as he filled his lungs with the chill air. Even the nearby stream smelled of the red earth of this place. He listened, frowning suddenly.

Stepping closer to the stream, it was as if the red-colored water were telling him something not quite intelligible in its gurgling passage across the canyon floor.

He stood there listening to its words: almost a warning, it seemed.

Quanah jerked at the next shot, his heart seized in his throat at the third that followed on its heels. Spinning barefoot in the damp, dew-laden grass, the war chief felt a sudden flare of white-hot rage for Mamanti, the Kiowa with the owl medicine. The shaman had consulted his sacred stuffed owl days ago when the war bands had come to the canyon. Yes, the owl had told Mamanti—this is a safe place for the villages to stay the winter.

Other shamans, Cheyenne and Comanche, had concurred.

But then the soldiers had come marching. Still, Mamanti and the rest had vowed the yellowlegs would never find the canyon. Instead, Three-Finger Kinzie could be driven off by decoys the way a sage hen would feign a broken wing to draw the predator from her nest.

So his Kwahadi had rested in peace.

"Get up!" Quanah yelled to his wife and children.

Their eyes opened wide. Without question they were pulling on clothing and dragging moccasins over their feet.

"Take only what you can carry," he told them as Tonarcy handed him his rifle.

From the dew-cloth liner rope she pulled his medicine bag, then a quiver filled with arrows and his short bow. He knelt and stuffed his huge Walker Colt pistol into his belt, then stopped, lunging for his wife as their three children clambered out the lodge door. Quanah embraced her quickly, then held her face in his hands.

"Guard them with your life this day, woman," he told her.

Then bent his head to kiss Tonarcy, drinking in the taste of her as if it had to last him a lifetime.

"Go!" he said, pushing her through the door.

She turned, hesitant, the children calling to her. Then rushed into his arms once more, embracing him, her ear pressed against his pounding heart. His eyes moistening, he knew he would always remember the fragrance of her hair.

Tonarcy finally tore herself from him and disappeared into the shadows of lodge and tree and canyon wall.

In the distance he recognized the brassy-throated call of a bugle, knowing it would be the white man's summons to his warriors. This was the echo of Three-Finger Kinzie's challenge, fading slowly, drifting down this bloodred canyon.

This was no less than Kinzie's personal challenge for Quanah to come do battle.

Quanah whirled, straightening the quiver over his shoulder. He yanked up the single buffalo-hair rein to the dun-colored war pony he had staked beside his lodge and leaped atop the animal's short back.

Throwing his chin back, the Kwahadi war chief raised his death cry to the coming sun, the echo of its call reverberating back again and again around him like a physical thing, around and over his warriors as they flocked to him from every corner of their camp, raising their own cries.

The women and children were on their way into the deepest recesses of the canyon, fleeing the threat. His warriors were ready now. Unpainted as they were—they were ready.

They would cover the retreat of their families with their own lives.

From behind every tree and rock, the Kiowas were sniping at the excited Seminole and Tonkawa scouts as Lieutenant Thompson barked his orders, attempting to regain control of a bad situation.

"Front into line, goddammit!"

"They don't know what the hell you're wanting them to do, Lieutenant!" Donegan shouted above the clamor.

The soldier pursed his lips in frustration then nodded. "Charge! Just charge, goddammit!"

Then Thompson savagely sawed his mount about in a tight circle and kicked the frightened animal into motion. The rest were off like grapeshot from a cannon. Behind Donegan arose the confused jumble of orders and snorting horses and angry men mixed with a generous helping of gunfire and tumbling rocks kicked loose by those still winding their way down that narrow thread of a trail into Mackenzie's jaws of death.

As the scouts surged forward into the mist and shadows, the lodges came into clear view, beyond them the first of the horse herds. Already the Kiowa were falling back, firing and yelling to one another, covering the retreat of their families. They stopped and turned, firing from a boulder here, a thick cottonwood there—firing, reloading, and firing again before they hurried on like bits of ghostly flotsam among the mist and shadows and trees.

To Donegan's left a Seminole's horse screamed out, its head wrenching about cruelly as it pitched its rider into the mesquite brush, crumpling instantly, legs thrashing and splayed on the bloody grass crushed beneath it.

He had watched horses die before, more than he believed he could ever count. Three had gone down under him during those hours and days of manmade hell at Gettysburg alone. And all the others—he squeezed his mind off of it of a sudden, the way a man would squeeze dust from his eyes. Tears streaming, because he could not shake the pain it gave him to watch the great, graceful animals fall screaming in death. Donegan drove his own horse on into the canyon, through the lodges, racing in among the warriors.

His left thigh stung.

Suddenly the horse pranced sideways, lost its gait, then burst off at a gallop again as Seamus peered down at his leg. The canvas britches fluttered mid-thigh along the furrow that grazing bullet had slashed in his flesh. It burned with the cool breeze as the horse beneath carried him on, step by leaping step into Mackenzie's canyon of death.

He felt alone the next moment, and reined up. Bullets whined past as he turned about in a tiny circle, the horse fighting the bit. He yanked back on the reins once more, trying to gain control of the huge animal. Then heard a smack of lead against flesh. The horse quivered, shuddering as a dog would shed water.

A puff of smoke from the nearby rocks betrayed the

warrior. Pointing the Henry out at the end of his one arm, Seamus fired, whirled the repeater around in that one hand as he struggled to hold the reins in the other. He fired a second time, watching the bullet strike the warrior as the Indian rose to fire a second shot.

The air about him sang with lead as the great horse crumpled beneath him. Throwing himself out of the way, Donegan rolled in the grass, grunting with his fall as he came to a stop against some mesquite.

The Henry spat free the empty brass as he chambered another .44-caliber cartridge and plopped to his belly. Behind him came the reassuring brassy call of Mackenzie's bugles. Then he clearly heard the thunder of hooves beneath the horn's fading echo. Hundreds of hooves.

As quickly, he heard the nearby rumble rise down the canyon as well. Horses coming from the opposite direction.

From their hiding places behind trees and rocks, the warriors disappeared, melting into the dawn mist hung gauzy over the creek like some broom-swatted cats as the first of the Indian ponies raced toward the Irishman from the camps on down the canyon. Yells and shouts, the snap of blankets and the slap of pieces of rawhide—the Seminole and Tonkawa scouts had raced in among the coveted herds, surrounded them and started the ponies back up the canyon toward the soldiers.

Gazing over his shoulder, Donegan watched the charging troopers as they were forced to draw off to either side of the grassy defile to make way for the stampeding ponies.

Mackenzie's cavalry sat there, suspended temporarily in their assault, fighting to control their prancing army mounts as the ponies raced by. Most cheered the scouts, tearing their hats from their heads and hallooing as Thompson's Indians tore past—having captured the pride of those war bands of the southern plains.

Once again Mackenzie had put his enemy afoot.

driven off by the skirmishers and pickets, the Comanche began their traditional circling of the herd, feinting in and back out again, looking, probing, testing for a weak spot. After thirty minutes of panic and sporadic gunfire, the ghostly horsemen disappeared into the autumn night as quickly as they had come.

From time to time snipers fired into Mackenzie's camp, causing some momentary excitement here and there, then they were gone. Minutes later firing erupted elsewhere on the perimeter, successfully keeping everyone jumpy and jittery well past midnight when wagonmaster James O'Neal's long overdue supply train rumbled and squeaked into the canyon.

"Lucky they was," Donegan said later as he swabbed out the barrel of the Henry repeater. "Riding in here dumb as rocks, not knowing the country was crawling with h'athens."

While roaming bands of warriors kept sniping throughout the shank of the night, most of the soldiers tried to get some much-needed sleep, knowing the next two or three days would allow them even less.

As soon as there was enough light before dawn, more than three hundred warriors gathered along the ridges north of the camp, content for the time being to fire at long range.

"Grover!" shouted Lieutenant Thompson as he trotted up on horseback in the gray light of that twenty-seventh day of September, his mount parting some of the sleepy-eyed scouts just then being roused after less than three hours of rest. "You and Donegan come with me! We've got orders to go with Captain Boehm and drive those Indians off."

Quickly pulling pickets and loosening knots on the crosslines, the two joined some of Thompson's Tonkawas and Lipans as they led Captain Peter Boehm's E Company northward toward the ridge held by the Comanche.

The wind cut cold slashes at them as the sun first breached the horizon. The coming warmth felt good going down into his lungs as they loped up the broken, rocky slopes toward the taunting enemy. Bullets stung the air sporadically around Donegan as the Comanche began to fall back toward their ponies tied at the mesquite back among the narrow ravines that honeycombed the country north of Tule Canyon. A few kept firing until the soldiers were almost in among them. One beautifully dressed warrior stood his ground as long as he dared, covering the retreat of the others, then whirled, sprinting to his pony. He leaped atop it as a Tonkawa named Henry surged past the Irishman, firing his pistol rapidly at the Comanche.

The warrior spun and fell from his pony as Henry closed on his ancient enemy.

Reining up in a clatter of rocks, Henry stuffed his pistol in his belt, ready to take the Comanche scalp. But just as Seamus turned to leave, the Comanche had other plans for the hated Tonkawa.

Springing from the ground where he had been feigning death, the warrior yanked a much-surprised Henry from his army mount. Striking the ground so hard it knocked the breath out of him, the Tonkawa struggled to collect his senses as the Comanche yanked his bow from the quiver at his back and repeatedly struck Henry with it.

"Kee-yip! Kee-yip!!" the warrior shouted each time he counted coup on his enemy.

It was becoming one of the most amusing vignettes Seamus could remember seeing in his short but bloody time on the plains. He was laughing uncontrollably as Grover rode up. The older scout began roaring at the Tonkawa's predicament as well, while the Comanche unabashedly refrained from killing Henry, preferring instead to beat his enemy with the bow, shaming him.

"Why you no shoot?" Henry shouted at Donegan and Grover, along with a handful of soldiers who rode up, curious at the laughter and noisy racket.

"Something this damned funny gonna make me bust a belly seam, Seamus!" Grover said, laughing.

"Shoot bastard! Shoot bastard!" the Tonkawa demanded as his bloodied arms canopied his face and head.

"You had enough, Henry?" growled Henry Strong as he rode up in a clatter of pebbles and dust.

"Shoot bastard!"

38

Donegan shook his head as he watched Captain Sebastian Gunther order the men of his H Company to the base of the canyon wall, directing them to scale the cliff in order to dislodge a few snipers firing down on the cavalry's advance.

"Clear those bastards out!" Gunther roared.

As if in reply to the captain's challenge, the warriors rained even more bullets down on both of Gunther's platoons.

"Captain!"

Donegan jerked about, recognizing that voice. Mackenzie himself sat there atop his mount, waving his arm at Gunther.

"General?"

"What the hell are you doing?"

"Attempting to dislodge these snipers—"

"Goddammit—I'm countermanding that order, Captain!" Mackenzie shrieked. "You force these men to obey you: not one man will live to reach the top of that bloody cliff! Now, call them off!"

Gunther glared but a moment, then turned and trotted back among his men, shouting for them to retreat off the face of the cliff.

The Irishman watched Mackenzie rein away, wagging his head. The colonel had covered but a few yards when he stopped beside a soldier whose horse had been shot. The private was struggling to pull his saddlebags from beneath the dead animal.

"What's your name, soldier?"

"McGowan, sir!" the youth replied, his face blackened by frustration.

"Get away from there or you'll be hit!"

The soldier nodded, starting to move away as Mackenzie reined about to go. McGowan sneaked back toward the dead horse as the colonel glanced over his shoulder, reined up and flushed with anger. Bullets splattered the rocks behind them both.

"Soldier! I thought I ordered you to go before you were shot!"

Private McGowan stammered a moment, digging for words. "I need the ammunition in these bags, Colonel." A sheepish look crossed his face as he shrugged. "Got some chew in there too."

The colonel wagged his head. "If your tobacco is worth getting your head blown off, have at it, McGowan!"

The soldier lunged at the carcass, yanking again on the saddlebags. "Thank you, Colonel. Thank you!"

More bullets slapped the rocks behind Mackenzie as a squad of troopers galloped up. Cottonwood leaves rattled as lead stung through the branches.

"Colonel, sir!"

"Yes, Lieutenant?" Mackenzie answered as Donegan trotted up behind the soldiers on foot.

"Sir," and the officer licked his lips, his eyes glazed with fear and fatigue, "the bastards are opening up a new front on us—over there!" He pointed to the far canyon wall, where gray puffs of smoke dotted the red and pink and white striations. "How're we ever gonna get out of here, Colonel?"

"Get hold of yourself, soldier," Mackenzie said sharply, motioning the Irishman over. "I brought you men in here. By God, I'll take you out."

Seamus cleared his throat. "Colonel?"

"Donegan—take a dozen of the lieutenant's men here and clear out that nest of vipers up there." Mackenzie pointed at the far canyon wall.

"Only a dozen, Colonel?" asked the lieutenant.

Mackenzie looked at Seamus. "Do you need any more than that, *Sergeant* Donegan?"

The Irishman's back went rigid. "How'd you—"

"It's not that hard for one soldier to recognize another when it comes to a close fight of it. Besides, I've asked about you."

"Grover?"

Mackenzie nodded. "Now, tell me if you'll need more than a dozen of the lieutenant's men."

Donegan shook his head, smiling broadly. "We'll make short work of it, Colonel."

"Twelve of you!" Mackenzie called out, waving his pistol. "Count off and follow Donegan. Do as he says and you'll all be eating beans and hard bread for dinner tonight!"

Twelve of them, mostly privates, peeled off, trotting past Mackenzie, then dismounting as they called out their number. Each man lashed their mounts in the brush. Wasn't a one of them wouldn't do what Mackenzie asked at a drop of a kepi, even though the colonel had ridden their bottoms raw through the last month.

Donegan looked over them quickly, seeing their faces gone liver-colored with fatigue, then led the twelve forward through the litter of abandoned blankets and clothing, cooking utensils and collapsed frames the women used to dry meat. An Indian mule tore past, heading down the canyon, its hastily tied bundle come loose and slung below its belly.

By the time they made it to the jumble of sandstone boulders at the foot of the cliff wall, there were but two, perhaps three warriors remaining. The rest had scrambled down from their perches, escaping away up the canyon, or had chosen to disappear up the wall itself.

Donegan spread the dozen out, pointing out where he wanted fire concentrated from three directions on each of the warriors. With the deep-hued shadows, he could not be sure as the minutes crawled past—but one by one by one, each of the warrior guns was silenced. The soldiers did not see the enemy fall. There were no bodies to count. Only the relative silence come back at them from the canyon wall.

"Good job, sojurs. Time you reported back to your lieutenant," he ordered them.

As the rest passed by him, a young sergeant with three stripes on his arm stopped and turned, his red hair shining in the morning sun like Mexican copper. He saluted Donegan, saying, "I wasn't old enough to fight in the war, Sergeant. But I imagine I damn well would've learned something from you if I had."

Then the fire-haired sergeant turned and was gone with his men.

Those few words, along with the confidence of Mackenzie himself, sent a surge of pride coursing through the marrow of him as Donegan loped away from the cliff wall.

McLaughlin had led three of his four companies down the canyon trail to aid Beaumont's battalion in mopping up what resistance the warriors attempted. In less than an hour and a half, the bulk of the fighting was over. While an occasional gunshot echoed far down the canyon where the warriors were retreating before the pressure, Mackenzie already had his victory. He ordered the destruction of the captured lodges and everything in them.

"Colonel," a young lieutenant said as he reined up near Mackenzie. "Hord's been shot."

"My bugler?"

"He was riding beside you in the charge, Colonel."

"Hit bad?"

"In the gut, sir."

"Damn! Get him to the surgeon."

"Surgeon Choate is already with him," and then the lieutenant wagged his head. "He says Hord will likely make it."

Mackenzie grinned, turning to find Donegan coming up on foot. "By Lord, that is good news. Do you know of any other casualties?"

"No others reported at this time, Colonel."

"Very well. Tell Hord I'll be along to see him once we get these lodges put to the torch."

Donegan halted near Mackenzie, watching the troops from E Company assigned to pulling down the lodges into great piles and setting them on fire.

"Are you afoot, Donegan?"

"Yes, Colonel. Lost my horse in the fight."

He nodded, looking over the Irishman's great bulk. "We've captured what I figure to be over twelve hundred Indian ponies. I hope you can find something to ride among the enemy's herds. Go find Thompson's scouts and inform the lieutenant you have first choice among the captured ponies."

"Thank you, Colonel."

Mackenzie smiled genuinely, presenting his hand down to the Irishman. "No, thank you, Sergeant. That was awfully pretty how you cleaned out that nest on the cliffs for me. Triangulation of fire—very, very good, soldier."

Seamus shook the colonel's hand then backed a step from Mackenzie's horse, saluting. "Congratulations to you too, Colonel. For a while there I figured you had gone and spelled the end of the Fourth Cavalry, I had."

Mackenzie's brow knitted. "How's that?"

"Spreading your regiment out along that canyon trail. If these warriors had been up early, if they had pickets out—why, they could have wiped out half your regiment, picking them off the wall where there was nowhere to go but down. It turned out a damned fine gamble."

Mackenzie gazed for a moment up at the line of sunlight crawling down the red face of the Palo Duro. "Fighting Indians is just that, Donegan: a gamble. Some fights I've lost. Some big ones too." He grinned. "I just figured, what with as much of a gambler as I am—I was about due to win one of the big pots."

"Your daring paid off, Mackenzie. My hat's off to you."

"Go fetch you a horse, Sergeant Donegan. And make it a fine one at that."

Seamus turned to go, his voice loud in the canyon. "No doubt, Colonel—if it's courtesy the U.S. Army, it will be a very fine horse!"

There had been no time for the women to gather up the travois ponies, to tear down lodges, to pack clothing and utensils, dried meat and robes to ward off the coming winds of winter. With those first sinewy, warning yaps of the camp dogs, they had been forced to leave behind the ponies and the mules for the white man and the hated Tonkawa trackers.

Everything but their lives had been lost to Three-Finger Kinzie.

Doing what they had done time and again, the warriors

fell back slowly, firing, holding the soldiers at bay while they could. From every crevice in the canyon walls, from every rock and tree big enough, the warriors held while they could against the solid blue phalanx.

And through it all, Quanah was among them—Kiowa and Cheyenne as well as his own Kwahadi. He exhorted them, rallied them, bolstered them as they fell back—urging them to hold the line a little longer.

"For our women and children!" he shouted first in one tongue, then in another. "For our families! We leave our bodies here to protect the ones who flee!"

Back, back across the yucca and tiny prickly pear, across the white quartz studded in the red earth they retreated slowly along the upvaulted rock formations as hawks drifted overhead on the warming air currents.

Yellow-striped lizards scampered out of the way of his feet as his moccasins felt their way for him as he pushed back, fired, then pushed back a little farther, darting away like a puff of wood smoke. Birds chirked in protest against the constant, booming cacophony of the gunfire.

But for all the gunfire and noise and fear, for all the rage the warriors felt for this attack, they had seriously wounded only one soldier that Quanah was sure of—the bugler himself, his shiny horn pressed to his lips, riding beside the bearer of the flag. On the far side of the bugler rode the one who caught Quanah's eye. He was sure who the soldier was. It could only be Three-Finger himself.

To his shoulder Quanah had thrown his Winchester carbine, aimed and squeezed just as the bugler's mount stumbled. The horse pitched forward two halting steps, placing the horn-blower's body in front of Kenzie's.

The bugler spun out of the saddle and the soldier chief raced on, never knowing how close he himself had come to Quanah Parker's bullet.

The others were falling back along the north side of the canyon now. A half-dozen Kiowas struggled past him, bearing the body of Red Warbonnet.

"He opened the fight with the yellowlegs," a young warrior said proudly of the dead man slung across their arms. "We will sing his name in praises for many generations to come," Quanah promised, motioning them to pass quickly.

For more than four miles now they had held the soldiers back. From afar he heard the low, grumbling charge of the cavalry coming their way, so much like the sound of a mule with a bellyful of bad water. Now came time for the last of the warriors to disappear into the narrow washes and bent-finger arroyos wrinkled off the main canyon.

"Go!" Quanah hollered at them, waving them away with his rifle. "Disappear until we can regroup at the top."

It was there at the top of the canyon walls as the day's sun grew old and weary, seeking its rest beyond the far mountains, that the warriors parted when Quanah walked through their midst, stepping up to the powerful and well-known Mamanti and Lone Wolf of the Kiowa, Iron Shirt and Stone Calf of the Cheyenne.

"Why are you standing here?" he demanded of them angrily. How he wanted most to put his hands around Mamanti's throat. "You have families to protect. They are scattered like the cottonwood down across this prairie. Winter comes!"

"Go take care of your own, Quanah Parker!" snapped Lone Wolf, his old, yellowed eyes filled with fire. "Do not presume to tell us what to do."

"No, I would never attempt something so foolish as that!" His eyes raked them all, provoking them. "How can I presume to do that? I, Quanah Parker—the one among you who has never had a mouthful of the white man's food! The one among you who has never put his hand out and accepted one of the white man's blankets. The one among all of you great ones who has never put his mark on the white man's talking paper that gives our enemy the right to come take everything from us!"

Some of the Kiowa warriors crowded up, ready to protect their chiefs. A dozen and more of the haughty Kwahadi moved up as well, glaring at the others standing behind their chiefs.

"So tell us, you who know the white man so well,"

Quanah sneered, "tell us what my people are to do now. Is it better to go in to the reservations now? Or better to continue the fight? What say you?"

He looked over their faces. Their eyes unable to hold his there in the late afternoon light. For a moment there was a rustle through the great assembly. Some were pointing across the great chasm. More than two miles away on the south rim they could see the soldiers were beginning to climb out of the canyon once more. Quanah turned back to the Kiowa and Cheyenne chiefs.

"We are leaving, Quanah Parker," Lone Wolf finally admitted. "Hardest hit this day were our villages. Our warriors fell under the white man's guns. We have been robbed of—"

"Everything that belonged to my people lies down there!" Quanah roared, pointing into the Palo Duro. "We lost as much as the Kiowa, as much as any of you! Think on this as you return to your reservations where the Kwahadi have never gone—remember that more than blankets and robes, more than lodges and dried meat was left behind or burned by the yellowleg soldiers. What could hurt more than the loss of your ponies?"

Reluctantly, they nodded.

"More than half our herds," Iron Shirt replied.

"What are my people to do now?" Quanah asked rhetorically, for he raised his voice to the sky, knowing these mere mortals could not answer him. The answer to such a question had to come from elsewhere. "Am I now forced to take the road these Cheyenne and Kiowa take? To walk the road to the reservation where I have never once retreated, forced to shrink in cowardice just so my starving women and children have something to eat for their empty bellies when the winter winds come slashing across the cold breast of the land? How can I expect the little ones, the old ones, the ones who are sick—to face the coming winter without lodges and blankets and robes, even moccasins?"

"Soon you will have your answer," declared Stone Calf, the oldest of the Cheyenne chiefs.

His eyes turned to the Cheyenne elder. "Perhaps I will become a white man's Indian like you, Stone Calf." He glared at the Kiowa. "Like you, Lone Wolf. Like the great Satanta who gave himself up to the white man's iron chains. For what is a man to do when he cannot find food for his family—the buffalo are gone! Is a man's family to survive on his pride? Can they eat that warrior's honor?"

Stone Calf nodded sadly. "Times have changed us, Quanah Parker. This one day has changed our peoples more than most. How long can you and your Kwahadi resist traveling the white man's road when the reservation offers the only peace and safety in this land? How long, Quanah Parker?"

From their dark, questioning eyes, to the far rim of the canyon where the tiny figures of the yellowleg soldiers crawled across the prairie driving the pony herds before them, the Kwahadi war chief looked. Then eventually Quanah gazed at the setting sun in the west before he spoke.

"As you yourself said it, Stone Calf. Soon . . . I will have my answer."

Anticipating the very real possibility that the retreating warriors might block the exit of his troops from the canyon, at noon Mackenzie had dispatched Captain Boehm with companies A and E to the far end of the canyon to be sure that the Indians did not sweep back on a counterattack, then ordered Captain Gunther's H Company to ascend the dangerous trail to the top of the canyon to secure the south wall. Far away to the north across the chasm, Gunther's men watched the milling warriors dispersing like puffball dust across the prairie beneath the fading afternoon light.

A half-dozen Tonkawa women, wives who had come along on the campaign with their tracker husbands despite Mackenzie's prohibition on the women attending the march, frantically pilfered through the piles of captured goods the soldiers were stacking in each of the camp circles. The women laid claim to the choicest of the plunder: new reservation blankets, fine clothing, a pair of tin snips, copper kettles and bone china, Minneapolis and Osage Mission flour, along with bolts of turkey-red and multicolored calico cloth. As the women bundled their ill-gotten booty into manageable packs, their husbands were already consumed with taking their pick of the captured ponies.

As much as Mackenzie despised the practice of awarding the animals to his Tonkawa and Seminole trackers, the colonel explained to his officers, "I do so because it is the only way that it is practicable for me to get such dangerous work out of these men."

Before long greasy columns of black smoke were climbing up and down the twisting valley floor, the dark tracks of destruction rising more than a thousand feet to reach the level of the Staked Plain where the warriors and their families had fled, dispersing in a hundred different directions. For more than two miles along the Prairie Dog Town Fork, Mackenzie's fires choked the red-hued walls, swirling on the fickle afternoon breezes as the great destruction continued.

"Colonel, we found both of these among the refuse left behind by the escapees," declared Captain McLaughlin as he strode up. He presented two scraps of crumpled yellowed paper to Mackenzie.

Opening the first, the colonel read the message:

> Office Kiowa and Comanche Agency
> I.T., 4 Mo. 9, 1874
> Long Hungry is recognized as a chief among the Cochetethca Comanche Indians, and promises to use his influence for good among his people, while continuing to conduct himself in a friendly and peaceable manner. I ask for him kind treatment by all with whom he may come in contact.
>
> J. M. Haworth
> United States Agent

Mackenzie wagged his head as he stuffed the notice inside his wool tunic, unfolding the second, read it, then passed it on to the officers assembled around him:

No. 13—Kiowa and Comanche Agency
I.T. August 6, 1874

Wah-lung, of Sun Boy's band of Kiowas, is regis-
tered and will not be molested by troops, unless engaged in acts of hostility, or away from his camp
without special permission.

J. M. Haworth
United States Agent

He snorted sourly, jabbing the second note in his tunic.
"I'd say Wah-lung was damned well away from where he
should be camped . . . and without special permission!"

Around him, Mackenzie's officers laughed.

They were due, Seamus Donegan allowed. Damn well
due that laughter.

Although only three warrior dead could be confirmed,
the soldiers had suffered only one serious casualty, and
Private Hord would live. Yet more than inflicting casualties
on the war bands, Mackenzie's Fourth Cavalry had done
the tribes even greater harm than drawing blood.

Here, with winter racing down from the northern plains,
the colonel had driven the Kiowa and Comanche and
Cheyenne onto the prairie, without lodges, blankets, robes
and clothing, without ponies, and without any of the meat
they had dried against famine for the coming time of cold
and snow. Mackenzie had robbed them of everything but
their own lives.

So it was that Seamus Donegan laughed with those too
as one of the surgeon's stewards dabbed fumaric along the
raw, oozy bullet wound on his thigh. The soldier, a rotund
fellow with iron-crusted hair, and by his accent clearly a
former Confederate, began singing an old Civil War favorite as he worked the burning, hissing caustic into the Irishman's flesh.

"When I get to Heaven, first thing I'll do,
Grab me a horn and blow for Ol' Blue.
Then when I hear my hound dog bark,
I'll know he's tree'd a possum in Noah's ark.
Go on, Blue; go on, Ol' Blue!"

The steward eventually had Seamus singing along with him, gritting out the words to the song, if only to keep from bellowing out in pain. Damn!

This truly had to be as sweet a victory as Ranald Slidell Mackenzie had ever known.

39

November 1874

Late that night after Mackenzie's troops drove more than fifteen hundred ponies out of the Palo Duro Canyon, the cold rains of autumn returned.

Up and out of the canyon the colonel gave orders that his Fourth Cavalry form a marching square around the captured herd, then pointed his nose to the southeast, intent on returning to his Tule Creek camp. With every one of those miles crossed, Mackenzie grappled with what to do about those captured animals. How well he knew from his own firsthand experience that the warriors could at any time sweep back in and recover some of their herd. Chances were that they would not attempt it that first night, miles away as they were along the north rim of the canyon wall. Still, the warriors and their families were there, not that far off and scattering across the plains, almost close enough that Donegan could count them like flies gathered on a piecrust setting on Samantha Pike's windowsill.

But prairie warfare wisdom had taught the colonel that they would make the attempt, as they had so many times before. And this time Mackenzie didn't want to give them the slightest chance of succeeding.

He had decided he was not merely going to capture the enemy's ponies.

This time he was going to slaughter them.

With one company riding at the head of the march, two companies on either side of the pony herd in columns of twos, and a final company forming the fourth side of the marching square, Mackenzie's Fourth Cavalry finally returned to the Tule Canyon campsite and Lawton's wagon train shortly after midnight on 29 September. There the troopers turned the herd over to the infantry, who corralled the animals within the wagon corral while Mackenzie's cavalry ate, then slept for the first time in more than thirty-six hours. Some, like Thompson's scouts, had closed their eyes very little since the night of the twenty-fifth.

It was a bone-weary Seamus Donegan who pulled his head inside his canvas bedroll and let the rain batter the prairie, rocking him to sleep with its drumbeat. Nothing was going to interrupt the sweet, delicious sleep and his dreams of Samantha Pike. And dream he did that night, as helpless as any man who had gazed into those moonlit blue-green eyes the color of teal feathers. A man never fought the exquisite torture of such dreaming, Hell's own sweet sugar.

After breakfast around smoky fires the following morning, Mackenzie assembled his officers and announced his decision.

"Those of you who were with me at Blanco Canyon in 'seventy-one will remember how the warriors rode back in and reclaimed their herd from us," he told them. "And those of you who rode with me on the North Fork in 'seventy-two will remember how they did it to us a second time."

"We can keep them corralled for you this time, Colonel," sang out Lieutenant Lawton.

Mackenzie only grinned while some of his officers laughed. "No, fellas. This time is going to be different. I can't afford to be tied down guarding a herd of this size. We have a campaign to fight. And that means marching and fighting, then more marching and some more fighting. We'll sleep when we can and eat what we get our hands on. But guarding a herd of ponies is the last thing I need any of my men doing when there is work to be done fighting Indians. No, men—I have decided to destroy the herd."

While most of the officers and a few of the scouts murmured, the colonel turned to his adjutant. "Did you get the count I requested early this morning?"

The lieutenant nodded, referring to his small tablet.

"Yes, sir—1,424 animals. Of them, 1,274 horses. One hundred fifty mules."

"What have the scouts decided to take for themselves, Lieutenant?"

"Three hundred seventy-six. That leaves us with something over a thousand to . . . to destroy, Colonel."

He sighed deeply. "Very well, men. I've decided to assign this task to Lieutenant Lawton."

The quartermaster stirred uneasily. "Sir?"

"Assign some of your infantry to rope the ponies and take them to a spot you will determine for the slaughter. Designate others to complete the slaughter."

Lawton gulped visibly. "Yes, sir, Colonel."

From just past six o'clock that morning of the twenty-ninth, until after three that afternoon, the Springfield rifles of the Eleventh Infantry roared and gun smoke blanketed the prairie near that Tule Canyon camp. And when the ghastly gray pall disappeared on the chill autumn breezes late that afternoon, the multihued carcasses lay in steaming piles, the new stench already drawing the carrion eaters for miles around.

Just as he had vowed to his officers, Mackenzie was not about to retire from the field after the battle of Palo Duro Canyon. Instead he strove to press his advantage over the warriors he had just stripped and demoralized. Again and again in the following weeks he sent his scouts out, ordering them to search in wider and wider circles, each night analyzing their reports, then determining to follow one trail or another, bringing his troops into position to strike here, then there at the bands who refused to move east onto the reservations.

Mackenzie's Fourth lay on the south. Price and Miles operated from the west and north. Buell and Davidson probed along the east. Those last holdouts among the southern warrior bands had to surrender, or be crushed by one of the army columns.

In all throughout that autumn, the tribes on the Staked Plain lost more than 7,500 head of horses and mules to the army. Eventually most would be sold in auction. But without fail officers and enlisted alike would always speak of the great slaughter that took place after the fight at the Palo Duro.

As well, it was an evil thing often spoken of in hushed tones around lodge fires for many winters to come.

That night of the battle in the Place of the Chinaberry Trees, the rains had come, making the wanderers even more miserable. And the next day the bands continued their flight. Mamanti and Big Bow sought safety, so headed farther west onto the Staked Plain, where they ran into a large band of Mexican traders and Navajos. That band of larcenous Comancheros proved to be unfriendly and robbed the Kiowa of what little they had left after the fight.

Big Bow decided to turn back to Fort Sill with his people. They joined Big Red Meat's Comanches and limped onto the reservation as winter's icy maw began to close down on the southern plains with a vengeance.

A few days following Mackenzie's stunning victory far to the south in the land of Texas, a scouting patrol riding out of Fort Wallace on the Smoky Hill River in Kansas Territory spotted in the distance the blackened hulk of what appeared to have been a solitary wagon. It was the second of October when those scouts reined up at the bloated, bloodied, half-eaten bodies of the German family.

Among the few things discarded and scattered through the bloodstained grass by the raiding party before they set the wagon afire, one of the scouts knelt to pick up the trampled, dusty leaves of the family bible. In a fine hand, the names of nine family members had been written in the front. This did not tally with the remains of five victims.

On closer examination around the wagon, mixed in among the tracks of the unshod ponies, the scouts discovered several sets of small footprints. None of them wearing moccasins. It took little time for those scouts to conclude that four of the youngest German daughters had been carried off into captivity.

"They're Cheyenne," declared the civilian scout as he rose from the dust where he had inspected the hodgepodge of moccasin tracks. The young soldiers had finished the last of the shallow graves. As he dusted his hands off on his buckskin britches, the scout added, "I'll lay money on it."

"Just how much money do you have, Hickok?" asked one of the older soldiers.

"You don't think I'm right?" James Butler Hickok replied, grinning.

"Naw—I won't dare bet against you when it comes to knowing Cheyenne from Sioux from Kiowa mocs," the corporal replied. He stuffed the bible inside his shirt. "C'mon, Bill—we're heading back to Wallace with word of this. The army will want to know."

"You damn bet the army will want to know about this," Hickok echoed.

At the top of the knoll the young scout reined up, turned in the saddle for but a moment and gazed back into that little valley where they had scraped five shallow graves from the flaky Kansas soil. How he wished Bill Cody or Seamus Donegan were here now to help. Maybe together they could find those girls.

"God rest your souls," Hickok whispered as he put spurs to his horse once more, loping quickly to catch up to the soldiers. "May God rest your souls."

When the warriors had pulled them up on horseback with them, Sophia recalled how the naked warrior stank of rancid grease he had smeared in his hair. But then, she recalled how her own father and brother stank as well. With little opportunity to take a bath, she thought . . .

It struck her as funny now, months later, that she had even remembered such a thing. For she could not recall the last time she had been able to bathe, going week after week, brutalized by the squaws, gang raped by the warriors as she and her sister went for water or into the timber to gather wood. How she hated having to drive the camp dogs off as they continually sniffed her privates where the bloody, seeping stench had to be the strongest.

Sophia started to cry again, but this time she did it silently. How quickly she had learned to cry in silence. At first she had not, and had been beaten by the squaws for it. Now she saved her tears for the darkness as she lay under her scrap of blanket, shivering, her belly so empty it had ceased complaining, her soul feeling helpless and lost. Wondering if anyone knew she was here. Hoping someone was looking for her and Catherine. Praying that little Addie and Julie were all right. Wondering if the little ones were still alive.

It had been many weeks since she had last seen her youngest sisters. She caught herself sobbing. Praying that God would send someone to rescue them all.

South across the Canadian the raiding party had taken the four after the attack on the German wagon, climbing onto the high, flat divide between the Canadian and the Red rivers. Descending into the land of the Red, Medicine Water's war party again grew cautious, hiding at day and traveling only at night.

It was some time after they had reached this high, barren land that she last saw her two little sisters. For days the two had ridden behind the same warriors, on and off the same ponies. Then one morning as the bands were breaking up, Sophia recognized the two warriors and saw that her sisters were not with them.

Quickly she had swallowed down a cry of panic, calling out to God to bless their little souls, knowing that death would surely come as a relief to what they would have to suffer in the land of the living. As soon as Sophia had a chance that afternoon, she quietly said to Catherine, her older sister, "Julie and Addie—I think they are dead."

Catherine's dark, sallow eyes seemed lifeless already as she turned slowly to Sophia and replied, "They are better off than we are."

Then Medicine Water began to wander some more, moving often from place to place, warriors coming and going with great celebration. Sophia figured they were fighting someone—most likely soldiers.

In the deep canyon with the bloodred walls, it was quiet and peaceful. A good place out of the wind, she thought. But of a morning a sudden panic grew among Stone Calf's people and the tribe began retreating from the noise and commotion and shooting. How she yearned to go running to the soldiers who must surely be coming for her and Katie.

But the squaws pulled knives on the girls and beat them with rawhide ropes until both were forced to turn about and retreat into the dark shadows of the Palo Duro with the rest of the warrior bands. Fleeing once more with the Indians onto the trackless wastes of the Staked Plain. Now it seemed the women and even more of the men took out their anger with the soldiers on her and Katie.

After that Sophie wanted more than ever to die—of hunger, for they had little to eat now; of the cold, for they had abandoned blankets and robes and clothing fleeing from the canyon; of the severe beatings, because both warriors and squaws abused the two just short of death.

Sophie prayed that the hand of God would lead someone to rescue her and Katie. To rescue them . . . or that God would finally take their souls to Heaven to be with Mama and Papa.

The cold wind pushed roughly through the abandoned Cheyenne camp this eighth day of November. They hadn't been here long enough for a stench to collect.

Billy Dixon had been scouting for General Nelson A. Miles since August, yet it was only in the last month that Miles had become a man possessed. Not a day passed, not a conversation occurred, without the commander mentioning the possible fate of those four German girls. In fact, there wasn't a man who had come in contact with Miles over the last few weeks who didn't know how driven the colonel was to make that singular rescue.

So they had harried and driven and herded the war bands before them, never knowing for sure who had the four sisters. Kiowa, Comanche, perhaps Cheyenne. But they marched and fought and pressed ahead with the campaign, drawing ever tighter the noose Sherman and Sheridan wanted drawn around the last stronghold of the free Indian on the southern plains.

Then this gray morning, Miles had ordered the charge into what turned out to be a Cheyenne village. After a brief attempt to cover the retreat of their women and children, the warriors had fallen back and the Tonkawas and Delawares rushed in to claim the spoils. The trackers informed Dixon and the other white scouts that this had been the village of Gray Beard's band of Southern Cheyenne.

Already the soldiers were stripping the buffalo-hide covers from their poles, leaving the lodgepoles standing like so many skeletons against the winter sky, immersed in counting weapons and food and robes captured. As Dixon walked through the smoky village, marveling how these brown-skinned fighters kept moving, fighting, then moving again while dragging along their families and homes, a young soldier nearby jumped back, frightened by something in the pile of buffalo robes and greasy blankets he was digging through.

"Them . . . them buffler hides moved on me!" exclaimed the frightened soldier, pulling his service revolver.

"You likely scared some varmit, soldier," Dixon said, pulling his pistol as well. "Some critter just took shelter in there—Injun dogs can be a bit dangerous, you don't watch out."

Billy's jaw dropped as the first little hand pushed out from a gap among the hides. He knelt, peering closely into the shadows, seeing the pair of eyes back in the darkness of that hiding place.

"You . . . you're white?" asked a little, frail voice.

"My name's Billy," he said, tears starting to sting his eyes. He leaned forward as the second set of eyes appeared beside the first. Dixon gently pulled back some of those heavy hides the Cheyenne had abandoned in their rush to retreat before the attack of Miles's troops.

Both sets of frightened, furtive eyes squinted up and blinked into the dull gray light of the heavily overcast sky threatening to snow. Their faces were smudged, scratched and streaked with blood, their hair hanging in greasy sprigs.

"It's all right now," Dixon soothed, forcing himself to speak as he held out a hand to them both. "There's just two of you?"

The oldest of the small girls nodded her head, her chin

quivering as she started to sob. The younger girl clung to her sister like a tick, keening loudly as a small crowd of soldiers gathered.

Quickly he tore off his own coat, motioning for one of the young soldiers to do as well. They wrapped the two small girls in them, the bottoms of the coats dragging the ground. Then Dixon gathered them both against him as the cruel November wind whined, slashing brutally through the abandoned camp.

"Is your name . . . German?"

The oldest of the pair nodded. Her eyes focused more on Billy. And the younger one quieted her sobbing a little.

"Get them something to eat, will you?" Dixon asked the growing crowd.

"Lord deliver," one of the older soldiers murmured prayerfully, pulling some dried beef from his haversack and handing it to the grimy little hands that snatched it from his.

Hands so thin they reminded Billy of birds' claws. He looked up around the gathering of faces, men jostling and shoving to get a better look at the two tiny girls. A few men silently, openly cried, others angrily swiped at betraying tears. A few turned away to hide their feelings. But there wasn't a man there, hardened soldier or veteran scout, who was not moved by the sight of those two tiny victims of this cruel war.

Out there, he thought—somewhere out there in the midst of all this wilderness—the other girls were still captive.

"Yes," Dixon replied as the two youngest of the four German sisters gobbled down strips of salted beef. "We have two of them back now. The Lord does deliver."

40

New Year's Eve, 1874

For the first time in three days, the snow and wind had stopped. Seamus and Sharp lost no time in bundling into blanket-lined canvas mackinaws, gloves and wool mufflers,

before they pressed through the door into the icy drifts that corduroyed Sharp's yard.

Needing first attention was the stock they fed in the ramshackle pole and shake barn Grover had plans of expanding come spring. Then they set about sawing and bucking more firewood. The supply inside the cabin's tinderbox had been dangerously depleted during the past few days. By the time they were nearing the end of their labors over the sawbuck, the sun even made a bright appearance, bringing a sparkle to the snow's white scurry.

"We get back inside, you gonna bring out more of that fruit brandy you keep tucked away out of sight?" Donegan asked.

"Damn right I keep it tucked away," Grover replied. "You had your way, you'd drunk it all the night we got back."

Seamus snorted. "No cause for celebration, that."

Grover stopped and sighed, a grin creasing his face. "You're right, Irishman. We both had cause for celebration —getting back here whole and of one piece."

After destroying the pony herd, Mackenzie had moved his command northward once more, marching around the head of the Palo Duro Canyon then back down south to the North Pease River by the middle of October. From there he continued on back to his supply camp on the Freshwater Fork, continually probing with his scouts the country of the Brazos, up toward Mound Lake in the caprock country of the Staked Plain, then back north to Yellow House Creek through November. In early December, as the weather began to close down and word came that two of the German girls had been rescued from Gray Beard's band of Cheyenne, Mackenzie redoubled his efforts, pushing men and animals while he still could, sweeping southwest to Cedar Lake, then eastward across the Colorado River and back to the Brazos.

From time to time Donegan and the rest came across sign of small parties of Indians, warriors and travois too, fleeing this way and that. They came across campsites, halting temporarily where the escaping bands had killed a settler's cow or slaughtered a few buffalo, simply made meat

in a herd of antelope. But for all Mackenzie's efforts, it was as if the Indians were ghosts. No more were they gathering in great numbers as they had at Palo Duro Canyon. No more were they staying in one camp for more than one night.

Mackenzie had them on the move, not allowing them time to dry meat for the winter, to flesh hides to replace lodges lost, destroyed, burned. Then on the nineteenth of December, a day after ten of Lieutenant Thompson's scouts had a brief skirmish with more than fifteen hostiles, Mackenzie came to the smoky breakfast fire where Grover and Donegan boiled coffee over wet wood.

"We're not far from Fort Richardson, fellas," the colonel had said, yanking his gloves from his hands, warming them over the low flames.

"You figure on turning back from here?" Grover asked.

Mackenzie nodded. "It's time to put in. They're transferring me."

That caught Donegan's attention. "Where they sending the Fourth now?"

"Sill," he had answered. "Enough of the war bands have been surrendering, they want us to come in and reinforce the troops from the Tenth up there. Just in case of trouble."

Donegan nodded, dragging the coffeepot off the coals before he threw more grounds into the water.

"So, I figure you fellas won't mind having these," Mackenzie said, his hand dragging two folded notices from inside his wool coat.

"What're these?" Grover asked.

"Pay vouchers. I signed 'em this morning."

"You're firing us?" Donegan asked, a strange grin crossing his smoke-smudged face.

"Yeah, you might say so, Sergeant. You too, Sharp." Mackenzie stared back into the low flames a moment before going on. "This part of the campaign's over. We've done all we're going to do for now. We'll just have to see about getting Quanah Parker's Kwahadi band come spring."

"You're going to winter up at Sill, is it?" Sharp asked.

Mackenzie nodded. "But we'll never be closer to Richardson . . . to Jacksboro than we are now, fellas."

Donegan found Grover looking at him with a wide smile. "Why, Colonel," the Irishman declared, "I do believe you've got a heart."

The soldier flashed a grin quickly, pointing to a stack of tin cups. "Suppose one of you pour your commander a cup of that coffee looks done now. We'll share one last pot of the Irishman's devil brew before you boys are out of a job and got to ride back home for the winter."

They had come riding back to Grover's little spread late on an afternoon a week ago. Christmas Eve. As the light had faded early, Donegan found nothing more heartwarming than the four red candles lit in the front window as the two ice-crusted riders dismounted stiffly and knocked snow off their boots, when suddenly the door flew open and two teary-eyed, shrieking women burst onto the porch, bringing with them the fragrances of baking and cinnamon and vanilla.

Not to mention the just plain good smell of a woman, wrapped around a man, all arms and legs and moist, warm lips kissing and kissing and kissing some more as Mackenzie's former scouts were dragged into the warm, cozy cabin while night closed down on the southern plains that twilight before the day they would celebrate the birth of the Lord who had once more delivered both Donegan and Grover from the hands of their enemies.

The day after Christmas, Sharp and Seamus had taken a ride on over to Richardson to present Mackenzie's vouchers to the fort's paymaster. It was a bad time of the year, the officer told them, but he could likely pay them a part of what they were owed. With new vouchers for the balance in their pockets, the pair returned to Grover's spread and began to repair the battered cabin and barn for winter, as the air changed and the wind swept out of the north, foretelling the coming of a winter storm.

"The older girls likely with Stone Calf's band," Grover declared now as he leaned on the huge, heavy maul he was using to split the firewood Seamus was sawing in the buck. "And he's likely headed south."

"Will he sell 'em?" Donegan asked, his eyes narrowing.

Grover pursed his lips. "Chances are he might. Those Comancheros like white-skinned women. They'll fetch a pretty price if Stone Calf runs onto any of them Mexican or Navajo traders."

The glittering dance of snow crystals bobbed and weaved on the cold breeze in the bright January sunshine. Seamus dragged the saw back and forth through the firewood a few minutes, then turned back to the older man as Grover drove the maul down into a chunk of wood.

"You ever worry, Sharp," he began, then sighed, as if searching for words, "ever worry about Rebecca, about Samantha being here alone while we been away from the place?"

Grover laid both wrists over the end of the maul's handle and stared at the cabin for a moment. The windowpane frosted, a curl of gray wood smoke rising from the stone chimney. His own breathsmoke slowed as he turned back to the Irishman.

"No, Seamus. And that's honest. I never worried about Rebecca. Not once. She can take care of herself, Rebecca can. But there was a time or two that Samantha crowded my worries some."

"Well, if Rebecca can care for herself, then likely Samantha will be fine too."

Grover snorted, dragging his mitten under his reddened nose. "I'm not talking about someone else coming out here and doing the women harm, you stupid jackass. I'm talking about me being worried about Samantha's safety—when she's around you."

Donegan straightened, leaving the saw in the cut he had made. "When she's around me?"

"Neither one of 'em are dog-shanty, cow-ranch women. And you're plainly a dangerous man to Samantha Pike, Seamus. I . . . don't want to see that woman get hurt."

He wagged his head as if he could not believe what he was hearing his old friend telling him. "You don't think I got feelings for her?"

He stared at the Irishman a moment before saying, "You damned well never spoke of 'em, Seamus."

"Well, I—"

"But it's about time you did," Grover snapped, suddenly sounding very protective of his young sister-in-law. "Just what the hell are you planning on doing about that woman who's gone all cow-eyed over you?"

Donegan's hands moved a little in front of him as he released the long cross-cut saw, his lips moving too, but without any words coming out.

"What is it, Irishman? Of a sudden you've gone fiddle-footed and shy, eh?"

Only the muscles along his jaw were moving now, making tiny ripples below skin the color of smoked buckskin, ripples trembling all the way down into his dark chin whiskers. Then finally Seamus said, "It ain't like I haven't thought about it, Sharp. The saints preserve me, but I have, and thought about it a lot. Problem is, I worry about what I can give her—the kind of woman she appears to be. Samantha deserves a lot."

"Damn right she does. But more than anything else, she deserves to know where she stands with you, Irishman. You gonna tell her what she means to you? Or you gonna keep that woman tortured, in suspense all winter long while you figure out what it is that you want?"

Seamus swallowed, hard. All autumn into winter he had ridden across the Staked Plain with Colonel Mackenzie, free to dream and ponder and plan—but now he had to put up. No more it seemed did he have the luxury of merely dreaming of possibilities. As he had been free to do when he searched out dreams of gold and tracked down one uncle after another, from the high plains of Colorado Territory to the far, misty land of southern Oregon. As he had done first with auburn-haired Jennifer Wheatley and now with golden-haired Samantha Pike. No one had ever made him put up before. If any man could, Sharp Grover was that man.

"Why, jus' look at you, Irishman," the old scout said. "You growed as rosy as a Georgia belle at her first ball."

His brow wrinkled, struggling with it inside. Seamus had fought his way across this land with his fists and with lead. He had ridden hard and loved hard and never shied from giving back what he figured had been give to him. "What . . . what you think I ought to do?"

"Damn you," Sharp said quietly. "Seamus Donegan asking me what he ought to do? You're a man never asked another what to do."

Seamus shrugged, suddenly feeling helpless. He glanced at the frosted windowpane and those four red candles the women lit every night near sundown.

"What you ought to do is make Samantha your wife and get Rebecca off my back where she's been riding me cinch and bridle to get you convinced that her sister will make you as good a wife as any man's bound to find, and far better than you deserve."

"She . . . Sam's a fine woman," Seamus replied finally, his stomach turning flips the way a starling would dive and swoop after a moth. He looked away thoughtfully.

"I figure every woman's equipped about the same, Seamus—to one degree or another. They all have the same God-give power, and to one degree or another they know how to use those God-granted gifts to make a slave of a man," Grover continued. Then he sighed. "She'll make you a fine wife, as fine a partner in your life as she has been a warm and willing partner in your bed."

"You know?"

Grover shrugged a shoulder, gazing at the ground. "I didn't. I suppose us men never really do. But Rebecca knew, even before she was able to drag it out of Samantha."

"Damn! How am I gonna face your wife now? How am I gonna face either of 'em knowing that they talked about me like that?"

Grover suddenly laughed. Seized so suddenly and so hard, he doubled over. Leaving the Irishman to sputter in dismay, bewildered.

"Lookit you—acting like a schoolboy caught pulling a young girl's pigtails! This man who's charged into the muzzle of the best the Confederate army had to aim at him. This man who's stared down the finest light cavalry this world will ever see—be it Sioux or Cheyenne Dog Soldiers or Quanah Parker's Kwahadis. And this man is of a sudden

378

all afeared of what two soft-skinned women gonna say about him? Damn, Irishman!"

Donegan grabbed Grover's coat in both his gloves, suddenly shaking the older man as Sharp went back to laughing uproariously. "Tell me, what am I gonna do?"

"The human eye is not for future-seeing, my mama always told me, Seamus."

He let go of Grover's coat. "I think I'd rather face Confederate artillery or Roman Nose's horsemen than walk back into that cabin and face them two."

"Then you just damn well better go off to the barn right now and saddle up, Irishman. Because it appears to me you got two choices: ride off and never show your face around this part of the country again. Or . . ."

"Or what?" he shrieked, grabbing Grover again, shaking him in the snowdrift at their feet.

"Or, you walk back in there with an armload of firewood and fill that tinderbox. Then stroll over to Samantha Pike and take her smooth hand in yours . . . and tell that pretty woman you've got something to talk to her about tonight after supper."

41

April 1875

All through the late fall and into the early winter, the army columns crossed and recrossed the Staked Plain, from the Canadian down to the Rio Colorado, forcing the war bands to stay on the move. Sometimes Sophia saw Katie on their long marches with Stone Calf's village. Sometimes she did not see Katie for days at a time. Sophie prayed as the Cheyennes kept their noses pointed steadily to the southwest, marching farther and farther away from the soldiers.

By the last week in January, Nelson A. Miles figured what bands had not come in and surrendered to their agents were about done from the constant harassment and lack of food. It was upon looking at the small cabinet photograph Surgeon Powell had asked W. P. Bliss to take of the two little German girls that Miles decided what to do next.

Sophia was startled that cold February day when the Mexican-Comanche half-breed had eased over beside her there in Stone Calf's village and spoken to her quietly, his dark eyes constantly moving, wary that he would be discovered. In broken English he explained that the chief of all the soldiers in this part of the country had promised him a lot of money and four fine horses if he found the white girls who had been captured in Kansas many moons before.

Then he asked her, "Are you German?" His eyes touched her briefly, then flicked away, watchful.

"I am . . . Sophia German," she answered. It had been so long since she had said her family name.

He smiled, his browned, crooked teeth flashing in the winter sunlight as he reached beneath the smoke-blackened Navajo blanket he had cut a hole through and pulled over his head like a poncho. From somewhere inside his smelly clothes the half-breed pulled a small photograph wrapped in the folds of some crumpled oiled paper.

The tears instantly stung her eyes as she looked down at the serious faces of her two little sisters.

Sophia touched them both with her callused fingertips. "Addie," she said aloud.

He shushed her harshly.

Then she gently touched the face of the other sister. "Julie," she whispered now.

In the chromo they both wore simple smocks, clothes clean. Both had well-scrubbed faces and hands. Sophie glanced at her own, cut and dirty, the blood caked around her fingernails like dark crescents. Both Adelaide and Julia had on small frock caps and dark capes. Julie sat, her legs tucked under her smock; Addie stood beside her, her hand gently laid on little Julie's shoulder, a table behind them.

Sophia found it difficult to keep herself composed, starting to cry as she brushed her fingertips back and forth over the faces of her sisters, knowing they were safe now, that someone had given them a bath and fed them and made warm, clean clothing for them to wear, and even took a photograph of them.

The half-breed reached for the photograph, ready to take it from her.

"No!" she growled, fighting him for it as he struggled, his eyes wary again.

He grabbed her wrists as she cried out, hissing for her silence. She let the small rectangular photograph go, sobbing as she watched it pass into his hands.

"Good," he said, then smiled. But it was not a cruel smile, like so many she had seen the Cheyenne wear in the months she had been separated from her younger sisters. This was a kind smile.

Surprising her, the half-breed turned the photograph over and handed it back to Sophia. She stared at the writing on the back for a long time, disbelieving at first, then finally took the photo into her own hands once more, cradling it across both trembling palms as she read:

Headquarters Indian Territory Expedition
In the field, January 20th, 1875
To the Misses Germaine: Your little sisters are well, and in the hands of friends. Do not be discouraged. Every effort is being made for your welfare.
(s) Nelson A. Miles, Colonel and Brevet-Major
General, U.S. Army
Commanding Expedition

"May I . . . may I keep this?" she asked in a gush, holding it to her breast.

He smiled that smile again, then nodded.

"I want my sister to see it," Sophia said. Her eyes looked over the half-breed's shoulder. "Have you seen her? My sister, Katie? Catherine German?" She tapped the photograph with a dirty finger. "Have you shown this to her?"

He shook his head, shrugging. "No. I do not see her yet. You keep." He gently touched the hands she held against her breast then rose. "I go talk with Stone Calf now. General Miles wants you home . . . soon."

It had such a good sound to it. *Home.*

Yet in all her joy at seeing the faces of her sisters in that photograph, in all the hope she experienced in reading and rereading the words of the soldier who vowed to rescue her, Sophia felt a twinge of cold emptiness. She doubted that with all that had happened to her, witnessing what had happened to her family, experiencing the cruelty of the women who beat her and the men who repeatedly brutalized her in unspeakable ways—Sophia German doubted she would ever again feel truly safe.

For what was a home after all? If not a place where a person was supposed to feel safe and loved.

She cried silent, bitter tears that fell on that sepia-toned photograph of little Addie and Julie German. Praying now that God would take away the bitterness and the pain, and allow her once more to be someplace safe.

To Chief Stone Calf and his head men, the half-breed presented the colonel's formal demand for surrender— along with the stern declaration that the two white girls were to be brought back to the reservation alive. Stone Calf said he would consider Miles's demand and told the half-breed emissary that in the interim he would take charge of the two prisoners to assure their safety until he had decided the course his people would take.

Through the excruciatingly cold days of February, a few more small bands of Cheyenne trickled into the Darlington Agency in Indian Territory.

Stone Calf's band broke camp as soon as the half-breed rode off to the northeast. The Cheyenne marched to the south for days, then began circling, circling back to the northeast themselves. Sophia caught a glimpse of her older sister, Katie, one cold afternoon as the Cheyenne were going into camp. And though they did not speak to one another, Sophia knew from the look on Catherine's face that she too had seen a copy of the photograph, and knew the army knew where they were—preparing to rescue them. Katie laid a hand over her heart, to signal something to her younger sister, but with the next breath an old squaw was upon her, beating her with a quirt, driving Catherine back among the jumble of camp gear.

Sophia stood there as long as she could, her hand held over her own heart as well.

It was a time of extreme cold when the Cheyenne village marched back to country where there were more trees and vegetation and there were places on the ground where the snow had been blown clear as they trudged along the frozen creekbanks. Her feet grew so numb she knew her toes were going to fall off, lost out the open, cracked sides of her dry-split broughams. There seemed to be much excitement in the band over the last few days. Warriors came and went, and Sophia believed they were preparing to do battle with the soldiers once again.

But old Chief Stone Calf had taken a delegation of a dozen or so warriors with him from his village and rode in to see the agent and the soldiers at the Darlington settlement. Two weeks before, he had sent in Gray Eyes, Mad Wolf, Cedar and Red Eagle with word to the soldier chief that he was coming in, with a request not to send out yellowlegs to hunt his people down now that they were drawing so close to the reservation. With word that he was in fact returning the two white girls to the Cheyenne Agency.

And now, with Stone Calf saying it with his own lips through the interpreter, Colonel Thomas H. Neill immediately dispatched an ambulance to go with Mad Wolf and Gray Eyes to Stone Calf's village.

So it was that there arose a rustle of some excitement at the far edge of camp that early afternoon, the first day of March. Her muscles crying with fatigue, Sophia stood from the work she was doing at the fire. She did not mind cooking for the old women. It kept her warm, like the shred of old, greasy blanket she had been given never could.

Suddenly Long Back was over her, beating her with his rawhide shield. Then Long Back's first wife was beating her too. Sophia collapsed to her knees, crying. This must surely be the end—for she had so little strength to go on.

Please, God, she prayed then, huddling fetally beneath their brutal blows in her tattered clothes and dry-split shoes, just let them kill me now and be done with it.

Then she heard a foreign voice, a woman's. And she blinked through her swollen eyes and tears into the bright winter sunlight, watching warriors dragging a shrieking

383

Long Back and his woman off her. And saw for the first time in many days the face of her sister, Catherine.

Katie was smiling. Behind her other warriors held Catherine's angry captor, a warrior named Wolf Robe. They grasped him as if he were a prisoner, the same way they restrained Long Back now. Then there were gentle hands lifting Sophia. At first she jerked away, afraid, for they were big, strong hands just the same. But then she realized she had not been touched this way in a long, long time. With gentleness.

She blinked her swollen, teary eyes and looked into the bright light, seeing first the glimmering brass buttons, rows and rows of them swimming against a sea of dark blue. Gold braid and stripes and shiny rifles and gleaming black belts and holsters. They had beards and mustaches and blue eyes and green eyes and . . . then she realized they were her people.

No matter that she did not know their names—these were her people.

Word drifted down from Darlington through the blue grapevine to Reuben Waller at Fort Sill that Agent John Miles had been so distraught upon seeing the condition of the two elder German girls that he could not bring himself to speak, much less question them about their five and a half months of brutal captivity. He left that part of his duties to his wife Lucy.

Days later, when he had been given the details of Lucy's interviews with Catherine and Sophia, an enraged Miles penned his report that their Cheyenne owners had hired the young women out as prostitutes.

> While Long Back who held possession of Catherine had not himself treated her brutally, yet he had permitted his Lodge to be visited regularly by the young Bucks of the tribe—He no doubt realizing a pecuniary benefit . . .

Ironic as well that a few days later, when, as promised, Stone Calf's band finally reached the agency to surrender to Colonel Neill, the agent's rage would mellow to such a bitter sadness at the sight of those destitute Cheyenne. At the end of that momentous day, Miles wrote to his boss, the Indian Commissioner:

A more wretched and poverty-stricken community than these people presented after they were placed in the prison camp it would be difficult to imagine. Bereft of lodges and the most ordinary cooking apparatus; with no ponies or other means of transportation for wood or water; half-starved, and very little to eat, and scarcely anything that could be called clothing, they were truly objects of pity; and for the first time the Cheyennes seemed to realize the power of the government, and their own inability to cope successfully therewith.

There was a palpable and explainable joy among the Tenth Cavalry down at Fort Sill when they learned that the agent's wife had asked the German sisters to help in identifying the warriors who had murdered members of their family, as well as those warriors who had brutalized them in an unspeakable manner. In Reuben Waller's barracks a cheer went up among those buffalo soldiers when they learned that those two young women had courageously walked down a line of Cheyenne warriors and pointed out at least fifteen of the guilty.

Perhaps there was some justice in this part of the frontier after all, Reuben thought that night as he lay on his cot, the winds of winter still howling outside in the blackjack oaks along Cache Creek. Justice that didn't come at the end of a white racist's rope, nor at the muzzle of an army carbine, much less the tip of iron arrow point.

As the late winter wound down into a rainy spring, the Tenth Cavalry concerned itself with adjusting to the news that they would be going south and that a new commanding officer would be stationed at Fort Sill—Colonel Ranald S. Mackenzie of the Fourth Cavalry. Too, every soldier from Camp Supply down through the distant string of Texas posts were shifting the emphasis of their duty from fighting Indians to feeding their wards and seeing that the tribes did not wander back to the Staked Plain where the last few holdout Comanche still roamed.

The warriors who had caused blood to flow from the Smoky Hill down to the Rio Grande were coming in and giving themselves up to the army. Back near the end of February, Reuben's own H Company had watched as Lone Wolf himself rode into Fort Sill with Mamanti and Poor Buffalo. In abject, stony silence they had laid their weapons at the feet of the soldiers standing at attention there on the windswept parade, then reluctantly allowed the buffalo soldiers to take away some four hundred ponies, all they had been able to save when Mackenzie's scouts captured the herds grazing in the Palo Duro Canyon.

One by one the bands had come in, their property piled up and put to the torch, their ponies and mules sold at auction to pay reparations to the cattlemen of Texas. The women and children were escorted to the swamp beside Cache Creek where Kicking Bird's loyal suffered disease and despair, while the haughty warriors of the Kiowa nation were led to an unroofed, unfinished stone icehouse being built at the foot of a hill east of the post. There, once a day, a wagon rolled up to the outer wall and stopped while soldiers threw raw meat over that wall to the inmates. When no more warriors could be accommodated in the icehouse, the buffalo soldiers had to turn the new prisoners over to Kicking Bird.

Now at the beginning of April, Colonel Davidson and his Tenth Cavalry were on their way south to garrison the posts of southwest Texas. Carpenter's H Company was the last to leave, here to watch the arrival of the men who had crushed the spirit of so many warriors with their fight at Palo Duro Canyon. And for the first time, Reuben laid eyes on the thin, pale hero of that battle, the man who had gambled heavily in sending his men down into that mist-shrouded crevasse to hand the tribes a dawn surprise.

On 18 April the Comanche war chief Mow-way rode in to Sill with nearly two hundred of his people. The following day saw the stunning surrender of the powerful Comanche warlord, White Horse, and his band of holdouts. One of the greatest, one only, remained among the canyons and the bluffs of the Staked Plain—where he had been born and raised by his Comanche father and his white mother. Quanah's people ran and hid, sleeping when they dared, taking game when they found it. Living life on the run, as Mackenzie had wanted to force them to do all along.

Reuben Waller was glad too that he and his H Company were now marching south. There was little pride that a soldier could take in the role of prison guard to a defeated people.

For now it would be troopers from the Fourth Cavalry, and not the Tenth, who would escort Kiowa, Cheyenne and Comanche prisoners from Fort Sill down to the ancient Spanish Castillo de San Marcos, what had become known as Fort Marion in Florida—stone walls built near a stagnant, mosquito-infested swamp . . . a hot, sticky land so far from the stark beauty of the Staked Plain where the prairie wind blew strong in a free man's unfettered hair, day and night, winter or summer.

42

June 2, 1875

Little had Sophia German known a year ago just how much her life would change in so short a time.

Here she sat on the leather-covered, horsehair-stuffed seats of this railroad passenger car, her head craned out the open window, wind whipping and snarling her hair, her eyes smarting with the black smoke and fiery cinders flung back from the belching smokestack atop the huge, wheezing locomotive pulling her east atop these two iron rails. So much new in the last two days, foreign tastes and smells and textures. The odor of damp steam and coal smoke, of cinders and warm oil. This railroad was a marvelous, magical thing, she had decided—providing as it did the single heartbeat each day to so many small Kansas towns clustered along the tracks stretching from horizon to horizon. From nowhere and gone again.

"Get your head in here, Sophie," admonished her older

sister. Catherine had always taken on that role with her younger sisters, and especially now that Katie had recently turned eighteen.

Next month Sophia would observe her sixteenth birthday. She and Catherine had come to talking about it in that way: *observe* instead of using the word "celebrate." There still seemed to be little to celebrate, even birthdays, which for a girl in her teens should be more than enough cause for great celebration and joy.

So she pulled her head back in past the green roller shade and dropped back to her seat, sweeping the hair from her eyes, grinding the tears and cinders from them as well. She had so tried to wrench a little joy from every day, from everything she did, from every person met. But Catherine was certainly not like that Lucy Miles who smiled incessantly and made you happy to be around her, an Indian agent's wife.

No, Catherine was still sad about what had happened to them.

Sophia did miss Papa and Mama and Stephen and Joanna and Rebecca. Mostly Stephen and Papa. They were happy all the time, and now they were gone. That amazed her a bit, that she should allow herself to remember, where for so long Sophia had refused the memory a place within her, holding it at arm's length and refusing to turn her head in its direction, as if . . . it simply did not exist. But just then, she had remembered. There was really no helping it, for she really did remember all the terrible, bloody aftermath of that awful day among the rolling, grassy hills.

Sophia often thought, as she did now, on the feelings she had for her captors and tormentors, for the men who had abused her so horribly. And repeatedly.

After she and Catherine had silently marched along the lines of warriors with Lucy Miles and a clearly inebriated Lieutenant Colonel Thomas Neill, the fourteen whom the girls had pointed out were separated from their people, and there began a process of finding more whom Neill could use to fill his quota, putting them in iron shackles in preparation for their long trip to Fort Marion near the ocean in faraway Florida. Sophia had also pointed out Buffalo Calf Woman, Mochi, telling what role in the murders and later torture was played by this wife of war chief Medicine Water. But Stone Calf himself escaped punishment due to the protests from the two German girls that the old chief had done what he could to protect them once he could read the writing on the wall and saw that surrender was inevitable.

So much time had it taken that sixth of April, a cold, blustery, spring day, that near sundown Lieutenant Colonel Neill grew irritated and quickly brought the chore to a conclusion by ordering eighteen warriors arbitrarily taken from the line without any evidence or testimony of their guilt. He had his half-breed interpreter, Romero, explain that he would find the guilty parties at a later date, that he was using these eighteen only as substitutes for the time being.

But for the next three days Neill did nothing to have the Mexican-Cheyenne Romero interrogate the prisoners further.

On 9 April the lieutenant colonel explained to Agent and Mrs. Miles that one Cheyenne was likely as guilty as the next, and that he had decided to let his selection process stand. Thirty-three prisoners were ordered out of their holding cells and escorted over to the blacksmith's hut to be fitted with the white man's iron shackles.

That mid-morning, Sophia stood at the window of the school, watching the process as one by one by one the warriors stepped forward between a pair of guards and submitted to having the straps of heavy iron riveted around their ankles and wrists. Throughout the whole process, Cheyenne women had gathered among the nearby trees, taunting their men, shaming them for submitting. Yet while the eyes of the warriors held much hate for their captors, they did not protest.

That is, until Black Horse was shoved forward with the butt of an infantryman's rifle.

Sophia brought a hand to her mouth, knowing the haughty Black Horse would likely cause trouble. He had refused to abuse the four white prisoners, saying instead

389

that a true warrior found no honor in humiliating children, even women.

She had watched his back straighten as the Negro blacksmith named Wesley gripped Black Horse's wrist and yanked it down onto the anvil where he enclosed it in a tight bracelet. The warrior turned to the women who were tormenting the Cheyenne men and suddenly cried out his war song. No more would he take this shame heaped upon him. As Wesley glanced up from his work at the sudden commotion, barking something to the Cheyenne warrior, Black Horse slapped the heavy shackle into the blacksmith's face and bolted off.

As if that cold day were only yesterday, Sophia remembered the shouts and orders from Captain Andrew Bennett's soldiers as they brought their weapons to their shoulders, aimed and fired. How the puffs of smoke burst from the muzzles and Black Horse stumbled, fell to his knees then struggled to his feet to run again, bleeding horribly as more of the Cheyenne men struggled to escape.

At the same time, other warriors who had been among the women back in the trees began to let fly a hail of iron-tipped arrows at the infantry soldiers still guarding more than thirty prisoners destined for Fort Marion in the Florida swamps. As more soldiers bolted from the barracks and mess hall, the Indians melted back into the trees and disappeared, fleeing into the nearby sandhills on the south side of the North Canadian River. It was there the army later learned that the Cheyenne had secreted most of their firearms prior to surrendering earlier that spring. Among the highest of those sandhills, the warriors and women threw up what breastworks they could and prepared to receive the soldiers charging across the river.

By that time, reinforcements had hurried the two miles from nearby Fort Reno, built just the previous year. Captain William A. Rafferty, Troop M of the Sixth Cavalry, also brought with him a Gatling gun he struggled to get into position to spray the enemy village. While the mules were hauling the ten-barreled gun into position, Troop M under Captain S. T. Norvell and Troop D under Captain

A. S. Keyes of the Tenth Cavalry rode up, crossed the river in fours and dismounted to join in the fray.

Despite the army's numerical advantage and the Gatling gun, the Cheyenne turned back every charge Neill's troops attempted, until the light drained from the cold, spring sky. At twilight the lieutenant colonel suspended the fight and, in leaving a cordon of troops around the sandhills to prevent escape, withdrew with his wounded: eight white troopers, eleven buffalo soldiers, six of the brunettes wounded seriously enough that surgeons doubted they would survive the night. In the bloody fight several Cheyenne were undoubtedly killed or wounded before most of the survivors later drifted back to the camps of Little Robe and Whirlwind at the agency.

But during that cold, stormy night however, 250 Cheyenne did not choose to return to Darlington. Instead they slipped past Neill's troops and turned toward western Kansas, fleeing toward the land of their Northern Cheyenne cousins.

Neill prepared his forces to attack the village at dawn, but found it deserted when his troops marched in unopposed on the morning of the tenth. Among the sandhills on the far side of the village, they found only seven dead bodies—six warriors and an old woman.

That hot June afternoon on the train, Sophie bought a bottled drink that fizzed when the vendor opened it for her. It tasted good and sweet, like nothing she had ever had before.

She wondered now why Catherine had been so silly a goose to ask if Addie and Julie would recognize them. Such a strange thing for Katie to say—they had only been separated less than half a year. People didn't change in half a year, did they?

Had what horrible things they had suffered changed them so much that their little sisters would not know them?

With a sigh, she sank back into her seat, recalling the morning she was visiting Lucy Miles at the agent's house, the day before the prisoners were scheduled to leave for Florida. It had been a heartrending day, as Lieutenant

R. H. Pratt of the Tenth Cavalry, who would be leading the prisoners' escort, appeared at the agent's office with interpreter Romero and two of Sophia's captors.

"Gray Beard and Minimic want you to write their words in a letter, Romero tells me," Pratt had explained to the agent. "They want you to read their words to their people after they are gone to be punished in that land far away."

The two war chiefs spoke at length, often interrupted by interpreter Romero, and Miles wrote down at length what he made of the rambling discourse:

> Your Gray Beard and Minimic want me to write you to tell their people to settle down at their Agency, and do all that the Gov't. requires of them. They say tell them to plant corn, and send their children to school, and be careful not to get in any trouble . . . that we want them to travel in the white man's road. The white men are as many as the leaves on the trees and we are only a few people, and we should do as the white man wants us to, and live at peace with him.

Many, many things Sophia decided on that long, hot rail trip east to Leavenworth, many things had changed.

And would never be the same again.

Far south of the Kansas Pacific rail line where Sophia and Catherine German rumbled ever eastward that second day of June, 1875, Sergeant Reuben Waller stood again on the parade at Fort Sill, I.T. But this time he was a visitor.

Waller had arrived here yesterday, carrying dispatches for Colonel Ranald S. Mackenzie along with mail for the last two companies of the Tenth Cavalry still stationed in Indian Territory. This morning he had planned to saddle up his escort and head north to the Cheyenne Agency at Darlington where Troops M and D were posted. In their ranks Reuben had lost a couple friends in the April ninth skirmish among the sandhills south of the North Canadian River. He wanted most of all to visit their graves, hoping they were marked. If they weren't, Waller had vowed, he would himself carve a cross or a marker to place at the head of each.

A man needed to be remembered when he had been brave enough to walk this dangerous land. This was the promise Reuben Waller made to every trooper who fought with his H Company under Captain Louis Carpenter. None of his men would ever go into battle and fall, to have his name forgotten as he was buried. Reuben had seen enough of that nameless anonymity already while he was but a private in the newly formed Tenth U.S. Negro Cavalry back to 'sixty-six.

Waller remembered how many times he had carried a small notebook and the stub of a pencil with him into those early campaign battles on the plains, how the others would line up in the hours before marching out to fight, asking him to write their names on those little slips of paper they could pin to their tunics, so should they fall during the fight against the Indians, someone would know their names when prayers were said over their lonely graves hastily scraped from the sandy soil in this wilderness.

He remembered now, and felt his heart rise to his throat for it. No man who served with Reuben Waller had ever fallen and not been remembered by his fellows. There had always been friends to gather at the side of those shallow pits, friends to sing a spiritual or the Old Hundredth, someone who would use the departed's name in that final prayer before returning dust to dust.

So now this Wednesday morning, in what the Comanche themselves called the Moon When the Grass Is Tall, it seemed fitting that Reuben held his half-dozen here at Fort Sill before leaving, for there was much excitement electrifying their former station. Mackenzie's Fourth Cavalry proudly told the visiting buffalo soldiers that their colonel finally had what he had wanted most: the Kwahadis had promised to ride in and surrender this early summer day.

Not long after arriving here back in April to take command of Fort Sill, Mackenzie had dispatched Dr. J. J. Sturm with Sergeant John Charlton and two of the agency's trusted Comanches to attempt finding Quanah

Parker's Kwahadis. On the far western side of the Staked Plain, Sturm and Charlton had eventually located the warrior band clinging desperately to their old ways and tenacious in their desire to be left alone. The white men and friendly Comanches had been immediately disarmed and led to a lodge where the head men began three days of intense discussions with the peace delegation.

Sturm offered Mackenzie's two guarantees: if the Kwahadi came in, they would be allowed to retain some of their ponies, and none of their leaders would be sentenced to prison; if the Kwahadi refused, Three-Finger Kinzie vowed he would hunt down and exterminate them to the last Kwahadi.

How could Quanah trust the word of the white man when so many promises had been made, only to be broken?

Sturm reminded the Kwahadi of who had captured more than a hundred of their women and children three winters before, then did as he had promised—protected the Comanches from a lynching by the Tehas citizens of Jacksboro before releasing those prisoners, allowing them to return to their people. This was the same Three-Finger Kinzie.

A man of honor, as was the war chief of the Kwahadi, Quanah Parker.

It was with no small sadness that Reuben had laid in the steamy darkness of the barracks last night, staring at the top bunk and thinking back on his own time as a slave, a slave to a white man. Brooding on how it had felt to have nothing, to be robbed of everything by the white man. Yet, thinking too how he had persevered and come west to become part of this new Army of the West. How this land was now as much his as it belonged to any man, red or white. Here, on the frontier of a rapidly growing nation extending from sea to shining sea, Reuben Waller hoped one day to find a woman to share the rest of his life, to raise children who would enjoy the fruits of what he and others had fought so hard to win for their descendants, no matter their color.

To plant roots here, as the Kwahadi and the other warrior bands had sent their roots deep so many generations before. His roots, like theirs, would be free, for he had fought to open this land and make it safe for settlement.

He had closed his eyes last night, fighting back a few tears, as he prayed these years he had given to the Tenth Cavalry were not how a few white soldiers joked: that the white man had brought the black man west to fight the red man, taking his land away from him . . . so the white man could eventually settle on this country once bled over by black and red.

Into the bright, morning sunlight he now stepped off the porch in front of the massive mess hall, a place he had taken so many of his meals in years past. From the trees fully leafed in summer green, the sounds of celebration echoed. The commotion was growing across the creek, coming nearer now from the place where the Comanche would live with the Kiowa in a place filled with croups and agues and festerations, troubled by constant putrid fevers and tick-sicks.

The air buzzed with a new level of excitement as Colonel Mackenzie himself stepped onto the porch from his head-quarters office, resplendent in his freshly brushed uniform. He slowly squared his hat on his head and pulled on his antelope-hide gauntlets before he descended the steps to the gravel walk ringing the grassy parade.

With a contingent of officers from his Fourth Cavalry, men who themselves had battled the powerful and wily lords of the southern plains in four campaigns, Mackenzie stopped beside the tall flagpole that stood at the center of Fort Sill, I.T. There he would await the leaders of the hold-outs.

Cheering, beating drums and singing their war songs, the Kiowas and those Comanches who had already surrendered lined the road and pressed through the trees, dogs barking and chasing about with children who beat on tin plates or cups with twigs.

Then Reuben saw him.

Riding as proudly as he had ever seen any Indian ride a wild pony. The two, man and pony, looked as one: both bred on the windswept reaches of the Staked Plain. Horse and warrior. This pair like no other.

He led more than four hundred of his people, ready to surrender more than 1,500 ponies to the army, knowing he had chosen as a free man to surrender. Let no man ever make the mistake of declaring that the U.S. Army had defeated Quanah Parker.

Through the parting crowd he rode slowly, never looking at the cheering warriors and women, the children who poked their heads between legs to catch a glimpse of this famous warrior. Never did he look at the staring, gawking soldiers or the white women who watched from behind the safety of parasols.

Instead, Quanah Parker never took his eyes from the man he had sparred with so many times in the past five summers.

At long last his bare brown knees tightened against the pony's ribs. The proud animal immediately halted at the edge of the gravel walk that led to the central flagpole. Quanah slipped his left leg over and dropped to the ground, standing there but a moment, as if getting accustomed to the feel of this gravel beneath his moccasins, before he stepped onto the manicured lawn and strode purposefully toward the blue and gold and brass assembly of officers.

With only a wave, he halted his warriors from following, commanding them to remain behind among their war ponies. Silently, Quanah Parker walked on alone, carrying his brass-studded Winchester repeater across his arms, clutched there with his fan of eagle wing feathers.

Mackenzie took a step forward, then turned slightly, motioning wordlessly that his officers were to remain behind as well.

As the two met, alone, there beneath the summer sun and that red and white striped flag snapping in the hot June breeze, the crowd fell silent as if a great hand had passed over them all, red and white alike.

For a long moment the two simply beheld one another, face to face at last. Then Mackenzie smiled, yet not the smile of conqueror. It was instead the gaze of respect one courageous warrior gave another.

It was a look that gave Quanah Parker the confidence

that he had indeed done right to bring his people in, to save them by putting their feet on the white man's road at long last.

Slowly he knelt in the shadow of that snapping flag, laying down the rifle at Mackenzie's feet, then stood to find the stoic soldier chief's eyes misting, to find Three-Finger Kinzie saluting him.

Epilogue

He yanked again at the starched celluloid collar one of
Sharp Grover's friends in nearby Jacksboro had loaned
him. The suit was a little tight, but if he didn't do much
moving around in it, Seamus Donegan figured he just
might get through this hot afternoon.

Then he could rip off the tie and collar and shed himself
of this burying suit, all of it making the Irishman itch and
sweat even more here in the heat of this midsummer's day
in North Texas.

The collar was the worst part of it all, he decided, sticking a couple fingers back inside it and stretching again. As
big as Grover's friend had been, his neck still wasn't as
thick as Donegan's.

Every now and then a breeze came along, bringing with
it the scent of lilacs Rebecca had planted along the walls of
the cabin years ago. It was a delicate fragrance that readily
made him think on Samantha. He smiled now, knowing
not a single one of these others would know why he smiled:
thinking now how she always placed a drop of that lilac
water between her breasts, right where she knew he loved
to dip his nose and drink in the fragrance of her. Breasts so
smooth, like the soft belly of a newborn puppy—

By the saints, what that woman had given him.

And again his mind wandered in these moments as the
murmuring crowd grew restless, warm and restless, his
thoughts wandering back to just what it was that his two
uncles had given him.

Liam would have loved to hear this fiddler, Seamus decided, watching the man's nimble fingers stride up and

398

down the neck, his elbow like a piston as he drove the bow back and forth over the catgut strings, accompanied by another, shorter man, energetically pumping out accompaniment on his concertina. Yes, indeed—he decided as he put one big foot to tapping lightly the hard-pounded earth of Sharp Grover's front yard, Liam would have loved this music. And likely were he here, his big brawling uncle would have one arm already clamped around the waist of some comely, likely colleen, her hand clutched securely in his roughened paw as he swung her 'round and 'round to the amusement of some and the befuddlement of others.

A lively, lusty soul, this Liam O'Roarke, not given to finding fault with most any man, least of all finding fault with any member of the fairer sex—he had unwittingly passed down much to his nephew.

Seamus looked over the gathering Sharp had called forth, friends and erstwhile business associates from Jacksboro and the surrounding countryside. There were soldiers here from Fort Richardson. A few others of the army trade who were able to ask for and be given leave, marching all the way down from Fort Sill or up from Fort Concho. Once more he looked through the milling crowd hanging back for these moments of prelude in the shade of the great spreading oaks and cottonwoods. Seamus found that singular black face, creased now in middle age like his own, worn with worry and the war map of his own far travels on these plains, nonetheless brightened by those eyes that had seen the glory and still believed in one Union after all.

Reuben Waller's eyes found that Seamus was watching him from afar. The sergeant, dressed in his freshly laundered uniform, those gold chevrons bright at his shoulder, smiled, his whole face gleaming, just as it had been that autumn day on the parade at Fort Wallace eight winters gone as Seamus and his fists stepped between a lone buffalo soldier and seven bullies from George Armstrong Custer's Seventh Cavalry.*

The face might have begun to sag a little, what with the years and the miles the army had asked of the man, but

* The Plainsmen Series, vol. 3, *The Stalkers*

those eyes and that smile would likely never be brighter. From across the shady yard Waller hoisted his tin cup in salute to Donegan as the Irishman stood with Grover, waiting.

His heart filled again with gratitude to have such friends, men like Reuben Waller, who had come all this way from Fort Concho to be here this morning after receiving word on the wire from Richardson's post telegrapher. Men like Sharp Grover too, who now stood beside him, perhaps to support Donegan in this great undertaking. Perhaps, Seamus believed at times, to keep an eye on him, to keep him from bolting.

And what of Uncle Ian O'Roarke? he asked himself again as a woman from town came out the front door and down the steps, walking quickly across the yard to whisper something in the ear of the fiddle player. Donegan grew gray-gilled and his heart pounded all the more as he thought back on the happiness Ian had found with one woman—seizing the chance and fighting for her, staking his claim not in gold or silver, but in love of a woman for life. Ian had risked his hide and heart, and for it he had won Dimity.

Now they lived at the edge of the Lava Beds, raising crops and cattle and a passel of five children. And while Liam had been happy of a time in his own way, Seamus had to admit that Ian had something that his younger brother had never laid claim to: that peace and contentment a man could possess when he found at long last the piece of ground where he would make his stand.

So both uncles had given him much, not only during those hard years in Ireland while young Seamus was growing up fatherless—but even more of late, realizing now as he did that he had gone in search of them and ultimately found them both when he was supposed to find them all along. When each had even more to teach him about life. It was a shame, he said to himself as he looked over the children in the crowd, darting this way and that, scolded and chased by their parents through the dapple of shadow and sunshine, a shame that a man has to spend so many of his years before he learns what it truly means to live.

Silhouette SPECIAL EDITION

That SPECIAL *Woman!*

She's friend, wife, mother—she's you!
And to thank you for being so special to us,
we would like to send you a

FREE

Romantic Journal

in which to record all of *your*
special moments.

To receive your free ROMANTIC JOURNAL, send four proof-of-purchase coupons from any Silhouette Special Edition THAT SPECIAL WOMAN! title from January to June, plus $3.00 for postage and handling (check or money order—please do not send cash) payable to Silhouette Books, to: **In the U.S.:** THAT SPECIAL WOMAN!, Silhouette Books, 3010 Walden Avenue, P.O. Box 1396, Buffalo, NY 14269-1396; **In Canada:** THAT SPECIAL WOMAN!, Silhouette Books, P.O. Box 609, Fort Erie, Ontario L2A 5X3.

087 KAS

NAME: _____

ADDRESS: _____

CITY: _____ STATE/PROV: _____ ZIP/POSTAL: _____

(Please allow 4-6 weeks for delivery. Hurry! Quantities are limited. Offer expires August 31, 1993.)

That SPECIAL *Woman!*   Proof of Purchase

087 KAS

Silhouette

SPECIAL EDITION ®

Once there were seven...

Seven beautiful brothers and sisters who played together,
and weathered adversity too cruel for their tender ages.
Eventually orphaned, they were then separated. Now
they're trying to find each other.

Don't miss Gina Ferris's heartwarming

FAMILY FOUND

Sunday's child may be fair and wise but she has a lot to
learn about love and trust. And who better to teach her than
a sexy, mysterious man from her past? Read all about
Lindsay, as this youngest Walker gets her own story in
FAIR AND WISE (SE #819).

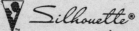